THE QUIET POOLS

THE QUIET POOLS

MICHAEL P. KUBE-McDOWELL

ACE BOOKS, NEW YORK

THE QUIET POOLS

An Ace Book
Published by The Berkley Publishing Group
200 Madison Avenue, New York, New York 10016

Book design by Arnold Vila

First Edition: May 1990

Library of Congress Cataloging-in-Publication Data
Kube-McDowell, Michael P.
  The quiet pools / Michael P. Kube-McDowell.
      p.   cm.
  ISBN 0-441-69911-1
  I. Title.
PS3561.U184Q5   1990
813′.54—dc20   89-18150
                                                                            CIP

Printed in the United States of America

*With love,
for my father, John,
and my son, Matthew,
each of whom, in his own way,
has given me life.*

ACKNOWLEDGMENTS

THE AUTHOR WISHES TO THANK DR. JORDIN KARE OF
Lawrence Livermore National Laboratory, for discussing his
work on laser-sustained-detonation launch systems; Mike
Resnick, for lending his expertise on Kenya; Stan Dale and all
those who shared their experiences with open relationships and
extended families, especially Sharon, Mike, Pat, Mark, Mary,
and George; Sandy Mikalow III of the Northwest Astronomy
Group and Ellen Louise Saunders, for their help with research
in and about Columbia County, Oregon; and Francis Crick,
for *Life Itself*, and Dr. Helen Fisher, for *The Sex Contract*,
both of which helped crystallize the speculations which are
fundamental to this story. Any errors or amendments of the
facts are my responsibility, not theirs. Thanks also to Gwen,
for a thousand gifts of the spirit; the Ann Arbor gang and my
compufriends, for moral and immoral support; my parents, for
CARE packages and helping keep the wolves from the door;
my local Pepsi Cola bottler; Mike & The Mechanics, whose
wonderful song "Living Years" seemed to come on the radio
at all the right times; my editor, Beth Fleisher, for her
patience and for caring as much as I did; and G.Z. and S.F.,
who didn't know they were helping that weekend in August,
but did anyway.

BEGIN CHAIN: AUG⊢

BEGIN CHAIN: AUG–

—|GAU|—

"This is Jeremiah . . ."

FROM THE ELEVATED GUARD STATION AT THE MAIN ENTRANCE to Allied Transcon's Houston center, a young corpsec monitored the truck trundling up Galveston Road toward NASA Boulevard. With his televiewer, he could see that the rider cabin of the robot tractor was empty. The dull silver tank trailer bore the familiar logo of Shell Chemical.

"Traffic on the board," his watch partner said suddenly as the truck crossed the security threshold. His watch partner was an artificial intelligence personality named Isaac, one of eight personalities making up the center's Sentinel system.

"I've got it," said the corpsec. A squeeze on the grip of the televiewer brought the reply to the station's radioed interrogative into the finder in pale yellow lettering. "ID's okay. Shellchem local hauler, running empty."

"I have confirmation from the National Vehicle Registry," Isaac said. "The registry is valid and current."

"Okay." The corpsec idly continued to track the tanker in the glass, trying to read the graffiti scrawled on its flanks. In the course of their four-hour shift, more than a hundred wheeled cargo vehicles would slide by on the old surface road, shuttling between Galveston and Houston. Except for the occasional burst of imagination or artistry in the graffiti, they were hardly worth notice.

Besides, ground traffic was the least of Corporate Security's concerns. It was far more likely that someone seeking to penetrate Allied Transcon would try to hop the triple fence in a flyer; far more likely that someone trying to destroy it would lob a

3

screamer from the forest of scrapers downtown, or from a boat bobbing somewhere on the poisoned waters of Galveston Bay.

And even those possibilities were hard to take very seriously at all—right up to the moment the Shellchem tanker suddenly veered right and roared up the ramp onto NASA Drive, accelerating all the way. At the top of the ramp, the tanker swept an unsuspecting two-seat flyer aside and hurtled down the entrance drive toward the barbican.

"Jesus," the corpsec said unbelievingly. "It's going to crash the gate."

There was little else for him to do, for the silicon reflexes of Sentinel had already taken over. In less than a microsecond, the AIP declared the tanker a threat, activated the gate defenses, and transmitted an alert to corpsec throughout the grounds.

"Now sending kill-Q," said Isaac.

A half dozen flyers were queued up in the accumulation lane outside the barbican's tunnels. They settled to the ground as one as Sentinel abruptly took command of their pilot systems. But the tanker kept coming, its systems refusing the insistent commands. In seconds the tanker would smash into the stalled flyers and their human occupants.

"It's stall-shielded," the corpsec realized.

Sentinel had already drawn the same conclusion and made the only possible decision. With almost tangible reluctance, Sentinel exercised what control it had, and the flyers suddenly rose up and scattered like a flock of birds. That ended the risk to life. It also cleared the way to the gate.

"Fire authority," snapped the corpsec. "Blow it off the bridge."

"Road sensors show the tanker is fully loaded. There's no way to know what's in it," the construct said. "Sorry."

The corpsec swallowed hard. "Jesus, I hope they built this tower good—"

At the end of the bridge, spikes rising from the roadbed shredded the tanker's tires, but could not halt it. The tanker reached the final concrete apron outside the twin tunnels of the barbican, now sealed by heavy doors, and abruptly slewed into a sideways skid. Moments later it slammed into the wall of steel and stone.

The corpsec grabbed for a handhold as the tower shuddered and swayed. But there was no explosion, no alarming creaking and rending. The corpsec looked toward Isaac's room scanner with a look of relief and drew a deep breath to clear the poison of fear from his lungs.

"That wasn't so bad," Isaac said.

"No," said the corpsec, going to the window. Peering down at the barbican, he saw the tanker crushed sideways against the entrance gates, bleeding a yellow-brown soup from its belly. The fast-running pool of liquid had already reached the east edge of the apron and begun to spread across the hard earth and brown grass.

Grabbing his viewer, the corpsec trained it on the spill. Wraithlike white wisps played in the air above its surface. "I don't like the looks of that."

"The HazMat team has been notified."

"Should I evacuate?"

"No," was the answer. "Remain at your station. You'll be given further instructions when HazMat evaluates the situation."

The corpsec frowned. "I'm not settling for that," he said. "Let me listen to E-1."

Emergency channel 1 came on the speaker just in time for the corpsec to hear the chatter of excited voices fade under a storm of static and then vanish beneath the clean white hum of a pirate jammer. Then a voice spoke, a solemn, sonorous male voice that commanded their attention and tugged somehow at the emotional chord labeled *father*.

"This is Jeremiah, speaking for the Homeworld . . ."

"Shit."

"This is an unauthorized transmission," Isaac said.

"Shut up, Isaac," the corpsec said irritably. "I want to hear what they've done to us."

As always, Homeworld had worked hard to make certain that the corpsec, Allied Transcon management, and as many of Earth's eight billion as possible heard.

This is what they heard:

"This is Jeremiah, speaking for the Homeworld.

"From the first, I have been a student of history. The truth of the present can be found in the past, if you seek it. Enemies hide their evils in the mists of the past, if you allow it. The winner is the player with the longest memory.

"For more than a hundred years, the bandits of Allied Transcon have insulted the Earth, our gentle mother. The trail of Gaea's pain begins with Allied Transcon's sorry heritage, with names to which such shame attached that those names were abandoned and hidden.

"We have not forgotten. Rockwell built weapons of war, abetting the mindless devastation of fragile ecologies. We have not forgotten. Exxon bled the earth of its precious stores and poisoned the waters and the air with chemical wastes. We have not forgotten. Mitsubishi supplied the tools to turn once-beautiful Japan into a mechanized warren and to ravage the grand tropical forests of Indonesia and the Philippines.

"The bastard of the mating of these soulless parasites worships at the altar of the same shallow profit principle. I look on your works and weep. Thirty square miles of the Amazon Basin transformed from lush jungle to dead, sterile pavement. A dozen gigawatt power plants generating million-year poisons. An endless parade of LSD freighters ripping through the atmosphere, carrying away the riches of the Earth.

"And the worst insult of all, that all this is done only so that we might reach out for more worlds to despoil.

"Today, we have returned the insult. We returned to Allied Transcon a tiny fraction of the poisons it creates in a single day—a few seconds of death and disease. At six-fifty this morning, a tank truck emptied five thousand gallons of life-hating industrial pollutants at the main entrance to Allied Transcon's American headquarters in Houston. We have rubbed their noses in their corporate excrement.

"We have heard it said, even by those who agree with our goals, that we have committed a crime, and become like our enemies. We accept this judgment, with one distinction.

"Allied Transcon's crimes are crimes against Nature. They harm the body and spirit of Gaea, immanent in the fabric of life. Our crimes are crimes for Nature. We harm only those who bring harm to our common home. We steal their wealth. We destroy their tools. We stand against them, and for the silent Earth.

"This is Jeremiah, speaking for the Homeworld."

The jammer in the Gulf ran for just over six minutes, pumping two and a half repetitions of Jeremiah's announcement out over E-1, G-1, and three Gulf State commercial bands before its power cells died. Float jammers in the South Atlantic off Brazil and the Mediterranean west of Sicily delivered the same message to Allied Transcon's primary launch center at Prainha and the European administrative center in Munich, respectively. Off-planet, Aurora Sanctuary's official broadcaster carried the announcement for the benefit of the sixteen satlands, following it with a two-hour debate on environmental activism.

There were failures: A relay jammer located across the street from Allied's Tokyo facility was picked up in a security sweep twenty minutes before the tanker reached NASA Drive. And a reliable old Homeworld trick finally played out its string: The rom ora on the main feed for ComNet 3 cut in on schedule, replacing the broadcast of "Personal Combat" with Homeworld's earth-globe logo and Jeremiah's voice. But a ready controller blacked the net before more than a few words could go out.

A new trick, however, worked very well indeed. A routine stack upload into the Direct Information Access Network for North America suddenly showed itself to be a Trojan horse, commandeering nearly half of DIANNA's data channels and piping Jeremiah's announcement out through the terminals of more than six million surprised users.

And the ComNet blackout and DIANNA incursion together ensured the kind of attention Homeworld craved: a minute on the Current News stack, and a moment in the lives and thoughts of uncountable millions of Earth's children.

On balance, Jeremiah was pleased.

Christopher McCutcheon rose early, escaping from a restless and unrewarding sleep, hoping to escape from encountering either of his wives. He padded softly through the big house on Denham Street as though a trespasser. Which, in truth, was how he felt that Monday, even though he not only lived there but held four-tenths of the fractional mortgage.

The door to Loi's bedroom was still closed, which helped. It closed out the inevitable sounds of morning—running water and the muted voice of the housecom, the gurgle and hiss of the kitchen appliances. And it screened Christopher from the sight of Loi and Jessie together, though not from the memory of the sight of them last night.

He had stood in that doorway a long time, hammered by the tangled limbs, murmuring voices, and the raw fragrance of sex. The rumpled sheets, tousled hair, and skin-glisten of sweat had told him that what was happening was not a beginning but an encore. He had been in Freeport since midday; they had had more than enough time.

Stunned, silent, Christopher had watched Loi's experienced hands exploring Jessie's sleek secrets, her mouth ravening Jessie's throat and breasts. He watched with pain, not pleasure, feeling as though he should be part of what was happening before his eyes, and yet knowing that he was not welcome. Waiting to be noticed, and yet knowing that to wait one moment longer was to invite more misery.

And then he had been noticed, Loi catching sight of him as she turned her lithe body on the bed, opening herself to Jessie's touch. Her eyes fixed on him challengingly, reproachfully.

He did not withdraw. He could not move.

"Chris is back, Jessie," she had said finally. Her voice was empty of apology or embarrassment.

Jessie had twisted her body toward where he stood, showed a mischievous smile. "Hi, Chris."

Loi gave him no chance to read a greeting as an invitation. "Chris, would you close the door for us? I think Möbius must have pushed it open," she had said, naming the family's elder cat. "Oh, and you have some mail on the com."

There was nothing in her words that he had not already foreseen, and yet he had felt sudden fury at being sent away. He remembered yanking the door shut with all the force he could muster, rattling the framed pictures hanging in the hall. And then fleeing to his room at the opposite end of the upstairs hall, expecting his distress to lure one or both of them to follow.

But neither did. He lay in the dark fighting to close out the sounds of Jessie and Loi's pleasure—never sure if he was hearing or imagining them—and bleeding from a wound he had thought had closed over forever.

A miserable moment. A miserable night. And in both, more than enough reasons to avoid facing them that morning.

Christopher satisfied himself with a speedshower and a muffin from the warmer, then slipped quickly into his gray two-piece. When he was ready to leave, the house was still silent, Loi and Jessie presumably still cocooned in Loi's bed. But he felt too acutely that he was running away, and in rebellion against the feeling stopped in the family room to retrieve his mail.

He was glad he had. There were five messages for him on the housecom, the last a brief notice from Allied informing him that the main entrance was temporarily closed, and asking that pools and dropoffs use the north entrance and that everyone else ride the tramline to work. Riding the tram was an annoyance, but less of one than reaching the main gate in his flyer and being turned away.

The price of his rebellion was high, however. By the time he shut down the display, there were footsteps on the balcony behind him. He turned to see Loi descending the stairs in her robe, her eyes sleepy, her short blond hair robbed of its usual sculpted look by her pillow. It was only in the morning that Loi's true age showed. On the lee side of breakfast and her morning rituals, Loi usually passed for ten years fewer than her forty-six.

"Good morning, sweet," she said. "I almost missed you."

"I have to leave," he said defensively. "I'm riding the tram."

"You have time for a hug, don't you?" But he was stiff in her embrace, and she drew back to study his face. "I wanted to see if you were all right this morning. I guess that tells me."

"You might have thought about it last night."

"Chris dear, you have no right to be angry with me, or with Jessie."

"You shut me out," he said sharply.

"As you do when you and Jessie take time together, as we do to Jessie at other times. Is there any difference?"

He frowned sulkily. "I didn't know you were interested."

"Jessie is a beautiful young woman, full of interesting energies," Loi said. "How could you think I wouldn't be attracted to her? And how could you not have noticed what's been happening when the three of us are in bed together?"

For a moment, Christopher was silent. "Look, I've got to leave."

"Not yet," Loi said, grabbing his hand as he tried to turn away. "Yes, you met Jessie first. Yes, you were the one who suggested her as our third. But you don't own her—or me, for that matter. I want a family in which we all share our lives and our selves, freely, without contracts, without artificial boundaries. I thought you wanted that, too."

"I wasn't expecting this," he said angrily. "I didn't think I'd have to fight her for your time. All I thought about on the way back from Freeport was coming home and making love with you. Except you were already busy."

"Did you think that being the only male in this trine made you the center?" Loi retorted. "We're not going to work like this, Chris. Not with you reacting to our love with jealousy. If you can't find a better place to be on your own, maybe you'd better make an appointment with Arty."

"I've got to leave," he said firmly, pulling away.

This time she let him go. "We'll talk tonight, then," she said, "all three of us."

"I'm not interested in a conversation on the subject of How Foolish Chris Is Being," he said, his back to her. "Thank you *very* much, but no thanks."

She came up behind him and slipped her arms around his waist, cuddling close and resting her head on his back. "I had in mind a conversation on how we can all help each other with the hard parts," she said softly.

Christopher shrugged out of her embrace. "It still adds up to Let's Help Chris Adjust," he said bitterly, pausing at the door. "And I'm just not sure that I'm the one who's wrong."

Mikhail Dryke hated traveling almost as much as he hated being trapped for days on end in his office suite in the green-glassed administrative warren at Prainha. The former was pure impatience; the latter, the natural resistance of a hands-on field investigator who had been promoted too many times.

The last promotion had left Dryke chief security officer, Diaspora Project, Allied Transcon. His first accomplishment in the new post had been to locate and hijack a triumvirate of lieutenants who could handle the administrative end without him. His second had been to acclimate the Diaspora Project Director, Hiroko Sasaki, to the idea that he would be absent from Prainha more than he would be present.

Sasaki had not needed much convincing. It was trouble that took Dryke away, and Allied Transcon and the Diaspora were facing a full menu of trouble these days. The Homeworld hit on the Houston center was part of a panorama of problems that ranged from labor sabotage at the Kasigau Launch Center to an endless parade of would-be stowaways attempting to make their way onto the starship *Memphis*.

Named, like its predecessor, for a great city of antiquity, the second of the Project's five great generation starships was nearing completion in high orbit for a planned 2095 departure. A third larger than *Ur*, which had sailed eleven years earlier, *Memphis* was a small city in space, and a world of problems unto itself. Dryke gladly left the protection of *Memphis* in the hands of Matthew Reid, who was based at Takara, the satland building the ship for Allied Transcon.

But any problems earthbound belonged to Dryke, and this morning Jeremiah and Homeworld were at the top of the list. He had caught the flash alert from Sentinel in his flyer and immediately rerouted from the tower to the field. Jeremiah's message came through while he was waiting out prep on his Saab Celestron; ten minutes later, he was in the air.

Prainha to Houston was one of those especially annoying intermediate hops—barely six thousand kilometers—that took longer to complete than a trip covering twice the distance. The apogee of the arc traced by Dryke's pop screamer was well within the stratosphere; the max velocity was a plodding 4,000 kph; the e.t. nearly two hours.

Only the skylink kept the time from being a total waste. The analysis of the spill came in shortly after take-off: dioxin, methylene chloride, benzothiazole, PCBs, chloroaniline. By the time the Texas coast crystallized through the hanging haze, Dryke had collected reports from Munich, Tokyo, and Kasigau, and an excuse from Washington. The Trojan horse's final act had been to wipe itself from the system, and DIANNA operators were still trying to reconstruct where it had gotten in and how it had done what it did.

Nobody knows anything, Dryke grumbled to himself as the Saab flashed across the center boundary and floated in, nose high, over the end of the runway. *An old story. Getting very old. Jeremiah finds us with our backs turned, hits us, and then slips away clean. Very clean. The son of a bitch.*

Spinning wheels touched rushing pavement, and Dryke swung the skylink console back out of the way. *Six times they've hit us. Six times I've had to pick through the mess they left. The red dye in the water in the Munich offices. The data center fire in Kasigau. The launch laser that blew up at Prainha. Never anyone killed. No victims except Allied Transcon. No enemies for the friends of the Earth.*

The Saab rolled to an open slot in the bunkerlike hangar, and a blue corpsec flyer scooted up alongside. At the controls was the local chiefsec, a bird-necked, mild-tempered man named Jim Francis. *I don't like always being one step behind,* Dryke thought gruffly as he climbed down from the cabin. *I don't like being outsmarted. How do they do it? Who the hell are they?*

It was unlikely that any answers awaited him at the disabled gate, but Dryke was obliged to go through the motions. "Thanks for meeting me," he said with a nod.

"Sorry you had to make the trip," Francis said. "We've got the tanker sealed, and we're about ready to lift it out of there. But there's roughly thirty-five hundred gallons of a very nasty soup soaking into the ground, and that's going to be a whole hell of a lot harder to deal with."

Dryke nodded gravely. "Let's take a look."

• • •

Running parallel to the highway it had largely replaced, the Harris County tramway was a concrete ribbon on stilts, a fifth as wide as the fifty-seat silver and blue cars which skimmed atop it. From below, it looked fragile, the cars precariously balanced like eggs on a knife-edge. But inside, the ride was stable and smooth, even as the slope-nosed tram car left the main track to Galveston and slowed sharply for the T-spur to Allied Transcon.

Christopher McCutcheon took advantage of the slower speed and his seat on the right side of the tram car to peer out the window at the odd congregation by the main gate, a quarter mile away. He was not the only one to do so. The half-filled cabin grew noticeably quieter for the forty seconds or so that the gate was in view.

They saw two bright yellow mobile cranes standing outside the barbican, their long booms making an X in silhouette against the sky. Two red Flight Services trucks sat at odd angles on the side slopes; Christopher thought one might be a foamer, but he wasn't sure. A pale blue HazMat van blocked the middle of the bridge, and most of the figures walking among the vehicles seemed to be wearing full-body environmental suits.

"Looks like somebody missed the runway," he said conversationally to the round-faced woman in the adjoining seat.

"Didn't you hear the news?" she asked indignantly. "It was those Homeworld people. They tried to blow up the shuttle. What's wrong with them? Don't they realize what they're doing?"

It was then that Christopher noted the binoculars dangling from the woman's neck. Forewarned, he limited his reply to a sympathetic smile; there was no such thing as a brief conversation with a starhead. He'd learned that lesson very early in his three-month tenure with the Project.

When the tram car came to a stop a few moments later, Christopher watched to see where the woman went. As he expected, she passed by the escalators to the ground level and the base entrance and continued down the platform toward the observation area. By the time Christopher reached the bottom, she had joined the other starheads at the plex, peering out toward the field where a barrel-bodied ESA Pelican sat being readied for launch to orbit.

Not too surprisingly, the line at the staff gate pass-through had stalled, since—always vigilant after the fact—corpsec was not only checking for employee IDs but checking everyone's ID through the verifier. While he waited, Christopher found himself thinking about the woman on the tram.

There was something simultaneously delightful and pathetic about the starheads. They knew the launch schedule for the center's one LTO runway better than most Allied staff, knew the difference between a Pelican and its near-twin Martin Rendezvous, knew the nine satlands and the governor of the Mars colony and the latest news and gossip from *Ur*. They came to the ob deck at Johnson Field as a solemn pilgrimage and then turned into wishful, wistful children, noses pressed to the window on a rainy day.

Christopher had no doubt that the woman and everyone else on the ob platform that morning owned a selection option for *Memphis*. Those who were old enough had probably owned one for *Ur* as well, that prized certificate which had been so proudly hung on so many walls when there was no Homeworld to prick at the conscience. Back when being a pioneer candidate conferred status, when even those with no intention of leaving wanted to be able to say, "I could have gone if I wanted to."

Things were different now. It had been years since Christopher had seen an option certificate on display, and mentioning Allied Transcon, *Memphis*, or the pioneers among strangers had become a good way to invite a passionate harangue. But nothing had changed for the starheads, except that *Ur* was already gone. One down, four to go.

Christopher had every reason to doubt that the woman or any of her peers would be selected for *Memphis* or any of the ships to follow. Anyone that set on leaving Earth would have done so already if they had any skills to offer. There were 200,000 people living off-planet—Technica and Aurora Sanctuary, Takara and Horizon, the Mars colony and Heinlein City on Mare Serenitatis. The starheads were obsessed with dreams they could never fulfill, and so came to touch with their eyes the only piece of that dream they could reach.

Or was it that they viewed the satlands, the Moon, even Mars as shabby substitutes for the only goal that mattered? If so, Christopher did not understand their desperate longing. It did not seem either real or realistic, and he could not quite stop himself from seeing the starheads as fundamentally irrational.

But then, he felt like a curiosity himself sometimes. When he had come to Allied Transcon from the San Francisco offices of DIANNA, it was almost like being an agnostic entering a community of believers. He had come there for the work, a chance to be part of the most ambitious library science project ever, the

Memphis's unabridged hyperlibrary. They had come to join a cause.

A curiosity. Oh, he knew where he had been on June 28, 2083, just like everyone else—watching *Ur's* long-delayed departure, the unimaginable power of its superconducting metal-ion engines driving it slowly up out of the solar system toward Epsilon Eridani. But he did not own an option for *Memphis*, would not have even if his father had not so clearly disapproved. It was such a long road, so few would be chosen, and the rewards that awaited the selected seemed so empty.

He just did not understand—any more than he had understood why, two months after *Ur* left, one Deryn Falconer had abandoned Oregon, her husband, and a fifteen-year-old nurture-son named Christopher for the satland called Aurora Sanctuary.

The environmental suit stank of chemwash and disinfectant, leaving Mikhail Dryke to wonder cynically whether he was really any better off inside it than he would have been going bare-skin. In any case, he was glad to retreat at last beyond the hazard boundary with Dr. Francis, endure the pummeling spray-down, and then strip off the heavy helmet and breather.

"They got us good," Dryke said, mopping the perspiration from his face.

The local security chief nodded glumly. "My site engineer says three months to clean it all out and open for business again."

"Nonsense," Dryke said. "Run a bypass right across there," he said, pointing and swinging his finger in an arc, "cut a triple gate through the fence, and you can be back in business in a week, flyers only. Nothing wrong with the guard station—you can cover the bypass as well as you covered the drive."

"Which wasn't very well, as it turned out," Francis said. "Do you really want us to go back to sentries and turnpikes? The human factors—"

"Yes, I really do," Dryke said shortly.

"We can't leave the spill. They're telling me we've got dioxin, chloroaniline—"

"Don't leave it. Seal it. Use the old Kansas Technologies method. You inject the whole site with a neutralizing binder—blend it in with augers—and stabilize the spill in place. We had to use it after the fire at the plastics plant in Lyons a year back. Talk to your site engineer. He ought to know who to bring in."

"People are going to worry about contamination."

"Then you'll have to educate them. We're not going to rely on the north entrance and the tram for three months. We're not going to let him put us under siege." Dryke pulled at the neck band of his environmental suit. "I want out of this thing. And then I want a tank so I can face-to-face with the Director."

"I'll get someone to run you back—"

"You run me back. You can't do anything here now. This mess belongs to your engineer now."

The faintly sheepish look on Dr. Francis's face betrayed him. "All right."

But Dryke had already turned and started down the drive toward the flyer. Francis hurried after, the environmental suit squeaking as one surface rubbed against another. "Mr. Dryke—"

"What?"

"There's people here that need to know. Should we have hammered the tanker on the ramp? Should we have used the rockets?"

Dryke stopped and shook his head. "You couldn't," he said bluntly. "That's where he beat us. You want to do something useful, stop posturing and beating your breast and start figuring out what other ways he's come up with to fuck us over."

One moment, the other half of the holo tank was dark, except for the yellow eye of the imager. The next, Hiroko Sasaki sat facing him, seated cross-legged and straight backed in a large fixed armchair identical to Dryke's.

The chair made the president of the Pioneers Division look diminutive, but Dryke knew better than to let that deceive him. Sasaki was more of Takara, her birthplace, than Japan, her parents'—an efficient, demanding, uncompromising administrator with tremendous personal energy and intensity. What else she was she kept to herself. Dryke had worked for her for seven years and still could not say if he liked her.

"Yes, Mikhail."

"Reporting on the Houston incident."

"Go ahead."

"It was a blind spot, not a system failure. The tractor was grabbed from a yard in Angleton no more than an hour before the hit, and the report got screened out by a remora somewhere between the cops, Shell, and the NVR. Probably they picked up the tanker in a side-of-the-road swap, dropped the stall screen in it at the same time. We've got the box. Black market, police version—take maybe fifteen minutes to install. Nothing on it, but I'm having it shipped to the labs down there just in case.

"The jammer was a float and went to the bottom in five hundred feet of water. They could have dropped it anytime in the last ten days—you wouldn't want to take a land flyer out over the Gulf, but you could. I'd like authority to send the Gulf rescue unit's submersible after it."

"Given."

"Thank you," Dryke said with a nod. "Without it, we don't have much to put into the puzzle. The tractor's navigator is scrambled. DIANNA's still backing and filling on the penetration. Sanctuary is being close-mouthed as usual."

"Do you have an estimate of how many Homeworld activists were involved?"

"On a principal-contribution analysis, six or seven. Physically? It could have been as few as one."

"Jeremiah."

"You might as well say so."

"You continue to reject the opinion of your counterterrorism subdirector that Jeremiah is a figurehead, representing no real person."

"I do," Dryke said. "Homeworld has many hands. But it thinks with one mind."

"Perhaps. See that your prejudice on this matter doesn't lead you down false trails," Sasaki said. "As to this incident, what prospect is there for locating the 'hands' responsible?"

Dryke shook his head, frowning. "I hesitate to promise. They work very clean. But they can't be everywhere without leaving footprints. They've been forced to use more and more hardware. We'll go back along that path and try to find out where it's coming from."

"That seems to be where they are most vulnerable."

"Yeah. Except they know that, too. It's going to be an inch at a time, with no help from outside. We took a hit. We'll take another, and another, and another, like as not. But one of these times I'm going to get there first. I promise you that, Hiroko. One of these days I'll bring you Jeremiah's head."

CHAPTER 2

- GUA -

"... for the Homeworld."

THE ESA PELICAN *SILESIA* SAT AT THE TOP OF THE RAMP AT the west end of Johnson Field's runway 1E like an overladen and aging beast of burden. Its twenty-four massive tires were spread wide by their million-pound burden, the delta wings and fat fuselage streaked and stained from five hundred previous missions. Four trunklike umbilicals extended up into *Silesia's* underbelly from the ramp, as though the freight shuttle belonged in a hospital ward rather than on the flight line.

The notion that in a few minutes it would be in orbit was as ludicrous as the prospect that a corpulent, comatose man might leap out of bed to perform a breathtaking *pas de bourrée*. Yet that was exactly what was to happen. Like its namesake, the Pelican was a different bird in the air than on the ground. Aloft, it was stable and tireless, even graceful, equal to both the leap of faith and the leap to space.

In the shuttle's cabin, the three-man crew laughed and joked among themselves as the autopilot counted down through the preflight checklist. Flight controllers in the tower warned all air traffic away from the field and from *Silesia's* flight path with the call "LTO red, LTO red, five-mile interdiction now in effect." Around the perimeter of the field, suppression teams checked their screens and weapons one last time.

A half mile from where the Pelican waited, Dola Martinez waited patiently on the observation platform for the launch. Nearly a dozen waited with her, watching the runway for the first sign. When a puff of white gas appeared under the shuttle's wing and quickly dissipated in the hot breeze, there was a muted cheer. With binoculars, televiewers, or merely squinting with eyes sun-shielded by a hat brim, they watched as *Silesia*'s umbilicals detached themselves one by one and retracted below ground.

But three late arrivals to the platform showed only cursory interest in the shuttle. Dola had noticed them, two men and a girl, none older than twenty, and marked them as virgins—idle curious, drawn there by what they thought was chance. The two men took seats high on the bleachers; the girl lingered near the entry, looking back down the platform toward the tramway, as though she were expecting someone. Just like virgins to keep themselves apart, uncomfortable with the camaraderie of the regulars.

Dola remembered her first time, thirty-eight years ago in Florida, at the then-verdant Cape. Dragged there by the family to visit the museums, and remaining at her father's insistence that they witness a fortuitously scheduled launch. It was the most inconsequential flight possible, a robot heavy-lift full of specialty metals bound for Horizon, then under construction. And yet, watching it—no, *feeling* it—roar into the cloud-dotted sky on a triple column of fire, she truly grasped for the first time where it was bound, and understood what that meant.

"It's rolling!" someone cried, and Dola forgot the virgins. The stay cables had been released, and the Pelican lumbered down the ramp, gravity providing the initial acceleration. At the foot of the ramp, the idling transonic engines came to life, the boiling schlieren in the transparent exhaust the first clue, a thunderous roar the confirmation.

There was applause, there were tears. Dola felt her own heart soaring as the Pelican rumbled ever faster down the runway, half bouncing and half floating as it teetered at the balance between lift and gravity. She lowered her binoculars and watched with naked eyes as *Silesia* rose and the ground fell away, ten meters, a hundred, the massive landing gear vanishing swiftly to trim the shuttle's ungainly profile.

It was at that moment that someone seized the strap of her binoculars where it rested on her neck and yanked violently. The hard-shelled glasses flew out of her hands and smashed against her face, the pain as sharp as it was unexpected. Dola cried out, her nose and mouth bloodied, as she ducked and

THE QUIET POOLS

49

twisted to escape. A moment later the binoculars vanished, torn away as she collapsed to her knees.

"Take them," she pleaded blindly. "I don't care."

Her vision clearing, she looked up and saw one of the virgins standing atop the first row of the bleachers, whirling the binoculars over his head like bolas, his face a grim and twisted mask of hate. A few feet away, his companion shoved Archie, harmless little Archie, facedown on the concrete platform and then trampled him underfoot in pursuit of Eleanor. She quickly went down under a hail of punches.

"Fucking starheads," the youth with the binoculars snarled, and leaped forward. "Fucking starheads."

Dola ducked away from the whirling weapon and started to scramble toward the tram platform. It was then that she saw the girl standing in the exit, blocking the way with the aid of the black-tipped scrambler in her right hand. Her eyes were glowing with excitement, challenging, daring Dola to try to flee.

Then a kick exploded in Dola's midsection, and she sprawled flat on the platform. The binoculars whistled through the air and came down on the back of her skull, driving her face down hard against the concrete. The snap of breaking teeth and the pop of shattered cartilage blended with the screaming, animal and angry, that filled the observation deck.

As Dola's attacker looked for other prey, blood began to puddle beneath her, running freely from her torn and battered face. A sick, queasy chill raced through her, sucking the strength from her muscles, the spirit from her heart. She tried to raise her head once, a foolish, futile effort. Then, vision graying, she let go, escaping into unconsciousness, only realizing at the last that the most wrenching screams had been her own.

Mikhail Dryke stood rigid, arms wrapped across his chest, body vibrating with barely contained fury, as he watched the transit medics roll the last of the injured past him to the waiting flyer. The bloody parade had included four women, three middle aged men, a handicapped teen, all battered and bewildered.

"What did we do?" one woman had asked beseeching as she was led away. "Why did they hate us so much?"

Because you still have dreams, Dryke had thought impulsively. The medic attending her did not attempt an answer. His soothing words were empty balm, and, in that, were doubtless kinder.

Jim Francis stood silent and uncomfortable beside Dryke, vacillating between empathy for the victims and concern for himself. The report had come in from the north gate as he and Dryke were reviewing system security. On his own, Francis would have merely acknowledged it and carried on. His office was his domain; the gates and fences belonged to those who worked for him.

But Dryke had insisted on responding, and Francis had been obliged to trail along. The moment they were close enough to read the streaky red lettering smeared across the observation deck's plex, Dryke's countenance darkened. When they mounted the platform, hard behind the first medics, and saw the litter of bodies, he had gone white.

The ambulance lifted and roared away toward the city, and Francis took a step forward. "I don't think there's anything we can do here," he suggested.

With a wordless look of contempt, Dryke started down the platform toward the observation deck and the trio of city police still working the scene.

"Officer," he said, accosting the nearest, "I'm Mikhail Dryke, Allied Transcon security."

"You folks made the call on this?"

"Yes. If there's something we can do—"

"You did it."

"Did the medics give you any report on the injured?"

"Nobody's dead, if that's what you mean." He checked the screen of his slate. "The Martinez woman is about the worst of them—ribs, spleen, facials, concussion." The officer shook his head. "You'd think the word'd get around," he said. "You'd think they'd learn."

Dryke's brow wrinkled. "This has happened before?"

"Third time I know of. First for that, though," he added, gesturing at the plex and the sun-baked graffito FOR THE HOMEWORLD.

Dryke stared. "I didn't know," he said.

"Well, this should be the last. City manager'll probably recommend we close this up," the officer said. "We can't have someone here all the time, after all."

"*We* can," Dryke said firmly. "Would that step on anyone's toes?"

"Not mine," the officer said with a shrug. "You'll want to check with Lieutenant Alvarez. Transit Division."

"I'll do that," Dryke said. "Excuse me."

Francis saw Dryke returning and brightened; he was eager to leave the platform. Then he saw how Dryke's expression had hardened and began to quail.

"Your office," Dryke said curtly as he stalked past.

But Francis's office could not contain Dryke's rage. It spilled over into the adjacent hallway and the Building 1 courtyard, into a cascade of whispers and gossip.

"Why didn't our people respond?" Dryke demanded, backing Francis toward his desk. "They were right there—they could have stopped it."

"The observation deck's not Allied property," Francis said defensively. "It's not our responsibility."

Dryke balled his fists as though he were about to strike Francis, then caught himself and turned away. "Son of a bitch," he muttered.

"Besides," Francis went on, emboldened, "it could easily have been a diversion aimed at getting through the north gate. In fact, we don't know that it wasn't. The standard gate complement is three. If two of them go racing up to the platform to play hero, that's as good as throwing the gate wide open. And considering what happened this morning, prudence—"

Whirling, Dyke raged, "What about the last time? And the time before that? What excuse do you have for them? And why the hell didn't I see something about this in your monthlies?"

"That's not Allied property," Francis began bravely. "None of our people were involved—"

"They should have been, goddammit, aren't you listening?"

Francis tried to stand his ground, though it had turned to sand beneath him. "I don't believe that these incidents are properly the concern of Corporate Security."

" 'For the Homeworld' painted in blood and it's not our concern? Christ, would I have even heard about this one if I hadn't happened to be here?"

"These incidents are off-site, only outsiders are involved, and there's been no threat to our people or our operations—"

"A moment ago you were trying to convince me that there is a threat," Dryke said coldly. "You can't have it both ways."

Francis surrendered, the resilience leaving his body as he slipped down into his chair. "There were three incidents before today, not two," he said. "The first time, a woman alone up there at night was raped. We didn't know about it until it was

over. The second time involved a couple, about thirty, who got
roughed up a little. The third time, a couple of thugs scattered
a pretty good crowd with pepperguns. I didn't see where any of
it touched us. If I was wrong, I was wrong.''

"You were wrong,'' Dryke said curtly. He flexed his shoulders and sighed. "All right. We've got some making up to do.
Find out who those people were. I want flowers in their rooms
by visiting hours. Sympathy and our sincere regrets. And if any
of them have exposure on the medical bills, I want them to know
we're going to cover it.''

Francis squinted questioningly at his superior. "Mr. Dryke,
I understand the gesture, really I do. But isn't that just going to
make it seem like we're admitting responsibility?''

"We are responsible,'' Dryke said. "If you don't see that yet,
you're even denser than I thought.''

"I was just concerned about liability—''

"Let them sue us. We should have done more. *Will* do more.
I want two of your people stationed on the ob deck around the
clock, starting immediately. In uniform. I want them to be a
presence,'' Dryke said. "But a friendly presence—find some
people with personality. Those folks that come to watch our
ships fly are our friends. And we're damn well going to start
taking better care of our friends.''

CHAPTER 3

-|UAU|-

"... a student of history ..."

SITTING BACK IN HIS BOWLLIKE OPERATOR'S CHAIR, CHRISTO-
pher McCutcheon studied the center pair of the ten standard
displays arrayed before him in the darkened archaeolibrarian's
booth. His gaze flicked from the upper screen to the slim green-
bound volume resting on his lap, then back. Frowning, he
pressed the black bar on the right armrest.

"Come on, Ben, you've got to have some cross-reference,"
he said. "These guys didn't come out of nowhere, write this
book, and then vanish."

"I'm sorry, Chris," replied Benjamin, the most agreeable of
the library's AIP constructs, "I find nothing with the search keys
'A. Privat Deschanel' or 'J. D. Everett.' I do find entries for
the Lycée Louis le Grand, the Academy of Paris, Queen's College in Belfast, D. Appleton and Company of New York—"

"What's the closest match on Deschanel?"

A third display sprang to life to display a double-column list
of names. "A Paul Eugène Louis Deschanel was the tenth President of the Third French Republic in 1920," Benjamin said as
a monochrome photograph appeared on a fourth display.

"Birth date?"

"February 13, 1855." The text of a biography took over a
fifth screen.

"Too late," Christopher said. "All right. New entry." All
five active displays blanked momentarily. "Key to title, author,
coauthor, associations for both. Cross-link to physics, history of
science, natural philosophy, mechanical engineering, technol-

23

ogy. There're a lot of cutaway drawings and diagrams in this one, so let's make it an image upload with text call. Give me the null reference list on the big screen.''

"I understand," Benjamin said, and a slotlike drawer opened in the sloping semicircular panel below the bank of screens.

Christopher leaned forward and laid the green volume in the drawer. "And be careful with that one," he added. "It's almost two hundred years old."

"Always, Chris."

It took bare seconds for the source upload to begin and the results to be reflected on the quiescent displays. Christopher sat back and watched the "picture window" display high above the center of the operator's panel. As the library's engine began analyzing the contents of *Deschanel's Natural Philosophy*, thirteenth edition, 1898, the list of terms which had no reference anywhere in *Ur*'s library began to build: Atwood's Machine, Vase of Tantalus, Morin's Apparatus.

What good any of it would do the pioneers when they reached Tau Ceti was neither Benjamin's nor Christopher's concern. Their task was to help assure that the starship carried with it the most complete and most accurate library of human thought and experience available—a fully interlinked hyperlibrary drawing on sources neglected even by DIANNA and her counterparts DIANE in Europe and DIANA in Asia.

There were a hundred scavengers in the field, supported by a public appeal campaign paying finder's fees to donors of material on the team's Red List. More than two hundred of Allied Transcon's Houston complement were working part- or full-time on the library, including forty archaeolibrarians.

Adding in the staff in Munich and Tokyo, as well as the scratch squad on *Memphis* herself, more than a thousand people were devoting their energies to building the pyramid. The *Memphis* library was already forty percent larger than that which had sailed with *Ur*, and exponentially more complex.

Even so, there was a crisis atmosphere in Building 16, a sober urgency which belied the fact that the target sailing date was still fourteen months away. Part of the urgency came from the realization that larger did not necessarily mean better. More than a quarter million errors had been found in the *Ur* library in the years since it sailed, and management was determined to produce a cleaner product the second time around.

The balance of the urgency came from the knowledge that

Memphis's sailing date was an absolute deadline. Data time on the starship's thousand-channel laser link and the five-channel neutrinio was too precious for all but the most crucial corrections and updates. There would never be room for the likes of *Infantry Drill Regulations 1911*, the novels of Michael Hudson, or *Deschanel's Natural Philosophy*.

"Excuse me, Chris," said Benjamin politely.

Christopher pressed the black bar. "Yes?"

"I see that the current volume is marked 'Part One,' and there are references in the text to a Part Two, a Part Three, a Part Four, and the topics covered in those volumes. Are those sources also available at this time?"

"No," Christopher said. "Like I said, it's almost two hundred years old. We are lucky to find this one—it turned up at an estate liquidation in Michigan. Nineteenth-century science texts are about as welcome as acid-based paper at the Library of C."

"I'll make secondary entries for the missing volumes with the information available," Benjamin volunteered.

"Do that," Christopher said.

"Shall I add them to the Red List as well?"

"No. But you can find me a current hydraulics instructional. A lot of these nulls look like demonstration gadgets. They may correspond to some of the computer models used later on."

The instructional came up on a blank display a moment later Christopher leaned on the red bar and began navigating through the full-color animated sequences with half-whispered commands, seeking a match for the pen-and-ink drawing on the adjacent screen. It was several minutes before he noticed the blue mail window up on display ten, and the one-word message therein:

LUNCH?—DK

"Send to Daniel," Christopher said, touching the white bar. "Sure. I'll come there. I can use the walk."

The mail window dissolved into Daniel Keith's sandy-haired and smiling visage. "Wrong, wrong, wrong I need to get out of this zoo for an hour a lot more than you need to exercise. I'll come to you, Twelve-fifteen."

"Food's better at the central cafeteria," Christopher reminded his friend.

"If you get a chance to eat it," Keith said dryly. "It's three weeks until the first batch of selection notices. A selection coun-

selor's got about as much chance of enjoying a quiet lunch as
Jeremiah has of being named captain of the *Memphis*.''
    "Read and understood," Christopher said with a grin. "I'll
see you downstairs in a bit." He touched the black bar. "Ben,
show me the Bramah Press again, will you? And let me know
when it's ten after.''

    The rumble of a departing Pelican echoed in the garden court-
yard just as Christopher McCutcheon and Daniel Keith were
settling at a small table shaded by a broad-leafed tree.
    "I'm serious," Keith was saying. "It's like they think the
rules are different now than they were a year ago. I've had all
kinds of offers this last month—and that's from *our* people. God
help me if anybody outside finds out what I do.''
    "If you want to keep the secret, you'd better watch where you
flash this," Christopher said, reaching across the table and tucking the bottom half of Keith's ID inside his shirt pocket. "We
know what goes on in Building 37, too. You'd probably get accosted just on general principles.''
    "I don't doubt it," Keith said, cracking his soup container
open.
    "So, did you report the offers?''
    "A few. The serious ones. The scary ones.''
    "Take any offers?''
    Keith's mouth worked wordlessly, then turned up in a sheepish
grin. "No. And I don't know if that makes me a saint or an
idiot," he said.
    "Depends on the temptation in question, I guess," Christo-
pher said, amused.
    "Ranged from truly sad to died-and-gone-to-heaven.''
    "Oh?''
    "I'll have to show you. One woman mailed me sixty seconds
of very—uh, wet video. On reconsideration, I *am* a saint," Keith
said. "Look, you must have something to talk about that doesn't
have anything to do with *Memphis*. Tell me about Jessica. Tell
me how wonderful it is to wake up next to something like that.''
    "Don't tell me *you* want her, too," Christopher said dourly.
    Keith shrugged. "Hair down to here, tits out to there—what
did you expect?'' Then he caught the unhappiness in Christopher's eyes, and his demeanor changed. "Don't tell me there's
a problem already.''
    "Yeah. Me.''

"Huh?"

He toyed with a spoon before answering. "I found out I don't like sharing Jessie."

"No surprise," Keith said. "Nobody does. Your woman lies down with someone else and your genes start screaming at you for not protecting their interests. No matter how noble and rational you're determined to be, there's a little program running in the back of your mind saying, 'No, you idiot,' and worse."

"I know."

Keith went on, "This can't have been a surprise, though—even though she's only been living with you for, what, two months? A woman like that's going to attract a lot of attention, and you three aren't contracted. And hasn't Loi had other lovers all along?"

Christopher nodded. "I couldn't do anything about that. That was clear going in. That's why she wouldn't go for a closed contract." He paused, then added quietly, "I guess that's part of the reason I wanted Jessie in the house. I thought she was going to be all mine."

"While she had to share you with Loi?"

"I said it was what I wanted. I didn't say it was fair." He sipped at his iced tea. "So maybe it's justice, after all."

"What's justice? What exactly happened?"

"Loi and Jessie happened. While I was playing my usual Sunday gig down in Freeport."

"Oh-*ho*."

"Which means?"

"Which means I could have seen that one coming."

"This makes sense to you?"

"Sure," Keith said. "My moms were closer to each other than to either of my dads. Same thing happened with Brenda and Jo. As far as I can tell, if there's two women in the house, they either form the strongest bond in the family or they split the family apart scratching at each other. Mostly the former."

"I don't have the benefit of your experience," Christopher said. "My only other trine was two men and a woman."

"What about your own family?"

Christopher shook his head. "My mother died three years before I was born—"

"Excuse me?"

"Frozen embryo. They took some eggs when my mother took sick, just in case."

"Huh," Keith said. "Interesting. Right out of the soaps."

Tight-lipped, Christopher nodded and said, "Anyway, De-ryn—she was my host and my nurture-mother both—was the only woman in the house when I was growing up."

"You have a sister, don't you?"

"Doesn't count."

"I suppose not," Keith said. "Look, did you bring this business up hoping for some free advice?"

"Did I bring it up?" Christopher asked. "Never mind. You can play relationship technologist if you want. *Doctor* Keith."

Keith smiled. "It's nothing brilliant. It just seems to me that what happened was still inside the family, even if it was kind of a rude surprise. And along the lines of what I said earlier, you've probably got to take it as a good thing."

"You're talking to the guy up here," Christopher said glumly, tapping his temple. "And he knows all that." He touched the center of his chest. "It's this guy that's having the trouble."

"Evict him," Keith said with mock solemnity.

"I tried. He's got a long-term lease."

"Bribe him, then. See if you can buy him off with the erotic possibilities of two women together."

"No chance. We were playing three-in-a-bed the first week Jessie moved in. He just feels left out." Christopher shook his head. "I really love both of them."

"Try 'loving' them a little less and trusting them a little more," Keith said wisely. "It's a better mix in the long run."

"Yeah," Christopher agreed. "Fine. But how do you do it, Daniel? How the hell do you get from here to there?"

Keith smiled, chewing. "I only do theoretical, Chris. Practical's up to you."

Though music was playing throughout the house when Christopher McCutcheon arrived home, he seemed to be alone there. But Jessica quickly appeared as he entered, her body tucked into black slacks and blouse, her long hair pulled together at the back of her neck into a golden waterfall.

"Hello, Chris," she said cheerily, intercepting him near the door with a hug.

The hug lasted until it triggered recent memories, and Christopher stepped away. "Where's Loi?"

"With a client, previewing a commissioned piece. Barring

disaster, she'll be home at seven or so. Can you survive without dinner until then?''

He shrugged. "I guess so."

"I haven't seen you to talk to since Sunday morning. How did your set at Alec's go?"

"Not too badly, I guess," he said, continuing past her. "Alec seemed happy, anyway. Of course, all he cares about is that he does more business with me there than he was before I started."

"Did you do 'Caravan to Antares'?" she asked, following.

"Yeah. Last song of the night. Just me and the hard-core."

"And?"

"I don't think they quite knew how to take it."

"It's a terrific song," she said earnestly.

A crooked smile, thrown back over one shoulder. "So long as no one from Allied hears it. I'm going to check mail, okay?"

She stopped following and let him escape. "Okay, Chris." Her poignant expression was wasted; he did not see it as he settled in front of the housecom.

"Mail," he said, absently noting Jessica's footsteps on the stairs behind him as the sole message came up.

"Hello, Christopher," said William McCutcheon, looking out at him from the display.

His father's face was not a friendly one—eyes too piercing, jaw too stern and angular. But his voice, warm and cultured, moderated the effect.

"I'm sure you won't be surprised to hear that Allied was in the news today," the senior McCutcheon continued. "This business with Homeworld reminded me that you haven't been up to visit since you started there—what, six months, seven months ago? Why don't you come up this weekend." Not a question. Something closer to a command. "You can tube up Friday night and leave early enough Sunday not to disappoint your followers. Don't bother with a rental. I'll pick you up in Portland."

The display dimmed, and Christopher sat back in the chair, thoughtful. The break had been more complete than his father had acknowledged. There had been no meaningful contact in nearly three months. Moreover, it was not mere neglect, but a conscious choice not to risk an open fight, not to face his father's fury.

Even at twenty-seven, on his own for a dozen years, Christopher dreaded his father's disapproval. When he decided, after much agonizing, to come to Allied, Christopher had not sought either his father's permission or his approval. Permission was not required, and approval was not likely. Not from the man who had made Christopher refuse the selection option won in a tenth-grade cybernetics contest. Not from the man who had spent *Ur*'s sailing day climbing Saddle Mountain, safely out of touch with the net and out of the reach of any Diaspora zealots.

Christopher had sent the news wrapped in a tissue of justification, and his father responded with an acknowledgment empty of both criticism and congratulation. The rules of the compact seemed clear: You are my son and I love you, but I cannot love this choice you've made.

But now his father had broken the contract of silence with an invitation. A summons, couched in the civilities of family. The confrontation Christopher had thought he had avoided loomed before him.

"Chris?" Jessie's voice, timid and tentative, intruded on his thoughts.

He twisted in the seat to see her sitting on the stairs, halfway between floors. "What's the matter?"

"That's what I was wondering. Are you mad at me?"

"Why would I be mad?" he asked, delaying an answer.

"About last night."

He pursed his lips, polled his feelings. "Nah," he said, and shrugged.

"I could use just the littlest bit more reassurance than that," she said.

"Like?"

She stood up, a far more flattering pose for her figure. "Will you come upstairs and make love with me?"

He hesitated, polling another set of readings. "With pleasure," he said, bounding out of the chair wearing a playful smile.

It wasn't too difficult to see that they were still involved when Loi and seven o'clock arrived.

CHAPTER 4

-|AUC|-

"... the bandits of Allied Transcon ..."

IT WAS CALLED THE DIRECTOR'S RESIDENCE, BUT IT MIGHT AS well have been called the Director's Refuge. Located on the western edge of the compound, three kilometers from the cluster of towers and pyramids which housed the Diaspora staff, the small white Minano-designed bungalow was off-limits except at the explicit invitation of its sole occupant, and such invitations were rare. No more than a half dozen of Prainha's 35,000 residents and employees—including those whose task it was to clean the bungalow—knew how Hiroko Sasaki lived.

Sasaki had no kin or roots on Earth, no purpose but the Project, no life outside of Prainha. Anything else that might be, that might be desired or desirable, was on hold, tabled until that which must be, was. For now, she was what she did. She spent as many hours as she could in the warren, driving herself and the Project staff toward efficiency, toward excellence, demonstrating by example the level of commitment she expected, the Project demanded. When she felt herself reaching her limit of patience or energy, she withdrew, retreating to the bungalow to rest and restore.

To serve effectively in that role, the bungalow was, as it must necessarily be, a world apart. Her world, private and personal. Its thick soundprooted walls closed out the sound of the multigigawatt laser lifting the T-ships skyward. Its only windows, a broad expanse of sloping plex across the face of the overthrust second story, faced the jungle, as though denying that the entire Prainha compound existed.

But that was as close as Sasaki cared to get to what remained of the great Amazonian wildlands. Born in the first of the satlands nearly half a century ago, Sasaki had never learned how to live with or in large spaces. Even the bungalow was uncomfortably, embarrassingly spacious. She used only three rooms of the bungalow's fourteen, and spent most of her time in just one, the second-floor greatroom behind the wall of plex.

Sasaki had filled the spaces she did claim with objects she loved, with as much beauty as could harmoniously coexist there. From the Sorayama original on the north wall, a chrome dolphin gracefully leaping from the sea, to the pastel rice-paper *bunjinga* by Gyokudo which filled the south, the greatroom was a living museum. The Imari porcelain, the bronze of the Galloping Horse of Kansu, the pre-Revolution Valenciennes lace—each image, each piece, vibrated with life. Each was one breath of the yearning, one thread in the weave. She touched them, and they touched her. And the touch helped make her whole.

So, too, did the touch of Lujisa, one of the few who were not only permitted but invited to enter the Director's Residence. Sasaki had an ageless body, supple and sleek. But at the end of a sixteen-hour day filled with Jeremiah and the Homeworld, negotiations with Beijing to lease the *Memphis* hyperlibrary and with the astronauts' union to avoid a threatened strike, and conferences on six of the six thousand suits pending against Allied Transcon, enough stress had penetrated through her meditative calm to knot muscles and snarl the flow of energies through her body.

Sasaki stood at the window, gazing out at the fading purplered glow of what had been a disappointingly banal sunset, waiting. The colors in her Kanja silk robe were more vivid even in the waning light than the sky colors had been at their peak. A hint of the simple dish of shrimp and rice which she had prepared for herself still hung in the air.

When the housecom announced Lujisa's arrival, Sasaki let the robe slip from her shoulders. Unselfconsciously nude, she crossed the room to the raised futon as Lujisa appeared at the top of the stairs. Sasaki offered no greeting, nor did Lujisa expect one. She followed Sasaki wordlessly to the tablelike bed; while the Director stretched full length, facedown on its unyielding surface, the masseuse opened her small bag and retrieved oil and a thick soft towel.

The massage began with Lujisa's hands passing slowly over

Sasaki's body as though floating on a cushion of air, as though feeling for the shape of her body rather than the substance. Whatever Lujisa was touching, she learned from it. Her hands hovered, hesitated, probed.

"Heat here," she said. "And here."

"Yes," Sasaki acknowledged.

Then, her hands slick with fragrant skin-warmed oil, Lujisa began her magic. She worked the muscles and the chakras at once, relaxing the former, clearing the latter, opening the channel from root to crown with a touch which shaped and molded the energy of Sasaki's body as skillfully as it shaped her flesh and muscle.

Sasaki surrendered herself to the invasion, opening and releasing, until it seemed as though she, too, were floating on a cushion of air. The pain of shiatsu, Lujisa's strong fingers knowingly savage on the soles of Sasaki's feet, the palms and joints of her hands, was transmuted by that surrender into bliss and balm elsewhere in her body. She was clay, without will, with Lujisa as sculptor.

When it was over, Sasaki lay on her back, eyes closed, savoring the balance and clarity in her body, the world reduced to that space encompassed by self. It was in this state that Lujisa would leave her, quietly collecting her kit and absenting herself.

But this time, Sasaki called her back with a single word, half whispered.

"More."

Lujisa turned and wordlessly returned to the table. This time the hands were gentle, though just as knowing. Oil-slick fingertips slipped between sweet-slick labia, found and caressed the swelling nub concealed within. Sasaki lay with eyes closed, legs together, her only response at first a slight quickening of her breath, the rise and fall of her boyish breasts.

Floating upward, mind still clear, body still calm, she allowed the warming wave to spread outward from her center, to rock all of her being to a single rhythm. She was egoless and empty. She was all and alive. Her legs parted, a wordless invitation. Her lips parted, a wordless exultation.

But Sasaki's cries were measured, polite, bare hints of the soaring of her soul. Her pleasure was her own. She did not share it with Lujisa, did not invite her within. Though she craved the release, shame kept her inside herself, rejecting intimacy.

She told Lujisa only in the silent signs of her body's own

language, in tensed hands and flushed skin, in quicksilver wetness, of the spiraling energy within. Lujisa read the messages
and answered in kind, her touch faster, firmer, more insistent.
And at last Sasaki's body arched, seized, gasping, grasping the
white light at the top of the spiral. There was a long moment of
unity, of focus, and then she was floating downward, tranquil,
content.

Her eyes flicked open, and she found Lujisa's face. "Thank
you," she said.

Lujisa showed a small smile, then quietly left her.

It was only what Sasaki needed, not all she wanted. She
wanted more—more of laughter, more of love, more of self,
more of silence. She wanted empty days in which to rediscover
what she wanted. But there was no time. And there would be
no time for such indulgences until the starship *Memphis* broke
orbit and was on its way at last.

CHAPTER 5

-|GCC|-

"... *our gentle mother.*"

FRIDAY FOUND CHRISTOPHER MCCUTCHEON A RELUCTANT traveler, Oregon-bound.

The New Orleans–Houston–San Antonio feeder loop of the tube was still a year from completion, so he was obliged to make the 200-mile-plus run to DFW in his skimmer. By the time he reached the transplex, it was after seven o'clock, late enough to escape the commuter bulge, though not enough to dispel the air of chaos.

But then, it was never really quiet at the Dallas–Fort Worth transplex. Not with the confluence of the third busiest airport in the world, the ninth busiest spaceport, a mainline station for the primary southern tube, the metroplex's own double-line tramway, plus flyer and surface traffic to boot. DFW was a traveler's rite of passage, a nightmare despite the load cycling and smart-guides. Locals avoided DFW whenever possible; survivors asserted blackly that its initials stood for "Don't Forget to Write."

Humor was a good weapon, patience a better one. Christopher ran into a ten-minute hang at the flyer storage stack, a twenty-minute backlog at the security checkpoint. On escaping those lines, he found that the slidewalk to the tube station was out of service, obliging him to walk the half-mile connecting corridor.

It was like running a gauntlet. Seven years in San Francisco had given Christopher a don't-bother-I'm-not-buying look which discouraged most ordinary panhandlers and deadweight. But DFW's parasites were bred for persistence. Discouraging look or not, Christopher was accosted four times—by a Mormon re-vivalist, by two canvassers for the Greens, and twice by joybirds working N Corridor's bed-box hotel. The revivalist was the hard-est to brush off; the whores were the most entertaining, offering to perform acts Christopher suspected were physically impossi-ble in the confines of a sleep capsule.

The final hurdle was the annoyingly slow-moving line at the tube fare machine, where an attempted cut-in precipitated a shoving match violent enough to attract the rentacops. But once inside the station, matters proceeded more smoothly. An esca-lator carried him down to a half-filled lounge; five minutes later, his train was called, and he continued down to the chutes.

One moment the track was empty, the red and green lights above each boarding chute marking the number of seats available on the approaching train. Then the great interlock separating the station from the evacuated stone tunnel opened, and the massive red and white cylinder slid through the aperture, its entry almost silent save for the rushing air. Boarding was swift and efficient. Christopher took the last seat in compartment 11, tucking his night bag in the underseat basket. In less than two minutes, the train continued on its way.

The cities flew by like subway stops: El Paso–Juarez, Phoenix–Tucson, the San Diego–Los Angeles sprawl. Christopher's com-partment emptied, filled, and emptied again. From outside San Diego north to the California border the trains ran on the sur-face, at half their underground speed—no one wanted to have to rebore a five-meter tunnel after an earthquake. But the scattering of lights glimpsed at high speed through tiny windows was little distraction from his thoughts.

Christopher tried to concentrate on the unfinished lyric of a new song, tried to interest himself in an odd little book on neo-teny, halfheartedly tried to engage the jet-eyed Filipino woman who boarded at Sacramento in conversation. He was successful at none of those efforts, which left him sitting half curled in the half-darkness, thinking about Oregon. Thinking about William McCutcheon.

It had always been a mystery to Christopher how he could feel so uncomfortable in the presence of someone he loved so much. He had found it difficult living in the Vernonia house with his father, the more so as he left childhood behind. William Mc-Cutcheon was a magnet toward which everything turned. When he was home, it was clearly *his* home, and he filled it with his

unequivocal expectations—expectations of excellence and, less
nakedly stated, of obedience. Lines of force, radiating outward
to bind everything in their reach to he who stood at the center.

When his father was absent—as he often was for business, for
a month or more at a time—the house was calmer. Christopher
felt a better balance with Deryn, who threatened none of his
ambitions. In the glare of his father's light, Christopher had trouble seeing his own. Against the weight of his father's opinions,
Christopher had trouble holding his own.

In one of their few conversations on the subject of William
McCutcheon, Deryn had told him, "Your father doesn't know
how to be anything other than what he is. Try to appreciate
what's best in him, and try not to take the rest personally."

It had seemed an odd thing to say. His father's flaws were not
the problem—it was his own flaws that Christopher felt so
acutely. Measured against his father's accomplishments, Christopher found his own achievements shabby and wanting. It was
the same at fifteen, at twenty-five, as it had been in the open-
eyed infant years. Mere age and physical stature had changed
nothing. He could still only see his father by looking up.

Even more, Christopher knew that he did not yet truly understand his father, that he did not yet see him clearly. There were
unresolved paradoxes in William McCutcheon. Quick-witted, but
he used his humor as a weapon. An incisive thinker, but close-
minded and stubborn. A genteel, well-spoken man who could
turn curt and coldly dismissive in an eye-blink. Who drew people to him, and yet had opted to live alone for the last dozen
years.

Somehow, he was all of those things. And the pieces would
not fit together, frustrating Christopher's quest to close with this
man who still, at more than a decade's remove, from half a
continent away, piped the tune to which Christopher danced.

William McCutcheon.

Father.

The moment it cleared the Portland flight-restriction zone, the
Avanti Eagle carrying William and Christopher McCutcheon
home soared skyward five hundred meters and surged forward
at full thrust through the night. The diffuse glow of Hillsboro
and Beaverton, the scattered lights of the wheelies and skimmers
bound to Highway 26, fell away below and then behind them.

Still Christopher pressed his face to the window, more hiding than watching.

His father had not met him at the gate, but paged him instead from the pickup curb. That was both annoying and merciful—merciful because it avoided any waiting-lounge hugs or other embarrassing efforts at intimacy. All Christopher had to do was clamber in, flash a quick smile and say "Hello, Father" to the man driving, and settle back in his seat.

The Eagle, a six-figure six-seater appointed with expensive natural fibers and a whisper-quiet extended-range flight package, was new since Christopher had last seen his father. Letting him relate its pleasures and mysteries had avoided the inevitable awkwardness for the first few minutes; sight-seeing and reminiscing had postponed it still further. But his father did not do his part in fueling the idle chatter, and Christopher had run out of landmarks.

"Not much to see out there," his father said.

Innocent enough words from anyone else's mouth, the observation struck Christopher as a reproach. "More than I saw the whole way up," he said truthfully.

"But what's to see from the tube?" William McCutcheon asked. "Houses stacked one upon the other like cancer cells, and serving as little purpose. Consider yourself lucky, Christopher. The railway designers were kind."

"I think the engineers had the last word, not the designers."

"If the engineers had had the last word, there'd be no windows in the cars at all," McCutcheon said, downshifting into a lecture. "If you want to look out, look up. You'll never see a night as clear as this one in Salem or Sacramento or San Bernardino, not with the haze hanging and the sick-sodium halo."

"Maybe so," Christopher said, heading it off. "But I wish it was daytime. The stars are the same here as in Texas. What I'd like is a look at Mount Hood."

"I expect it looks more or less like it did the last time you saw it," McCutcheon said.

"Wyeast," Christopher said. "That's what the Indians called it. Did you know that?"

"Wy*est*," his father said, correcting his pronunciation. "Yes, I knew that." He shook his head. "Why I know it, I couldn't tell you."

The correction irritated Christopher. "Maybe Deryn told you," he said, the mention of her name a bold bit of defiance.

"She used to tell me Nisqually and Okanagon stories—how the Coyote made the Columbia, the story of the Changer."

"Did she," His father's voice was cold.

"I'd forgotten until a few weeks ago, when I indexed a book of Indian legends." He laughed. "It's odd. The Indians were here for hundreds of years, but we name the mountain after a British admiral who never even saw it. Doesn't seem right, somehow."

" 'Das Weltgeschichte ist das Weltgericht,' " his father quoted. "The world's history is the world's judgment, now as in Schiller's time. We're here—where are the Nisqually? Mount Hood will do for us. Or are you rewriting history down there in Houston as you compile it?"

"No," Christopher said. "But there's more than one history of the world, I'm discovering. And the Nisqually's version has a place in the library along with ours."

To Christopher's surprise, his father surrendered the point. "Fairly answered," McCutcheon said. "How is your work going?"

Another surprise. Christopher felt as though he had wandered into conversational quicksand. "There's too much of it, and not enough of us," was his cautious reply. "Or enough time."

"That's regrettable," McCutcheon said. "The work you're doing is valuable. It is, to my mind, the only worthwhile aspect of the Diaspora Project."

Allowing his surprise to show, Christopher said, "I didn't think you approved of my being there."

"You're not going to Tau Ceti," McCutcheon said matter-of-factly. "You're not even helping those who are going to leave. What you're doing is helping us find knowledge we've lost."

"On the payroll of Allied Transcon."

McCutcheon gestured with his right hand as though waving off an irrelevancy. "Do you realize how many people believe that everything we know is in DIANNA? That it's the first and last source? The Authority. But it only contains the tenth part of everything we are."

"It's a digest. An electronic encyclopedia," Christopher said. "That's all it was ever meant to be."

"And the more we come to depend on it, the more its weaknesses show. Washington knows that. And Allied Transcon knows that. It's inevitable that DIANNA will be upgraded with the *Memphis* hyperlibrary. The only issue is the price."

Christopher was slow to answer. "I'm surprised to hear you say that."

"That I value learning? That I believe in the Twenty-ninth amendment? Access to information doesn't mean much when all you have access to is rewritten secondhand truth."

"That's not what I meant," Christopher said. "I'm just surprised to hear that you support anything that Allied is doing. In fact, I imagined you celebrating what happened this week."

"Celebrating? Why?"

"Because of what you've said before."

"What I've said is that I object to the obscene expenditure of energy—human and otherwise—on such a dubious enterprise. And you agreed with me, as I recall. Have you changed your mind?"

"No," Christopher said, wondering if he had agreed or merely acceded. "It's just that I thought you'd be happy to see the Project stopped."

"Did *you* celebrate?"

"No—"

"Why not?"

Christopher considered. "I suppose because I don't think it can be stopped. All Homeworld can accomplish is to make it more expensive. And maybe convince a few pioneers to change their minds and stay here."

Ahead, a single light atop a dark tree-covered ridge marked their destination. It seemed as though William McCutcheon fixed on it and did not hear. Then he shook his head.

"Earth is better off without them," he said, his voice cold. "She is full, and she is tired. Why should we try to stop them? They're the ones who want more from her than she has left to give. I don't begrudge their leaving. We give them up gladly."

There was an edge in his father's voice, a finality to his words, that warned against any attempt to disagree or even to continue the discussion. But as the flyer curled downward toward his father's hilltop hermitage, Christopher wondered in silence why the words and the emotion behind them sounded so familiar.

It was a cliché out of a storybook family life Christopher had not lived, and he did not take note of it until after the fact.

"Would you mind if I took the skimmer? I'd like to run down to Vernonia for a little while."

His father did not mind. Saturday was the same as any other

day to the self-employed, and William McCutcheon was already settled before the comsole in his den, attending to some of the myriad details of his multiple businesses.

"Be back by noon, though," McCutcheon called back over his shoulder. "I want to hike across to the fire tower and see if that last storm finally did in the roof. But I have a couple of hours of work in front of me here first."

"Okay." It would take them two hours to traverse a distance the Avanti could cover in ten minutes, then two more hours back, but Christopher did not object. He had wondered how they were going to fill the hours until Sunday morning; a walk through the forest was among the most attractive options.

The skimmer, a five-year-old Saab, gave no sign of having been used since Christopher was last there. As he stowed the cover and ran through the power-up sequence, he found himself wondering exactly what his father would be doing while he was gone.

Christopher had never been invited to share the fine details of family—that is to say, his father's—finances. He had never been offered a clear picture of where his father's money came from— nothing as simple as, say, his grandfather Carl, who had been a millwright, or his great-grandfather William, who had been one of the last of the logging-truck drivers to work the twisting high-ways and narrow dirt roads of southwest Columbia County.

As best as Christopher understood, his father was at once a land broker, a biomechanical engineer, and a political consul-tant. The engineering had come first and was the only profession which could be deduced from the contents of his father's den-office—the shelves and walls featured models and drawings of clever and impossible gadgets, as well as the certificates for the two nanotech patents McCutcheon held in his own name.

Profits from the patents had apparently led him to land and then to brokering, which seemed to take the most time, return the most headaches, and generate both the most income and the least discussion. The consulting had come along but recently, growing out of ever-more-healthy contributions to the Oregon Greens and the Republican National Party. Christopher was not sure exactly what his father had to offer them beyond money, nor how much he had had to do with the successes of "his" candidates for governor and, in the last election, U.S. senator.

But whatever the source, there was no question that there was money, in more than adequate supply. The host contract with

Deryn had run to six figures (he had found a copy playing teen-hacker games with the housecom files), and the nurture contract had probably more than doubled that. His sister, Lynn-Anne, had gone to Bennington, Christopher to Salem Academy at fifteen and then to Stanford, all institutions with if-you-have-to-ask tuitions. And though the house, a double-dome Fuller in redwood and seal-shingle, was modest to the eye, it sat in the heart of more than six thousand acres of fir forest which had not seen a saw for a century—and to all of which his father held title.

It had never been a silver-spoon life. But if his father had ever had those tastes, it probably could have been.

Once a sodden mud track beaten down by an endless parade of heavily laden trucks, the old logging road leading down to Vernonia Road—which the state insisted on calling Route 47—was long since impassable for a wheeled vehicle. The forest had a tumbling-over-its-heels vitality, an irrepressible fecundity that had reached out to claim back the right-of-way the moment it was abandoned, a dozen, a hundred species of plant conspiring to soak up the scattered sunlight and heal the wound.

All that remained to mark the road was a serpentine trench of young trees winding through the taller Alpine fir and lodgepole pine blanketing the ridge. Taking the skimmer down it was a challenge to its ground-hugging flight system and to the reflexes of its driver. The reward was seeing the forest the way it showed itself best—from below, surrounded and looking up.

It was five miles and fifteen minutes to the bottom. At times the ranks of evergreens to either side seemed like the pillars of a grand cathedral. The air was humid and rich with the scents of life and decay. Christopher drew it in and breathed back out the tension in his muscles, the tightness in his chest. *If only I could relax with him,* he thought. *If only he could see me as I am.*

A hailer marked the end of McCutcheon property, and a few hundred meters farther the logging road met the highway. It had been at least a decade since 47 had been maintained for wheelies, and the ancient pavement of Vernonia Road was cracked and fissured and carpeted with moss. Most of what little traffic the artists and cityfleas of Vernonia generated had taken to the air, though the moss bore the crushed tracks of the fat-tired

omnis which brought freight in from Forest Grove, fifty kilometers to the south.

Christopher cruised slowly, noting with idle interest how fun-
gus and rot were fast pulling down what had been a home near
the roadside, that one nearly denuded hillside was beginning to
come back from the fire that had blackened it, where a sterile
new white package house had been tucked in among the trees
above tumbling Beaver Creek. But it was less than half a year
since his last visit, and little had changed except the season. His
pace was set less by the desire to sightsee than by the fact that
he really had nowhere to go.

The house on B Street had been his home for fifteen years. A
dozen years had passed since he left there, long enough for all
of his peers to have moved on or mutated into strangers. As for
adults, Jimmy, who had given him his first guitar lessons, and
Nick, the haiku poet who had befriended him, both still lived in
town, so far as Christopher knew. But he had not progressed
very far along the path that either man had urged on him, and
he did not think either would think much of the path he was on.

As he headed north toward Vernonia, Christopher considered
stopping at old Hamill Observatory, the one-time private astronomy center sitting on a thousand-foot ridge just to the east, a
mile up McDonald Road. In its prime, the observatory had been
a mecca for amateur astronomers, and its presence had helped
retard development in the forested Nehalem-Pebble Creek watershed for half a century.

But it was an idea whose time had passed. Astronomy now
belonged to the satlands brightening Earth's night sky. While
Christopher lived on B Street, Hamill was limping along, inglo-
riously, on tourists' curiosity and pay-per-view satland-
sightseeing. And while Christopher was at Stanford, Hamill's
owners finally bowed to the inevitable, retiring its ninety-year-
old telescopes and shuttering the silver domes. There had been
talk of making it a county museum, a state education center, but
nothing had come of the talk. Christopher let the turn-off flash
by. There would not be much to see now.

Then, rounding the last big curve south of town, his attention
was caught by the red-rusted gray steel of the Nisqually trestle.
There had been dozens of bridges and trestles along the old
narrow-gauge logging spurs through Columbia County, as both
the river and the railway switched back and forth at the dictates

of the land. Most had been torn down; a few had been preserved as part of the Columbia County Linear Park.

But the trestle just south of town was *the* trestle, a temptation and a challenge to every child of Vernonia. The rails were long gone; the timber approaches had rotted away to stumps. Inertia and engineering kept the rest there, a giant box bridge beam hanging just two meters above the flowing waters, anchored at either end by concrete footings.

On impulse, Christopher pulled off the road and parked the skimmer. He clambered out and studied the span with a smile, remembering how much higher and longer it had seemed when he was seven and ready to cross it for the first time. The metal had been slick with condensation, the river surging from a recent rain. *But I was most afraid of being caught,* he thought. *I had no idea that I could die here. I was fearless then.*

The last thought stuck uncomfortably in his ego, and before he quite realized what he was doing, he was standing atop the north end of the trestle, looking down through the web of metal at the river and across at the thicket of birches into which the roadbed vanished.

What the hell, he thought, and took a step forward. By the time he reached the far end he was laughing with rediscovered childhood joy. By the time he returned he was crying, and the reason was the same.

CHAPTER
6

"The trail of Gaea's pain ..."

THE HOUSTON POLICE FOUND ONE OF THE TRAMWAY THUGS before Allied's submersible found the Gulf jammer, but only just. Reports of the two captures reached Mikhail Dryke within an hour of each other. Either would have been sufficient reason to make Houston his next stop; both together were compelling enough for him to set aside his business in Munich and go there directly.

Dryke's Saab touched down at Houston in pitch-darkness, a few minutes after one. A young driver wearing Allied green picked up Dryke at the hangar and ferried him to the hardware lab, where he found the jammer sealed in an immersion tank and under guard by a gnomish sentry named Donovan. No technicians were in evidence, nor was there any sign that the unit had been touched.

"What's going on here?" Dryke demanded. "Why hasn't that jammer been torn down yet?"

"Mr. Dryke, Mr. Francis gave instructions that we were to hold it for your arrival," the driver said.

"Where is Francis?"

"I don't know, sir," Donovan volunteered. "He said that he would be back before you arrived, sir."

"When was that?"

"About seven o'clock."

Dryke muttered something unintelligible and stepped forward to look down into the tank. Though only shreds remained of the jammer's float bladder, the blue-green pear-shaped metal casing

45

gave no evidence of its five-day immersion in 160 feet of warm Gulf brine. Nor did it bear any obvious identifying marks.

But Dryke recognized it all the same. *Float jammer, Teledyne-Raytheon K-14 style, military model. Made by fifteen manufacturers in eleven countries. Knock-offs and licensees both. About as generic a piece of hardware as you can buy—*

"Who's the lab director?" Dryke asked, turning back to the other men.

"Dr. Kimura," they said together.

"You," Dryke said, pointing at the sentry. "Donovan. Call Dr. Kimura. Tell him I want him in here with his best technician by the time I get back. Tell him I want to know where this came from."

"Yes, sir."

"And you," Dryke said to the driver. "You're taking me downtown."

The driver nodded, and they started toward the door. But before they could reach it, Jim Francis appeared there.

"Mr. Dryke. I'm delighted to be able to bring you back with *good* news. It's in perfect condition—hardly even a scratch from the manipulators—" His voice trailed off as he saw the annoyance on Dryke's face. "Is something wrong?"

"May I see your gate ID, please?"

Puzzled, Francis retrieved the card from an inner pocket of his suit coat and handed it to Dryke.

"Donovan," Dryke said, folding the card in half with one hand until it snapped in two with a sharp crack. "Mr. Francis has just left the company. See that he leaves the grounds."

"What?" protested Francis. "You can't fire a man for being late—"

"Yes, sir," said Donovan, stepping forward.

Dryke nodded and turned away.

"Wait just a minute," Francis said angrily. "You owe me an explanation—"

Whirling, Dryke snapped, "If you were bright enough to be worth keeping, you wouldn't need an explanation. You've made it clear that you don't really understand what's going on. You've got your head buried in procedures and schedules and you just don't *see*. That makes you dangerous, Francis. I want you gone."

"I have fourteen years experience in corporate security—"

"And you haven't learned a thing from any of it except how

to dot your *i*'s." Dryke crossed his arms over his chest and shook his head in disgust. "Get him out of here."

Mikhail Dryke studied the picture on the security monitor—a high corner view of Dilan Elo White slouched with arrogant casualness in the sole chair in Interview 3, Transit Division, Houston Police Department.

"Cocky," Dryke said at last, looking up at the soft-faced, hard-eyed woman standing beside him.

"He's street," said Lieutenant Eilise Alvarez. "Country manners and city morals. Good ol' boy with an attitude."

"How did you find him?"

"We picked his fingerprints out of the blood smears on the plaz," Alvarez said. "He won't dean on the other two, though. Not even with four years in front of him and a Victim's Lien waiting for him when he comes out."

"How is the Martinez woman?"

"Last I heard she was still in intensive care. She got racked."

Dryke nodded and looked back at the screen. "This one have family?"

"No. Just relatives."

"Any leverage at all?"

"No," she said, and shook her head. "Twenty-one and as cold as they come. I don't think you're going to get any help from him."

"I want to be alone with him."

Alvarez nodded, "But the monitor stays on. I can't sanction any hands-on. He's in our custody. He'd walk. And you don't want that. Besides, this kind has thick calluses."

"I understand the rules."

"Okay," she said, standing. "Let's go."

Alvarez led him down the hall to the guard station at the interview suite, and the guard in turn escorted Dryke into Interview 3. White looked up lazily as he entered.

"So you're the fuck that's cheating me out of my sloop," the youth said, his mouth twisting into something that was half-sneer, half-scowl.

"Yeah," Dryke said, advancing toward the table. "I'm the luck."

"You're no cuff," White said, squinting. "Must be collar."

"I'm both," Dryke said. "Allied Transcon security."

White pursed his lips and waggled his hand in a mocking

gesture. "Little cuff, big collar," he said, folding his arms across his chest and closing his eyes. "Nothing to me, beershit. Not worth my sleep."

"I can get you out of here," Dryke said.

"Scammer."

"I can. Tonight."

In a vaguely reptilian manner, the youth's left eye opened slowly and regarded Dryke curiously. "Why?"

"That's the magic question," Dryke said. "Why?"

The other eye opened, wary. "Why what?"

"Why you and your friends came out to the observation platform Monday and racked the starheads."

White pulled himself up out of his slouch and twisted on his chair until he was facing Dryke. "You cute cuff psych, want to draw a pretty of my head?"

"I told you who I am. Why'd you do it?"

"Didn't."

"Scammer. You're not here for the food."

A shrug. "Fagging cuffs can lie from A, who catches 'em? It's their world."

"Fine," Dryke said, straightening. "Nice talking to you." He started for the door.

"Hey," White called. "Hey, collar. What d'you care?"

Dryke turned and regarded the youth coolly. "It's none of your business why we care," he said. "All you need to do is listen to the questions and roll out answers. You scam me, I walk. You help me, you walk. Choose."

A self-satisfied smirk spread across White's face. "Sure. Sure, we racked the 'heads. Pure gold Olympic. Fagging top jazz."

"Whose idea was it?"

"Who d'you think, scammer?"

"What gave you the idea?"

White shrugged. "Saw the hit on the wire, looked like good jazz. Thought we'd join the party and make our own hit." He laughed to himself. " 'Heads seeing stars now."

Dryke's face was a mask. "Tell me about the 'heads."

"Bore."

"Tell me."

"D'you know what I hate?" White said, coming up out of the chair, his body suddenly a coiled spring. " 'Heads got going-away eyes."

"What do you mean, going-away eyes?"

"Like they're with you but they're already gone. You seen 'em. They got their fagging noses in the air and their eyes blind with Starshine and they don't *see* you. Like you're a fagging ghost." His face was hard and prideful. "Well, we made 'em see us. We gave 'em a proper good-bye."

"They aren't the ones who are going," said Dryke. "The pioneers haven't even been selected yet."

"They're all the same," White said. "All the same to me."

"Tell me about Homeworld."

"Nothin' to tell."

"What about 'For the Homeworld' on the window?"

The youth sank back down into his seat and his casual slouch. "Jeremiah is cool jazz. You know brotherhood? He and me see the straight together."

"Who is Jeremiah?"

"You know—Jeremiah. Man, he is the fucking Avenger. The knife in the night. And sweet. You can't touch him."

"You believe what he believes?"

"You hurt anybody who hurts you or yours. I believe that, aces."

"Who did the starheads hurt?"

"They're so fagging greedy. They get nine zeros handed to them and don't even think about us," White said. "What makes one of them worth a billion chits, huh?"

Months ago, a popular satiric comedian had added the Project to his list of favorite targets. Taking a recently published—though inaccurate—estimate of the cost per colonist to build and launch *Memphis*, he began asking his audiences, "So—what did you do with *your* billion dollars?"

It was inaccurate. It was unfair. Within Allied Transcon, at least above the work circle level, it was worth your life to admit that you found it funny. But outside the company, especially among those under twenty-five, the routine struck a chord. It had taken the comedian from the club circuit to the big arenas, and the question had joined the slanguage as a catch phrase.

The catch phrase had in turn spawned a hundred variations, from "When I get my billion . . ." to "He/she must have gotten my billion by mistake . . ." So it wasn't much of a surprise for Dryke to hear another variation from Brian Elo White. But it wasn't much of a pleasure, either, and Dryke had to fight off the temptation to give a sharp answer.

"Do you want to go?" he asked instead.

White snorted. "Hell, no."

"Are you sure about that? What if I came here to offer you a chance to leave on *Memphis*?"

"Scammer." White scowled. "You'd never take someone like me."

"What if, Brian?" Dryke persisted. "Do you want to go?"

For a brief moment, White hesitated, caught between hope and skepticism. His eyes softened enough to admit a hint of wonder, and his face became that of a pensive child. Then the scowl returned, a cloud across the sun.

"You think I'm like them, beershit?"

"Do you want to go?"

"Spend the rest of my life with a bunch of 'heads, going nowhere fast? The hell with that. Fag 'em, fuck 'em, and rack 'em up. That's all they're good for. You understand?"

Nodding, Dryke said, "I understand." Then he sprang forward, catlike. His right foot lashed out, catching the knee of the youth's left leg and driving it downward. With the limb pinned between floor and chair, the knee hyperextended, then shattered with a horrible wet tearing sound that left the leg bent backward and started White screaming.

Writhing and wailing, White slid forward off his chair to the floor, clutching helplessly at the grotesquery. The steel toe of Dryke's left shoe swung forward in a swift arc that intercepted the youth's unprotected groin. White's screaming ended with an explosive cry and a strangled whimper, and his already pale skin went shocky white. As Dryke stepped back, the youth disintegrated into a huddled, twitching mass on the floor.

"That's for Dola Martinez," Dryke said quietly as a furious Lieutenant Alvarez and several other Transit cuffs burst into the room.

"I promised him he'd walk," was all he said.

They held him for more than an hour, first while they unraveled the status of a Russian-born British citizen carrying Brazilian diplomatic credentials, then while Lieutenant Alvarez balked at accepting the conclusions of that inquiry. He walked out of the station knowing that he had made no friends by what he had done.

But he also knew that only Mikhail Dryke and Hiroko Sasaki could rightly judge him, and that at least one of them believed that he had done nothing wrong.

• • •

Yotama Kimura led Dryke to the back of the clean room, where the jammer lay in pieces on a tear-down table. "This is Anna Romay," he said, introducing the technician hovering over the dissected machine. "Anna, please show Mr. Dryke what you found."

The technician reached for the articulated arm of the microviewer and pulled the screen forward. "There were three identifiers. The first was on the controller chip. The chip had been fried, of course, but they must have used an off-the-shelf bracket—see, here," she said, turning it over under the lens of the viewer.

Dryke studied the screen, the block lettering stamped into the foillike metal. "Yes, I see it. 'Inex, S.A.' South Africa?"

"No. Inex, S.A., is a chip shop in Mexico City. An old Intel subsidiary, specializing in standard X-ray burns. They have a lot of customers, but the South Africans aren't among them.

"So this points toward Taiwan or Chile. Or one of the guerrilla shops in California or Arizona."

"If you'll be patient, I can do better." She reached for another component. "Standard hardened hex-head lock screw. Eight-millimeter, forty-thread. Taiwan uses ten-millimeter, forty-thread."

"So it's from the West."

"I thought so as soon as I saw the controller chip. This was the clincher," she said, punching up a graph. "I did a mass spec on the casing. It came up with a mix that's in the base as U.S. Government bronze, spec H. Very old formulation. There's only seven mills around the world that still make it—three of which are owned by the Chilean government's National Metals."

"So it's Chile."

"I'd say so. Probably right out of military stores."

Thoughts tumbled through Dryke's mind. *Could be a straight sale, which won't take more than a bribe to track. The Chileans don't worry about much past seeing that your money's good. Or it could be black market, same reason. Or a sympathizer. That'd be the toughest. Give me greed over idealism any day—*

"I hope that is adequate, Mr. Dryke?" asked Kimura anxiously.

Dryke nodded, a satisfied expression on his face. "That's all I needed," Dryke said. "One step closer to Jeremiah. One step at a time. I hope that you've pointed me in the right direction."

"We share that hope," Kimura said.

"I want you to document what you've shown me, then pack up the jammer and send it down to Brazil for safekeeping."

"Immediately," Kimura said. "Is there anything else that I can do?"

In the last five minutes, Dryke's body had begun to remind him that he had had no sleep in thirty hours. "You can point me toward a bed," he said.

Kimura smiled. "There are sleep tanks in Flight Operations and in Building 7."

"Flight Operations, please," he said. *Because when I wake up, I'll be leaving for Santiago.*

-|CAG|-

"... fragile ecologies."

IT WAS THE VOICE OF AUTHORITY VEXED, CARRYING DOWN THE corridor of Syncretics' suite and through the open door of the small counselors' lounge.

"Malena? Is Gregory here yet?"

Inside the lounge, Malena Graham looked up from her book. She was not pretty, but art and artifice had made her attractive. A spill of chestnut hair framed a young, mannish face. Her blue flower-print dress was long enough to hide her useless legs.

"I haven't seen him," she called in reply.

The owner of the unhappy voice appeared in the doorway. "Didn't he say he was coming in this morning?"

"I don't know," Malena said. "I ran late with my three o'clock regression, and he was already gone when we were done."

A petulant look crossed the facilitator's face. "I swear he said he was going to resculpt Mr. Barton's cues." She shook her head and gestured past where Malena sat in her airchair. "When you get a chance, try the Normandy water—I swear it tastes sweet this time."

"I did," Malena said. "It tastes like they didn't flush the linc. Or like what they used to flush it."

The facilitator made a face and disappeared.

Malena returned to the book that she had been reading—a fantasy about the vengeful return of the Inca gods. Reading was the best way to forget where she was, to absorb the minutes remaining before her first appointment. Reading demanded her full attention. At times, it was hard work. Unlike with dyna-books and vids, she had to build all her own pictures from the author's sketchy words. Sometimes it seemed more like her book than theirs. Distractions from life, Mother Caroline called them.

But Malena thought that she had every right to her distractions. Twenty years old, and no part of her life was what she wanted it to be. She was still a prisoner of both the airchair and her family's solicitude, and the continuing lesson of her employment seemed to be that, in the real world, excellence was not always rewarded.

She had excelled in the personal development track, then chosen the thirty-month intensive at Adrian College (over the five-year relationship technology program at Virginia Technical) as the best and fastest route to employment and independence. At Adrian she learned that she could use her differently abled body as a wedge to crack open her clients' emotional windows. At Syncretics, she often succeeded with those whom other counselors had pronounced truth-deaf.

I'm good. The largest regulars list on the staff, in just three years—so many that she could rarely take any walk-ins. She had no knack for channeling, but she was the best spiritual motivator in the branch, better even than Kirella. She could find the spark inside them and blow it into flame. *They leave me better than they came to me.*

And yet she was still here, in the smallest Syncretics franchise in the South Bay area. The counselor's lounge itself said everything that needed to be said. It was no bigger than one of the five little encounter rooms at the front of the suite, half the size of the therapy rooms at the back—and six of them had to share it.

Nor did the lounge earn points for luxury. Its appointments consisted of a few soft chairs arranged around the periphery and a drink tap with waters, juices, and one choice from a rotating selection of caffeinates. That was the price of working for a franchise branch. *The price of working for Syncretics, the McDonald's of mind and body training.*

At the company-owned Virginia Beach office, on the other hand, each counselor had his own Network cube, the charge pool was reserved for their use from eight to ten every morning, the sense therapy room from four to six every evening. But one Syncretics branch wouldn't hire a counselor away from another—professional courtesy. (Bondage by conspiracy.) And the facilities at Interdynamics—she could only dream. You had to be a full R.T. to even think about working there.

That would come, three or four years down the road. It always took longer to catch up when you'd taken a wrong turn.

Kirella breezed into the lounge. "Hi, Malena," she said, dropping a bulging armbag and herself into adjacent chairs. "How did things go Thursday?"

"Like death. Like slow poison," she said, tucking the slate into a side pocket on the airchair.

Kirella laughed. "They didn't like him."

"They never gave him a chance," Malena complained. "None of my fathers can think straight on the subject. It's so obvious. They're so used to protecting me from the health Nazis and self-pity that they automatically extended the coverage to my virginity."

"A little late for that, aren't they?"

Malena smiled mischievously. "Just a little—not that I can tell them that. Not that they'd listen. They won't listen when I try to explain to them why they're being such asses. Father Jack even had the nerve to ask to see Ron's medical record."

"I hope he refused."

"He did—which is when open warfare broke out." She shook her head. "Ever since I met Ron on the net, the family's been delighted that I finally had a flick friend worth locking them out for. It'd be too much for them if I was sexually repressed on top of everything else. But let him show up in person, flesh and blood instead of shimmers in the cube, and suddenly it's bar-the-door Katie. Fear and loathing."

"My old roommate had pet rats named Fear and Loathing," Kirella said, chewing idly on a stick of strawberry.

"Your old roommate was a mutant."

"No argument."

The slate chirped from its pouch. "Malena—your nine o'clock Buddhist is here."

" 'kay," she said, and the airchair lifted off the floor. "My favorite," she said cynically. "Koan flakes for breakfast."

Kirella grimaced and looked for something to throw. "*You're* the mutant," she said pointedly.

"No argument," Malena said with cheerful insouciance. "Later, love."

• • •

The encounter room was dark save for the single candle on the floor between Malena and the young man seated cross-legged and bare-chested facing her. His eyes were closed, his head tipped slightly back, his arms floating as though weightless a few inches above the floor, his hands palm up and open, fingers loosely curled.

Pretty, she thought. *Pretty. If only he was willing to try a few more of the eight Paths—* "The negative energy is black and heavy," she continued in a low, warm, patient voice. "Look inside and find the dark places, the heaviness. The pain of your guilt. The sadness of your loss. It is only your choice that holds them there. Release them. Choose not to keep them, and they will drain from your body. Choose to keep them and they will become part of you. Find the dark places and open them to light. Find the weight and release it. Feel it leaving your body, discharging into the Earth. Feel your body become light. Feel the light within."

As she spoke, the young man's hands dipped slowly toward the floor. When his knuckles brushed the wood planking, it was as though a static charge had grounded. A hundred muscles in his body relaxed, and his face at last looked peaceful. She felt him floating, freed, and floated with him. She heard his silent half-sobbing laughter of release, knew the moment that he achieved ephemeral egoless *being* and the moment it was permissible to call him back.

"Jeremy," she said.

He opened his eyes and sought hers.

"We're finished for today."

A deep breath left him smaller and sadder. "Thank you, Malena," he said, skirting the candle and coming to hug her.

Unwanted hugs were an occupational risk for counselors, and all the more so for her, a prisoner in the chair. This hug was not unwanted, and yet it made her uncomfortable all the same, for she had to wonder if she had projected her earlier thought. She accepted the embrace self-consciously and kept her contribution as chaste as possible, considering that the object of the hug was nude.

"I'll leave you to get dressed," she said finally, and the air-chair lifted. *Way to go, bozo. Let him know that you noticed he was naked. Very professional—*

The counselor's lounge was empty, and she shut the door behind her in the hopes of keeping it that way. *Hormones from hell,* she fussed at herself as she drew a glass of hot cinnamon tea. *Ron, you'd better be there tonight, or I'm going to end up drooling on Father Brett again—*

It was not until several minutes later, when she retrieved her slate to resume reading, that she saw the V-mail marker blinking. The message was from Karin Oker, Supervisor of Selection, Diaspora Project, Allied Transcon.

She watched the message once, then immediately watched it again. For a long moment, she sat in her chair clutching the slate against her breasts, eyes glittering, hands trembling. Then she let out a whoop and sent the airchair into a dizzying spin.

The door flew open, and Kirella, the branch chiropractor, and the branch manager piled up in the doorway. "What's the matter?" Kirella demanded, approaching. "Are you okay?"

Smiling beatifically, Malena tipped her head back against the rest and closed her eyes. "Cancel my appointments," she said dreamily.

"What?"

"Cancel my appointments," she said, opening her eyes to let the tears run free. "They picked me. They picked *me*, Kirella. I'm going to Tau Ceti."

Ten thousand for Tau Ceti.

However euphonious it might be, the unofficial motto of the Selection Section was not quite accurate. Counting the core crew of roughly five hundred, drawn equally from Allied and Takara, plus between one and three hundred "discretionaries," split between paying passengers and other payoffs, plus a handful of creative stowaways, the final outbound head count would be closer to eleven thousand.

And that was only if you discounted the quarter million frozen eggs (five per donor) and five myriad frozen sperm samples which would also make the trip—consolation prizes in the starbound sweepstakes. In all, Karin Oker would get to say "Congratulations" not ten thousand, but a hundred and ten thousand times. (Lesser Selection officials would say "Sorry" to more than ten million.)

But it was the ten thousand pioneers who were the focus of most of the energy, most of the urgency, most of the romance, most of the anger. They were the elect, the chosen. They were the ones who would pass, knowingly and willingly, through what one popular commentator dubbed "the one-way door." To those

who would stay behind, the pioneers were humanity's hope, or
its arrogance; its idealism, or its idiocy; but most often, all of
that and more.

It was different in Houston and Munich and Tokyo, in Brazil
and Kenya, on Takara, on *Memphis* herself. To Karin Oker and
the rest of Selection, to Hiroko Sasaki and the whole of Allied,
the pioneers were the moving pieces in a complex ballet too
serious to be a game. Ten thousand to pluck from homes and
families across six continents. Ten thousand to process through
the training and transshipment centers. Ten thousand to lift skyward a hundred at a time and ferry to the great sky city which
would be their new and possibly last home. Ten thousand to
meld into a working community that could survive fifty years in
the crucible of interstellar flight.

Ten thousand for Tau Ceti.

There was no way of avoiding a Graham family conference
on Malena's news. And once the conference began, there was
no way to avoid splitting the family into warring camps.

It had started tranquilly enough. Unflappable Mother Alicia,
possessor of a wonderful matter-of-fact pragmatism which had
made her the emotional keel of the family for as long as Malena
could remember, was alone in the main house when Malena got
home, and so was the first to know.

"We'll need to talk about this as a family," she said on hearing the news. "I think all of the adults will be home tonight, so
no point in delaying. An advisory, of course, not a decision
conference. You are twenty, after all. But this does affect all of
us, so it's only right that we talk about it together."

As the other parents arrived home, Mother Alicia took them
aside and informed them of the news, asking them to hold their
thoughts until the conference. Malena hid in her room, reviewing the information files that had been attached to her selection
notice. The only intrusion was by Father Brett, whom she had
wanted to tell personally. It was Brett who had given her the
chance, transferring his own option to her after he failed to make
the cut for *Ur*. He responded to the news with an ecstatic, enthusiastic hug that did much to fortify Malena for the ordeal to
come.

Several hours later, with the family's three youngest children
in bed and the other four asked to respect the closed door of the
family room, the adults gathered, and the issue was joined. By

then it was already clear that both her blood parents, Father Jack and Mother Caroline, and Father Michel were united in their shock and opposition. Only Mother Alicia's thoughtful emphasis on the ground rules for an advisory conference as she opened discussion checked what might have been a summary execution.

"We can't tell Malena what to do, of course, any more than if she had announced that she was moving out or marrying," Alicia said, concluding. "Our place is to help her explore the dimensions of the decision, so that she can make the best possible decision. Malena, if you choose to accept their offer, what does that mean?"

"Mine is a staff selection," she said. "I'll be part of the counseling staff on the ship. That means I have to report sooner than the regular selections—in no more than thirty days."

"Where will you go?" asked Alicia.

"To the center in Houston."

"And how long will you stay there?"

"It'll be in Houston for sixty days of ground training. Then they'll give me ten days off for personal business—packing, good-byes—before I move up to the ship. From what I've been reading, we'll only be on board for a few weeks before the first group of pioneers moves in."

"Only ten days?" asked Michel. "Not very much to say good-bye to a whole world."

"We'll get another ten days closer to departure," Malena said. "If we want them."

Mother Caroline edged forward in her chair. "Malena—why do you want to do this?"

Malena turned the question on its head and fired it back at the source. "Wouldn't you want to if you could? Wouldn't you go if they wanted you?"

"Could I take Jack, and Michel, and you, and your brothers?" asked Caroline, knowing the answer was no. "Could I take this house, and my friends, and the Bay? And if I couldn't, what would I be getting in return that could be worth giving all that up for? Nothing. No, I wouldn't go. And I don't understand why you want to."

"We understand that you're flattered," Michel said, playing Tweedledum to her Tweedledee. "Anybody would be flattered to be picked out of such a large group. But this seems a little like winning a sweepstakes and then having to sell the prize to pay the taxes."

"To you," said Brett, coming to her defense. "But her life isn't your life, or yours, Caroline. She's still living in the world we created for ourselves. Of course we're comfortable here. But she's only just starting to make her own choices and shape her own world."

"Why don't you just shut up?" snapped Jack. "You've influenced her enough already. Everything you say is just an apology for yourself."

It was an old wound, reopened by the blow of Malena's news. Alicia stepped in to try to blunt the confrontation. "The issues here are present and future, not past. And everyone has a right to be heard, Jack."

"I'd like him to hear me," Jack retorted, jabbing a finger in Brett's direction. "He made this happen. When we let him in ten years ago, he picked out Malena and tried to make her his daughter—"

"I *am* his daughter," Malena said.

"You were happy enough about that when it was convenient for you," Brett said at the same time.

"—because he didn't have one of his own. And as for Malena living in the world we created, that's him talking for himself again. You were the last one on the scene. And if you didn't like what you were getting into, you shouldn't have contracted with us."

Brett refused to back down. "And if you didn't want me, you shouldn't have offered the contract. Or did you think that I would just take care of Alicia's needs so you three could go on ignoring her?"

"What does any of this—" Malena began.

But Caroline trampled over her attempt to reenter the conversation. "You've never stopped trying to make us feel guilty over Michel and Alicia growing apart—"

"Growing apart? The way I hear it, you came to every little crisis between them like a shark to blood—"

Malena watched, first with astonishment, then with growing dismay, as the compromises and accommodations which held Raven House together dissolved in the acid of harsh words. Finally, her frustration turned to fury, she skidded thc airchair into the middle of the circle and dropped it to the floor with an emphatic thump.

"Stop!" she demanded. "Stop, all of you! This isn't about you. This is about me. Doesn't anyone here want to talk to *me*?"

The display won a moment of awkward silence, brought an embarrassed look to Michel's face, and elicited a pursed-lip nod of self-recrimination from Brett.

"I'm sorry, Malena," Alicia said gently. "What did you want to say?"

She looked slowly from one face to the next, fixing finally on Father Jack. "I really hate the way you have to turn every conversation into a contest, and every conference into an excuse to drag out every old family argument and grudge. I've heard all of this until I'm sick of it. Michel neglected Alicia. Alicia drove Michel away. Caroline's a bitch. Jack's selfish. Brett's the thief of hearts. This one neglected the kids. That one spoiled the kids. This one doesn't pull his weight. That one's always trying to take over. Did you ever talk to each other, or was it always yelling? Don't any of you ever put anything away for good?"

"Listen, child," Jack started threateningly. "You can't talk to me like that—"

"Oh, no—I'm not going to let you shut me up by making me small," she said warningly. "I hit my majority five years ago—"

"It's true. Malena does not have to be here," Alicia said. "It's because she loves us that she's willing to share this with us and listen—"

"Mother Alicia, I can speak for myself," Malena said, irritated. "Father Jack, in case you haven't noticed, I have three fathers and two mothers, and have had for quite some time. I can talk to any of you any way I have to, to make you understand. The fact that you and I are blood doesn't give you any special right to say no to me, or to tell me who I can and can't respect. Every one of you has helped me. Every one of you has influenced me. And every one of you has hurt me, too."

Surely you don't mean me, Caroline's eyes said. Father Jack looked away and grunted.

"That goes with being family," Brett said finally.

"Maybe it does," Malena said "I don't really know, because this is the only family I've ever seen from the inside. I love you all, but it *is* your world, just like Brett said. I would have left it by now, if there'd been some place or way to go. I've been here too long."

"Is that your answer, then?" asked Caroline accusingly. "You want to go because you want to get away from us?"

She did not shy from the accusation. "That's not my best

reason. But I have to admit it's part of it, yes. It might be nice to be alone for a change.''

"What about Ron?'' asked Alicia.

That was a jolt, and her face betrayed it. "I guess,'' she said slowly, "I guess the fact that I didn't think of him all day until just this moment tells me something.''

"It should tell you that you haven't thought this through,'' said Michel.

"Or maybe that whatever needs Ron answered will be answered as well or better by going to Tau Ceti,'' said Brett. "Can you answer me this, Malena? Do you understand yourself? Do you know what this means to you?''

"Did you know, when you bought the option?''

His expression turned inward, reflective. "It seemed like the most exciting thing anyone could do,'' he said. "Like if you didn't want to, there must be something wrong with you.''

"Would you go now?''

He looked at Alicia before answering. "No.''

"Why not?''

"It's not important.''

"It *is* important. Is it because you grew up? Because you see things more clearly now? Do you look back and think you were silly, naive? Do you think I'm naive?''

"Too many questions,'' he said, shaking his head. "No easy answers. Sometimes I think it's because I grew old, inside. You have to travel light to get anywhere. The more you're afraid to let go of, the fewer your choices—until your only choice is to stay right where you are. My luggage got too heavy somewhere along the road.''

He looked up, taking in both Malena and Alicia sitting side by side. "I'm not unhappy, you know.''

Alicia smiled a sweet, sad smile. "I know,'' she said gently. "I also know that part of your heart broke when *Ur* left and you weren't on it.'' She turned to Malena. "If you know your heart, and your heart says go, I think you should listen to it and not to us. I think you should go.''

Bright tears spilled down Malena's cheeks. "I don't know *why* I want to go,'' she said. "I only know that I do.''

"That's enough, sometimes,'' said Alicia, reaching out and taking Malena's hand.

It was not enough for Caroline, who came to her feet and stood, indignant, looming over her daughter. "Do you really think life's as easy as that? That you can leave everything and everyone behind and be happy?''

"I don't know," was Malena's answer, "I don't even know how happy I am now."

"You're going to tell them yes." Father Jack's words were a harsh accusation.

Malena nodded and blinked back a tear. "I already have."

CHAPTER
8

-|GGG|-

"We have not forgotten."

IF IT SEEMED ODD SOMETIMES TO OUTSIDERS THAT THE DIRECTOR of the Diaspora hyperlibrary project was not a librarian but a historian, it usually seemed less so when they found out who the historian was.

Thomas Tidwell was that oddity which seemed to come along once in a generation—a popular writer-director who also had the respect of his more reserved peers. The British-born, Oxford-trained Tidwell had earned respect through more than thirty years of work on Millennial culture, including two standard reference works, *Global Technocracy* and *Faith and Fear*. But he gained notoriety with a single work, a series of nine videssays on the sexual mores of the last pre-AIDS generation.

Curiously, *A Summer in Eden* was seen as validation by both the most conservative and the most experimental elements of society. For the former, it was a cautionary parable, a warning of dire consequences if the rigid mores of the AIDS era were recklessly abandoned. For the latter, it was an exhilarating manifesto, an invitation to abandon now-irrelevant conventions and re-create a lost age of sexual freedom. The two poles had been fighting a war of opinion ever since—more than twenty-two years.

One voice that did not join the debate on either side was that of Thomas Tidwell. In an early interview, he said simply, *"Eden* is no more important than any other of my works, and everything I have to say on the subject is contained within its nine segments. That was, after all, the point of making it."

64

But that did not end the questions, nor restore to Tidwell even the tenth part of the blissful invisibility which he considered one of his two most important working tools. His next work, a serious study of the 2042 Amerussian "Peace Police" treaty, was mispromoted by a syndicator eager for another licensing bonanza and misreviewed by nearly everyone. Popular media condemned it for dullness; dull journals condemned him for his popularity.

Tidwell had no more to say about the reception of *The Guardians* than he had that of *A Summer in Eden*. And if the ego-crushing reception given the former was as painful for Tidwell as it would have been for any normal man, not even his friends were allowed to know it. A few, including his wife Marion, even suspected that he had deliberately and calculatedly set out to puncture the balloon of his own fame.

But for what happened next, they might have continued to suspect that.

In the preceding months, Tidwell had rejected two offers from Allied Transcon to become official historian of the Diaspora Project. But he had continued to listen with interest. The opportunity to write the definitive account of what would either be humanity's greatest leap or its greatest stumble, to create what amounted to the cultural memory of an entire new community, was tempting. Almost tempting enough to coax Tidwell to surrender his other precious tool—his autonomy.

Almost, but not quite.

Then came *The Guardians*, and on its heels a new offer from Allied which contained new guarantees of access and independence. This time Tidwell signed, insisting, perhaps even believing, that it was the latter that swung the balance.

"I intend to take a thousand-year view of the Diaspora—five hundred years into the past and five hundred years into the future," he had said at the press conference announcing his appointment. "I will be loyal to the truth and no one else. Allied understands this. I will have the full cooperation of the principals and the freedom to write what my conscience and professional judgment dictate."

But guarantees were paper things, easily crushed by bureaucracies, frayed by time. It was periodically necessary to breathe life into the cold, precise legalisms. That was the task which faced Tidwell now, which had drawn him from his comfortable manor house near Halfwhistle, within sight of Hadrian's Wall, to the executive suites of the Selection Section in Prainha.

Waiting for Karin Oker, Tidwell stood at the window and looked out at the spaceport. The contrast between the place Tidwell had left and the place he had come to could hardly have been sharper. The North Country was all rounded edges, a much-tramped land littered with history. Prainha was all hard edges, carved in relatively youthful memory from the Amazon forest.

The fairy-castle mountain of the Kare-Kantrowitz launch tower was a garish superposition on the denuded forest, the spacecraft which screamed away from its four-kilometer summit harsh substitutes for the parrots and macaws they had displaced. The blanketing rectenna, which sprawled across more than sixty square kilometers, was a metallic parody of the former jungle canopy. Spreading its "leaves" wide, it captured precious energy from space; in its shadow, a bustling ecology of technology thrived.

Tidwell wondered if they saw what they had done here, if they recognized the truth in Jeremiah's charges. *Someday I will have to ask Sasaki—*

The inner door of the suite opened, and an olive-skinned man emerged, followed closely by a pale, willowy blond-haired woman. "Thank you, Raja," she said. "We'll take it up at the weeklies." Then she looked past her companion to Tidwell. "Professor Tidwell?"

"Yes."

"I'm Karin Oker. Welcome to Prainha, Professor." She nodded toward the window. "Quite a sight, isn't it?"

Both the honorary title she used and the assumption that this was his first visit to Brazil were in error. He noted the lapses, but did not trouble himself to correct them. It was enough to learn from them that she was ignorant of who he was and that she viewed meeting with him as a necessary annoyance.

"I was just contemplating that fact," he said, settling in a chair facing away from the window. "Will we have privacy here?"

"If we ask for it," she said, selecting her own chair. "Privacy Level Two, please."

The offcom acknowledged with a musical note.

"There," she said. "We won't be interrupted except by the Director or a base emergency."

"Thank you," he said with a polite smile. "I appreciate it

the more for knowing that I, too, am an interruption. I very much regret finding it necessary to come here. But this seemed the most direct way of ending the running battle between your people and mine."

"Battle?"

"My staff's struggle to collect the information I require, and your staff's struggle to keep it from us. It's a sorry business when one branch of Allied has more difficulty getting cooperation from another branch than it does dealing with outsiders who have no reason to help us."

"I wasn't aware that you were having such problems," Oker said. "If there have been, I'm sure that they're based on misunderstandings. What have you been denied?"

"I'm less concerned about what we've been denied than with the fact that the working relationship between us has turned for the worse. We were partners with you. Now we are treated as supplicants, and reasonable, routine requests are met with excuses, delays, denials, and half-answers."

Oker was unhappy and unpracticed at hiding it. "Professor Tidwell, surely you understand that Selection's work is the most sensitive area of the Project. Much of the data, even the procedures we use, is personal or proprietary. Obviously, any release—even to the Historian's Office—needs to be screened and reviewed. And just as obviously, some requests might need to be denied."

Drawing himself up in his chair, Tidwell said in measured tones, "I am responsible for creating the definitive history of the expedition. That includes the personal histories of every pioneer. Remember, please, that this history is not only for us but for them. I have to anticipate questions which may not be asked for fifty years."

"I have to ask again—what have you been denied?"

"Personal histories include genetic histories. But we have been told we may not have access to your genetic library," Tidwell said. "And when we request a briefing on the final selection criteria, I expect more than a copy of the application file you made available to prospective pioneers."

Oker was shaking her head. "Hordes of lawyers are poised waiting to file suit on behalf of unsuccessful candidates. Every lawsuit has the potential for disrupting the prep schedule, or worse, taking the selection decision out of our hands."

"We are neither lawyers nor litigants. What has that to do with us?"

"There are thousands of Allied employees holding options," Oker said stubbornly. "Letting detailed selection data out into the corporation is an invitation to trouble."

"Perhaps, being comparatively new to the Project," said Tidwell, "you don't realize that this sort of information *was* made available to us for the *Ur* library."

"Times are different now," Oker said.

"Not in any meaningful way. Surely, the first thing that any competent lawyer would do is subpoena our records."

"And he would fight any order to release them. We would destroy them rather than release them."

"Interesting," Tidwell said. "Are the selections that subjective? Are we afraid to defend our selection practices in public?"

"No," Oker said. "They're as objective as possible. They're blind selections, made by AI engines at the proc centers."

"According to what criteria?"

"By the criteria spelled out in the application file—skill training, psych screenings, genetic screenings, intelligence and adaptability—"

"Weighted."

"Of course."

"What are the weightings?"

"The weightings are necessarily subjective," Oker admitted. "But that doesn't mean they were set casually. And I'm not about to let the process we went through to set them be picked apart by a know-nothing judge or a well-meaning but ignorant layman."

"That seems arrogant, Dr. Oker."

She bristled. "We don't even tell the nominees why they've been chosen. Or the rejects why they weren't. Why should we tell you?"

Tidwell studied her. "Are you afraid of the genetic discrimination issue?"

The question seemed to surprise her. "Of course," she said, recovering. "Almost half of our options are held in countries with antidiscrimination or bodily privacy laws. The American law is particularly troublesome."

"And yet it's well known that you've expanded your genetic screening since *Ur*."

"Is it?"

"Your staff chart shows the section has sixty-five more geneticists than it did six years ago, when you arrived. The obvious conclusion is that the genetic factor has become more important."

"We were understaffed when I arrived. And we *are* more thorough now with the genetics. We do full genotypes for every candidate, for example."

"I know," said Tidwell. "But why you do them, and what you look for? These questions you have not answered, except in generalities. 'For screening.' 'To create a healthy gene pool.' I must have better answers."

She shook her head. "I can't release that data. You'll have to do what you can to work around it."

"It's not your decision to make," Tidwell said. "The decision was made by Director Sasaki fifteen years ago. My right of access is unrestricted."

"Times are different now," Oker repeated. "We're prepared to upload standard adoption biographies for each of the donor packages, sometime before departure. The living passengers can obtain private testing and see to their own genealogies, if they think it important."

"I see," Tidwell said, sitting back. "Apparently, there was no misunderstanding, after all."

"You don't understand what you're asking for, Professor."

"For the record, it's *Doctor* Tidwell, twice over, in history and sociology," Tidwell said, crossing his right leg over his left. "You see, we are educable, Dr. Oker—not a one of my staff is dead yet."

Oker flushed, the first sign of an emotion other than anger. "This isn't personal, Doctor," she said. "We have a monopoly on the kind of expertise needed to interpret the raw data. I know, because if we could have found more experts, we'd have put them on staff, too."

"Then you should be prepared to make one of your experts available to us along with the data," Tidwell said, rising.

"If the Director requires me to."

"She will," Tidwell said. "Aren't you aware that the Director intends to sell the genetic library to at least three governments as a research base?"

Oker went white. "That hasn't been announced," she said stiffly.

"But it's so, all the same," Tidwell said.

He saw in her eyes that she knew she had underestimated him; she saw in his that he would not gloat in victory. "The raw data is almost unimaginably voluminous," she said slowly. "A single genotype is hundreds of thousands of genes, millions of codons—"

"I would imagine we can make do with something less than the full library," Tidwell said. "Perhaps the selection algorithm and the scoring of the successful candidates will prove sufficient. And you might wish to designate a contact person with authority to answer inquiries, not evade them."

Reluctantly, she said, "I think that could be arranged."

He nodded. "Then I've taken enough of your time. The details can be worked out by staff. Thank you, Dr. Oker." He bowed slightly and withdrew toward the door.

He had taken just five steps when she called after him. "Dr. Tidwell—"

"Yes?"

She was standing, and her eyes were clouded by an emotion Tidwell could not quite define. "You wouldn't do anything to harm us, would you?"

"Pardon me?"

"The Project. You wouldn't endanger *Memphis*."

Puzzlement wrinkled his brow. "What could endanger it?"

"The truth," she said. "Sometimes the truth can be a very dangerous thing."

Tidwell retraced his steps. "What will I find if you open your files?"

She looked down at her hands, out the window at the spaceport, everywhere but at him.

"Privacy Level One," she said at last, lifting her head and gazing levelly into his eyes. The offcom chimed. "Sit down, Dr. Tidwell. I'm going to rewrite your history for you."

Tidwell listened for nearly an hour, growing paler and smaller with each passing minute. He did not interrupt or quibble, protest or resist. Nor did he make any sign of acknowledgment. He listened so passively that presently Oker interrupted herself to ask if he was all right.

"You've asked me to declare my life's work irrelevant," he said with a sad smile. "If what you've said is true, I've been a charlatan. I've built a career describing the symptoms of history while the cause went undiagnosed."

"You're hardly alone in that," Oker said. "Less than a hundred people know."

"Sasaki."

"Of course," Oker said. "She was the one who told me, six years ago."

Tidwell shook his head. "I thought I understood the impulse. That part was written years ago. The unsuccessful search for extraterrestrial life. The sense of cultural mortality created by AIDS. The rechanneling of a post–Cold War economy."

"All true. Just not the whole story. Another layer, lying underneath."

"Yes—the curiosity! The unflagging, insatiable curiosity. The challenge to the spirit. From Lucretius to da Vinci to Tsiolkovsky to von Braun to Armstrong to Morgan. The dream they shared."

"No," Oker corrected. "The genes they shared."

"I thought I was tracing the history of an idea. Now you claim that all I've done is track an infection."

"Too harsh a word," Oker said. "We are what we are."

"Biology is destiny." It was said with a cynical scorn.

"Hardly. We might have failed. Might still fail. Others did."

"Others?"

"We're not the first species to carry the Chi Sequence. Only the latest."

"How far back?"

"To the beginning, perhaps. Life is a chemical reaction with audacity. And the meaning of life is to make new life. Nothing more. We just never understood the scale on which the drama was being played."

"It isn't our story. It never was," Tidwell said hoarsely.

"It is now."

Tidwell retreated, regrouped. "There is no proof."

"No. Not for the past. But enough for the present."

"Enough to make machines of us? Enough to make a joke of the will?"

"No. Do you know how hard it is to link complex behaviors and simple genes, even now? The Chi Sequence is a challenge, a call—you used the word *impulse*. We answered because we could."

"Not because we chose to. You make my point."

"No," Oker said forcefully. "A marriage of choice and destiny. Dr. Tidwell, I didn't accept this easily or happily. I did not

want to be convinced. I was a Catholic. This has cost me my
God.'' She showed a faint frown. ''You don't have to believe,
Dr. Tidwell. But the world is as it is. It doesn't much care what
we believe.''

''This is guiding policy?''

''Yes.''

Tidwell paused. ''I want to talk to Sasaki.''

Oker nodded. ''I'll call her.''

The closest thing to an expression on Hiroko Sasaki's face
was a slight knitting of her thin black eyebrows.

''You lied to me,'' Tidwell said plaintively.

''I did not.''

''She said you knew about the Chi Sequence,'' he insisted,
gesturing at Karin Oker, who was orbiting about him in Sasaki's
huge office at a psychologically safe distance.

''Yes.''

''How long have you known?''

There was no hesitation. ''Nearly ten years.''

''Since before you recruited me.''

''Yes.''

''Then you lied to me.''

Sasaki looked across the room and pinned Oker with her eyes.
''Doctor, what instructions did you have concerning Dr. Tidwell
and the Chi Sequence?''

''To tell him what I knew—no, I think you phrased it 'what I
believed'—if ever he should ask.'' She looked at Tidwell. ''I
thought that was a mistake.''

''To keep it from me?''

''To tell you. Even now that it's done, I'm not sure that it
wasn't a mistake. It's nothing personal, Doctor. But if this gets
out, everything we have planned is in danger.''

''Why is that?''

''You have the degree in sociology, Doctor,'' Oker said. ''Is
it that hard to see? To brand ourselves the elect—''

''Yes,'' Tidwell said, recalling the promise she had tried to
extract from him. *You wouldn't hurt us, would you?* ''Yes, of
course.''

Sasaki rose from her cushion. ''Thank you, Dr. Oker. Would
you leave us now?''

Nodding, Oker moved toward the door. ''I'm sorry, Dr. Tid-

well," she said, pausing. "I really am. I didn't enjoy waking
you."

"I know," he said.

She left, and Sasaki turned to Tidwell. "Thomas, will you sit
with me?"

They sank to the cushions together. "I hope that you can
understand," she said. "Karin must believe. I must question. I
need to know if I am making decisions for one generation or for
all generations."

"Does it matter?" asked Tidwell. "Can you do anything different for knowing?"

"Yes. I already have," she said. "Thomas, I know that your
pride has been hurt by what you view as deception—"

"Why should she know?" he burst out. "You tell her—you
tell a *hundred*—and keep it from *me*. I considered you a friend,
Hiroko."

She reached for his hand, covered it with her own cool skin.
"Karin is a talent, a gift, in her field. Her work for the Project
required that she know. Yours required that you not know. I
could not tell you, not if you were to do what I needed you to—
what I still need you to do."

"You presume too much."

"That is pique speaking," she said. "Thomas, I asked you
to write our history because I knew that if this thread was there,
you would find it on your own. That if the history you wrote
and the history Karin has built coincided, that I would have my
proof."

"So what do you want?"

"Read your own writing. Ask yourself if reason and hubris
and lebensraum and frontier fever are enough to explain it, to
carry us from Olduvai Gorge to here. Or whether those are all
synonyms for some other cause. Whether what we have done
makes more sense or less for what you've heard today."

"You think you know the answer."

She bobbed her head in disagreement. "You misread me,
Thomas. I hope that Karin is wrong."

"Why?"

A faint smile. "Because I do not know that I am equal to a
billion-year burden."

"One starship has already sailed."

"One is not enough," she said. "One is a frail reed. You
must help me, Thomas. Reflect. And then come and tell me

what you see, so that I will better know what it is that *I* must do.''

He sighed, covered her hand with his. "You ask a great deal."

"From you, as from myself."

Tidwell squeezed her hand and then freed it. "A question?"

"Of course."

"Do I carry the Chi Sequence?"

Sasaki answered without hesitation. "I do not know," she said. "You were never tested. Do you wish to be?"

His breath caught and he looked at her wonderingly. He had expected an answer, not a choice. *Tell me yes, tell me no, and then I'll go away to worry about what it means. To look inside myself as well as my history.* Then he saw with sudden insight that he had been given a gift. *Yes, yes—what song does your body sing, and where did you first hear it?* It was not something he should have to be told. He would find out for himself.

"I think not," Tidwell said. "Not yet."

He could not decide whether he was pleased or annoyed by Sasaki's approving smile.

CHAPTER
9

-|CUA|-

"I look on your works and weep."

THE NEXT TIME CHRISTOPHER MCCUTCHEON LOOKED UP, August had vanished, leaving very few tracks on his consciousness. It had been a nothing-much month, one day folding unnoticed into the next, time evaporating in the summer Texas sun.

Even the aftertaste of July's crises had faded into gentle memory. His father, conscience or curiosity satisfied by Christopher's visit, had pursued no further contact. And Christopher's brief panic over Loi and Jessie subsided as his worst fear—that of being excluded when all three of them were home together— failed to materialize. The worst crisis at Kenning House that month was the discovery of a nest of Formosan termites in the backyard

But in the world around him, and in the greater world beyond, August had been a busy, sometimes turbulent month. At work, the new front gate was opened, freeing Christopher from dependence on the tram. Thomas Tidwell, titular head of Christopher's division, made not one but two visits, events rare enough by all accounts to be a curiosity. One of the center's archaeolibrarians was picked for *Memphis*'s staff; two others quit, and one—a woman named Barbara Manly—committed suicide, when they learned they were not

None of those events had touched Christopher more than tangentially. He recalled them with no sense of involvement or emotional investment, not even that which a witness might feel. Not even for Manly. She was an older woman, a fiction and theater specialist, working in a different project circle in a dif-

75

ferent part of the building. He was a casual spectator, a passive
bystander, the distance between him and her death as great as
the distance between him and an image on the multimedia.

He wondered at his own reaction. After the first moment of
shock, he could find little more than puzzlement inside. Why
had she done it? Building the library was a contribution, a way
of taking part. Why was that not enough for Barbara Manly?
Daniel Keith had cried for her. Christopher had not. He could
not sympathize with the incomprehensible.

Too, part of the distance was numbness. There was too much
death to grieve over each departed. All month, the news seemed
to cater to a morbid, obsessive fascination with the many and
varied ways that people find to die. The running blood in the
street, the raglike bodies lying crumpled on the savanna, the
burned, the broken, those who went fighting, those taken by
surprise—they were all ways to touch the untouchable, to hold
in one's hand the idea of one's own mortality. How will I die?
Like this? Like this? How awful, how sudden, how unfair, how
noble, how right. How unready I am—

Death. The world was more peaceful than at any time in a
century, and yet there was no end to the dying. The Peace Police
were back in West Africa, but not before more than three hundred fell in clashes along the Mauritania-Mali border. A fire in
Phobos Station killed three astronauts and left the second largest
Martian outpost uninhabitable. One of the Global Environmental Watch's high-altitude ozonator barges fell out of the sky over
the Antarctic, condemning three of its crew to a fiery death and
the one who succeeded in ejecting to a slower, icy end. And so
on.

Christopher watched the news of the airbarge crash cuddled
with Jessica on the huge brown family room couch, with Möbius
in turn sprawled on Jessica's lap in one of the classic boneless-
cat positions which had earned him his name. It was the last
Saturday of the month. He should have been rehearsing for Sunday's gig; he could have been at an end-of-summer court party
at a residential center just three blocks away. But he had the
energy for neither.

Besides, Jessica needed the company. Her left foot was
sheathed in an air cast and propped on an ottoman. Inside the
cast was a freshly broken ankle, painful trophy of yesterday's
spill down a shopping center escalator. And Loi was in Brussels
for the debut of a commissioned sculpture at the Alianti Gallery.

So they cuddled together wordlessly, snacking at crackers and cheese, sipping at a fruity Piesporter that one of Loi's lovers had sent as congratulations. When the news was over, the screen returned to its normal cycling display, now a Brinwell animate of faces in a flickering fire.

"Aargh," she said. "Switch off."

The screen blacked, and Jessica sighed relievedly.

"Do you want to watch something else?" Christopher asked, kissing the top of her head. "We have that new Mojembe film in the capture queue."

"Loi wanted to see that most," she murmured.

"That's right," Christopher remembered. "No point in paying for two showings. Well—what about Loi's *Hearkentime*? It's a good lazy-evening kind of timesculpt, and I've only done it once."

"Are you bored with me?"

He kissed her head again. "Heavens, no. I just didn't want you to be bored."

"I like cuddling," she said. "Möbius and me. We just kind of gravitate to warm places and cuddly people."

"McCutcheon Heat & Friction, Ltd.," he said in an affected voice. "You've come to the right place, ma'am. No client too female or too furry."

"What if they're female *and* furry?"

"There's a surcharge."

She chuckled and snuggled closer. "Chris?"

"What?"

"Can you get into the library from here?"

"The *Memphis* library?"

"Um-hmm."

"No," he said. "There are no external ports to the system. For security. I wish there were. Some days I'd like to be able to work at home like a normal person."

"If you could work at home, you two'd have stayed in San Francisco, and then I'd never have met you."

"True. I'll try to remember that the next time I trudge off to work feeling like a tradesman instead of a professional."

"What was that you were doing this morning?" He had spent three hours in Loi's office after breakfast.

"Logs and mail and such," he said. "Documentation. That's different. Different system. Why?"

"I was just wondering if you could look me up."

"Hmm?"

"In the library. I was just wondering what it said about me."

"Oh," he said. "No. I can't do that from here."

She twisted her neck to look up at him. "Can you do it Monday? When you go in?"

He looked down into her eyes curiously. "I could. Why does it matter? What made you think of this?"

"I don't know," she said, turning away from his scrutiny and resting her cheek on his chest. "I guess I just wondered what they'd know about me, when they're living out there wherever. Do you think I'm in it?"

"Everyone's in it."

"What do you think it says?"

Discomfort stirred McCutcheon's emotions. "Well—your birth will be in the Vital Records stack, linked to your parents and your brother, at least."

"That's all?"

"Could be worse—it could have your death, too," he said. She did not laugh, and he quickly added, "Seriously, if any of your relatives is chosen, as far out as third cousins, there'll be at least a short biography and a still picture."

"Have all the selections been named?"

"About half of them by now, I think. It's hard to find out."

She shook her head, a quiver against him. "I guess it doesn't matter. The only one in my family with an option is my uncle—my mother's brother. And there isn't any way that they'll take him. He doesn't know how to do anything. All he's got is a head full of dreams."

His answer sounded patronizing even to his own ears. "It's a huge library, Jessie. You might be in it a dozen times. A sound-off in the *New York Times*—your Clean Teeth Club Award for sixth grade—anything."

"Loi will be in it. They'll probably have a whole set of her sculpts."

"I suppose they'll have a few."

Jessica started to cry. She was a quiet crier, not even troubling to wipe away the tears that tracked down her cheeks and dampened his shirt. "I just know I'm not in it. And they'll never even know I was here."

"I know you're here."

He meant the words to be comforting, but they only cut deeper.

"It's not fair," she said fiercely. "Everyone ought to be able to go. Or no one should go."

"Slow down, Jessie," he said. "There's no way that everyone could go. We couldn't even get everyone as far as the Moon. It's a seventy-five-year project just to build five ships the size of Angleton or Freeport. Everybody calls *Memphis* a city in space. It's just a little town, about to become the ultimate one-stoplight rural Hicksville."

She straightened up and pulled away from him, sending an indignant Möbius to the floor. "I don't really want to go," she said in a little voice. "I just don't want to be forgotten."

He reached out and touched her cheek tenderly. "Who knows us in Bangladesh, or even Boston? What does it matter if a few people on a one-way trip don't have stories to tell about Jessica Alexis Cichuan or Christopher McCutcheon?"

Eyes cast downward, she folded her hands in her lap. "I guess you're right," she said. "But I don't have to like it."

Christopher smiled and tugged at her hands. "Come here."

She returned to his embrace with a sigh of sadness and gratitude. "I just want to count for something," she whispered.

"You count here, with us. With me."

This time she accepted the comfort of his words. "You count with me, too."

"One, two, three, four—"

She pinched him, and laughed when he yelped. They settled in comfortably together again like two pieces of molding clay, holding hands, Christopher planting soft kisses wherever he could reach without dislodging their position.

"Maybe we could watch a skinner," he said presently. "What was the one you liked? *Tantric Fusion?*"

"I don't need to," she said.

"My apologies, ma'am."

"But I think I'd like to make love."

He smiled. "My pleasure, ma'am. Comfort the crippled, I say. They're so grateful—"

"But I might change my mind if you don't shut up."

"Shutting up, ma'am."

Fingertips lightly grazed bare skin where it could be found, teased and combed hair. Lips met in soft kisses, not yet fired by the impatience of passion. Hands played, locked together. A thumb rubbed the center of a palm. Teeth nibbled an earlobe, the nape of a neck. Their bodies in harmony, riding the rising curve that would soon take them upstairs to the big bed—

"Christopher."

"Mmm."

"Will you make a baby with me?"

He felt his body suddenly go rigid, his connection with her break. Children had never been an issue with Loi, ten years past fertility. And they were not supposed to be an issue with Jessie yet. "Now?"

"We could," she said. "I ovulated yesterday."

"What happened to your implant?" It almost sounded like an accusation.

"It ran out last month, or went bad," she said, and snuggled closer. "I didn't notice until it was too late to replace it."

Christopher's emotions were screaming protest, his body recoiling from contact with her. *Oh, no,* they said, *oh, no, you're not going to turn me into a father for the price of a cuddle-fuck.* He did not have time to analyze those responses, so he made an effort to subdue them. "You never talked about wanting a baby now."

"I've been thinking about it," she said. "I'd love to have someone to take care of. I think we'd be terrific parents."

"That's a family decision," he said, still desperately trying to back away from her proposition. "We can't make it for Loi."

"Let's call her, then. We could call her."

"Jessie, that's a fifteen-year contract."

She finally sat up, pulled away from him. "I didn't ask you for a contract—"

"There's an implied contract the minute we're naked together with you fertile."

"—I just asked you to make a baby with me."

"That's not something you ask in the middle of a cuddle that's heating up. It's something you talk about when the sun's up and your head's clear."

"You don't want to," she said accusingly. "All these excuses just mean you don't want to."

"I *don't* want to," he said plaintively. "Not this way. Not now. And I don't understand why you do."

"A woman who hasn't had a baby doesn't count."

"You're just taking a hormonal hit—"

"No, I'm not," she said, struggling to her feet. "I'm not a

machine. Even if you wish I was. That's what you want me to be. A nothing. A fuck-pillow."

That Jessie, soft-voiced and smiling Jessie, would use such language revealed the depth of the betrayal she felt. "Jessie—"

"No, I don't want to hear it. I'm going to bed," she said.

"Jess—"

"And don't even think about following me. Sleep in your own damned bed."

It was only after she was gone that, replaying the conversation in his head, he began to wonder if it had been woven from a single thread, if the dead men in Antarctica and the hyperlibrary and the cuddling and the baby they weren't making that night were somehow all of one piece.

If he said he understood why they were, he would have been lying. But he knew that it was so all the same, and there was no shortage of time alone that night to wonder on it.

The *Memphis* hyper could be accessed from Christopher's entry terminal, or even, in a limited way, from an ordinary graphics station—just as DIANNA could be accessed by a lowly DBS phone in a pinch. But it was best accessed from a hyper booth, with its desk-sized flat-table display, wraparound sound, digital holo tank, and full voice command.

The only hyper booths in the complex which were on the *Memphis* net were those belonging to the Testing Section, on the first floor of Building 16. There were twenty of them, and they were almost always busy. Besides Testing's own staff of verifiers, the booths served a parade of outsiders recruited to test the hands-off interface or wring out the stacks in their particular specialty.

Only the fact that it was a Sunday gave Christopher hope of catching a booth free. Had he waited until Monday, he would have had to settle for using his entry terminal. But waiting did not seem like a good idea. Saturday night's chill had persisted into Sunday, with Jessie vanishing without explanation soon after rising. He stayed in the house and spied on her, monitoring her skimmer's locator and Jessie's family subaccount long enough to follow her to LifeCare and see a health services charge appear.

Then guilt took over, and he left himself, partly to avoid being there when Jessie returned, as least until he had satisfied the one request he could cheerfully accommodate. He took the tram in and walked to Building 16 from the stop, risking the bright poison sun after three days of the gray clouds, wind, and soaking rains of Tropical Storm Jennifer.

"Staff. Any booths open?" he asked, waggling his identification badge at the scheduler.

"Sure," the woman said without looking up. "Three of them. Take your pick."

He settled in 11, waited until the door glided shut, and asked for Biographical.

"Ready."

"Find Jessica Alexis Cichuan."

The hyper's response was ordinarily instantaneous, but the table remained black for a long two seconds. Then the system chirped and the results came up:

1. JUANITA INEZ CICHUAN,
   changed to JESSICA ALEXIS CICHUAN April 9, 2085
   FHS Registry #TD-0943-3912
   b. Brownsville, Texas, 06:26 CDT, April 9, 2070
   • Mother: Dolores Maria Cichuan (deceased)
   • Father: Duane Allen Kent
   • Siblings: Luis Cichuan

"Huh," Christopher said in surprise. "She changed her name. Find English equivalents, Juanita, Inez."

JUANITA → pet form of Spanish JUANA
JUANA → Spanish of • JANE • JOAN
INEZ → Spanish of AGNES

"Huh," Christopher said again. *A butterfly named Joan Agnes. No wonder—* "Return. More."

END OF THREAD

"Visual."

NOT AVAILABLE

Frowning, Christopher opened the door and walked back down the corridor to the Testing desk. "Are all the bio stacks up?" he asked.

"For what population?"

"Contemporary."

The woman turned to her terminal. "They're all up."

"You're sure?"

"Unless they're lying to me. Problem?"

"I guess not," Christopher said uncertainly. He retreated back to booth 11 and cocooned himself there with his doubts. Briefly, he considered looking up Jessie's parents, but decided not to. *It'll be hard enough pretending I don't know one family secret.* He heard himself telling Jessie, "They know your name and when and where you were born. Sorry, that's it." *No comfort there. Better to say nothing. Better to lie—*

"Find Loi Lindholm."

The full expanse of the table was filled by the response. There was a still photo, life size, flattering. *From San Francisco, maybe two years ago—about the time I met her,* he thought. *Before she cut her hair short. Before the cheek tattoo.* There was a lengthy biography, with her apprenticeship to Rolf Dannenberg highlighted. There was a list of Loi's major sculpts, a partial list of her clients, an exhibition record. And there were thirty or more bullets noting where more information was available. *A rich thread.*

Looking at the picture, Christopher realized belatedly that while living in San Francisco, where self-definition by dress and demeanor were survival arts, Loi had stood out by being defiantly conventional. But since coming to Houston, as conservative a major city as remained in the United States, she had taken pains to be anything but conventional. The raked haircut. The hammered silver collar. The tattoo, a delicate thing of ink and silicone. The open trine, her young man on one arm, her young woman on the other.

Playing to her audience. Playing the iconoclast artist. Playing the Lady From the West. Give them a show. But looking at the picture, he also realized how much he preferred the way she had looked then to the way she looked now, and how little say he had had about the changes.

That was an unhappy thought, and he had had enough of those for one weekend.

"Clear," he said, and the table blanked.

He tried to think about Jessie and what he could do. There were mechanisms for correcting errors, but this was not an error. Jessie had done nothing to earn her any larger place in the archives of her species. It was not a slight. It was the truth, but one she was poorly equipped to either overlook or accept.

It had not been a trivial request. She would not forget. It might be a few weeks before she would ask again, but she *would* ask again. It's not fair, she had said. I don't want to be forgotten.

But she would be. And Loi would not. Loi lived through her creations. A trick of transcendence, the artist creating the art, the art re-creating the artist.

Jessie would find no comfort in that. But if she looked, she would find a great deal of company. Within their circle of friends there were two, perhaps three, who would merit a longer notice in the hyper. The rest, himself included, were merely part of the census. This many born this day, that many died.

A lie invited—but he had no ammunition with which to lie. He racked his memory for details she had offered in conversation these last few months, and then gave up, knowing that to be caught in a lie would be worse than telling the truth. He would tell her matter-of-factly, and show her a dump of his own entry so that she would know she was not alone. Loi was an exception, was exceptional. As was William McCutcheon.

If it was painful, well, he knew what that felt like. He would help her grow through it. Pain was a pointed lesson in living, a reality check for the beclouded.

"Find Christopher Thomas McCutcheon."

The entry was as it had been the first time he looked himself up in the hyper. He earned one extra line for being staff, one extra line for having had both donor and host mothers, lost one for having been content with his name, but otherwise it was a copy of Jessie's, simple, short, and shallow.

He was pleased.

But only for a moment.

Then, perversely, he began to think about what was missing from the display. He had earned two degrees, in Salem's grueling general studies program and Stanford's comparatively easy Information Sciences. He had won a Hastings Award at sixteen, a songwriting contest at nineteen. He had signed a marriage contract and dissolved it. He had written an essay for the *Oregonian*, played guitar on KSFO's *Tunnel Visions*. And more. A whole life, not just a moment of birth and a diagram of blood relations.

But there it was:

1. CHRISTOPHER THOMAS McCUTCHEON
   FHS Registry #OS-1029-0349
   b. Vernonia, Oregon, 23:40 PST, May 16, 2067
   • Mother: [Donor] Sharron Ria (Aldritch) McCutcheon
              (deceased)
              [Host] Deryn Glenys Falconer
   • Father: William Lowell McCutcheon
   • Siblings: Lynn-Anne Aldritch
   Library Staff, Diaspora Project, Houston

"Print and clear," Christopher said.

He took the dump and left the booth, wondering what was wrong. He had expected it to be brief. He had seen it before. What he didn't expect was that, this time, he would care.

CHAPTER
10

-|UGC|-

". . . a few seconds of death . . ."

FLYING INTO THE KASIGAU LAUNCH CENTER, MIKHAIL DRYKE could not fail to note how dramatically different the company's Kenyan spaceport was from its Brazilian kin. Though both served the same function and embraced the same basic facilities, the facilities were counterparts, not twins.

The difference began with the setting. Kasigau had taken over not former rain forest, but the *nyika*, the wilderness of dry mountain highlands southeast of Tsavo National Park. This was land that for centuries had known drought and famine better than rain and plenty. Land that had been picked over but rarely fought over, for the prize was too meager. Allied had paved its runways and sprawled its structures across a landscape which had scarcely any ecology to disrupt. Taita's elephants and rhinos were already long gone when the construction crews arrived.

At Prainha, the incredible guy-and-column mountain of the launch tower rose nearly four kilometers above the river plateau. The tower was the unchallenged centerpiece of the Pará. At night, its fairy-castle lights were visible from Macapá and Belém, and even from ships in the Atlantic off the coast of the Ilha de Marajó. The nearest natural feature that could compare with it was half a continent away.

The aperture of Kasigau's launch tower stood as far above sea level as Prainha's, above as much energy-stealing atmosphere. But it stood not on river plateau, but atop Kasigau Rock, a small round-topped mountain. Consequently, the tower's central beam tube was half the height, and the shrunken fairy castle clung to the contours of the mount like a great spindly-legged insect which had paused there in its wanderings.

And if that were not enough to diminish it, there was Kilimanjaro, its dramatic volcanic profile rising from the Masai Steppe to the west. Inbound to Kasigau, the Celestron slicing down through the high thin air, Dryke had been gifted with a long look at Kilimanjaro's steep western face and rugged snow-capped summit. Against that memory, the Kasigau cannon looked like the unfinished skeleton of a mountain, a child's backyard imitation of the real thing.

"That's one heck of a scenic outlook you folks built for yourselves," he said to the air controller.

"Only view of Kilimanjaro anywhere in the *nyika*," came the answer. "Four thousand meters up and not a cloud in sight. Not that anyone ever gets to enjoy it, except the tube monkeys and mirror mechs."

Dryke understood. For Kasigau was strictly freight, its ten-gigawatt compound laser array hurling a steady procession of pilotless T-3 capsules on one-way journeys into orbit. No pilots' colony, no astronaut union or joybirds here. Kasigau belonged to the working class, to the high-energy laser techs and the mirror mechanics, the loaders and launch bosses of the self-named "HELcrews." The complex mechanical ballet they performed, sending a fully loaded T-3 skyward every twenty-two minutes, day and night, was the only show in town.

One launch every twenty-two minutes. Almost three per hour. Sixty-five a day, lifting thirteen hundred tonnes of electrochemicals, microphysics, and human consumables from ground to orbit. But even at that pace, Kasigau was running at less than fifty percent of design capacity. Prainha was regularly topping ninety launches a day, with an amazing peak record of one hundred twenty-two.

Most of the difference was infrastructure. Prainha was thirty-five years old, mature, settled. Kasigau was just thirteen years old, gangly and growing. The airways, roadways, railways, and seaways which fed it were still unequal to the task of supporting Kasigau's design capacity. Especially the seaways. Even with the recent upgrade of the railhead and freight handling, the port at Mombasa was overwhelmed.

The transshipment bottleneck was not, at heart, a security problem. But Site Director Yvonne Havens was looking to Dryke for a solution all the same. What Havens wanted was to stream-

line the cargo security procedures enough to boost the schedule
to eighty or more cycles a day. To Dryke's annoyance, Sasaki
had endorsed the request, obliging Dryke to come to Kenya and
study the options.

"Most of the company's reserve launch capacity is there, at
Kasigau," Sasaki had reminded him. "The long-term solution
is here, with the new launcher proposed for Almeirim. But the
company can't justify the capital investment in a third spaceport
under present conditions. So we must look at Kasigau. A single
additional lift a day means another seven thousand metric tons
a year. We can use the capacity, especially since the mix here
must shift toward passengers when we begin ferrying colonists
to *Memphis*."

Havens was a plump fast-talking black woman who wore the
wound-wire bracelets and patterned cheek scars of the Rendille,
the most popular of Kenya's revival tribalisms. Using her smile
as a commentary, she underlined Sasaki's point while she and
Dryke toured the spaceport together.

"Kasigau is insurance—leverage," she said as they walked
through the cargo assembly center. "We're what keeps the Bra-
zilians from jacking the transshipment taxes on Prainha. We're
what helps keep the can drivers in line. We could fly T-2s out
of here with no one at the stick, and they know it. But it's all a
bluff if we can't run at capacity."

"If you compromise security and have to close down for a
few months because of a hit, you won't even have a bluff."

"I don't want our security compromised," she said, smiling.
"I want it factored out of the traffic stream."

The conversation continued in the skimmer. "I looked at your
incident log before I came here," Dryke said. "The cargo inspectors stopped a half dozen bombs and booby traps in the last
six months. Your perimeter defense smothered a shoulder SAM
and two planes so far this year."

"I'm very proud of our security team. Homeworld hasn't
touched us."

"Homeworld hasn't tried. All you've seen so far are amateurs.
Shiftas. Bandits."

"Amateurs do not own shoulder-launched surface-to-air mis-
siles," she said stiffly.

"Anyone can own one, if they've got a hundred thousand
dollars and a contact in Chile or South Africa," Dryke said.
"And besides, only an amateur would try to use a shoulder SAM

against a T-ship. You've got ten gigawatts of laser energy to play with and a mirror system up in the castle that can split a dozen secondary beams off the main beam. Anything that gets within a thousand meters of a capsule on the beam is going to be fried. I'm not worried about someone shooting down a T-ship. It's a surprise package in the cargo that worries me.''

They had reached the operations center entrance, but Havens made no move to leave the skimmer. "It's a trade-off, Mr. Dryke," she said, smiling. "I need another hundred tonnes a day. I could use another four hundred. Balance that against a slightly greater risk of an accident—''

"Not an accident. A terrorist hit.''

The smile widened. "You're not the only one who's been reading, Mr. Dryke. I've looked at your report on Jeremiah and the Homeworld. They're not terrorists. They're protesters. They're playing a public opinion game. They've never killed anyone. They're not going to strike blindly at Kasigau. And you've already said they can't knock down a can. So why are you tying my handlers up in knots?''

"To make sure that Jeremiah isn't tempted by opportunity.''

"There are no guarantees, Mr. Dryke. Make it difficult for him. That will be enough.''

Dryke frowned. "I won't know if I can agree with that until I've seen more.''

"What do you want to see next?''

"I think Mombasa.''

"We can go there now, if you like.''

"Now is fine," Dryke said. "But I'll go by myself, thank you.''

"As you prefer," she said, cracking the skimmer's door open. She climbed out, then turned and squatted to peer back inside at Dryke. "Please try to remember, Mr. Dryke—it's not that we're reckless. We're desperate. And that changes the rules sometimes.''

Dryke nodded. "For Jeremiah, too,'' he said.

In the choppy waters of Formosa Bay, two hundred kilometers from the fences of Kasigau, a small fishing boat flying the flag of the East African Union rode a sea anchor against a gentle breeze. The nameless craft had made its way up the coast from Zanzibar over the last sixteen hours, running the Pemba Channel under a blazing midday sun and passing Mombasa in the night.

It was rigged and outfitted for anchovy fishing, with fine-mesh purse seines, brails, and buoys. But none of the five men aboard were fishermen.

Throughout the morning, one of the five had stood on the bow, scanner raised to his eyes, watching the freighters from Kasigau tear across the sky. The launch trajectory for the T-ships carried them nearly overhead, bright sparks against the blue sky, already two hundred kilometers up and moving two thousand meters per second, racing for orbit.

The column of light on which the freighters climbed was invisible. Only at its base, where the beam shattered stray dust particles into clouds of ions, could it be seen, a pale glowing needle anchored to the top of the launch tower, barely visible on the far horizon, and pointed unerringly at the streaking spark of the spacecraft.

While one watched, the others removed the nets which had concealed the massive sea-green canister lashed against the stern gunwale. The canister was as long as the boat was wide and half a meter in diameter. It was heavy enough to take the concentrated efforts of all four men, aided by the boat's net winch, to raise it off the deck and carefully lower it into the water off the stern.

There it turned end-up and bobbed like a half-filled bottle, a bare thirty cents showing above the gentle waves. A wire-rope tether stopped it from floating away with the light current.

A second man joined the first on the bow. "Everything's ready."

"The Zodiac ready?"

"It'll take five minutes. Do you have the mark?"

"I have it. Easy as skeet-shooting."

"I'll make the call."

In a tiny belowdeck cabin, he hunched over a small military comlink, addressed its output at a private satellite in synchronous orbit over Sumatera, and sent a sixty-character code burst. He had no idea where the message went from there, only that some ten seconds later he had his answer.

He shut down the comlink and stowed it, then rejoined the man on the bow. "Jeremiah says the 2:20 and 3:05 launches are the best targets of opportunity, if we can wait."

The man with the scanner swept the shoreline, the sea. "Six months to get this far," he said at last. "We can wait. We can wait at least that long to do it right."

• • •

Mikhail Dryke's initial tour of Mombasa had yielded little of value.

All he carried away with him were a few glimpses of the little island city as it might have been five hundred years ago, as the Portuguese were concluding their hundred-year conquest. And of the city as it was fifteen years ago, before it became the primary port for Kasigau. The massive masonry of Fort Jesus, the Portuguese stronghold, recalled the former epoch. The outdated and undersized berths of the Kilindini anchorage recalled the latter.

The spaceport at Kasigau had conquered Mombasa more thoroughly than any invader in its thousand-year history, more than the Shirazi, more than the Omani, more than the Turks, more than the British. Kasigau had transformed Mombasa's focus. A pair of great white elephant tusks, too large to be real, still arched over Moi Avenue—a quaint and somewhat bittersweet anachronism. But the city that once controlled the trade routes to India was now a way station on the trade routes to space.

No, he corrected himself. A bottleneck. Neither Havens nor Sasaki had exaggerated. Dryke had seen container ships anchored offshore, awaiting an open berth at the quays. Between the backlog, the Allied inspectors, and the Kenyan tax and customs officials, the trip from ship's hold off Mombasa to the belly of a T-3 atop the castle was the longest, slowest leg of the journey.

Returning to the spaceport, Dryke rebelled at finding himself entangled in questions of corporate finance and cargo logistics. Sure, they could move inspections from quayside to Kasigau. Sure, they could open the center's runways to outside aircraft, to wide-bodied A-50s and Caravans from Al-Qahirah and Kiyev and the Ruhr.

But every instinct in Dryke screamed "No!" All it would take was one mistake. One robot kamikaze passing up its landing to crash into the operations center for the HFI complex. One pocket nuke concealed in a T-3 cask, one sloppy or hurried inspection, one little kiloton explosion at the top of the castle. One mistake could put Kasigau out of business for a year, or even forever.

Dryke left the highway at Mackinnon Road to enter the Kasigau compound at the Rukinga gate. He reached the gate just as the crackling thunder of a T-3 being ejected from the catapult rolled over the complex. The guard detail waved him through, which obliged him to stop and deliver a harangue on complacency.

He had just managed to inspire the desired degree of contrition when alarms began to scream from the gatehouse, the sentries' pagers, and the skimmer's radio. While the sentries raced to seal the gate, Dryke dove back into the skimmer.

"What's happening?" he demanded.

"The center is under Code Black rules," a curt voice answered. "Keep this channel clear."

"This is Mikhail Dryke. Tell me what's happening."

"I'm sorry, Mr. Dryke. I don't know."

"Is it Jeremiah?"

"Mr. Dryke, I don't know. *Please* keep this channel clear."

"Goddammit," Dryke muttered. "Goddammit."

Ten klicks from the gate to the castle, another three to the operations complex. He had covered less than half of it when a cold white flash which made the sun seem dim flooded the landscape from somewhere high in the sky. Half-blinded, Dryke was forced to slow his vehicle. He was still struggling to see when a deep-throated rolling thunderclap, dwarfing even the report of the castle's catapult, shook the skimmer and filled its cabin with deafening black noise.

Jesus Christ, was that a nuke? Oh, please— Twisting his head, Dryke risked a squint through the side window to reassure himself that the castle was still standing. It was. Puzzled, he sped on, fearing he was too late. He was. By the time he reached operations, Freighter T-3/E49851 was falling toward the Indian Ocean, and in Formosa Bay off Ras Ngomeni, a small fishing boat was down by the stern and burning.

The ballet begins. They wait in the wings in the kilometer-long tunnel from the cargo assembly center, tapered fat-bodied gnomes five meters in diameter and nearly seven meters tall, inching forward to the head of the line. They wait for the clamps and the hook and the long ride to the top of the castle, climbing the outside of the central tower like aphids climbing a stem.

T-3/E49851 had been built three days ago, its shell cut and curved and welded by the CAM machines in the fabrication center. It had been delivered to the cargo assembly center twelve hours ago, filled, sealed, and cycled into the launch queue six hours later, mated with its thrust disk of reinforced ice barely twenty minutes ago.

At five minutes after two, E49851 started its dizzying trip up out of the catacombs, bursting into the sunlight at the foot of the tower at a brisk fifty kilometers per hour. Even at that clip, the ride up the side of the tower took longer than the ride to space which was to follow.

At the top, a handler crane grabbed the spacecraft and lowered it gently into the catapult. In the launch operations center, a dozen stations ran a checklist of a hundred queries. The first clearance was from Laser Control, the last from Security; when it came through, the computers took over.

In a sudden convulsive moment, the T-ship was in motion, dragged upward by the accelerator ring, boosted from beneath by a giant's breath. At the mouth of the tube, the accelerator ring split and fell away, and the capsule shot skyward, flying free.

The instant it cleared the launch tube, the T-ship began to slow, fighting drag and gravity, trading speed for altitude, tracing a trajectory familiar to every child who had ever hurled a stone at the sun.

Half a kilometer away, the HEL bank, twenty parallel half-gigawatt free-electron lasers under one sprawling roof, waited the call. When E49851 was five hundred meters above the castle, Unit 9 jumped to life, sending a five hundred-watt pilot beam out through the bank lenses, along the nitrogen-filled beam tunnel, and up through the center of the castle to the mirrors. Guided by the tracking system, a single mirror directed the pilot beam against the broad base of the capsule.

Still the capsule climbed, still the capsule slowed. Two kilometers, three, three and a half. Any moment, it seemed, it would begin to fall back. And then the great bank of lasers came to life as one. The ten-gigawatt beam filled the full diameter of the beam tube, caught all twenty mirrors, and leaped across the sky to the broad base of the freighter

The first pulse vaporized an almost invisibly thin layer from the ice disk, forming a vaporous sheet of pure, clear, super-heated steam. A second pulse, a microsecond later and a hundred times stronger, shattered the molecules of water vapor into an atomic cloud of raw hydrogen, oxygen, and electrons, a plasma hotter than any chemical rocket flame, hotter even than the surface of the Sun. The plasma expanded savagely outward, kicking the spacecraft upward, as though it were the piston in a bizarre engine.

A thousand times a second, the lasers cycled through their double pulse. The awesome seamless roar of the closely spaced explosions was moderated only by distance, the pitch changing as the capsule accelerated, Doppler-shifting into the familiar falling, fading scream of a T-ship.

In the launch operations center, what little tension there could be in a routine repeated more than sixty times a day had evaporated when the thrust beam picked up the T-ship. The T-3 was riding the beam now, accelerating toward orbit, safely out of reach. Even the launch security officer, the man in the loop on Kasigau's air defenses, sat back in his chair and reached for his drink.

The failure of the AI protocols in the Houston incident had led to the LSO being given unprecedented responsibility. Now, the AIPs could kill. The LSO had gone from being the only station that could call down the fire from the mountain to the only one that could stop it. Which meant that the LSO's errors now would be errors of commission, not omission.

Yusuf Alli had not welcomed his newly elevated status. Kasigau was ringed by airports—the big one at Mombasa, the fields at Voi and Malindi, and fifteen rural airstrips within the primary air control area. The air traffic swarmed like bees around a hive. But every time a red light came up on the board, Alli had thirty seconds to call for a hold, and then one minute to make his decision. If he made a mistake, people would die.

Through the first three weeks under the revised protocol, Alli had dealt with his anxiety in a straightforward way. He always called for a hold, and then always gave the target a green. He had yet to be wrong. He knew there was some risk, but if any air traffic managed to reach the threat envelope of a T-ship on the climb, the defense system would bring it down without getting a second opinion. It was, he thought, foolproof.

Then the contact alarm sounded, and Alli jerked forward in his chair, choking on his tea.

"Hold," he sputtered. "Hold!"

"Tracking missile," said the board. "Threat category three. Risk category: moderate. Time to intercept: twenty-one seconds."

Alli wasted three seconds staring at the track of the streaking missile. "It's a clean miss," he protested. "It won't get within fifty klicks of the can."

"Risk category: high. Time to intercept; eleven seconds."

Alli's eyes danced frantically over the displays. "What's the danger? What can they hit?"

"Possible beam occlusion. Time to intercept: five seconds."

At the same time, someone was screaming at him, "Burn it! Burn it! They're going for the beam!"

Ashen-faced, Alli brought his palm down on the fire mushroom. One of the twenty lasers abandoned the synchrony of the launch rhythm, as atop the castle an auxiliary mirror rotated a few degrees. A defensive beam locked on the hurtling missile, and an instant later the missile exploded.

"Got it!" exulted Alli.

But the alarm kept sounding, and the displays continued to track something—now a cloud of a hundred smaller objects, still climbing as they fanned out. Then each of the smaller objects seemed to explode, and the missile was now a scatter of marble-sized projectiles. Moving nearly as fast as the missile itself had been, the chemical buckshot intersected the beam.

The first pulse heated the binder holding the projectiles together, and they blossomed into a dense cloud of aluminum dust. The next pulse, striking the fine particles, lit a myriad of tiny plasmas that quickly merged into a huge, sun-hot flare, dissipating the beam's energy as light and heat. Only a tiny fraction of that pulse got through to the T-ship. The echo, used for tracking and guidance, was smothered completely. The next cycle was completely choked off.

At full power, the launch cannon could have burned through the cloud in a matter of seconds. But with no positive track on the target, no reflection back from the T 3, the laser controller declared a scrub and shut the HEL array down.

Three hundred kilometers away, the freighter began to fall, as though the string holding it aloft had been cut. Before long, it reappeared on the radar displays, no longer eclipsed by the dissipating cloud.

"Can we get it back?" the launch boss asked, little hope in his voice.

"She's tumbling from the drag," reported one station. "There's no target."

"Can we burn it?"

"No. Too much atmospheric absorption, and we're losing the angle."

"Jesus Christ," the launch boss said. "Where's it coming down? Indian Ocean? God, just drop it in the ocean—"

The answer was slow in coming. "South China Sea."

Relieved expressions blossomed throughout the room.

Then the tracking officer added, "Maybe landfall in Malaysia. Singapore. I can't be sure."

"Damn," breathed the launch boss.

"Can't we warn them?" a sweaty and pale Yusuf Alli burst out.

Silently, his mouth tight with anger, the launch boss shook his head. "And tell them what?" he asked. "To put up their umbrellas? It's coming down hard. There's no place to hide."

The freighter was a hurtling meteor of ice and steel, thirty-two tons of inert mass tracing the arc dictated by the forces which had acted on it. Its fall through the afternoon sky went mostly unnoticed across the eastern third of the Indian Ocean, except by a navigational satellite in high orbit, the commercial radars at Colombo and Djakarta, and a Chinese warship in the Gulf of Thailand.

As air friction tore at the tumbling spacecraft, the great disk of reinforced ice shattered, jagged chunks of it spinning away as it passed over the island of Sumatera. One piece smashed into a tree-covered hillside near Siabu, scattering a family of civet cats. Another buried itself dramatically in a rice paddy on the flats near Dumai, scattering a family of farmers.

But the freighter itself remained whole, its dive becoming steeper as it neared the surface. Sumatera slid away beneath, then the islands of the Strait of Malacca and the tip of the Malay Peninsula.

By now the spacecraft was lighting up the radar screens at Paya Lebar Airport in Singapore. Controllers there watched in astonishment as it dove toward the Singapore Strait at more than four thousand klicks per hour.

The pilot of a Boeing 350 which had just taken off from the airport saw it as a fiery streak which bisected the sky less than a kilometer in front of his plane.

A million people heard the thunder from a cloudless sky, the death-rattle shattering windows all across the city. A hailstorm of glittery razor-edged fragments rained down to the streets from the jagged wall of high rises facing the harbor.

Thousands on the Singapore waterfront witnessed with amazement the spectacular fountain and plume of steam that erupted as the T-ship plunged into the waters of the strait.

But then it seemed to be over. There was much pointing, many voices raised in excitement, a few raised in hysteria. Those who had missed the moment rushed to hear the story from those who had witnessed it. The waterfront was a carnival of questions.

And then the waters of the strait rose up in a sudden rolling, roiling surge. Like a miniature tsunami, the concussion wave smashed small boats against each other and swept onlookers from floating piers and sea walls.

By the time the surge drained back into the strait, E49851 had become a killer many times over.

-|CGC|-

"We accept this judgment . . ."

NIGHT IS THE WINTER OF THE AMAZON, AND DAWN ITS SPRING.
Shortly after 5 A.M. each day, Hiroko Sasaki left the Director's
Residence to make the twenty-minute walk in the clammy-warm
tropical air to the headquarters tower. The walk was her morning
tea, awakening her mind, and daily constitutional, unlimbering
her body.

On reaching her office, she would hide behind a Privacy One
cocoon to read the active files, compose policy drafts, and update her own logs. Unlike the time she spent at the Director's
Residence, this was a working hermitism.

Word of the Singapore disaster found Sasaki there reviewing
the October dispatch from *Ur*. The first report, from Prainha's
operations monitor, was annoyingly sparse—a launch anomaly
in Kenya, a T-ship down.

She tried to call Havens at Kasigau, but was told that the
center was under Code Black.

"Search all sources," she told her com system.

Moments later, a single window came up on the display wall.
The Current Events stack of DIANA, the Asian information net,
had a report of a plane crash in the Singapore Strait. By the
time Sasaki reached Havens and Dryke at Kasigau, DIANA was
calling it a meteor strike, and Panasian television was offering
the first pictures of capsized boats, broken windows, and the
anguish of shaken and grieving survivors.

Havens looked chastened, guilt-haunted, and confused. Dryke

seemed more under control, though he was tight-lipped, his body coiled anger.

"Mr. Dryke, is the port under assault?" she asked

"No. It's over. We—"

"Are the facilities intact?"

"Kasigau wasn't touched."

Sasaki allowed herself a moment of relief. "What can you tell me?"

"There was a missile launched against a T-ship. Against the thrust beam, I mean. An occlusion trick. They had salvage fusing, beat the castle defenses. The moment our burn beam lit it up, it blew like a fireworks rocket. Everything we did after that just made it worse. Like judo. They went after our weakness and used our strength against us."

"More facts and fewer metaphors, please, Mr. Dryke. Site Director Havens," Sasaki said.

Havens raised her eyes toward the camera.

"Have you suspended operations?"

"Yes. We shut down immediately."

"Please resume launch operations at the first opportunity."

Her face wrinkled in puzzlement. "Resume—"

"At first opportunity. Priority is to be given to *Memphis* cargoes."

In helpless confusion, Havens looked to Dryke for support. But Dryke understood, as Sasaki expected he would "Yeah, I agree," he said, nodding slowly. "If we shut down we're doing them a favor. If they try to hit us again now they'll be doing us a favor. Fire up the lasers."

Havens's face twisted unhappily. "I have some very shaky people in flight operations—"

"Then rotate a new shift in," said Sasaki. "But get the freighters flying again. Refer all outside inquiries here. All statements are to come from me."

"Yes, Director."

"I will expect a more complete report from both of you in thirty minutes."

"We're on it," Dryke said.

There were six windows on the display wall now. Arms crossed over her chest, Sasaki stood before the wall and surveyed them. DIANA had corrected its story once more; the falling object was now a satellite. Orbital flight controllers on Highstar had provided Allied with a flight track confirming the aborted launch from Kasigau. Nikkei Telemedia had joined Panasian at the scene. The Kenyan commerce minister was demanding a conference. Panasian was demanding a statement.

But of Jeremiah, there was no word.

Sasaki was able to placate the Kenyan commerce minister with five minutes of earnest concern and a promise of more. That duty discharged, she composed a brief statement for the media:

"Reports reaching me indicate that at approximately eleven twenty-five Greenwich Mean Time this morning, an Allied Transcon T-3 freight capsule launched from Kasigau Launch Center in Kenya crashed into the Singapore Strait. Allied has begun an immediate investigation into the circumstances surrounding this most unfortunate event. We are deeply concerned by reports of damage and loss of life in Singapore harbor. Allied will extend every possible assistance to the government of Singapore and to those touched by this incident."

It said too much and too little, but it was better than silence, and would keep the dogs at bay for a time. She recorded it and sent it out to the European and Asian information nets and to Newslink, the private media clearinghouse. Within five minutes, Sasaki's face had appeared in three of the windows on her display wall.

By then, her staff sociodynamicist had answered her call and joined her in the office. Oker was not far behind. They watched the feeds together, quietly sharing their perceptions, until the Kenyan President called and Sasaki banished the others from the room.

That conference was longer and more difficult than the first. It took nearly half an hour before Jomu was satisfied, and the price this time was much higher.

Havens and Dryke were waiting for her when she finished with Jomu. But she kept them waiting, calling the sociodynamicist back into her office.

"There is still nothing from Jeremiah."

"There could be many reasons for that," the sociologist said. "Not least of which are the dead in Singapore."

"Could it be that he was not involved?"

"Why don't we ask Mr. Dryke that?"

• • •

"I can tell you that we *are* launching now," Yvonne Havens said, appearing calmer and more in control. "Operations resumed twenty minutes ago."

"Very good," Sasaki said,

"And we do have some further information. The cargo was made up of environmental and navigational subsystems and other black boxes for *Memphis*. I don't know how serious the loss is. I'm waiting to hear from the construction office on Takara."

"Please forward their answer to me when you receive it."

"I will. Director—what are you hearing from Singapore?"

Sasaki nodded. "My latest information indicates sixteen dead and at least twenty-six missing. As you might expect, I am being pressed for statements, explanations. I have expressed regret, but I will need to say more soon. Mr. Dryke, what can you add?"

"We have what's left of the boat," Dryke said. "We have the canister—it was a thirty-year-old bottle rocket, Korean manufacture. Whoever pulled this off has disappeared. We're searching the coastal area, Malindi. We're getting some help from the Kenyans on checking sea traffic."

"Do you expect to find those responsible?"

"I'd like to say yes. But the truth is we may well not."

"Have you any evidence that Homeworld was involved?"

"It has Jeremiah's fingerprints all over it. He hits *Memphis*, he hurts Allied, he gets people wondering about the safety of the T-ships just as the colonists are starting to report. The deaths in Singapore underline the point. All he really lost was a chance to get up on his soapbox."

"Do you believe that he intended those deaths?"

"Yes," Dryke said firmly. "At the very least he knew the risk was there, and went ahead regardless. They could have launched sixty seconds sooner and dropped the can in the middle of the Indian Ocean. I think he wanted a good show, a big scare, and rolled the dice."

"I agree," said the sociodynamicist.

"I value your opinion," Sasaki said to Dryke. "All may be as you say. But the moment demands more. An accusation without proof will appear to be an excuse. Can you offer any evidence of Homeworld involvement which the world press would find persuasive?"

"No," Dryke said reluctantly. "Not yet."

She nodded. "Thank you."

"Hiroko, we were on top of this," Dryke added. "We were very close to having him. We would have stopped him, except that one of our people reopened a door we'd closed."

"That, too, offers little to me now," she said. Sasaki turned to the man beside her on the bench. "I am ready for your counsel. How should we deal with this?"

"Hold our nose and take our medicine," was the answer. "I was looking at lightning polls in the outer office. We'll be seen as responsible whether or not we blame Homeworld. And if we blame them, we publicize our vulnerability to Homeworld tricks—and probably the details of the gag they used against us. In my opinion, it's marginally better for us to be seen as fallible than as weak."

"Yes," Sasaki said. "I agree."

"Perhaps something can be worked out with the Kenyans."

Sasaki nodded. "I have already consulted with the Kenyan government," she said. "They understand the true circumstances and are willing to be helpful. For appearances, they will insist on a suspension of launch operations while an investigation takes place. But I have been promised the restoration of our license, with certain cosmetic changes in the inspection and oversight provisions, in no more than ten days."

"Wait just one moment," Dryke interrupted. "Are we talking about taking the blame for this ourselves?"

"Yes," Sasaki said. "I have decided to issue a statement accepting full responsibility for the accident. Mrs. Havens, we will need to agree on a plausible failure scenario."

"Yes, Director."

"What in the hell are we doing this for?" Dryke exploded. "They're the murderers, not us."

"We can't win the war of opinion," the sociologist said simply. "We have no credibility. This is Robin Hood we're up against. Who listens to the Sheriff of Nottingham?"

"This is wrong," Dryke said, shaking his head in disgust. "This is dumb wrong."

Sasaki sought and held his eyes. Her focus made it as though no one else was with them. "This is reality," she said. "We must win the other war. We must persevere, and complete *Memphis*."

"This is a crime," snapped Dryke. "A bloody crime. And you want to wash it away."

"No, Mikhail," Sasaki said softly. "We will not forget, no

more than we forgot Dola Martinez. You must find Jeremiah and put an end to his interference. You made a promise to me. I am counting on you to keep it."

His eyes questioned, then accepted, her meaning. "There are some threads I can follow."

"Then do so," she said, her voice still soft, but her eyes hard. "It is clear that Jeremiah can hurt us. He must not get a chance to try."

CHAPTER
12

-|AUU|-

". . . the fabric of life."

LIKE A CHILD EXPLORING THE SCAR LEFT BEHIND BY A BAN-
dage, Christopher McCutcheon traced his finger along the nearly
invisible crack on the back of his ancient Martin steel-string.
The luthier had lovingly healed the wound in the century-old
rosewood dreadnought. McCutcheon strummed a chord, and the
mellow-voiced guitar sang as sweetly as always.

The club audiences preferred the bright sound of his Mitsei
electronic, which was just fine with Christopher. The Mitsei had
a versatile effects kit, could go six- or twelve-string at a touch,
and still looked more or less traditional. Most important, unlike
the Martin, it could easily be replaced should anything happen.
Christopher did not want to expose the fragile antique to the
rigors and risks faced by a working instrument, much less vio-
late it by having a performance port installed.

But there were certain songs and certain times that demanded
a softer, richer voice. And when he played for pleasure, more
often than not it was the supple-actioned D-42 that came out of
its case. The luthier had asserted that a wooden instrument held
all the music that had ever been played on it, and said that
Christopher's Martin had been played well. He was not inclined
to argue.

Almost of their own volition, his fingers found the opening
chords of "Caravan to Antares." "Look at me, I'm flying free,
living in the stars," he sang, head down, eyes closed. "Signed
my name and set my sights on a destination far—"

Sometime between the first verse and the last, Loi came to

his room. He opened his eyes to discover her leaning lightly against the wall near the doorway, folded hands pinned behind her, listening. Though it was barely eight, she was wearing a short black nightdress which showed much leg and shoulder and clung slinkily to the rest.

"Haven't seen that for a while," he said. She had bought the nightdress for herself on an early dinner-and-shopping date in the Embarcadero, then proceeded to take him home and show him that no visual aids were necessary. As play wear went, the nightdress was demure, but the associated memories were still potent.

"Are you busy?" she asked in her thoroughly direct and un-coquettish way.

"I was planning to be for a while," he said, gesturing at the guitar. "I just got Claudia back."

"Too busy to help a friend in need?"

A crooked smile. "Is that a proposition?"

"Of sorts. I think Jessie could really use both our attention. Unless you think Claudia will be jealous."

Christopher frowned, hugged the guitar to his chest. "I don't think Jess wants my attentions."

"I think she's been missing them."

He squinted uncertainly. "Did she say that?"

"If I had to wait for her to speak her mind plainly to know what she's feeling, this family would be in serious trouble," Loi said with a smile. "But you don't have to, if you're uncomfortable. I'd rather you didn't if you're uncomfortable, if you've still got business to work out with her."

"I just don't want to make her say no."

"I don't think she will," Loi said. "She needs what you can give her, Chris." She smiled affectionately. "I don't think you realize how much good you can do."

Her words were processed through a filter of self-image that removed most of the compliment, but left intact the hope of being worthy of it. "Sure," he said finally, setting the guitar aside. "Let's see if we can't put a smile on Jessie's face."

She came toward him. "Hug me first," she said. "Let me find you. Then we can go out there and remind her what she's part of."

It was hard to say what each of them brought to that joining that made it so special. But it was the best they'd ever been together, intense and intimate, loving and sharing. It was like they'd never shared a bed before; it was like they'd always been lovers. Everything was new, a discovery. Everything was familiar, seamlessly easy.

There was little said. Hunger and healing, doubt and reassurance, all were given purely physical expression. Eyes and smiles and mingling energies did the work of words.

Christopher let Loi take the lead. Smiling mischievously, the older woman settled beside Jessie on the couch and purposefully began to undress her. Christopher joined in the task from the other side, determinedly plucking at buttons and tugging at sleeves.

Though their movements were unhurried, their focus and intensity gave them an urgency flavored with inevitability. Together, Loi and Christopher wrapped Jessie in a timeless, dreamlike experience of sensuality. Any surprise, any resistance, boiled away in the growing sexual heat.

Naked, Jessie surrendered, releasing all Mind, embracing Moment. Four knowing hands caressed her soft cool skin and silken folds. Two hungry mouths tattooed gentle bites along a shoulder, sought crinkled nipples to tease. She opened to their touch, their energies. She took a kiss from Loi, long and hungry, and passed it in turn to Christopher, warm and forgiving.

In barely noticed pauses, Loi shed her nightdress with a shrug, and Christopher his shirt. Skin to skin to skin they embraced, dry tinder for the fire that ran through them.

Sometime in that span, Christopher let go of calculation and plan, centering in the immediate—the rich scent of Jessie's excitement, the soft sounds of pleasure, the warm touch of a hand, his own pounding blood.

A three-way kiss dissolved as the two women's mouths sought his nipples, their hands working in partnership to free him from his jeans and briefs. Loi went to her knees and briefly took his arching erection into an embrace of soft lips and swirling tongue. Then she sat back on her heels and pulled both Jessie and him down to the floor with her, seeking a larger canvas for what she was creating.

Without ever seeming to give direction, Loi orchestrated the rising crescendo. Sitting cross-legged with her back to the couch, Loi cradled Jessie's head in her lap while Christopher lay between Jessie's thighs, happily tasting her sweet slickness. From above, Loi caressed Jessie's full breasts, tugged and teased her nipples, stroked her hair and her cheeks, bent forward to cap a moan of pleasure with a kiss.

But when Jessie reached up for Loi's body, Loi captured her hands and forced them down, pinning them to the carpet. A gasp escaped Jessie's lips, and her eyes closed. His mouth melded to Jessie's sensitive center, Christopher rode with her on the rising curve, answering her excitement with a feverish intensity.

Then, as Jessie writhed and mewled under their combined attentions, Loi called Christopher forward with her eyes. He rose up and crawled toward her, their mouths meeting in a fragrant kiss as his cock entered Jessie. She moaned, a deep guttural animal sound, her body drawing him in, hips rising to meet his thrusts.

Finally, Loi, too, surrendered to no-mind, rocking forward to her knees and lowering her sparsely furred patch over Jessie's eager tongue. The trio soared together, reaching, the energy spinning through them, Jessie to Loi to Christopher to Jessie and around the other way as well. They flew faster and faster, pushing against the barrier, then suddenly broke through, one after another.

Jessie was first, her body seized by a fierce, twisting orgasm that triggered Christopher's own furious release. Not long after, the double charge and Jessie's flicking tongue lifted Loi to her own arching, blissful break. Christopher's body tingled, jangled, in sympathy.

They fell apart like toppled rag dolls, drained, bodies limp. In their breathless haze, they shared smiles of shy delight, of childlike giddy joy. They held hands, laughed, questioned each other with eyes that asked amazedly, needlessly, *Did you feel that?*

And as breath and strength returned, they began to look at each other with hope and hunger, for the pleasure, the moment, had been so exquisite that they could not help but try to touch it again. They adjourned gleefully to Loi's big bed and soon began again.

It was long after midnight before the edge of longing at last gave way to happy fatigue, and they fell asleep entangled in each other's arms.

For a long time, Christopher was unable to name the warm feeling that he woke with that next morning. It was as though there were a happy little spark lighting him from within. He didn't mind being the only one of the three who was expected elsewhere early. He kissed them good-bye as though they were sleepy children and found himself smiling as he went out the door.

Neither the police checklane on the U.S. 75 en route to Allied nor the endless section conference once he got there tested Christopher's patience that day. The smile came back at intervals, and with it crystal-clear sense-rich memories.

But he was scarcely aware of his own state until lunch, when one of the other archaeolibrarians wryly announced to the whole table, "I don't know what stack Christopher's been working in lately, but I wish he'd stop grinning like a contented idiot over it. I'm starting to feel left out."

That was the word. That was the feeling—contented. "Sorry, Angela," he said, the smile embarrassed this time. "Didn't know I was broadcasting."

"That's all right," she said with a wink. "It's good to see you happy."

But the spark was blown out almost the moment he got home. He found Loi and Jessie in the family room, and it was obvious at once that they had been talking about something serious, and equally obvious that they were waiting for him.

"Hi," he said tentatively. "What's up?"

"Jessie and I have been talking about the family," Loi said. "About what we want and where we're going. We were hoping you'd join us."

"Can I hit the bathroom first?"

"Of course."

Scrubbing his face, Christopher scrambled for emotionally secure ground, trying to anticipate the blow before it came. What could be wrong? What could have happened since last night? Jessie had been crying, and Loi was in her mother-therapist mode. He did not want to rejoin them scared, but scared he was. There was a tremor of change in their faces, and change was the enemy of the contentment he had enjoyed all day.

But he could not hide. Summoning a calm he did not feel, he rejoined them, settling by himself in a chair across the pit from them. "That feels better," he said with a false smile. "Who's going to bring me up to speed?"

Loi looked expectantly at Jessie, who ducked her head,

frowned uncomfortably, then looked up into Christopher's eyes. "We were talking about what rights I have here."

Surprise registered on Christopher's face. "The same as any of us."

"I mean, how far does it go?"

Oh, God, she's talking about the baby. "How far do you want it to go? It isn't just rights for any of us. It's rights and responsibilities."

"Don't lecture, Christopher," Loi said quietly. "Listen."

"I'm waiting for her to say what she means," Christopher said edgily.

"I have the privacy you promised, and the freedom," Jessie said. "I like making a home for you two. You've been more than generous with my family share—I feel guilty sometimes because I don't think I give enough back to deserve it."

"You do," Christopher said.

"But you're both so busy. I'm here alone more than not." She smiled shyly. "Last night was wonderful. But it made me sad, too, because it made me realize what I was missing."

Christopher silently waited for her to continue. He could not make himself ask the polite question.

"I just feel like I need somebody for me," she said.

"Don't you feel like Christopher is yours?" asked Loi.

"Oh, I don't mean you don't share him, like last night. But when you're here, he belongs to you. He only ever wants me when you're away."

"That's not true," Christopher said reflexively.

"Look at the way you got jealous about Loi and me making love," Jessie answered. "You got angry at her for being with me. You didn't get angry at me for being with her."

"That's not what that was about."

"It's okay," Jessie said. "I understand. You two have the most history together. It's natural. And I'm not saying I don't think you both love me. But I need more if I'm going to be happy. I need someone who belongs to me the way you two belong to each other."

"I spend a lot of time with you," he protested. "This last month I know I've seen you more than I've seen Loi. I even think we've made love more often than Loi and I have."

"When it suits you," Jessie said with a sudden chill. "When it suits you, you're more than ready."

"Be fair, Jessie—"

"There's a perspective problem," Loi was saying. "Christopher, you have a full-time job and a time-consuming hobby. You spend a lot of what's left over with Jessie. But that's a much smaller part of her life than it is of yours."

"Am I supposed to not work?" he asked indignantly. "Are you saying you feel neglected, too?"

"Jessie and I have different needs," Loi said. "You know that I've never expected you to fill all of mine. I don't feel neglected. You've always been just what I wanted you to be. But I'm not the one who's unhappy."

Christopher could not keep his expression from souring as he looked to Jessie. "I think this is really low, for you to lobby Loi behind my back. We talked about this once already."

"No, we didn't."

He snapped, "We did, too, when Loi was in Geneva. Did she tell you about that?" The last was aimed at Loi.

"This is a different subject," Jessie said.

"What?"

She looked down. "You were right about the baby. I wasn't being fair to you that night."

"Well—" Christopher was nonplussed. "Then what are we talking about?"

"I want to know if I can propose a new addition to the family."

Christopher felt a sudden wave of panic, which he made a noble effort to suppress. "I don't understand something. Is this a theoretical discussion? Or are we talking about someone specific?"

"Don't be dense, Christopher," said Loi. "Jessie would like to ask John Fields over Saturday for dinner and a discussion."

"The cyclist? From the club?"

"Yes. He was here once—you met him."

"Are you fucking him?" he asked, incredulous.

"Not yet. He wants all of us to talk before we get involved. He's very principled."

The door to Christopher's sympathies, which had been weakly propped open, suddenly slammed shut. "No," he said harshly, jumping to his feet.

"Chris—" Loi began warningly.

"No dinner, no discussion, no John Fields. We're just learning how to be three. We're not bringing someone else in."

"Chris, if Jessie is unhappy, we may lose her," Loi said. "Is that what you want?"

"What does she have to be unhappy about? She's had everything handed to her. She said it herself—she's got freedom, privacy, a comfortable home, money—our money. She's got time enough to go cycling every day, to watch every damn crier made in the last century, to go looking for sparking buddies in every neighborhood inside the loop—"

"Christopher," Loi said sharply.

"I thought you liked John," Jessie said meekly.

"I like John all right for somebody I spent ten minutes talking to once," Christopher said. "But that's a long way from saying, 'Sure, come on, move in, by the way, Jessie likes it hard.' "

"I didn't ask—"

"You'd better figure out what's wrong with you. You're grabbing for people like zoners grab for pills. First Loi, then a baby, now John—people aren't teddy bears, goddammit, you can't start a fucking collection. Does John know what you're going to want from him? Does he know that six months from now you're going to whisper, 'Guess what, I'm fertile,' just as he's about to come?"

Christopher was shouting at the end, but barely aware of it. The room was suddenly chaos—Jessie crying, cringing, Loi shouting and trying to drag him away from her. He shook off her grip and turned on her, his angry words a snarl. Loi grabbed at his wrist again, and only then did he realize that he had been shaking a clenched fist at her, at Jessie, that his body was coiled and charged to strike at them, to smash them down.

In horror and shock, he backed away, dropping awkwardly into the chair where he'd been sitting. Jessie took that moment to escape, running up the stairway and disappearing into her room.

"Jesus," Christopher whispered, covering his mouth with his hands and staring at the carpet.

"Where did that come from?" Loi asked, her voice hard and unsympathetic.

"I don't know," Christopher said. "You know I've never done that before—"

"Once is enough." She frowned unhappily. "I never thought I'd see you come on like lord and master of a feudal castle. What in the world is going on with you?"

"I—I just got a little too wound up. The way Jessie's been—"

"You can't blame this on her."

"Everything I said is true," he insisted. "I just—didn't say it very well."

Loi shook her head dismissively. "I don't think you said one word about what you really feel."

"We've got what we need right here," he said, looking up at her with a plaintive expression. "If we have to make some adjustments, all right, we'll make them. But bringing someone else in is crazy. That's going to change everything."

"Don't you realize that you just changed everything? You lost control at just the idea of *talking* about expanding the family. You went so blood-crazy that you were ready to hurt us to have your way. That isn't healthy, and you know it."

"I don't have to do this and I'm not going to," he said stubbornly. "You can't guilt me into saying yes."

She shook her head. "I'll tell what you have to do," she said softly but firmly. "If you want to stay part of this family, you're going to have to go to an R.T. and start working on this."

Christopher was numbly silent for a long time. "This scares me, Loi. I don't know if I want to know what's inside me that could make me do something like this."

"You scared *us*."

"I know," he said.

Loi studied him. "I'm going upstairs to be with Jessie," she said finally. "Let me know what you decide."

"I think she needs to go, too," he said as she started away.

"You're not in any position to set conditions," Loi said pointedly.

"I wasn't—"

"You were. Get your own house in order, Christopher. Then maybe your opinions on Jessie will matter to me again."

CHAPTER 13

-|UUC|-

"... for the silent Earth."

EYES CLOSED, HIROKO SASAKI ENDURED THE FINAL TOUCH-UP of her makeup and powder. The corporation's image doctor, a round-bellied American named Edgar Donovan, hovered nearby, fretting.

"You have to remember that no matter how much Minor smiles at you, he's not your friend," Donovan said. "The smiles don't go out to the audience. When they cut to him, it'll be for a raised eyebrow or a frown."

"I will remember."

"And don't be surprised if he tries something to provoke you. You took a lot of power out of his hands by insisting on a live interview. He's going to try to get that back."

"I fully expect so."

"I'm not saying you were wrong, mind you," Donovan added. "The board's delighted that you finally agreed to come out of the shadows and stand up for the company. And I'm delighted with the conditions—live, ninety minutes, and here at Prainha. That's as close as we can get to a level playing field. Which tells us how much RCA wanted this one."

"Yes," Sasaki said. The makeup artist stepped back, her work finally complete, and Sasaki opened her eyes. She looked around the inner office until she found Mikhail Dryke, a silent spectator in a window well. "Are you ready?"

"We're ready," Dryke said.

Sasaki smiled a brave smile. "Then I will go face the jaguar."

• • •

Except for his eyes, Julian Minor, senior correspondent for RCA Telecasting's *Newstime*, looked more like a terrier than a jaguar. Barely 170 centimeters tall, with a round-heeled walk and close-cropped fuzzy beard, he seemed unequal to the attention he received when he entered a room.

But on camera, the walk and the height were irrelevant, and the beard became a mask which served only to focus attention on Minor's eyes. His eyes unmasked the hunter in him. They could punctuate a comment with an angry flash, puncture a defense with a skeptical smirk. From just a meter or two away, the challenging intensity of his gaze could paralyze thought.

It was a candidate for the Russian presidency who had given Minor his nickname. Emerging from what would be a career-ending interview with Minor, Sterenkov had complained bitterly that to look across into Minor's eyes was like looking into the tall grass and seeing the gleam of a jaguar's eyes. In time, Minor's reputation itself became a weapon; later victims sometimes destroyed their own credibility simply by trying to avoid his gaze.

For all that, Minor enjoyed a reputation for fairness. He was tough, direct, and aggressive; if you were strong, direct, and honest, you could survive, and might even earn a sympathetic hearing.

Or so Donovan promised.

Centered and calm, Hiroko Sasaki sat in the bergère armchair Donovan had chosen for her ("You disappear in a big, soft couch") and waited for the interview to begin. On a monitor a few meters away and angled toward her, the introductory backgrounder on the Diaspora Project and the Singapore "disaster" was continuing.

Almost certainly, the backgrounder was infuriatingly slanted and misleading. But Sasaki was not watching. She had already succeeded in making herself not see the screen, had drawn in her focus until it and the camera operator and the Skylink engineer disappeared. Once the interview began, there would be no temptation to watch herself.

Minor looked up from his notes and smiled at her. She became a shadow and let the smile pass through her like a breeze.

"One minute," someone said. Sasaki tugged the sleeves of her red blouse (Donovan again: "Dress international. Let's not play to latent racism by looking ethnic") down to her wrists, rested her elbows on the slender wooden armrests, folded her hands in her lap. The next time Minor looked up at her, she met his gaze and answered his smile with a bow of her head.

"Good evening," he said to his camera. "This is Julian Minor in Prainha, Brazil, the busiest spaceport on the globe. Just five kilometers from where I sit, a launch cannon identical to that blamed in the tragedy in Singapore is busy hurling twenty-ton shells into the sky.

"With me is Hiroko Sasaki, Director of the Diaspora Project, a division of Allied Transcon, which owns and operates this spaceport. Director Sasaki, are we safe here? And how can you be sure?"

"No one is ever perfectly safe, anywhere, anytime, Mr. Minor," she said smoothly. "But you are safer now than you would be waiting on a railroad platform for a train or crossing a city street. You are safer now than you were when flying from New York to Belém last night for this interview. Every year, more than two hundred thousand people die worldwide in transportation accidents. Space flight is the safest form of transportation, and the T-ships are the safest form of space flight."

The eyebrow arched. "Is your answer to the families of the thirty-seven dead in Singapore that they were just unlucky?"

"Mr. Minor, when I heard what happened that day, I wept," Sasaki said. "It was a terrible moment, and one I deeply wish could have been prevented. But—"

"But you could have prevented it," Minor pounced. "Isn't that true? Don't your own operating rules, Allied's own documents, anticipate exactly the kind of failure that took place? If you knew it could happen, why didn't you take steps to prevent it?"

Launch services were the responsibility of Allied's Starlifter Division; Sasaki and the Diaspora Project were, properly speaking, merely their customers. But Donovan had warned her that there was no point in trying to draw fine distinctions or correct every misstatement.

"But of course, we did," Sasaki said. "Unfortunately, there is no such thing as a perfect machine."

"That's certainly true of your launch cannon," Minor said. "I have reports here of more than sixty launch failures. It seems to me that the only way you could feel safe here is not to think about it."

Sasaki frowned. "In thirteen years of operation at Kasigau and thirty-five years here, Allied has launched more than a mil-

lion payloads. There have been just sixty-one launch aborts.
And only once has an abort resulted in any loss of life. I regret
the Singapore accident. But I don't see where I need apologize
for the safety record of the Kare-Kantrowitz launchers or of Allied's Launch Services Division.''

Minor settled back in his chair. ''I notice that you avoid calling these systems 'launch cannon,' an expression which is in
such widespread colloquial use that it's in every general lexicon.
Why is that?''

''I resist the coinage,'' she said. ''It's misleading.''

''Well, now, I've heard those launchers at work,'' Minor said
with a convivial smile. ''They sure sound like cannon to me.
Isn't this linguistic legerdemain an attempt on your part to mask
the military origins of Allied's technology, what Jeremiah calls
your bloody heritage?''

''I find an interesting irony here,'' Sasaki said. ''Yes, nation-
alist tensions drove the technologies that lifted us into space. We
use high-energy lasers and tracking systems created for a ballis-
tic missile defense. The first all-points aerospace plane was designed as a bomber-interceptor for the United States Air Force.
The first space station was a Russian spy base. The first moon
landing was a political power play. The first boosters began as
weapons of war.''

''Then you admit—''

She did not pause. ''I am prompted to wonder at times where
we would be if we humans hadn't been fighting each other tooth
and nail. I am not ashamed of the pedigree of our tools. On the
contrary, I think that in many cases we have redeemed the cre-
ators of those tools by finding better uses for them than those
for which they were originally intended.''

''I hear in that answer exactly the kind of arrogance of which
Allied stands accused—''

''Stands accused by whom, Mr. Minor?''

''By Homeworld. By public opinion. Isn't arrogance implicit
in the fact that within an hour of the Singapore tragedy, the
Kasigau cannon was back in operation?''

''What's implicit is necessity,'' she said calmly. ''Prainha and
Kasigau are lifelines for the orbital communities—for Technica
and Horizon and Aurora. All of the aerospace vehicles owned
by all of the planet's governments and corporations could not
make up the shortfall if Prainha and Kasigau shut down—''

• • •

Donovan and Dryke had been monitoring the broadcast from Sasaki's private inner office, using the center four cells of the display wall. While Donovan sat self-evidently at ease, lounging back in Sasaki's Swendon club chair, Dryke stood, sometimes pacing by the windows, sometimes standing close enough to the display that its changing patterns of light played on his face.

"Come on, come on," Dryke muttered to himself.

"She's doing wonderfully," Donovan said. "She's absolutely fine."

"I wasn't talking to Hiroko," Dryke said.

"Director Sasaki, how much has *Memphis* cost?" Minor was asking.

"How much does a city cost?" Sasaki replied.

"Excuse me?"

"Before I answer, I want to know that you'll have something appropriate to compare it to. How much is invested in a modern community of ten or fifteen or twenty thousand? Draw a circle around one and tell me. How much in their roads, their businesses, their homes? How much in their play yards and factories? Don't draw the circle too small—"

"Attagirl," Donovan said, sitting forward and beaming.

"—don't leave out the land that grows their food, the quarries and mines and wells that supply their stone and water and steel. How much for the endless maintenance to keep what you've built whole? How do you value the man years of unpriced labor? How much did it cost to bring it all together? How much has it cost to keep it alive?"

"Not a billion dollars a person."

"That's your figure, not mine," Sasaki said. "How much, Mr. Minor? Everything that goes into *Memphis* has a price tag, because it's all being done at once, by one organization. I know what building this city cost. But that number would mean nothing to you or to the audience, because you don't know the value of what you've inherited yourselves."

If she said more, neither Donovan nor Dryke heard it. There was a buzzing sound, which Dryke later decided sounded like electric butterfly wings. The four-cell display seemed to collapse toward its center, then stabilized with a new image: a red-haired, bearded man perhaps forty years old.

"Of course you know what *Memphis* costs," said the image. "A good thief always knows the value of what he steals—"

"Yes," Dryke said approvingly. "There you are."

"What the hell is that?" Donovan demanded, brow wrinkling.

Dryke walked forward a step and studied the face. "Not what, Mr. Donovan. Who."

"And who is—"

"Jeremiah."

Recovering quickly from his surprise, Donovan scrutinized the display. "Any chance that's what he really looks like?"

"Not much."

"I thought not," Donovan said, then looked quizzically at Dryke. "Ah—shouldn't you be doing something?"

Dryke shook his head. "It's being done."

There was confusion in the outer room. The monitor at hand still showed Sasaki's face, but Minor was on his feet and demanding explanations for something he had heard through his earpiece.

"Are we on or off? Off? How—then give it to me here, goddammit, so I can see what's going on."

The image of a gentle-eyed bearded man replaced Sasaki's puzzled expression on the monitor.

"Sound," barked Minor. "I want sound."

"—it *is* arrogance, arrogance in the service of imperialism, which forgives such plundering," the man was saying. "They want, and so they take. They call their wants needs and justify their greed with necessity—"

"Jammed? From where? Are you sure this isn't their doing?" Minor demanded. "No—who? Are you sure?" He stared at the monitor. "Jesus," he said, turning to his crew. "Let's go back live."

"Nothing's getting through," the engineer protested.

"Do it," Minor snarled.

"—what do they want? More, always more. For those who are empty inside, there is no such word as enough. Never enough power, never enough wealth—"

The engineer shrugged. "On three. But you're talking to yourself. Three—two—one—"

Minor looked into the lens. "Jeremiah? Jeremiah, this is Julian Minor of *Newstime*. Can you hear me?"

"—never enough to satisfy the unsatisfiable need." Then he paused. "Yes, Julian," he said. "I can hear you."

"You're Jeremiah, leader of the Homeworld?"

"I am Jeremiah," said the pirate.

"Would you answer a few questions?"

The bearded man nodded. "Ask your questions,"

"Some have called you the John Muir of the Earth. You use an Old Testament prophet's name—a reluctant prophet with a flair for theater and an uncompromising message of danger and destruction. Do you see yourself as an oracle for the twenty-first century—"

"I am not important. Ask another question."

Minor blinked in surprise. "Very well. Jeremiah, why do you oppose the Diaspora?"

"It is those who support it, not those who oppose it, who must explain themselves," said Jeremiah. "Ask Hiroko Sasaki to explain. Explain by what right you squander your inheritance, the Earth. Explain what you have bought at such a dear price. The choking summers. The burning forests. The rising oceans. The killing rays of the Sun. You have trampled the Earth underfoot in your headlong rush to the stars."

Sasaki held her head high as she answered. "We are all collaborators in that crime. Not Hiroko Sasaki alone. Not Allied Transcon. But I, and you, Jeremiah, and you, Julian Minor, and each of those listening, and ten generations dead and departed. The Amazon forest was burning, the river poisoned by mercury, long before Allied began to build at Prainha. The Earth was warming, the ozone vanishing, when starships were only engineers' dreams."

The Starlink technician was shaking his head. "No," he said. "It's not going through."

"What?"

"He doesn't want an answer," Sasaki said quitely. "He only wants an audience."

"Jeremiah, this is Julian Minor again. I still have Director Sasaki here, on camera just as I am. Are you stopping her answers from being heard? Are you afraid of what she might say?"

"Hiroko Sasaki is programmed with lies," said Jeremiah. "She is abducting ten thousand of our brightest and best to send on a modern Children's Crusade. What can she say that we can believe?"

Minor looked to Sasaki. "What about that, Director? Have you taken a look at what the effects of giving up that many people of that quality might be? From a human resources standpoint, it seems that Jeremiah has a reasonable case."

"Jeremiah controls the airwaves. What point is there in answering?"

"We're recording here," Minor said. "If we have to, we'll put it together and rebroadcast it later. Director Sasaki, one way or another, I promise you that your answers will be heard."

She frowned, looked to the floor as she marshaled her thoughts, then up at the camera. "The pioneers are a select group of very special people," she said. "They have to be, to face and triumph over the challenges ahead. But they've chosen this for themselves, earned it for themselves. No one is being abducted. Thousands more would join them if there was only room.

"Even so, *Memphis* won't be leaving the Earth poorer. The Diaspora Project has been the single greatest stimulus to education and self-development since the invention of the computer. It's motivated people of three generations across every continent to say, 'I want to contribute,' and work to better themselves. Most of those people, and all of that human capital, will remain here."

Minor turned back to his camera. "Jeremiah, you can't dispute the fact that millions worldwide bought options for the Diaspora Project. The pioneers are volunteers, the lucky few. Why not let them go? Why is it important to you to stop them?"

"It is important to all of us," Jeremiah said. "We need what they represent. We need their will and energy here. There is so much work left to do, so much damage to repair. We need to focus on stewardship, not starships. Otherwise this endless expansionism will exhaust us and leave us empty. We have a choice between living in the Sun and dying in the dark. We must raise our voices. We must reclaim the choice from the corporations and their collaborators. It is *our* future."

"Director Sasaki—" Minor began.

"Gone," said the Skylink operator, shaking his head. "Nothing up or down."

Minor looked helplessly at Sasaki. "Director, believe me when I say that we had nothing to do with any of this."

"I do believe you," she said, rising.

"I can give you a chance to make a closing statement."

"Thank you. It's not necessary," Sasaki said.

"You're going to give him the last word? This story's going to be in the A queue for the rest of the week."

She turned and met his perplexed look with a gentle smile.

"My mission is not to win converts. My mandate is to build starships."

"Mandate?"

"Have you ever tried to push a string, Mr. Minor?"

"I'm afraid you've lost me."

"Do you think that the Diaspora Project is something that was created from the top down?" she asked chidingly. "This is not something that we are doing to the Earth. This is something I do *for* the Earth. Those who can, already understand. Those who do not, never will."

When Sasaki rejoined Dryke and Donovan in the inner office, the latter greeted her with a disapproving look.

"I should have been told," Donovan grumped. "The board should have been told."

"Told what, Mr. Donovan?" All sixteen cells of the display were occupied, and she began to scan them.

"Listen, I'm not an idiot. You set up this interview to sucker Jeremiah. Mikhail here spent the whole time itching and fidgeting like he was waiting for the main act to go on stage."

She glanced at Dryke, a hint of a smile on her lips. "Jeremiah is his own master."

"Bullshit. You were laying for him. You used the Singapore business as cover for changing your colors. The only thing I can't figure is what you got from doing it."

"I appreciate your help in preparing for the interview, Mr. Donovan," Sasaki said, gliding toward the display. "Please thank the board for making you available. You can relay to them that I do not expect to be granting any further interviews in the near future."

Donovan frowned. "Yeah," he said as he stumped out. "I'll tell them."

As the door was closed behind Donovan, Sasaki asked for Privacy One. "Well, Mikhail?" she asked. "How did we do?"

Dryke pulled the plug from his ear and broke into a smile. "We have a piece of him," he said. "A good piece."

"Tell me."

"The Jeremiah image was synthesized with a Palette III broadcast animator. Images, I mean. There were three different ones."

"Three!"

"An equal-opportunity air pirate. He blanketed Europe and

North Africa with a vaguely Mediterranean synth through SIRIO, fed the Far East with an Oriental bounced up through AUSSAT, and gave us the mountain man through Hiwire.''

"All things to all people," Sasaki said wryly.

Dryke continued, "The video lab says that if all three had the same root image, they may be able to correlate them and back-form a fair picture of the real Jeremiah."

"Is that all we have—a hope?"

"No," Dryke said. "More than that. You know, you can route a call to your neighbor around the world if you know how, and by ten thousand different routes if you want to be creative. Jeremiah knows how, and he was creative. All three images were scatter-routed to the uplinks in short bursts—too short to track back. Jeremiah used one hundred and eighty routes—good for three minutes. But thanks to Mr. Minor, he stayed on for seven. And with a second and a third look, we were able to map six of his routes back to a common entry node."

"Which is—"

Dryke looked up at cell 4, which contained a map of North America. "Monterrey, Mexico."

"Monterrey! Is that his base?"

"Almost certainly not," Dryke said, shaking his head. "He's not that foolish. But it makes the odds very good that his base is in the Americas. He needs land-line access to the node. Jeremiah's a neighbor, Hiroko."

"Or an insider?"

"Perhaps," Dryke said. "Can't rule it out."

Sasaki crossed her arms and nodded. "This is very heartening, Mr. Dryke. I can see progress at last. I am comforted that I did not endure Mr. Minor's questions and Mr. Donovan's molding in vain."

"I'm not finished," Dryke said. "There's one piece more. The best piece."

"Oh?"

"We always thought that Jeremiah's voice was synthesized. Nothing exotic to it," Dryke said. "But there's one kind of solution for a canned track like we've seen before, and another for a live exchange like we just had."

"The difference is important?"

"Very. For live work, the easy way is to give an AI translator—maybe an IBM Traveler—a cross-file of another voice, just like you'd give it a cross-file for French, say, and let it do the substitutions on the fly. But something interesting happens when you throw a word at a translator that it can't find in the file. It passes that word through unchanged.''

Sasaki looked suddenly hopeful. "Did that happen?"

"Yes. With Julian's name. Your name. And 'starships,' near the end," said Dryke. "All different from the rest. All in Jeremiah's own voice.''

"Can you do anything with so little?" Sasaki asked. "A few syllables—''

"It's as good as a fingerprint. It's enough to do a cross-match search in the *Memphis* hyper. Enough to set up a monitoring program on the corporate com net.'' Dryke smiled, a smile full of threat. ''You know, you can't hardly work for Allied without saying your name or 'starship' now and again. If Jeremiah *is* an insider, we'll find him very soon.''

"And if he's not?"

"A little longer. But not much longer. We're coming up behind him in the dark. One more gag and we'll have him.''

"What will it take this time?"

Dryke thought for a moment. "A sacrifice.''

CHAPTER
14

-|ACA|-

"I fight against myself ..."

IT WASN'T WORKING.

"Why do you want to go on *Memphis*?" Thomas Tidwell would ask the pioneer in the facing chair.

And more often than not, the person he was interviewing would freeze, as though seized by the sudden fear that the fix was not yet in, that somehow they could still lose what they thought they had gained. Anxious. Nervous. Defensive. It didn't matter if it was the first question or the last, whether he was friendly or formal, whether it was Tokyo or Munich or Houston.

"This is not a test of any sort," he would assure them. "Nothing you say to me can affect your standing in the Project."

And they never quite believed him.

"My name is Thomas Tidwell. I am supervising the definitive history of the Diaspora Project, including the personal histories of every pioneer. We need to understand what kind of people took up this challenge, what they wanted, what they hoped."

That helped a little, except that it tended to elicit the kind of answers he had found in the file of application essays—rambling anecdotes with the flavor of personal myth, inadequate and unconvincing except to the mythmaker. Why had they chosen to exile themselves from the only world they'd ever known? The answers remained buried in their individual psychologies.

A fifty-two-year-old American named Peg: "My great-grandfather was a mission specialist for NASA, flying the Shuttle back when it was all new. Joe Allen. He wrote a book about it—I read my mother's copy when I was ten. But I was never much

124

interested in space until the Project came along. It was all about as exciting to me as brushing your teeth. But this is different. This is like it was when my great-grandfather wore the blues."

Tidwell blinked, and the face changed.

A handsome, earnest young Tanzanian named Zakayo: "When I was twenty, I climbed to the Kibo summit of Kilimanjaro with an expedition of Australians. I thought I had done a great thing until night came and the stars came out to show me I had not climbed high enough."

Tidwell blinked again, and the room changed. Munich, not Houston. A blink. Tokyo, not Munich.

Realwadee, a Malay Thai woman, barely a woman at nineteen: "My option was a gift from King Adulyadej on my admission to Ramkhamhaeng University. My selection honors my father, my family, and my sovereign lord. Can I do other than go?"

If he questioned them further, probed for the reasons and emotions underlying the words, he lost whatever measure of trust and goodwill he had managed to manufacture. Either they were telling him what they believed was the truth, and resented his questions as a slight on their honor, or they were telling him what they believed they must, and retreated before his questions to protect their fictions.

It was not working, and Tidwell was frustrated. The immaculate synthesis of a lifetime's work had been smashed that afternoon in Sasaki's office, and he had been unable to reconstruct it.

He remained unwilling to revise it. Tidwell's private briefings with Selection's geneticists and counselors, arranged by Oker, had left him unsatisfied. It was too much like going to church with True Believers. And Tidwell did not believe.

Could not believe. He was the silent observer, the fair witness, the impartial analyst. He could not embrace anyone's passion. He was beyond or above or one step removed from passion, from this particular passion. When the great ship sailed, he would stand on the dock and wave good-bye without the smallest pang of regret.

But Tidwell could not suffer the thought of waving good-bye with the root question still unresolved. So when Oker's geneticists were finished with him, Tidwell had launched himself on a globe-spanning quest for answers. In the month since his visit to Prainha, Tidwell had spent all but four days away from Halfwhistle, continent-hopping like a tourist on a seventeen-city holiday.

After more than two years of reclusion, it was too much too

fast. By the time he reached Tokyo to interview a selection of pioneers being processed through that center, Tidwell was sick of travel, of strange beds and sleeping poorly, of fighting a balky biological clock. His health was faltering, and with it his concentration.

At the end of the Tokyo sessions, Tidwell retreated to Halfwhistle, his thoughts in disarray. In his garden he pruned away neglect and worried over faltering shrubs and flowers. In his journal he wrote,

> I fight against myself not to cast out this unwelcome intruder before he speaks another word in my ear. His voice is the voice of the banished—Lamarck and Baer, Spencer and Miller, Crick and Corning. There is only one history of the world. It begins with the rejection of mystery, with penetrating the illusion of purpose. The notion of purpose is meaningful only in the context of individual lives. Beyond that there is a synergy of chance and fate and individual purpose which is ultimately stochastic.
>
> Nothing is as it was meant to be. Everything is as it happened to be. We flatter ourselves with notions of progress. But progress is merely opportunism seen in hindsight. We salve our burning conscience with visions of Gaea, God become goddess become cybernetic superorganism. But Gaea is merely wish fulfillment, the newest clothes for an old craving. We await the return of the greater power to enforce the greater good, to save us from our selfishness.
>
> I have already written this story. This is the story of the power of a dream. Of that which is quintessentially human—the tug of curiosity, the spur of ambition, the heat of passion, the drive of hubris.
>
> Now Sasaki seduces me with a new delusion embracing an old and discredited idea. Where and when did purpose arise in a world of chance? At the beginning. Before the beginning. Purpose preexisted history. Purpose preordained history. All sins are justified by the imperative command. All crimes are forgiven in the name of necessity.
>
> This ground bears the footprints of lost souls. I must walk carefully.

The houses in the Nassau Bay residential complex were aging, inefficient frame structures, survivors from an earlier century's winding-street waterfront suburbia. Once a satellite community to the Johnson Space Center, Nassau Bay was now inside the fences, absorbed into Allied's Houston facility as a sort of decentralized dormitory.

Three score of the better houses were being used as residences by center staff, including the center director and several other Building 1 types. Two of the largest houses, one overlooking narrow Nassau Bay, the other on little Lake Nassau (now a captive lagoon) had been converted into pilots' hostels. And in the years between *Ur* and *Memphis,* several of the empty structures on Nassau Bay's quiet streets had been used as illicit lovers' rendezvous, giving the complex its nickname of "Noonerville."

But there were no empty houses now, and the streets were again full of life. Once again, Nassau Bay belonged to the pioneers—one to a bedroom, two, three, or four to a house. There were few amenities, but diligent—if minimal—maintenance had kept the complex clean and livable. And the energy and joyful camaraderie of its occupants turned Nassau Bay into a community.

"It's like a college campus the weekend before fall classes begin," Daniel Keith observed as he walked slowly down a Nassau Bay sidewalk with Thomas Tidwell. "Everyone's starting with a clean slate. Everyone's ready to meet and make new friends. It's like they get here and say, 'I know you.' The bonding rate is incredible. The sociology team really has to scramble to keep on top of it."

That was what had brought Tidwell there: the promise of a more intimate glimpse into the mind and heart of the *Memphis* pioneers. It was old-fashioned, dirty-fingernails primary research, contemporary field anthropology of a sort that Tidwell had not resorted to in thirty years.

"We've only got about four hundred pioneers in the center at the moment," Keith said as he unlocked the door to a little house, "so we've still got some room. Your housemates are all ship's staff. They've got a very intensive training schedule—don't expect to see them from six to six most days."

The house was a few degrees cooler than the sultry air outside. "I understand," Tidwell said, setting his small bag on the threadbare couch. "But I won't be here if they aren't. I intend to wait with them at the shuttle stops, sit with them in the cafeteria, huddle with them in whatever private spaces they've chosen. After all, I am Thomas Grimes, communications auxiliary—a correspondent for the ship's log." He smiled. "A flack for the ship's morale officer, more to the truth."

"I don't know that you're going to be able to hide who you are for long," said Keith. "There *are* people here who know you, Dr. Tidwell."

Tidwell nodded. "Perhaps not. I don't believe it will take long."

Shaking his head, Keith held out the key he had used to admit them. "Maybe this isn't my place, but I have to say that I think you're looking under the wrong rock, Dr. Tidwell. You won't learn anything from these people. They don't know, themselves."

Tidwell took the key. "That defies reason. How can they make such a monumental decision without knowing their own minds?"

"Because it isn't reason that drives them," Keith said simply.

"If so, then that will be the lesson I'll take from here."

"Will you know it when you see it?"

"What do you mean?"

"You're not like them. You've lived a life of the mind. You have more respect for the power of thought than most of us do for the power of God. I'm not sure that you can credit a motive that you can't understand. I don't know if you can see it in them if you can't see it in yourself."

Tidwell's gaze narrowed into a rebuke. "I'm familiar with the dangers of egocentrism."

"A story?"

"If you wish."

Keith folded his arms and leaned against the doorjamb. "I suppose you know that this used to be the headquarters for NASA's astronaut corps. For obvious reasons, we were interested in their astronaut selection procedures, and so we acquired their records. We found in looking at them that every time NASA announced openings, they got hundreds of applications from people who had to know that they had no chance to be picked, who didn't begin to meet even the minimum requirements."

"Dreamers and optimists," said Tidwell. "This is not surprising."

"Maybe not," Keith said. "One of our genetic historians got ambitious and traced the descendants of twenty of those dreamers. Every one of them has at least one blood relative in *our* selection bank."

"Chance. Each must have dozens of relatives. And millions held selection options."

"She traced two control groups from the same era as well. The correlation there was less than five in twenty."

"Which does not rule out chance. Nor the influence of the family environment."

"Skeptics can always fall back on chance," Keith said.

"Is there something wrong with being a skeptic, with insisting on evidence and causality?"

Keith sighed. "No. Dr. Tidwell, I'm not here to convince you of anything. You asked us to make these arrangements, and we did. I'll be available if you have any problems or needs."

"You are frustrated with me."

He shrugged. "Not my place to be."

"But you are. Why?"

"Because it's so clear to me, and you have so much trouble seeing it."

"Exactly what is clear?"

There were voices in the street, and Keith glanced over his shoulder in their direction. "That they don't really know why they're going," he said quietly. "They only know that they want to."

"What persuades you of that, Mr. Keith?"

Keith turned back and showed a faint smile. "Because I want to go, too, Dr. Tidwell. And I don't really know why, either."

When Keith was gone, Tidwell granted himself license to explore the house. The salutary effect of the house's enfeebled air-conditioning vanished the moment he started upstairs. The air there was stagnant and hothouse stuffy. Unless the nights were markedly cooler, sleeping would be a challenge.

He found the empty bedroom and, in it, his trunk of clothing, delivered ahead by the Selection office. Leaving for later the task of unpacking it, Tidwell extended his license to entering the other, already occupied bedrooms—two up, one down.

Tidwell did not see it as a violation of privacy. Most of the pioneers' personal belongings—250 kilograms each—would be shipped directly from their homes up to *Memphis* through Prainha or Kasigau. He reasoned that what his housemates chose to bring with them while camping out in Houston might reveal something of their personality, and so was germane to his purpose there.

Still, he was careful not to disturb anything that might betray his trespass, contenting himself with what he could see. He peeked in a closet, but not in a suitcase; at the objects arrayed on a wobbly-legged dresser, but not in its drawers.

He took note of several travel and geography volumes in a file of chipdisks—perhaps someone trying to plan how to spend their last days on Earth? He startled at finding candles and Wiccan icons in the single ground-floor bedroom—surely more appropriate to a Homeworlder than a pioneer?

All data were preliminary, all conclusions provisional. He would not judge them until he had met them.

The back windows of the house looked out on turgid Cow Bayou and the tall double fence running along its far bank. The fences marked the south boundary of the center; when he stepped out onto the small patio deck, he could see the south gate tower and bridge half a kilometer upstream.

He also saw something that surprised him. Scattered along the outer fence, all the way from the tower to where the bayou emptied into Clear Creek, were dozens of people standing in ones and twos and threes, almost like statues. The phrase "outside looking in" popped into Tidwell's head.

Starheads, Tidwell thought. *Those must be starheads.* Some of the groups closest to Tidwell noticed him and began shouting something unintelligible across the water. He raised a hand in acknowledgment and salute. *Perhaps I should talk to some of them as well, go and stand with them for a day—*

They were still shouting, but try as he might he could not make out the words, any more than he could make out their faces. He waved one more time and turned to enter the house. As he did, he caught a reflection of sound off the metallic siding, a shrieking high-pitched voice.

"Bastard," was what he thought he heard, "bastard pig bastard—"

His head whipped around and he stared, unbelieving. The three figures nearest to him, almost directly across the bayou, were contorted by the body language of hostility, jumping, fists raised. Others were hurrying along the fence to join them. Someone somewhere was beating on the fence itself, a metallic rattle like clashing swords.

From the direction of the gate tower came the muffled roar of a gasoline motor; moments later, tearing his gaze away from the enraged, now fifteen or twenty strong, Tidwell caught sight of a small boat racing bow-high toward the commotion. When he realized that the boat carried the Allied Transcon logo and the grim-looking men aboard it wore Security armor, Tidwell, still bewildered, fled back into the house.

Shaken, Tidwell watched from behind the heavy drapes shrouding the window of the onetime dining room as the Security boat slowly circled and the gathering slowly dispersed. Tidwell wished for some sort of binoculars; it almost seemed as though those beyond the fence were celebrating as they scattered, finding some sort of victory in the episode.

Fifteen minutes later, all was as it had been before Tidwell pulled back the sticky sliding door and stepped outside. The boat stopped circling and returned upstream. The watchers—not starheads, certainly, though Tidwell was at a loss for what to call them—took up their stations along the fence.

And Tidwell retreated to his room, where he hastily recorded an account of the episode and then began to unpack his luggage. From time to time, he would peek out through the drapes to see if the watchers were still there. They always were, and Tidwell found himself grateful when the first of his housemates returned and he was no longer alone.

Tidwell met them all that night. The travel books belonged to Evans, a tall, barrel-chested judge-arbitrator from Chicago. Genial as he was large, Evans plied Tidwell with questions as he swept through the house, scooping up what passed for a meal and changing into fresh clothing before vanishing out the front door a half hour later.

By contrast, Colas, the young Canadian environmental engineer, had as little personality as his room had revealed. His angular face had deep worry lines worked into it, and when he excused himself to go upstairs and study, mumbling something about having to work out calibrations for six systems, Tidwell made no attempt to deflect him.

Last to return was the most interesting of the three, the bodywork counselor, Malena Graham. Her airchair was as much of a surprise as the altar in her room had been. Her spirit seemed as light as her limbs were leaden.

Together they scouted the prepacks in the freezer, and then they settled together at the steel kitchen table to pick their way through the edible parts of their meals.

"We'll eat better than this on board, I trust," Tidwell said, eyeing his rubbery lasagna with suspicion.

"Never enough cheese in one of those," she said. "I should

have warned you. The cafeteria's lasagna is better. But if you really like lasagna, I ought to try to get you some of Mother Alicia's. Two inches thick and three kilos to a pan. It takes her all day to make enough for the whole family."

"My wife enjoyed cooking," Tidwell recalled. "Not Italian. Her specialty was sweets—poisonously rich desserts." He smiled. "A weakness that crosses all cultures."

"Real sugar and I have a pact," she said. "It doesn't jump into my mouth and I don't make it live on my thighs. Just because I can't walk around in high heels doesn't mean I can't be shapely."

"You are a very attractive young lady."

She clucked unhappily. " 'Young lady'—those sound like words you use to keep someone in their place."

"Habit of speech," Tidwell apologized. "I meant nothing by it. Except the compliment."

She smiled acceptingly. "I'm actually the youngest old woman you've ever met. I'm a crone at heart, waiting to grow into her role. I can hardly wait to be respected enough to be listened to."

"Do you have to look the part?"

"Or get paid for it. People take advice much better if they're paying for it."

"I must confess I've never been to a bodywork counselor," Tidwell said.

"I know."

"Excuse me?"

"I can tell by the way you police every motion. I don't think you're very comfortable in your body."

"It serves me passably well," Tidwell said, then his face reddened with embarrassment. "Forgive me—I didn't mean—"

"That's all right, Thomas. Everyone asks eventually, so I'll save you from working up to it," she said easily. "Did you know that about three in a million contract polio from their vaccinations? I'm one of them. Our family health worker is a nice man but a rotten diagnostician. He missed the early signs and then sent me to a chiropractor when he should have been feeding me virus-eaters."

Tidwell cocked his head and gazed at her appraisingly. "Are you truly not angry, or do you simply hide it well?"

"What would angry get me?" she asked. "I'm not a cripple. I can dress myself in the morning, fuck in three of the four most popular positions, and swim a 1:20 hundred-meters. But don't ask me to rumba. It's just not in my personality."

A surprised laugh fought its way through Tidwell's tightly drawn lips. "Well said."

"I didn't scandalize you? How disappointing."

The irony of attempting to shock the author of *A Summer in Eden* made Tidwell smile. "I'm afraid I'm no longer very easy to scandalize. But feel free to try again sometime."

"Veteran reporter has seen it all."

"Something like that," he said, recalling the afternoon's events. "But sometimes I can still be surprised." He gestured toward the drape-hidden doors. "There were people outside the fence today—"

"Ah, you've discovered the vultures. They're probably still there, in fact," she said. "Don't worry, the curtains are Kevlar weave, and anyway, Security says the vultures rarely have any weapons. Just don't tempt them by wandering around out back."

"So I learned," he said ruefully. "Malena, who are those people? Are they there every day?"

Her face took on a serious cast for the first time that evening. "Every day since I came here."

"There must be a hundred of them."

She nodded. "Fifty, a hundred, five hundred some days. The faces keep changing, but the expressions are always the same. *There's* anger for you."

"But who *are* they? Not starheads, surely."

"No. Not starheads," she said, shaking her head. "The starheads come to the west gate. They get protection."

"Then what?"

Instead of answering, she backed her chair away from the table, dimmed the lights, and crossed the room to peek out through parted curtains. "When I first moved in, I could feel them all the way over here," she said. "I had to ward the house so I could sleep at night."

"Feel what?"

"What they're sending at us." She straightened and let the curtains fall closed, then turned back to Tidwell. "Didn't you feel it when you went outside? There's two kinds of people over there, Thomas. Those that hate us for leaving—and those who hate us for leaving them behind."

CHAPTER
15

-|AAA|-

"... this unwelcome intruder ..."

THERE WAS ALMOST NOTHING CHRISTOPHER MCCUTCHEON
liked about coming to see Eric Meyfarth, R.T.

Christopher hated the ritual of signing Loi's complaint and
being called by Meyfarth for confirmation. He hated scheduling
the appointment and leaving work in midday. He hated the
walled canyons of downtown Houston, the warren-towers of plex
and chrome.

He hated the office manager's earnest cheeriness, and the tight
mouths and guarded eyes of the other clients waiting with him
in the twenty-sixth-floor lounge. No, not clients—patients. Patients that belonged in a back-street clinic, seeking treatment for
some embarrassing disease, deathly afraid of being asked why
they were there. That was how they behaved—no help to Christopher, fighting against the same feeling. Up went the walls,
driving Christopher back behind his own.

The little man in the pinstripe cap and white bristle-brush
moustache, raccoon eyes furtively glancing around the room,
retreating to the window when Christopher spoke to him. The
woman in the short white skirt and the glittery cascade of string
earrings, paging hopefully through a glamour magazine in search
of one more secret. The child-faced woman in the blue flower-
print dress, her toddler on a tether, a faraway look in her eyes
until she was brought back to her boredom by the tug of her
charge.

Never give them your eyes. There must a school which teaches
that as a survival skill, Christopher thought. When by chance

134

eyes met there was no contact. They stood mask-to-mask for the instant of surprise, before turning politely away. It was as though they held to their masks more tightly for knowing that beyond the door, they would be expected to let them fall.

So Christopher waited, unhappy and uncomfortable, for the part he hated the most.

Not that he had any personal enmity for Meyfarth. Referred by their former arty in Oakland, Christopher and Loi had come to see Meyfarth for baselining in the first weeks after arriving in Houston. They had come back a second time a few months later to introduce Jessie.

Neither session had been particularly demanding, and Christopher had come away with qualified good feelings. He would have preferred they sign with a woman, but the bearded and round-bellied relationship technologist had a calming presence and, it seemed, a genuine heart.

But then, Christopher had expected to see him only for periodic checkups and the odd arbitration, not with a major family crisis blowing. That pushed ugly memories to the fore, memories of the long, angry sessions when his marriage to Donald and Kristen was collapsing. Whether it was their arty's incompetence or his own intransigence, all he learned from that episode was that he resisted being dissected, and resented being made to feel a failure.

And there was no way that he would be able to escape either experience in the sessions to come.

With the unerring accuracy of a master archer, Meyfarth went straight for that discomfort in the first five minutes.

"How do you feel about being here?" he asked, twirling a pencil. "I always wonder when it's someone from an open family. All that legalistic leverage is absent."

"I'm not too happy about it," Christopher confessed.

"Not too happy because—"

"It's embarrassing."

"Like going to a proctologist?" Meyfarth asked with a smile.

"Somebody's always wrong. I just don't like it."

"How do you feel about refusing Jessie a baby?"

"I'm sorry I had to hurt her feelings."

"Should she have expected you to say no?"

"Well, yes—if she'd thought about it. If she'd thought about me."

"What about the argument last Tuesday? How do you feel about that?"

Frowning, Christopher allowed, "I'm not too proud of it."

"Why?"

"I lost my temper."

"Anything else?"

"It wasn't that big a deal."

"How do you feel about me being party to all your family secrets?"

"I like you all right."

Meyfarth sat back. "I can't work with forty percent answers, Christopher. And you can't learn anything from them, either."

"What do you mean?"

"That you haven't given me a soul-deep honest answer yet. 'Well—.' 'Not too happy.' 'Not too proud.' 'A little uncomfortable.' 'Something like that.' 'I'm sorry I hurt her feelings.' "

"Those *are* honest answers."

"Half-truths are lies, Christopher. It's far more serious when you tell them to yourself than when you tell them to me. But I'm far more useful to you when I know the truth. Shall we try it again?" he asked rhetorically. "You don't want to be here."

Surprised, it took Christopher a moment to get the word out. "No."

"But you think you have to be, to satisfy Loi."

Grudgingly, "Yes."

"You don't know me, you don't know if you trust me, and you think I'm going to be on Loi and Jessie's side, anyway."

A rueful smile. "Yes to all three."

"If you're pushed to the wall, you've decided to compromise on having a baby with Jessie. But you'll be damned if you're going to be talked into letting John Fields into the family. That's where you've drawn the line in the dirt."

Christopher stared. It was like having his thoughts read. It was like being naked. "Yeah," he said, almost a whisper.

Meyfarth nodded, satisfied. "That's better. Now we can start to work. Do you want your family to survive?"

"That's why I'm here," Christopher said. "That's really why I'm here."

"Are you prepared to risk discovering yourself?"

"What's the risk in that?"

"Easily said when you think you already know who you are

and what you want,'' Meyfarth said. ''But this won't be easy. Extended families are so damned complicated. Six vectors with three, twelve with four, not even counting second-order pair ings. And noncontract families are even more complicated, be cause you don't have all the crutches. Do you know, what you three are doing is actually closer to the original conception than most of my clients?''

''How so?''

''I've read Stan Dale's original treatises. I think he'd have been horrified to have people locked together by contracts rather than by love, and even more horrified to have his name hung on the result. But that's what happens when a bureaucracy crosses paths with a philosophy.'' Meyfarth shrugged. ''Ancient history. I'd like to see you succeed, Christopher. I really would. If you can do it without my help, more power to you. If you'd like my help, I'm ready to do what I can.''

Christopher sighed, a pale breath. ''This isn't going to be much fun.''

A polite smile. ''You never know,'' Meyfarth said. And he waited.

''I don't know why, but it's a hard thing to say,'' Christopher said.

''I know.''

Christopher frowned, looked up at one corner of the ceiling, then back at Meyfarth. ''I'd like your help.''

''Okay,'' said Meyfarth, sitting forward. ''Then let that be the reason that you're here. Not Loi or Jessie or John Fields or the baby. This is about Christopher McCutcheon. This is for Christopher McCutcheon.''

Christopher found himself with nothing to say.

''Does that feel better than the reason you walked in here with?'' Meyfarth prompted.

''Yeah,'' Christopher said, breaking into a smile. ''That feels all right.''

Christopher could no more stop himself from referencing the hyper than he could stop himself from breathing. Not only did he not need Meyfarth's explication of ''ancient history,'' but he probably could have taught a short course in it himself from what he had read in the last week.

The basic facts were simple. The profession of relationship technologist had grown up alongside the contract Dale family, which in turn had been given its life's breath by the turn-of-the-millennium AIDS epidemic.

Behind that skeleton was a fascinating and convoluted story. At the end of the twentieth century, every generation in memory had bowed to the nature of the beast and given tacit, usually hypocritical, consent to indiscretions of the flesh—men driven by old programs, women freed by new technologies. But consent was summarily withdrawn by HTLV-III and its mutant heirs, ruling final, no appeal.

With the wages of sin death, monogamy fast regained its fading respect—and collected a bandwagon's worth of champions. The new fidelity advocacy was an odd alliance comprised, at the most fundamental level, of those women whose security was threatened by male philandering and those men whose control was threatened by female sexual emancipation. Whether they wore cleric's garb, a doctor's coat, or the prim dress of a moral reformer, they embraced AIDS almost gleefully as the means to a final victory.

This was true to some degree in every Western nation, but particularly true in the United States, which at the time was already skating down the slope toward social repression. Testing for the damning virus followed the trail blazed by testing for drugs. The lid came down on prostitution, the rad-lib argument that it was a victimless crime rendered laughable.

Pornography, which might otherwise have flourished, fell under ever more restrictive laws, with the Trojan horse of a campaign against homoerotic and anal-erotic material leading the way to sweeping condemnation of all explicit expression. Hardening hearts victimized the afflicted a second time, shutting them out of medical care, jobs, and even the communities they had long called home.

But even in the United States, the victory did not last long. Like a dammed river in flood season, the accumulating sexual energy penetrated every crevice and eroded every point of weakness, seeking its own level.

To start with, the well-networked Womyn's community, its lesbian leanings anathema to both species of monogamist, was barely touched by the plague. It became ever more visible as a political constituency and ever more attractive as a sexual safe haven; it exercised its economic might by building Aurora Sanctuary, the smallest of the satlands.

Separatist hard-liners resented the influx of the "fashionably femme," but their presence made for a more credible voice and the leverage to win two-woman couples the right to contract "marriages" in five states.

Technology offered an even more important outlet. While the public media were drying up, the private media were heating up. Personal computers and SkyLANs, video camcorders and digital cameras, even faxphones and the lowly copier put more than enough resources into the hands of individuals to allow a revolution in home-grown co-op erotica.

What's more, those who took fantasy one step further found that phone dates and compusex meant that safe sex did not have to mean no sex at all; that there could be intimacy without intercourse. By the time scanning image telephones gave way to hi-band stereo com tanks, a whole new culture and etiquette had grown up around what unfriendly observers ridiculed as "secondhand sex" and "technology abetting pathology." Defenders cheerfully called it "masturdating" and went right on.

But the frontal assault on the new monogamy came not from without, but within.

The three key elements were in place almost from the outset, but it took a decade and a half for the synergy between them to jell. The brave notion that people are not by nature either sexually or emotionally monogamous was already in circulation, quietly promulgated by a new school of human-growth therapists such as the Dales and pioneer researchers like the Constantines. (Books by both were in the hyper, though Christopher passed on reading them.)

On the parenting front, with two-child two-earner families increasingly the norm and one-parent families still all too plentiful, there was a continuing crisis in child care. Millions were wrestling with the unhappy alternatives of toddler warehouses and the unrewarding solitude—for child and parent alike—of home.

And—the final straw—home was more likely than not to be rented space. The bloated national debt and a minor worldwide recession had blessed credit sellers with rates high enough to squeeze even the middle class out of owning a decent house. (Here Christopher ignored another lengthy side-thread, this time on the "leveraged prosperity" of the Conservative Revolution.)

All three problems had a single solution, and thousands of families found it on their own. A third person or second couple meant an extra income, extra hands, siblings for the solo child, sexual variety with security. For those who could solve the jealousy riddle, the "big houses" were stronger economic units, stronger emotional units—stronger families.

But it was not until a California woman named Jennifer Allison and her two husbands offered their relationship up for dissection that the question of group marriage entered the national dialog. With the assistance of the Bush Foundation for Freedom, the Allisons sued for the right to a contract marriage under their state's "lezzie law." The issues were the same—custodial rights, spousal rights, taxes and insurance, wills and inheritances—and the arguments on both sides had a familiar ring.

Even so, the story was a media sensation, and *Allison, Allison & Allison* v. *The State of California* went all the way to the U.S. Supreme Court before finally being resolved 6–5 in favor of the plaintiffs. The case turned on the narrow issue of what, for federal purposes, was a family and what was merely a household, with the Court's opinion introducing a genteel euphemistic coinage for the Allisons' arrangement: extended monogamy.

The ruling was less controversial than it might have been thanks to the influence of Sharon Ferraro's extraordinary novel *While Life Is Still in Us, Let's Love All We Can*, which had appeared earlier that year. A fictionalized first-person account of the trials and triumphs of Ferraro's own extended marriage, the book became a best-seller on three continents. Its title became a cultural catchphrase, a rallying cry for millions hungry for a taste of the riches of the heart.

In the wake of the *Allison* ruling, Congress rushed to regulate what the Court had blessed. Predictably, the central issues were muddied by irrelevancies: precontact AIDS testing; a schedule of renewals (with more testing) ranging from a one-year "compatibility" renewal running out to a fifteen-year "life" renewal; a counseling and mediation requirement.

The last was the work of the American Psychological Association's heavyweight lobbyists. For more than a decade, the APA membership had been in a professional quandary, with the meaning of the old labels "counselor" and "therapist" being debased and diffused by the likes of color therapy and spirit counseling on the one hand, and by AI query-psych engines with names like Sigmund, Eliza, and Dr. Chip on the other.

Developing the model curriculum and certification for "relationship technology" was the first step toward redefining the APA's mission and elevating their credibility. A clever campaign against the do-it-yourself psychware, pushing the idea that "people need people," was the second. Persuading the authors of the national Family Integrity Act to mention relationship technology in the section requiring family counseling was the clincher. Every Dale family—and, in time, a fair fraction of what were now called "pair" families—would have its "Uncle Arty."

Behind the high-tech label and its folksy derivation, though, was old-fashioned goal-oriented therapist-assisted self-examination. Be it transactional analysis or power dynamics, reality therapy or Klersen System, it still came down to inviting a stranger to tinker with your emotional machinery. And there was nothing in the hyper that could make Christopher any happier about that prospect.

Meyfarth allowed Christopher to tell his version of the baby-making blowup and the John Fields fiasco. The arty listened patiently and sympathetically, asking only a few questions to clarify minor points.

"I'm sure they told you I'm being selfish," Christopher concluded. "Is it selfish to want to be happy? Am I obligated to say yes when I don't want to? Why is it me that should have to adjust?"

"I'd like to come back to those issues a bit farther down the road."

Christopher eyed Meyfarth suspiciously. "I thought that was what we were here to talk about."

"And ultimately we will—when you're ready to answer your own questions."

"I already have answers. The problem is that no one accepts them."

"Including yourself," Meyfarth said, "or that fact would not trouble you."

"What troubles me is that if I follow my conscience I'll kill the family," said Christopher. "They've put me in a position where I can't win. And they can't lose. Either they'll turn me into the man they want or they'll turn me out and find another."

"Something like that has already happened to you once, hasn't it?" asked Meyfarth.

"No," Christopher said. "I left that one myself."

"I see. Perhaps this is a good time for me to hear about your marriage. You were living in San Francisco then?"

"I don't see what my marriage has to do with what I'm here to work on."

"The common element is you," Meyfarth said simply.

"But it's old news," said Christopher.

"Do you really think that a relationship that serious which ended that unhappily had no effect on how you approached your next bonding?"

Christopher looked away. "I know what effects it had."

"You were really quite young," Meyfarth said. "How did you come to marry Donald and Kristen?"

The question took Christopher away from Meyfarth, two years and two thousand kilometers away. "Donald was my friend," he said. "We were both working for DIANNA in San Francisco, in the updates group. I was a year out of school. Kristen—I met Kristen at a musicbox down in Santa Cruz. She was a singer, though I didn't know that when I met her. Terrific energy."

"What did she look like?"

A little smile. "Tall. Very tall. A graceful gazelle. Chestnut-brown hair, what people call laughing eyes. I'd phone her now and again, and things would get pretty warm. And sometimes she'd come up for an evening, a few friends over to make some music. One time Donald was one of them."

"So that's how they met."

"No. They already knew each other—they met taking a tour of San Simeon, the old Hearst mansion, of all places. They'd been dating for a few months and hadn't realized that they both knew me. We started doing things together, the three of us, and the one-on-ones kept getting warmer. She wanted us both, but she was old-fashioned—contract first, play later. So we ended up getting married and moving into a house in Santa Cruz."

"Was there love, too, or just sex?"

"I thought I loved her," Christopher said. "I don't know how to judge whether I really did. Three years later I was gone. What does that say?"

"Nothing," Meyfarth said. "Nothing by itself. Were you three happy?"

"Kristen was. Donald was. Most of the time I wasn't."

"Why?"

He hesitated. "Do you know what it's like to watch someone else make love to your wife?"

"What was that like?"

Christopher covered his mouth with steepled hands as he thought. "He was my best friend, and I ended up hating him."

"Because you had to share Kristen?"

"It wasn't bad at first," he said, looking up and coming back from his faraway place. "It was all new and very crazy. We knew we were safe, and we could do anything. There were whole weekends when all we did was fuck. We invented new ways to put two into one. Or at least we thought we did."

"Was there ever any sexual contact between you and Donald?"

"No," Christopher said. "Nothing more than a kiss."

"Isn't that difficult to manage with three in a bed? It seems to me that the incidental contact, the energy, would eventually lead to—"

"I didn't want that. I made sure he knew it. I'm not a bigot. It just didn't appeal to me."

Meyfarth shook his head. "Try again."

"What are you talking about?"

"That's a forty percent answer. Peel back one more layer. You were friends sharing a woman, pleasuring a woman—"

"Exactly. We were focused on Kristen. She was the center of attention. It was like a challenge to see how high we could send her. We were partners."

"At the beginning."

Christopher slumped back in his chair. "Yeah. At the beginning."

"And it never changed so you or Donald was the focus, the other two the partners."

"No. Not really."

Meyfarth frowned. "It's a bit astonishing to me that your lovemaking had but one pattern. You're in bed together, the three of you. Everyone shifts positions, and there's his cock at your mouth, or yours at his. You realize that's his hand on your buttocks, not hers—"

"I wasn't going to let him do that to me," Christopher said coldly.

"Do what?"

"He started trying to take over. He started trying to make Kristen look to him first. If I'd let him have that, too, I'd have lost everything he hadn't already taken."

"And so—"

"We'd started out even. I didn't care for the way things

changed. She liked both of us together. But she liked him alone best. How was I supposed to feel?'' he demanded. ''Why are we talking about this? What does this have to do with me now?''

''Do you really want to know?''

''If there is anything, yes, goddammit. If not, then let's move on.''

''I heard the answers in what you said. I'm wondering why you didn't.''

Christopher balked at the implied criticism. ''Maybe you're going to have to rub my nose in it.''

''All right,'' Meyfarth said calmly. ''I will. You drew a sharp line between yourself and Donald in your marriage and pointed everything toward Kristen.''

''Yes.''

''And you expected Loi and Jessica to do the same.''

''I—'' Christopher stopped in mid-denial, looking surprised. ''Maybe I did.''

''You wanted Kristen's position. You wanted to be the focus.''

''At least sometimes, yes. Is there anything wrong with that?''

Meyfarth ignored the question. ''You thought you chose both Loi and Jessica. You thought they were going to give you that.''

''Yes.''

''That being the only man would make you the focus.''

''Ah—''

''But the truth is that Loi did the choosing. She's the one at the center. She's where *you* wanted to be. And you're only just realizing it.''

Christopher stared at Meyfarth. His expression was half wild-eyed indignation, half wide-eyed revelation. His mouth worked and his eyes grew bright with moisture.

''God,'' he said in a hoarse whisper. ''Yes. I never saw it. I never saw it. She's just like Donald. Like Donald all over again.''

CHAPTER 16

–|GAG|–

"... the imperative command."

STONE-ROUGH AND PATCHY WHITE, THE SHEER VERTICAL WALLS of Fort Jesus were slowly crumbling, shedding their brittle masonry skin. Mikhail Dryke touched the brick above a narrow-arched cannon portal, and his hand came away powdered with dust and a smear of mold and yellow lichen.

Peering out through the portal at narrow Mombasa Harbor, Dryke watched as a small sailing ship passed unconcernedly under the cannon's one-eyed gaze. The sixteenth-century Portuguese fortress was a toothless dog, its black-barreled cannon resting on laughable fake carriages or lying uselessly on the ground in rows. There were no breeching ropes to restrain them, no powder, no linstock and worm, and the pyramided shot had been welded into mere decoration.

But the fort's command of the harbor, and the craft in its design, were still evident to Dryke's eye. The stronghold stood where Leven Reef pinched the navigable channel down to a few hundred meters' width. The guns of the lower gallery controlled the channel, while the high parapet commanded the harbor entrance and land approaches.

So simple, and so effective. For a hundred years, the garrison at Fort Jesus—rarely more than a few hundred men—had been the anchor of Portuguese power all along the East African coast. And when it finally fell, it took a three-year siege by an Omani fleet numbering more than three thousand men to win the victory.

Dryke walked slowly along the seaward parapet, trying to

imagine that moment. He had meant to come to Fort Jesus on his last trip to Kasigau, but the chaos of the Singapore incident had denied him the opportunity. He was not much interested in the museum rooms below, in the relics of Portuguese, Mazrui, Omani, and Muscat occupations. His interest was the equation of siege and fortification—war as a chess problem, in an age without aircraft, without rockets or computers, without lasers o. atomic weapons.

There was not much time for what might be called hobbies in Mikhail Dryke's life, but this one he could accommodate. On every continent there were walled cities, forts and castles, relics of that simpler time. As his travels allowed, Dryke indulged himself with side trips to explore them. It was somehow a restful exercise, somehow refreshing and yet somehow far away and foreign to contemplate two enemies who fought their battles face-to-face.

In his seven years working for Allied, he had managed visits to several dozen sites. A few would bear longer and more leisurely exploration. Eben-Emael, the first victim of the *Blitzkrieg*. Château Galliard, Richard the Lion-Hearted's cliff-top stronghold on the Seine. The Castel Sant'Angelo in Rome, where popes took refuge and Hadrian lay entombed.

And heading the list, the spectacular Krak des Chevaliers, the great fortress built by the crusading Knights Hospitalers in twelfth-century Palestine, near the border of Lebanon. Not even the regional wars of the twentieth century had managed to destroy its magnificence or bring down the towered walls. Against such standards, Fort Jesus was mean and ordinary, a rude structure with a dull history.

Settling on a low wall on the gallery level, Dryke began sketching his defense of Fort Jesus. The sketches were amusements, exercises—the adult remnant of a childhood game. He made no excuses for it, to himself or to anyone else. It seemed to him that he had come by both his career and his hobby honestly, led by blood and breeding both.

Dryke was born in Kaliningrad to a Russian mother and an English father—ironically, a few kilometers from the site of the thirteenth-century fortress of the Teutonic Knights, though he would not learn that until years later. Edward Dryke was an electronic intelligence technician in the Peace Force; Lina Koshevaia was a security officer at the Kaliningrad naval base where Dryke was attached.

When Mikhail was eight, Edward left the Peace Force for a job in the British electronics industry, and the family left Kaliningrad for Coventry, an hour from the Welsh border. Within a few months, they had begun taking weekend outings to explore the abbeys and castles of Wales—Cardiff and Caerphilly, Harlech and Valle Crucis. Drawing campaign maps and fighting imaginary battles in the back seat of the Leyland, Mikhail cemented his fascination with matters military.

And, in time, he learned a lesson that carried forward into adulthood, a lesson reinforced when a ruptured cerebral aneurysm stole his father's soul, when a Nexus flathead's gun spilled his mother's blood on a Birmingham street. The lesson was hard. Dryke had never verbalized it, but he had internalized it: *There is nothing that you cherish that cannot be taken from you, no treasure that cannot be lost—*

No matter how grand, no matter how imposing, the fortresses and castles had all fallen. Each had been a grand edifice in its time, bustling with the discords of life. Now they were dead museums, containing but a faint echo of their former greatness. The halls were empty, the walls unmanned.

It had been the same fight in every world and every time—against weakness and neglect and corruption, against tactics and numbers and valor and luck. And it was still the same in the present day.

Fort Houston. Castle Kasigau. The walled city of *Memphis.* Outside were the forces of chaos, swarming, massing, undermining the walls, building engines of destruction. Dryke carried the shield of his liege as captain of the queen's knights, looked out at the world through the dark, suspicious eyes of the besieged.

Except this time, there was a goal beyond mere preservation. A crusade was forming. If the walls held, if the attackers were repulsed, if the will did not weaken or the moment slip past, one day the gates would open, and the crusade would march out with flags flying to claim and conquer a new land.

Was it metaphor, or more? As he stood looking out from the high redoubt of Fort Jesus, Dryke could not say. He knew only that, for him as for the captain of the Portuguese guard, wondering what lay over the horizon and around the point, the waiting was the hardest part.

• • •

When he could, Dryke preferred to conduct conversations in person. The nature of his work meant that many of those conversations were sensitive; the nature of the world meant that none of those conversations could be guaranteed secure if any form of telecommunications was employed.

Split encryption, line-of-sight narrowcasting, dead-wiring, path-switching, all could be beaten. True, the message stream was like the Amazon in spring flood, and there was nothing easy about sieving the flow for one particular bit of electronic flotsam, much less decoding it.

But Dryke and Allied knew how, and it was only prudent to conclude that others knew as well. No one was saying, but the likely list included the intelligence arms of the Peace Force and several national governments, a smattering of the most technically inclined corporations, the best—and least principled—of the consulting and forecasting firms, a crime syndicate or two, and almost certainly Jeremiah's Homeworld as well.

Dryke would go to Houston, or Munich, even halfway around the globe to Tokyo for the company. But Matthew Reid on Takara was sixteen hours and 36,000 klicks away. Dryke had been to the "City of Builders" only twice, to the partially completed *Memphis* but once.

But those early visits had been sufficient for him to grasp the security parameters and to measure Reid, whom Dryke inherited from his predecessor. The situation and the man were well suited to each other, and Dryke had left them undisturbed.

There had to be communication, coordination, and there was. No less than weekly, reports and directives and updates were ferried back and forth between Prainha and Takara by courier. Twice a year Reid came back for working vacations—briefings and marlin-fishing off Brazil's Atlantic coast.

And at least once a month, on no fixed schedule, Dryke would call Reid and they would talk. The calls were nominally social, always informal, and quite probably monitored.

"Sounds like you folks had an amusing October," Reid was saying. "A T-ship fragged, a couple of midnight fire-bombings, half a dozen road shipments hijacked, and that business with the Canadian environmental inspector—I'm almost jealous. All we had up here were a couple of half-baked sabotage attempts and an old-fashioned drunken family murder."

"Just wait until we start sending you colonists a thousand at a time," Dryke said, smiling. "You'll get your share."

"Now, wait a minute, I was promised angels and Eagle Scouts."

"Nine hundred ninety-nine angels and one Javier Sala," said Dryke. Sala was an *Ur* colonist who smuggled the components of a forty-kilogram cyclotol-aluminum bomb aboard the starship in his personal effects. His plan to destroy the ship before the eyes and cameras of the world was foiled three days before sailing when *Ur*'s security, monitoring internal communications, uncovered Sala's ties to Spanish nationalists. Sala was quietly removed, and the incident never publicly revealed, but it remained a cautionary parable for Project insiders.

"Sporting odds, anyway," Reid said lightly. "You keep the number of fanatics and martyrs down to a round dozen or so, and we'll take it from there."

"That's big of you, Matt," Dryke said. "Considering that every second warm body—man, dog, and grandmother—seems to be pointing for us down here. And every damn one of them can reach us if they try."

"You need to recruit a militia. I hear the starheads gave a pretty good account of themselves in the Tokyo riot."

"Yeah. This time," Dryke said grimly. "It won't be the last riot, though. And the next one will be worse, for both sides. Next time both sides'll be armed."

"I never thought I'd see the starheads rallying to our cause with steel," Reid said, shaking his head. "That won a few hearts on Takara, I have to tell you."

"And probably lost us a few million down here. It's the old second-punch syndrome. Nobody saw it as five hundred screamers jumping fifty starheads and getting surprised. It played as Allied goons with stingers and blades carving up doe-eyed demonstrators."

"The media have swung that far over?"

"It's not what they said. It's the pictures they have to show."

"I don't know why you folks just don't pull out and move operations up here," said Reid. "Ninety-five percent of the ship is ready for occupation. And you folks are about as popular as the Plague down there. You've got more friends up here, you know."

"I wouldn't be surprised if the company does exactly that for *Knossos*," said Dryke. "Can't run Selection from up there, though."

"Sasaki could move West to Prainha and Central and East to Kasigau. Let the urban centers go."

"Maybe," said Dryke. "Be kind of like turning your back to a wolf, though."

"I suppose," said Reid. "Listen, I'd like to get as many of my people as possible some release time before things get crazy up here. Do you have anything that's going to need special attention programmed between now and the end of the year?"

Dryke considered. "You'll start to get ship's staff in two weeks," he said. "You knew that. They're finishing up the navigation and drive management software in Munich. That's the next critical pacing item. It'll be hand-carried up for installation sometime next month, six copies on three different flights."

"I hear it's about ready. Testing this week?"

"Yeah. Munich will put it up on a simulator, and Mission will go live with Prainha and the controllers at Horizon for a mock sailing and test program. Not our headache, thank God."

"How goes the mole hunt?"

"A couple more pelts in the Logistics Section, and a fistful out in the supplier community—Micronomics turned out to have a whole nest. I keep thinking we should be finding more, though. Houston's been clean for a year, Munich for two—makes me feel like I'm missing something."

"Hmm. Speaking of missing something—has this one reached you? There's a kind of oddball rumor circulating in Takara that Jeremiah is on Sanctuary."

"I heard."

"I haven't been able to put anything hard underneath it," Reid went on, "but it makes a certain amount of sense. Synthesized image, synthesized voice—no reason really to think that there's a real Jeremiah anywhere, or that he's necessarily a he. And the goals of Homeworld certainly are consistent with Sanctuary's politics."

"Yeah," said Dryke. "The thing that keeps me from taking it seriously is I think Anna X would sooner cut out her heart than use a male persona as Sanctuary's mouthpiece. But maybe that's my blind spot, so stay with it."

For the next ten minutes, they wandered off into other topics—a minor drug problem in the high-stress Tokyo office, a thrice-delayed test of *Memphis*'s shield lasers, a funny story about the starship's lead architect getting lost during an inspection tour—and then Dryke ended the conversation.

"Well—departmental conference in ten minutes, and I need to make a side stop on the way. So I'm going to let you get back to whatever I took you from."

"I *could* use a few more hours sleep," Reid deadpanned.

"Get it while you can," Dryke said with a sardonic half-grin. "The kids'll be home from school soon."

"That they will," said Reid. "It'll be nice to have the family back together again."

Dryke chuckled, shook his head. "I'll talk to you later," he said, and broke the link. Turning away from the blank wall, he looked toward the silent spectator to the conversation, seated in the far corner of the room. "Opinion? Too obvious?"

"Perhaps not obvious enough," said Hiroko Sasaki, rising and gliding toward him. "The Munich gateway has been open for three weeks without a single attempt at penetration."

"Trolling for big fish takes patience," said Dryke. "The bait has to be right, the fish has to be hungry, and you have to be lucky enough to run it past his mouth without him sensing the hook."

"You spoke of Javier Sala," she said. "We cannot allow Jeremiah such an opportunity. I am reluctant to permit any pioneers to board *Memphis* until Jeremiah has been found."

Dryke shook his head vigorously. "Delaying habitation would be a mistake. The closer we are to succeeding, the bolder he'll be in trying to stop us."

"But will he be more reckless, or merely more ruthless?"

"Truthfully? I expect both."

"*Memphis* is not replaceable, Mikhail."

"I know," he said. "But there's no safe way to gamble."

CHAPTER 17

-|CAU|-

". . . the voice of the banished . . ."

THE CALL ICON POPPED UP IN ONE CORNER OF CHRISTOPHER McCutcheon's work space, accompanied by a polite *cheep*.

"Who is it, Dee?" he asked his secretary.

"Lenore Edkins, Section 15," answered the AIP. "You last talked to him on November 8."

Edkins was a senior archaeolibrarian in the Culture Section. "I remember. I'll take it," McCutcheon said, suspending the error audit he had been conducting on the pre-Columbian thread of the North American Mythology stack. "Hello, Lenore."

"Morning, Christopher," said Edkins, a monk-haired black man with soulless eyes. "I've got some answers for you on that inquiry about your hyper entry. The *Tunnel Visions* telecast hadn't been reviewed, now has been. It won't be added to the hyper. Sorry."

Crestfallen, McCutcheon asked, "Any idea why?"

"You play well enough, at least so I'm told by people more accustomed to hearing antique instruments. But the quality of the recording is only fair, and the auditor says that, taken as a whole, the music you three performed on the broadcast has 'no significant entertainment or ethnomusicological value.' Pretty standard phrasing. I'm afraid your Project connection wasn't enough to swing the decision."

"No value? We did the Bach cello suites in the Segovia arrangement—"

"Which are apparently in the hyper, as performed by Segovia, Parkening, and the e-pop version by Helix."

"—'Mountain Storm,' by Michael Hedges—"

"Also in the hyper by the composer's own hand."

"—and Kristen's 'Elegiac,' which had everyone in the studio in tears."

"A nice piece. But it was never professionally recorded, never published, and this Kristen Carlyle doesn't come up in the stacks as either a performer or a songwriter. As near as I can tell, *Tunnel Visions* was as high as she ever got—thirty minutes on a regional arts showcase funded under USDC."

Christopher gritted his teeth. In the smug economic classism of the Los Angeles ent-art world, Department of Culture grants were viewed as welfare handouts, and the work they supported little more than vanity indulgences. He hadn't expected Edkins to show such colors. "What does any of that have to do with the music?"

Edkins sighed. "Look, you've done some work on the fiction stacks, haven't you? What gets something in? Impact. Impact is the final criterion. You look at sales, cross-media citations, major reviews. You look for seminal ideas, innovative techniques, representative examples. What did the work give us? How did it change us?"

"So it has to be popular and prestigious," said Christopher. "It's not enough to be good."

"It isn't even necessary to be good," said Edkins. "There are inferior fictions in the stacks because they added a single new word to the language, inferior songs because they caught everyone's ear one summer. It's not always fair. 'Elegiac' is a nice piece of work. I felt a tug, too. But it's foam on the ocean, and no one's going to miss it if it's not there. Sorry, but that's the truth."

Discomfiting as it was, Christopher knew that Edkins was right, and that arguing was pointless. He had gotten Biography to add his degrees and his Hastings Award; he knew what a victory looked like, and this wasn't one.

"All right, Lenore," he said. "Thanks, anyway. I appreciate your taking a look at it."

Edkins shrugged. "You're family. No thanks needed. Sorry I couldn't bring back better news. If you're interested, though, I'll tell you where the door *is* open."

"Oh?"

"Tidwell's holding a lot of space open for a Folklife stack on the Diaspora," Edkins said. "The impact arrow points the other way on this one—we're looking for what effect the starship Project's had on people's hearts and minds and muses. He's particularly interested in off-net material, according to recent memos. So if you've got any material dealing with the Project, make sure I see it.''

Christopher brightened. "I might just have something. I'll need to get a good recording made.''

"I can't make an unconditional promise, mind you, but I'd say there's a good chance that your musicianship and family connection would carry even a borderline piece in.''

"Charity, Lenore?''

Edkins shrugged. "I won't spin you. It's the back door. But it's a door. Do you want to live forever, or not?''

Christopher swallowed any further words of indignation, and with them a measure of his pride. "What's the timetable?''

"The sooner the better, I'd think. We'll probably close late, but we might have to be more picky toward the end.''

Christopher nodded. "Okay. I'll be in touch. Break, Dee.'' He sat back in his big chair, thoughtful, troubled. Is that what it was about, this ache? Living forever? Edkins seemed to see so readily something Christopher had not yet acknowledged in himself. Edkins presumed an understanding Christopher wanted to deny.

Living forever. A little piece of immortality. A mark, more permanent than a handprint in cement, than initials carved on a wooden railway trestle. More permanent than memory. More permanent than life.

He circled the thought cautiously, unwilling to embrace it. He had scorned and pitied Jessie for this same passion. It was hard to be more forgiving of himself.

But already one part of his mind was thinking, *Need to work on the middle eight—could use the date at Wonders—have to rent a v-cam, Greg can do tech—be nice to get some friends down for it—*

"Ego and hypocrisy,'' he chided himself aloud.

"Excuse me?'' asked Dee.

"Ego and hypocrisy,'' he repeated. "Not so different from Jessie, after all.''

Barely five minutes had passed when the phone cheeped again—little enough time that Christopher had barely found his place in the audit. Little enough time that he didn't bother to glance at the Caller ID, automatically concluding it was Edkins calling back.

"I'll take it, Dee," he said.

But it was not Edkins, not a call he would have taken had he checked the identifier. It was, in fact, a call he had been avoiding.

"Hello, Christopher," said William McCutcheon.

His father seemed to have a sixth sense for trouble in his life. Sure as sunrise, his father would call exactly when Christopher most wanted to avoid him—in the wake of crisis, calamity, or failure. Christopher half suspected his father of spying on him somehow, except he could not convince himself his father was sufficiently interested to take the trouble.

Probably it was just an accident of timing, a case of selective memory. All the same, the day after the blowup over John Fields, Christopher had directed his phone to divert any calls from William McCutcheon to V-mail. And true to form, in the two weeks since, there had been three such calls. Each time, his father had left an inconsequential message and an invitation to call back. Each time, Christopher had chosen not to do so.

It would not take William McCutcheon long to realize that he was being avoided. And Christopher should have known his father would not quietly accept that, would find a way to reach him.

Had.

Dee screened personal com everywhere—home, work, on the road. But Allied screened station com. Not that Christopher would have thought to post a divert on station com. His father had never called him at work before. Never in all the time Christopher had been in Houston.

"Hello, Father." His father looked tired, and fatigue had always softened his features. Christopher saw more of himself in his father's face at such times.

"Your friend Jessie says that you're not often home these days," said William. "She thought I might have the best chance to catch you here."

William always spoke of "your friend Jessie" and "your friend Loi." He refused to ratify the unconventional relationship by calling them Christopher's wives, as most older people would, or even his mates, the style book compromise. In part, that was simple moral stodginess. In part, it was a commentary on the trine.

"It's going to get worse before it gets better," said Christopher, declining to ask the reason for the call. "*Memphis* sails in six months."

"So the nets tell me, with painful redundancy. Have you begun to think about what you'll do when the ship is gone?"

There it was. Christopher looked at his father in surprise. "There's *Knossos* to come, and *Mohenjo-Daro* and *Teotihuacán* after that. Allied will still need archies. There'll be work here until long after I retire."

"So you're content to stay in Texas. I'm surprised. I would have thought you'd miss the woods more than you apparently do."

"I miss them, all right. Here you get bone-dry baked or flash-flood drowned. But this is where my job is," Christopher said, wondering. "I don't have the option to work where I please. Operations isn't about to allow dial-ups into the hyper. Not when a scissors virus could rip ten years work apart in ten minutes."

"There are three inches of new snow on the ridge," said his father.

A crystal memory of being ten and tracking deer and rabbits in the new snow suddenly flooded Christopher with unwelcome nostalgia. "You'll have to send me a picture. They tell me it hasn't snowed in Houston for sixteen years."

"I was nearly in your backyard not too long ago," he went on. "It seems that it was just as well that I didn't follow my impulse to come all the way. I probably wouldn't have found you there."

Another surprise. "You were in Texas?"

"Not quite. I had to go down to Albuquerque a month or so back to look at some properties. That was the first long drive I'd taken in the Avanti. Long overdue to check the GPS navigator. I timed it so I flew across the Colorado River canyonlands at twilight. Ever seen them, Christopher?"

"Pictures."

"Inadequate. Magnawall or stereo tank, it doesn't matter. Inadequate." A more familiar William McCutcheon, pronouncing his opinions with the authority of Truth. "A thousand meters up and a hundred klicks an hour, that's the way to see the Colorado watershed. If I had come to Houston I would have dragged you back with me so I could show you."

"I've been meaning to see it. But it's not exactly our back-

yard," said Christopher. "You're probably closer to the Grand
Canyon in Portland than we are here in Houston."

"Make the time. Do it." He shook his head. "Turquoise
blue lakes. Winding canyons like knife scars. Arrow-straight
fault ridges. Physical poetry, Christopher. The mesa cliffs are
fissured top to bottom like a giant cat clawed them. The rocks
are blood red, like a spill of paint in the dust. And when the
afternoon shadows move across them—you have to see it, Christopher."

"It's going to be awhile before I can think about taking sight-
seeing trips," he said, a hint of impatience slipping into his
voice. "I trust the Colorado'll still be there when I get to it."

"It's changing, now that people can fly in so easily," William
said. "There are five times as many people in southeast Utah as
there were thirty years ago. And they're leaving their mark as
surely as wind and water. Patches of irrigated green, self-
contained houses on top of the mesas, little communities in the
river valleys."

"I'll settle for almost virgin."

"It made me think about the white pioneers on horseback, in
wagons, on foot," his father went on, "reaching Denver and
seeing that wall of mountains. That anyone went farther west is
a complete defiance of sanity. It's astonishing to me that those
lands were ever crossed, much less colonized. They've never
been tamed."

"Have you been to Denver? I'd have kept going, too," Christopher said.

It was said lightly, a casual joke, but his father shook his head
dismissively. "Crowding doesn't explain it. Not the first wave.
Economic factors don't become meaningful until the second
wave."

"Maybe they kept going *because* it was hard."

His father cocked his head "Do you think so? Does that
make sense to you?"

Again, he was suddenly ten, but this time he squirmed uncomfortably at the familiarity of the moment drawn by his father into a duel of wits, stopped and subjected to a surprise oral
exam It could happen at any time. It had happened many times.

"Each generation went as far as its will would carry it," said
Christopher. "Sons and daughters crossed the barriers that had
stopped their parents."

"But they didn't all go. That's the puzzle. Some stayed to

make a life. Do you think that those who left were any happier, burned any brighter?''

Christopher's back was still up. "Probably they lived harder lives. I imagine some lived shorter lives. You'd have to ask them if they were happier.''

William McCutcheon shook his head. "*You* ask them, Christopher. You ask them if you get the chance. Aren't they there with you in Houston? Isn't that what the Diaspora is about? Aren't they one and the same?''

"Something like that,'' Christopher said lightly, unwilling to launch into a justification of the Project. "Except wagons are more expensive now.''

His father did not smile. "Much more. And we all have to pay for them.''

The conversation stumbled after that, and shortly Christopher escaped to his waiting work. But he was left puzzled and unsettled. It was the most curious conversation he could remember having with his father.

William McCutcheon was not comfortable with what most people called chatting—except with strangers, which was another matter entirely—and so he rarely bothered with it. When he spoke, he made speeches, conducted interrogations, issued demands, offered critiques.

None of the above. Christopher recalled his father's face from the capture queue to the display and stared at it. *Why did you call?* he asked the frozen image. *Why did you have to invade this space, too? To ask my opinion? To take my pulse?*

The sudden thought that William McCutcheon might be lonely prompted a curious state of wonder. *Mystery of mysteries, could it be you actually miss me?*

Christopher found himself growing angry without quite being certain why. He wanted to call his father back and say, *Don't change the rules now, goddammit. Everything else is breaking out of its box. You can fucking stay in yours. Don't make me care.*

But it was too late. He already knew that something was wrong.

It explained so much—his father's purposeless persistence, the odd emotional tone of the call. William McCutcheon would not be one to easily acknowledge a problem or admit to his own needs and weaknesses.

But it left unanswered the question of what was required of Christopher—what he was now bound to do.

One more problem to deal with, one more demand on his energy. As if there weren't enough. Someone else who wanted something from him. Someone else claiming a piece of him. And even though the claim was legitimate, Christopher rebelled.

After all, what if he were wrong? Wouldn't *that* be an amusing spectacle? No more foolish feeling than to try to hug someone who neither invited nor welcomes the embrace—

The decision was made. Did his father need him? He could not cope if it were so, and so he chose to believe it was not.

He would do nothing.

Eric Meyfarth looked up from his desk as Christopher entered the office. "Do you mind if we get out of here?" he asked, rising out of his chair. "I'm getting a bit claustrophobic."

Surprised, Christopher agreed. He followed Meyfarth down a back corridor into the floor's private section, where they commandeered an express elevator.

"Otis—Sky Room," said Meyfarth. The doors closed, and the arty leaned against the back wall. "How are things at home?"

"It's like being a bachelor with roommates."

"Jessie and Loi are closing you out?"

"I don't think it's them," Christopher said, shaking his head. "I think it's me."

"Oh?"

"I just can't be the same with them." He glanced at the display. "Where are we going?"

"The nearest spot that feels as little like an office as possible."

"Sky Room," said the elevator, and the doors opened.

"Here we go," said Meyfarth, leading the way out.

The top level of the Matador Building was a climoglas-enclosed forest micropark, complete with birds and bubbling water. Narrow paths led to private seating nooks. The air was slightly humid and carried the mixed scents of life.

"This is nice," said Christopher, craning his neck as he looked up toward the heat-blocking roof panels twenty meters overhead. The tallest trees nearly brushed them.

"Very expensive, very wasteful," said Meyfarth. "About eight percent of my lease payments go to maintain it. That's about fifteen dollars out of every appointment, if you're interested. I try to make sure I log my share of use. Anything like Oregon?''

"Just the smells."

They found an empty nook on the east side of the densely planted greenyard.

"You don't have any contact with your host mother, is that right?" asked Meyfarth.

"No. Not since I finished school."

"How did that happen?"

"She's on Sanctuary," Christopher said with a touch of impatience. "I don't have a lot of choice about it. I can't even call her. She had to call me."

"I understand that. Do you have any clue to why she stopped?"

"No. Is this important?"

"I was just refreshing my memory," said Meyfarth. "What does your father think about what's happening with your family?"

"He doesn't know."

"Really? When was the last time you talked to him?"

"This morning."

Meyfarth cocked his head quizzically. "So you chose not to tell him."

"It's not his problem. There's nothing he could do to help. So there's really no reason to bring him in." Christopher looked away and frowned. "Besides, it's just not something we McCutcheons do. It took him two months last year to get around to mentioning that an aunt of mine was dead."

"Forty percent answer, Christopher."

"I know. I really don't want to talk about my father just now."

"Guessing now—you didn't tell him because he has a rooting interest."

"Not that he'll admit to," Christopher said. "But it's true, I don't want to have to deal with his reaction on top of everything else. He's not fond of Loi." That was diluting the truth; the two were stone and storm. "I suppose he'd be happy to see me break with her and solo with Jessie."

"Which isn't what you want."

"No."

"Have you any idea why he feels that way?"

"I really don't know what he feels or why he feels it," Christopher said irritably. "Does this have a point?"

Meyfarth frowned. "Define your problem, Christopher."

"Look, there's a lot of old history there, and I don't much want to relive it," Christopher said, exasperation tingeing his voice. "The, ah—the emotions are still a bit confused."

"Did you quarrel often?" Meyfarth asked quietly.

A wistful look crept onto Christopher's face. "No. Not quarrel." He smiled, and the smile was eloquently bittersweet. "I didn't see enough of my father that I could afford to get angry with him."

The words seared his throat, stabbed deep into his chest. He was caught by surprise by his own thoughts. It was as though the words had leaped from his subconscious directly to his lips. Christopher looked plaintively at Meyfarth and found the arty's expression of empathy as distressing as the revelation itself. Rising, he walked to the edge of the nook, pretending interest in the plant identifier on a small pedestal there.

Meyfarth said slowly, "I think that's a piece of something important, Christopher."

"Do you?" asked Christopher, hugging himself as he stood facing the trees. "I don't. I don't even know that it's true. I have this habit of rewriting what I feel so it sounds more dramatic. And then when it comes out of my mouth it doesn't touch me at all."

Gently, the arty said, "I don't think this was one of those."

Christopher turned to face Meyfarth. "I don't think it matters," he said stiffly. "I don't think it has anything to do with what I'm here to work on. Damn you, I told you once already I didn't want to talk about my father. Can we get back to the main program, or are we finished?"

There was a long moment of silence. He felt Meyfarth measuring him.

"All right," said the arty. "My apologies."

Christopher frowned and waved a hand dismissively. "Listen, I'm not stupid. I know I'm going to have to look at it sometime. But I don't think I have enough banked just now that I can afford to make this the time. Do you understand?"

"Yes," Meyfarth said. "Can we talk about children?"

"Okay," Christopher said, returning to his seat. "I guess we have to."

"Loi has a son?"

"Einar. He's in San Francisco. Twenty years old."

"More like a brother, then."

"To me? I wouldn't know. I never had the experience."

"But you knew Einar?"

"I knew him. I didn't like him, but I knew him."

"Oh?"

"We had incompatible anatomies. He was an asshole."

Meyfarth's laugh was easy and genuine.

"Loi agrees," Christopher added.

"Enough of Einar, then," Meyfarth said, smiling. "Tell me about the last child under ten you liked."

Christopher shook his head. "I don't see many children. I'm not sure I like any of the ones I do see."

"No friends with adorable seven-year-old girls? All neighbors with brats?"

"Our upstairs neighbor in San Francisco had a boy while we were living there," said Christopher. "Cute, I suppose. Little odor factory, though. And they leak."

"That they do."

"Sometimes I see a two- or three-year-old toddling along with a parent and it'll make me smile. But a little older and I don't know how to talk to them. A little older than that and I don't trust them."

"Why not?"

"I was one, remember?"

"What kind of kid were you?"

Christopher laughed, surprised. "You'd have to ask someone else. I was busy being the kid."

"You don't have any notion?"

Frowning, Christopher considered. "A pretty good one, I guess. I wasn't much of a problem, wasn't much in the way. I liked learning, liked my ed plan and my schools. I spent a lot of time in the woods."

"Tell me what kind of father you think you'd be."

A wry smile. "Not a very good one," Christopher said. "I'm dividing myself too many ways already. I have an A job and my music and my family, and they all need more than I seem to be able to give them. If I divide myself four ways, I'll have even less for everybody." He shook his head. "I have too much growing up still to do. Look at why I'm here talking to you. Maybe someday. But I'm not ready now."

Meyfarth pursed his lips. "Christopher, the nastiest secret in life is that there's never a time when you understand it all, never a time when it's as easy as you were sure it was going to be. If that's what you're waiting for, you'll never be ready."

Blinking, Christopher stared at Meyfarth blankly. "I'm only twenty-seven. Jessie's twenty-five. We have lots of time."

"Every year you wait, you'll find more reasons to say no. Why not have the child and just let Jessie worry about it?"

"It's not fair—"

"I think if you ask Jessie, you'll find out that would suit her just fine—"

"No," Christopher snapped. "You're not listening. It's not fair to the *boy*. If I have a son, I'm going to be there for him. I'm going to be part of his life, not a sidelight to it. I'm going to watch him grow and make sure he knows how much I love him. I'm not going to raise him by remote control, turn him over to some kind of secondhand mom-for-hire."

"Like your father did with you?" Meyfarth asked gently.

There was a moment of soft-eyed surprise, a glimmer of hurt, a tinge of puzzlement, and then Christopher's face closed down hard. "Damn you, I told you I didn't want to talk about my father," he shouted, jumping to his feet and waving clenched fists. "I told you and you kept pushing me back there. My father's one person, and I'm another. And what I do has to do with me, not with him."

Meyfarth did not flinch or shy from Christopher's angry demonstration. "Then why did you start talking about a 'son'? Who were you thinking of when you spoke so passionately about the right and wrong way to parent? It wasn't a friend. It wasn't a neighbor. Wasn't it your father?"

"You said that," Christopher insisted. "You said 'son.' "

Meyfarth stood, half blocking the way to the trail, holding the younger man's eyes with his gaze. "No, I said 'child.' You're lying to yourself, Christopher. You brushed up against something that hurts and now you're lying to yourself."

"I don't have to explain my father. I don't have to apologize for my father. And I fucking don't have to talk about my father if I fucking don't want to.' As he spoke, he shouldered Meyfarth out of his way and stalked down the trail toward the elevator.

Meyfarth caught up with him there. "You have to look at it, Christopher."

"Shut up."

"You said you were willing to risk discovering yourself."

"Some other time, thank you," he said sarcastically.

"This has been playing in your head for twenty years. Don't you want to have a chance to decide if it belongs there?"

The doors opened. "My father loves me," Christopher said, backing one step into the car so that he blocked Meyfarth from entering. "Why do you want to make me think he doesn't?"

"This is about loving yourself, Christopher."

"What floor?" asked the elevator.

"Then what's my father got to do with it, goddammit?"

"Because he's inside your head. It's his voice you hear when you think you have to make your life perfect, yourself perfect. Did you hear yourself? You were a good kid because you liked school and stayed out of the way? I'll tell you why you don't want to have a child with Jessie. You're afraid that your son will disappoint you the way you disappointed *your* father. And you're afraid your son will think of you the same way you think of him."

"What way is that?"

"Answer that question yourself, and the answer will be worth something."

Christopher's bitter rage, which had momentarily faded as he listened, flowered in full blossom. "Goddamn you assfucker," he snarled, one many-syllabled word. "Otis—lobby."

The doors closed, the car began to drop, and Christopher closed his eyes in relief. *I'm not coming back,* he thought angrily. *We can find someone else. Or Jessie and Loi can find someone else. I almost don't care which. But I'm not coming back to have more tricks played on me.*

That resolve helped calm him. But he could not release all his anger, for the infuriating thing was that Meyfarth had been right. Christopher *had* brushed up against something that hurt, a black wraith that lived in an ugly place inside him. And try as he might to escape it, it shadowed his consciousness all the way back to the compound.

Work proved no amulet, anger no talisman. The wraith shadowed him all through the afternoon and into that early winter night, fragments of the session playing *tag-gotcha!* in his head until half a flask of Loi's Glenfiddich finally silenced what lies and bluster could not.

CHAPTER

18

-GCA-

"There is only one history . . ."

IT WAS TEN DAYS UNTIL THE END OF GROUND TRAINING, AND excitement was building in the village at AT-Houston. It was obvious to Thomas Tidwell, still sharing a house with three *Memphis* colonists. But it seemed to him that even a casual visitor to the compound could not fail to notice, would see it in the self-delighted smiles, the surreptitious winks and thumb-in-fist salutes.

Soon, the winks and smiles and salutes said, *soon*.

Soon the staff would scatter across the globe and throughout the orbiting worlds on a last sojourn home, for a final farewell to family and familiar. Even though the sailing date was still three months away, it seemed to Tidwell that the whole planet must soon echo with the ache of the tearing away, that the pain of those good-byes would surely more than cancel the giddy pleasure he was seeing on the faces of the villagers. But if that were so, he was the only one who saw it. When Evans or Colas said, "Ten more days," it was said with potent anticipation, as a promise and a bond between the elect.

The selection sociometricians had explained their strategy to Tidwell in elusive detail—how the ground training had less to do with technology than with psychology, with forging emotional links through shared homes, shared labors, shared goals. The demanding schedule only intensified the effect, an old work-shop leader's trick carried off on a much greater scale. The colonists would part on the last day saying, "See you on the ship,"

165

and that vow would help assure that most would keep the appointment.

Ten more days, they said. Ten more days until tomorrow begins. Ten more days until we can finally close the old book, open a new one.

And for Tidwell, ten more days until he could return to Half-whistle, the episode over, his mission concluded, though far from complete. Evans and Colas and Graham, reunited on *Memphis*, would count him as one who had faltered, who surrendered the dream in exchange for a tamer security—if they noted his absence at all.

No, he thought, they would not question it, or even be surprised. They had to know, just as he had come to know, living with them, that he was not one of them, one with them. They had to sense that he was deaf to whatever music pounded in their blood. There had been no lapse in civility, no attempt to exclude him. But they had to wonder why he was struggling, wonder if in his case Selection had made a mistake.

Tidwell would have thought they would shy from him, fearing that their own certainty would be contaminated by doubt. Instead, they had wrapped him in a gentle cocoon of silent sympathy and support, and went right on.

From within that cocoon, he watched them. He saw their naive energy and marveled as a parent marvels at the boundless energy of a child. He saw that they were helpless in the grip of their own dimly apprehended need, and happy being so. That selection counselor, Keith, had been right. Everything Tidwell had learned in his brief career as Thomas Grimes he learned that first day, except that he had rejected the wisdom.

They burned. He did not.

With each day, that gulf seemed wider, his estrangement from their passion more complete. They were leaving. He would stay. And in recent days it had become more important to consider what that meant to him than what it meant to them. New questions intruded on his thoughts: What becomes of the nest when the children have flown? What sort of world would the last of Allied Transcon's starships be leaving behind? How much energy of will, how much love of life, could five ships, a mere sixty thousand people, carry away with them?

For the first time, Tidwell wondered darkly if those who remained would have enough dreams to sustain them.

These were thoughts which would not have seemed out of

place in a tirade by the mythical Jeremiah, and Tidwell was
discomfited by hearing them rattle, homeless and unclaimed,
around his own skull. He had gotten too close; the charade had
gone on too long. He had lost perspective, lost the surety of his
own judgment. It was past time to withdraw, to regain the balance, to become the observer, to begin the synthesis.

And still not yet time. Ten more days.

Lying wide awake in his darkened room, the thinnest of sheets
covering his nakedness in the clammy warmth, Tidwell stared
ceilingward and tried to make sense of his day. *I no longer know
what questions to ask*, he thought. *I no longer know what matters.*

Point: his interview that morning with Carl Miller, the University of Texas systemist whose theory of "bioeconomics" had
caused such a flap in the popular media since October. The most
common spin on Miller's work was that it offered the first authoritative scientific support for Jeremiah's claim that Allied
Transcon was "bleeding" the earth.

Tidwell had put Miller on his schedule merely to fill time, to
occupy a block when "Thomas Grimes" was scheduled for
meaningless proficiency examinations. But Tidwell was unable
to put away what Miller had to say, unable to render it meaningless with logic or counterargument.

"I'm not a Homeworlder, Dr. Tidwell," Miller kept repeat-
ing. "I'm as excited about the Diaspora as anyone—I even
subscribe to the *Ur* journal, *Frontier*. All I've done in my paper
is analyze some of the issues in macroeconomic terms. And I
think I've demonstrated that this is, in fact, a one-sided transaction, building and outfitting these starships. In fact, I think
that it's time to revive the notion of the altruistic act."

"On whose part?"

"On the part of the entire species," said Miller. "I've heard
Sasaki claiming that Allied has paid its own way on this. But
that balance sheet is missing a lot of entries. If Sasaki wants to
amortize the cost of the Project against the entire future of the
colonial units, that's fine. But what about the knowledge that
these ships carry? What about the technical expertise required
to build them? That's an unvalued transaction. The cumulative
cost of that intellectual capital is by far the single largest cost
item on the ledger."

"Come now," Tidwell said dismissively, "that 'capital' can

be spent a thousand times over and never exhausted. It goes on *Memphis*'s ledger as a gift of great value and no cost. Every bit of knowledge that went into its conception and construction remains available to this community—perhaps even more available, considering the effort which we've put into collecting and organizing it. You're grandstanding, sir, with meaningless hypotheticals.''

''I understand your defensiveness,'' Miller said. ''I can't say it often enough—I'm with you, not against you. But where does intellectual capital come from? It's the product of an even more precious *emotional* capital. And emotional capital *can* be spent, because one of the multipliers is time. Is spent, every day, as we choose what to do with our opportunities. With our lives.''

''You are inventing realities again.''

''Are you familiar with CFS, Mr. Tidwell?''

''CFS?''

''Chronic Fatigue Syndrome,'' said Miller. ''It's a useful one-organism model for bioeconomics. CFS victims are achievers, ambitious, inventive. And then they reach a point where they can't keep the pace they've set for themselves. They're weary. They sleep too much. They're always sick, little nagging draining kinds of illnesses. The ambition vanishes. In short, they just don't care anymore. It happens to individuals. It happens to communities. It happens to civilizations. I think it's happening to us.''

''This is not economics,'' said Tidwell. ''This is political metaphysics. And you are aiding the Homeworlders, whether you consider yourself one or not.''

''Do you expect me to stop talking about this? We have a right to know what's coming. I think that Jeremiah is right about the price we're paying, about the decline to follow. But I think that he's wrong to try to stop the Diaspora. Because the decline will come anyway. The capital is spent.''

''We have survived the worst of our problems,'' said Tidwell. ''The human race has a long and fascinating future ahead of it.''

''Yes,'' Miller said. ''But not on Earth. For us, this is the end of the race. This is the finish line, coming up on us now.''

Point: the afternoon briefing from the *Memphis* mission planners.

It was not as though there was anyone in the Building 2 auditorium who didn't know where *Memphis* was headed. Sasaki's predecessor had announced the Tau Ceti system as the provisional choice for prime rendezvous eleven years ago, and Sasaki had reconfirmed the choice three years later, long before staff and community selection had begun. The Tau Ceti of *New Moon Over Barridan* and other popular fictions was well ingrained in the public mind.

But Training was fond of bringing the staff together, 300 people in a 270-seat hall, for this conference or that presentation, a seminar here, a briefing there. Never longer than a fast ninety minutes, the gatherings figured in Training's "unitary identity" strategy, a product of the best available sociometric and sociodynamic models. And an update briefing on the latest information on "T.C.," as Anglish slang rendered it, was as good an excuse as any.

The briefing was brisk and well organized. The lecturer, a polished presenter, recalled the relevant astronomical history, with the big Publook imager above him providing three-dimensional visuals. Listening idly as he watched the pioneers watching the show, Tidwell absorbed some details to which he hadn't attended during any previous exposure.

One of the nearest naked-eye stars, Tau Ceti had apparently been singled out early as a prime candidate for, in order, terrestrial planets, intelligent life, and Diaspora colonization. The first question was settled last, with the Hawking Space Telescope finally confirming seven planets in orbit around the G-class yellow star shortly after it went into operation in 2028.

An optimist could have taken a bet on the question of intelligent life more than a century ago, as the star had been a target of Frank Drake's unsuccessful OZMA, the first radio-based SETI search. Every extrasolar study since had yielded the same negative result. And that included the ongoing Allied-sponsored studies employing the big scopes on *Einstein*, the new U.N. research station in polar orbit around the Sun.

Nowhere in the sky had they found the handiwork of intelligent life. Nowhere but on Earth had they found the signature of biological systems, past or present. Life, it seemed, was precious and rare, and the universe a lonelier place than many had once believed. Every indirect evidence, every reasoned analysis, said that *Memphis* might find a Venus, a Jupiter, if they were lucky a Mars or Titan, but no lush garden worlds, no alien Earth.

"We'll go to Tau Ceti with a pocketful of options," said the lecturer, "and write our own story as we go. If we find an interesting planet with an unfriendly climate, we might establish a research colony of a few hundred volunteers and then continue on. If the parameters are marginal, we could found a terraforming colony of up to a thousand inhabitants before leaving.

"And if they're downright agreeable, we'll likely all go down, keeping *Memphis* in orbit as a lifeboat for a few dozen years until a new generation comes along to carry on where we left off. Because you can be sure that some of them will inherit our wanderlust, and you can be just as sure they'll think we're as stuffy and settled as some of us consider *our* parents." Laughter rippled through the room, self-knowing. "And they'll have us as proof that it can be done. Won't *that* be a moment to remember, when the first colony sends out its own colony ship?"

The question was answered by a swell of appreciative applause. Waiting it out, the lecturer smiled, nodded acknowledgment, and gave the thumb-in-fist salute. In a heart's breath, the applause doubled, and scattered members of the audience came to their feet.

"I want to leave you with the best new picture of Tau Ceti, which we received from *Einstein* just this morning," the lecturer continued as the applause faded. Above him, the Publook offered a dramatic image of a ghostly yellow star matted with the shadowy disk of one of its orbiting worlds.

"The best so far," he said, as the applause picked up again, at first scattered, growing as he continued into an almost tribal drumming of hands. "But there'll be better, and they'll come from us. No one will know Tau Ceti better than we will.

"I'm glad for the pictures Starwatch feeds us. It's amazing what additive digitizers and enhancers can do with a few photons captured ten light-years from their origin."

He paused and swept the room with his smile. "But I'm looking forward to seeing Tau Ceti for myself, without benefit of technology. And if wishes are horses, some morning I'll get to see it rise over a world that never knew life until you and I and the rest of the ten thousand arrived to make it our home." He stepped down from his dais, signaling the end of the assembly, as cheers and whoops and defiant cries punctuated the fevered ovation.

How gently he plucked their strings, Tidwell thought as he sat in his seat, politely applauding. *Yet how strongly they respond.* Just a few months ago, Tidwell would not have wondered at the scene. He would have written it off to passionate emotion and a skillful orator—no more mysterious than a preacher exhorting his flock, or a revolutionary inspiring his followers. No different.

We shall be delivered. The message was the same. And perhaps the passions were also the same. A ready well of courage, of commitment, waiting to be drawn on. Missionary zeal, waiting for a moment in time. Had the speaker spoken knowingly of inheriting a wanderlust or merely reached for a resonant idiom? No matter. The idiom recurred in the words of many speakers.

There is only one history, but there are many historians. Where was the truth written? The fire was lit. Where did it burn? In the hearts of men? Or in the cold nucleic chemistry of their cells?

Floating in and out of consciousness, Tidwell heard a sound in the hall and then at the open doorway. He was asleep enough to be puzzled, awake enough not to startle. Looking toward the sound, he saw a moving shadow, heard a breeze, or was it a whisper? The door swung shut with a hiss.

"Who's there?" he asked, rising to his elbows.

"It's me, Thomas." Softly, a woman's voice.

The shadow became a shape alongside the bed. The breeze carried the faint scent of flowers and something more to Tidwell's nostrils. "Miss—Malena—I am—"

A match flared in her hand, showing him the young girl's face. The black chemise she wore showed him more, even in the flickering light. She touched the match to the wick of a stout red candle, then set the candle on the end of Tidwell's trunk, which he had pressed into service as a nightstand.

He stared, and she smiled. "You told me to try and shock you."

"I—"

The airchair's mounting bar silently telescoped upward and out over the bed, and Malena reached up and gracefully lifted herself onto the bed beside him. Her hand touched his hip, scalding him through the light sheet. "Have you ever made love with a woman like me?"

"No," he said, too dumbfounded to challenge the premise of the question.

"Well," she said with a flame-lit twinkle in her eyes, "I may not be as agile as some, but I'm not fragile, and everything else is just as you'd expect. I like to touch and be touched," she said, her fingertips moving, burning a line across his abdomen. "I'll need to hold on to you or the bed or my bar when I'm on top, or I won't have any leverage. But we can take that as it comes."

He reached out and caught her hand, firmly but not harshly. "Malena, this is—I'm afraid you expect too much from me."

She brought his hand to her mouth and bit the ball of his thumb. Startled, he flinched and pulled his hand free, not in pain, but from the sudden charge of sexual energy, so alien and unfamiliar now.

"Please," he said, "it has been years—"

"I know," she said. She reached up for the bar again, and a moment later she was no longer beside him, but astride him, straddling his waist, the sheet still between them like a frail chaperone.

His breath caught, his hands shook. "Malena, please—you are a lovely girl. But how can I—you cannot understand the difficulty—"

Clinging to the bar with one hand for balance, she reached forward and pressed her other hand over his heart. She closed her eyes, as though listening intently, as though taking his measure.

"Let it back into your life," she said gently, opening her eyes. "You've waited long enough, invented enough fears. You don't have to hold yourself apart, Thomas. You have a right to permit yourself pleasure."

What door she had thrown open he did not know, but he suddenly felt naked before her, and panic began to rise in his chest. She sensed it in an instant and caught his face in her hands.

"Just be with me," she said gently, making him meet her eyes. "Just be here and let go of the rest. It will be all right."

"I don't know if I can—"

"Of course we can," she said, touching a finger to his lips and sitting back with a little smile.

Tidwell closed his eyes and sighed away his quailing, then looked up and beheld her in the candlelight. "You *are* lovely," he said.

"Thank you," she said with a hint of a blush. Purposefully, almost theatrically, she slipped the thin straps of her garment off her shoulders, one at a time. A fetching wriggle, and her chemise slid down to bunch about her waist, baring her young breasts, her upturned nipples. Tidwell swallowed his breath as he admired her.

"Do you like them?" she asked softly.

His drawn breath an anticipatory sigh, Tidwell confessed, "Yes."

Malena leaned forward, propping herself on her hands on either side of his shoulders, and lowered herself down to kiss him. Her lips were soft, yielding, melding, her taste the fresh-sweet peppermint of a too-recent brushing or candy.

"If you touch them, I can enjoy them, too," she said as she broke away from the kiss.

By then, Tidwell had caught enough of her playfulness that he could take it as an invitation, not a critique. "You did warn me you would expect that," he said, and reached for her.

Cooing happily as he caressed her nipples, Malena slid her body backward a few inches, until the bulge of his growing erection was trapped beneath her. She rocked her hips, rubbing herself against him, until the thin fabric barrier was velvet-slippery with their wetness, until Tidwell rose up, tore the sheet away, and took Malena to her back in an adolescent rush.

That was the first time: affirmation for her, release for him. The second time, with the knifelike edge of need gone for both of them, was a more leisurely, more playful ballet. Climbing a gentler curve of sensuality, fingers and mouths exploring, they became truly lovers. Her touch was new on his body and knowing on her own, their bodies sweat-slick in the heat, the humid air.

And though a second orgasm was beyond him, a second erection was not. When she straddled and rode him, leaning on his chest with one hand, being close to her and feeling the sensuality radiating from her was like being an old cat soaking up a spring sunbeam. When her body shook and clutched and she cried out her pleasure, his body was indistinguishable from hers, and he was part of what they made together, drawing from it a peace almost as profound as hers.

"You see," she said, blowing out the candle and snuggling against him, "I knew it would be all right."

And it was. But it could not last. When the moment was passed, the connection broken, all the thoughts which had been driven away while he lived in that moment, in a world of senses and sensation, returned to him. Joining them was an uncertain flavor of guilt and confusion, the deception which stood between him and the young woman in his arms tainting the contentment he might otherwise have felt.

"You're still troubled," she said, disappointed, as they cuddled together, legs entangled, her cheek on his chest. "I wanted to take that away from you."

Tidwell smiled in the darkness, wry and sad, as he stroked her hair reassuringly with his aged fingers.

"You took me away from it, at least for a while," he said. "And even that is more than I would have thought anyone could do."

CHAPTER 19

—|CCA|—

". . . the illusion of purpose."

WONDERS UPSTAIRS, SAID THE SIGN AT STREET LEVEL.

It seemed an outlandish claim for such an unprepossessing structure—a barnlike two-story wood frame building on a commercial street ten blocks from the Rice University campus. Downstairs was the Small Planet Grocery, a busy food and drug co-op which seemed to have an exemption from every licensing law and packaging code. Above, under the gambrel roof, was Wonders.

Daniel Keith recognized on first sight that the three-hundred-seat club was organically one with the co-op below—that is, Spartan, quaint, and inexplicably successful. Everything that wasn't handmade seemed secondhand. Half the seating was comprised of unpadded wooden benches, the other half of uncomfortable plastic chairs packed too closely together.

Most surprising, the only performance support was a twelve-channel sound system and an autospot. There was no net feed, no audio optimizer, no prompter—to say nothing of such cutting-edge technologies as a SyncScreen or harmonizer. But, as Keith learned when he editorialized aloud, that state of affairs was the result of the owner's philosophy, not his poverty.

"What fun is it if there's nineteen layers of insulation between me and the performer?" snorted Bill "Papa" Wonders, he of the great white beard like an Elizabethan ruffled collar. "That's like putting a tourist in a six-axis harness and a thrill-ride helmet and calling him a gymnast. My musicians work without a net."

The audience had somewhat better support: A little bar and

175

food counter in a glass-walled annex sold bottled drinks, light polypep, and a smattering of desserts—all of the crunchless variety, out of consideration to the performers.

But it was the music, not the menu, which filled the seats in Wonders at fifteen dollars per, six nights a week. Techjazz, English vocal, electric filk, revival rock, antitonal—everyone agreed that Papa Wonders had eclectic tastes. Most agreed that he also had good taste.

Which is why only Tuesdays were free for sampling new performers, two on a split bill, an hour set each with a break between. Tonight, the poster in Wonders's narrow stairway read:

Tuesday
December 20
8 P.M.
CHRISTOPHER McCUTCHEON
Traditional Guitar
✛✛✛
BONNIE TEVENS & AMBIKA
Synth Moods

At a quarter to eight, Keith slipped into the little room that served as the performer's warm-up room and found Christopher bending over his instrument with surgical concentration.

"What's up, guy?"

"Broke a string."

"Ah. Better here than on stage, eh?"

"Better," Christopher agreed. "How are things outside?"

"Greg has the recorders all ready to roll. The multi is audience center, fifth row, so he can do splits on your fingering, and the tank camera is front row left. And he's doubling sound with a digital MIDI."

Christopher shook his head. "God. He really went overboard."

"You ask a techie to help, you let them do it their way," Keith said with a shrug. "Nobody's going to think it's strange."

"No? Fifty thousand dollars of hardware and fifty people in the audience?"

"Says who? The room's filling up nicely. I think it'll be close to full."

Christopher was taken aback. "Really. Bonnie and Ambika must have a following."

Keith shook his head. "If they do, they're gonna have to stand in the back. There's a good dozen archies out there, and at least half the other faces look familiar. Looks like word got out around the center."

"That Greg's doing, too?"

Grinning, Keith said, "Well, not exactly. I didn't think you'd mind a friendly audience, after all the work you've been banking. And with graduation Friday and winter holiday coming up this weekend, I didn't have to twist any arms. We even got a few out from Noonerville."

Christopher sat back, the neck of the guitar held loosely between his knees, and looked sideways up at his friend. "Thanks, Daniel," he said. "I don't mind. I just hope I'm up to it."

"Just have some fun," Keith said. "They'll enjoy it if you do." He nodded. "You'd better finish with that."

"It's tuned," said Christopher. "You know, I've never done a whole set with just the Martin before. But that's what Bill asked for."

"High time," Keith said. "All that synth fill and bangbox stuff is for cowards."

"Who told you to say that?"

"Papa Bill did."

"He would." Christopher's expression darkened. "Just to save me from looking—I don't suppose Loi or Jessie—"

"Sorry. No," Keith said. "Not unless they came in while I've been in here."

Tight-lipped, Christopher shook his head. "I didn't expect them."

"Still at war?"

"Trenches and mortars. They won't pick a new counselor, I won't go back to the old one. We lob words back and forth at each other a couple times a day."

"Bad juju. But save it for later," Keith said, glancing at the clock behind Christopher. "Five minutes. I'm going to get out of here and let you collect yourself."

"Yeah."

"You all right?"

"Nervous," confessed Christopher.

"Nervous is good, I hear."

"I'm not used to playing for people who're there to listen instead of to get laid."

"If it'll make you feel better, I can try to get laid."

A laugh broke through the nervousness. "Oh, gee, Dan, it's awfully nice of you to offer, but I couldn't ask you to do that." "Sure you could," Keith answered with a grin. "Anything for a buddy. Break a string, huh?"

An hour alone on stage can be an instant or an eternity. For Christopher McCutcheon that night, it was an eternity, and Daniel Keith's heart ached for him.

The worst of it was that it was no one's fault but Christopher's. Papa Wonders kept his introduction low-key and discreet, careful not to oversell his inexperienced opening act or splash Christopher with the taint of Allied Transcon. And the friendly crowd gave Christopher a warm reception as he came down the aisle. The portents were all good. All he had to do was rise to the moment.

But when Christopher went to mount the small stage at the narrow end of the hall, he stumbled and nearly fell, cracking his guitar sickeningly against the steps. Collecting himself, he crossed to the stool at center stage and worriedly inspected his instrument.

"Is there a luthier in the audience?" he murmured, almost to himself, as he fingered a spot on the edge of the body. Finally satisfied, he looked up and out at the audience. "Good thing I don't have to walk and play guitar at the same time."

The honeymoon was still in effect; the weak joke got a stronger response than it deserved. Keith could only imagine what it felt like to look out from there and see more than two hundred people looking back at you expectantly.

"Anyway, thank you for the welcome. I'm going to try to give you about six hundred years of music in about sixty minutes," he went on, speaking quickly, "so I won't waste too many of those minutes talking. Just sit back and let me drive the time machine. And remember, if the scenery gets dull, you can always take a nap for a hundred years or so."

The laughs were noticeably weaker for the second jest. They had come to be entertained, and Christopher was parading his self-doubt before them like an anxious youth drafted for a recital before the relatives. His shaky confidence was understandable, but letting it show was a mistake.

So was the first number, a movement from the Bach cello suites, though Christopher forgot to announce it as such. Elegant and coldly precise, it seemed to Keith to steal the energy and enthusiasm from the room. It did not matter that Christopher played it well. The audience settled back into show-me mode, and though that was what Christopher had asked for, Keith wondered if he would be able to bring them back up to the higher pitch when he wanted.

If he wanted. Keith studied Christopher's face carefully, trying to read his emotions. It wasn't easy. Christopher rarely looked up, rarely made eye contact beyond the front edge of the stage. It occurred to Keith that perhaps Christopher was so uncomfortable with the audience that he preferred them at a distance, that he had to hold them down to hold himself together.

Ah, Chris, what are you doing here? Why did you let yourself in for this?

At the end of the Bach, the applause was solidly polite, but nothing more. Barely acknowledging the audience, Christopher introduced the next number as an Irish reel, and immediately launched into another instrumental. This one was up-tempo, energetic, and, to Keith's ears, monotonously repetitive.

Even so, the audience was good-naturedly clapping, more or less in rhythm, when Christopher's fingers seemed to forget their place. Though he recovered from the muff, he couldn't conceal it, and when the tune was done there was as much talk as applause. All around him, Keith could hear the registers falling in place, click-click-click. Whose idea was this? Say, where do you want to go afterward? What time is it, anyway? I think I'll go get another beer—

Come on, Chris, just look out here and sing to me, goddammit, Keith urged silently. *Pick a pair of pretty eyes and sing to them. You can't pretend we're not here.*

But Christopher did just that, through two more instrumental numbers. It seemed he did not have enough confidence to win their confidence, or enough concentration to survive being conscious of where he was. And so he withdrew from them, into himself, as though he were alone in his room.

Secure in that place, he played well, tight-jawed and sure fingered. But to get there, he sacrificed all emotional rapport with what had started out as an easy room. *You're a musician, not a performer, Chris my friend,* Keith thought sadly. *And you should have known.*

Halfway through his set, Christopher won back a few jury points with a bizarre story-song full of flashy harmonics, called "All Along the Watchtower." He immediately lost half the gains with an endless and mostly incomprehensible twentieth-century love song involving, as near as Keith could figure, a man, a woman, and a taxi.

His one "contemporary" number, the gloomy AIDS lament "Walls Between," was marred by a memory lapse that stretched out painfully until someone called out the next line from the audience. By that point, Papa Wonders was looking at his watch with an expression that did not promise any return invitations for the man struggling on stage.

And then something curious happened to that man, a kind of transformation. It was as though, knowing how poorly he had done, he suddenly felt no pressure. And he raised his head. He looked out into the room, looked around the audience. And he spoke to them the way Christopher would.

"One more and we're out," he said. "This is the song I really came here to do. I wrote the chorus almost six years ago, when I was still living on the Coast and hearing a lot from my father—none of it good—about the Diaspora Project. The funny thing was, even though I wrote this song for him, he still hasn't heard it. It never seemed quite right or quite good enough. Actually, it turns out, the problem was it wasn't quite finished. It wasn't until last night that I realized there was a verse missing. I like it better now. My father wouldn't, which means that maybe you will."

He began to play, simple chords, brisk and rhythmic, a cross between sea chantey and Irish folk song. The preamble was short, and for the first time that night, when he opened his mouth it was to sing *to* them, not *for* them:

> *I was sixteen years and I knew no fears*
> *When three ships' keels were laid*
> *And from the words of Captain Lee*
> *Sweet promises were made*
>
> *Come with me, you'll be flying free*
> *Living in the stars*
> *If you cast your stake and say you'll take*
> *The caravan to Antares*

Christopher sang the first few verses with an innocence, his voice shining with the bright joy of the song's narrator, strong with the narrator's bold confidence as his youthful dreams come

true. Christopher sang of a glorious sailing, a true cause, a steady
course, and they sang the refrain with him:

> Look at me, I'm flying free
> Living in the stars
> Cast my stake and said I'd take
> The caravan to Antares

As quickly as that, the audience—or at least the sizable portion from AT-Houston—was with him, caught up at last by
something that touched them in a familiar place. Though the
song was a romance in a fictional world, they saw, or thought
they did, past the disguise. Click-click-click. *He's singing about
us. He's talking about me.*

Keith watched with clinical detachment, knowing the turn
which was to come. And as Christopher's voice became harder
and the verses darker, the narrator battered by disappointments,
disillusionment, the faces of those around him began to be etched
by resistance, even anger.

They don't want to hear it, Keith thought. *You can't tell them
that it won't all be wonderful.*

When Christopher sang of a ship destroyed between the stars,
he struck them with a body blow. When he sang of hopes dashed
by worlds too harsh and too alien, of the survivors wearily
searching for a place that might be home, the chorus they had
so eagerly taken up had turned on them, its words now cynical
and mocking.

> My son was born on a sunless morn
> In the silent depths of space
> What his life will be I can hardly see
> In this hellish prison place
>
> Twelve worlds we've logged and the best was fogged
> With a filthy poison stew
> There's a year to go but today we'll know
> If the next world on might do
>
> Look at me, I'm flying free
> Living in the stars
> And I curse the day that I said I'd join
> This caravan to Antares

The solo riffs that followed had an anger that matched the words. Christopher wrung from the instrument and himself a fury of sound, all ringing strings and hammered notes. He forgot the audience once more, but this time they were with him, whether caught by disbelief or pain.

One crashing chord, and there was a moment's silence. When Christopher began again, the instrument muted, his voice cleansed of the anger, once more soft with innocence, strong with confidence, as he sang the new verse, the son's verse:

> *My father died on Alcestis Five*
> *My mother stayed on Pern*
> *Where we left a throng four hundred strong*
> *Its mysteries to learn*
>
> *And the Nina's docked in Kepler's lock*
> *Round the icy planet Hoth*
> *They'll warm the air and they'll seed the ground*
> *And build another Earth*
>
> *But there's worlds to know and it's time to go*
> *I was born to roam the stars*
> *And my crew has sworn that we'll carry on*
> *With the caravan to Antares*

With those few words, he gave them back their illusion, gave the struggle a purpose. And they threw their emotional arms around him and thanked him with an accolade that threatened to lift the slats from the club's wooden rafters. Keith saw tears on more than one cheek, felt the tightness in his own throat as he clapped and cheered.

Christopher himself seemed drained, overwhelmed. He stood and lifted his hand to them, but his expression was pained, and he did not stay long on stage. The trip down the aisle to the warm-up room had the smell of a panicky flight.

Keith slipped out into the aisle and followed him inside.

"Terrific," he said, clapping his friend on the shoulder. "You really got them with that one. A good finish."

"It's a lie," Christopher said, slumping in a chair.

"What? Listen, they're still clapping. You've gotta go back out."

"You don't *understand*," Christopher exploded. "It was

completely cynical. I don't believe a word of it. I thought they'd
cut my throat if I did it the way I always do. I wanted it in the
library. I wanted them to like me."

"Listen. They do," Keith said "Go on back out."

"I don't have anything more," he said hoarsely. "Tell Bill."

"Jesus, Chris—are you sure?"

"I just want to be alone. Can you be a friend and keep people
out for a few minutes?"

"Well—I guess," Keith said uncertainly, knitting his brows
in puzzlement. "Chris—"

"Please. Just get out."

Keith frowned, shrugged, and slipped out through the door.
The lights were already coming up, the audience getting up and
milling. He lingered in front of the door, winking and waving
to friends as they passed by in the throng, catching a thumbs-
up from Greg, who was hunched over the replay screen. Keith
decided he must look official: Someone asked if he could see
the guitar; someone else wanted to know if "Caravan to Antares" had been published. Both were disappointed that the answer was no.

Then he saw a face in the crowd that he had not noticed
before, a face he had not expected to see.

"Good evening, Mr. Keith," said Tidwell when he had drawn
close. "That last song was recorded?"

"As far as I know."

"Have a copy sent to Edkins in Culture. The young man is
inside?" Tidwell asked, nodding in the direction of the door.

"Yes—"

"I want to talk to him."

"Can you give him a minute? Chris is a bit wrung out."

"I understand that."

Keith hesitated. "He's an archie, in Building 16."

"So I understand. Is there a point?"

"You can catch him at your convenience—tomorrow morning, say—"

"Thank you. I would prefer to talk to Mr. McCutcheon now."

Keith swallowed, nodded reluctantly, and stepped aside. "He
doesn't know who you are," he added.

"Then I'll tell him," Tidwell said, and smiled a tight smile.
"Then he will know whom to blame for the intrusion."

• • •

Almost a third of the seats were empty when the lights went down for Bonnie Tevens and Ambika. Daniel Keith watched from behind the annex glass as they took the stage. Their high-gloss black clothing dazzled in the spotlight, but the sounds from their wind controllers were more subdued, aping a traditional flute (Bonnie) and oboe (Ambika).

Shortly, Greg emerged from the darkened club to join Keith at the window. "Where's Chris?"

"Gone," said Keith. "Dr.—Tom Grimes, one of the colonists, dragged him away." Tidwell had had, at most, a couple of minutes in private with Christopher before Ambika arrived and chased the two men from the dressing room. Christopher had little to say when he emerged, and his frame of mind was unreadable, except that he was obviously uncomfortable with the hail-fellow-well-met praise that swirled around him. He and Tidwell had left quickly, almost an escape.

"Is he coming back?"

"It didn't sound like it."

"Too bad," said Greg, rattling the plastic-cased chipdisks he held in one hand. "I made a couple of quick copies for him. Oh, well. I'm going to do some touch-up edits tonight, and he can have the whole banana tomorrow."

"Let me have one of those, then," Keith said.

"Sure. I can't break down until after the second set," the tech said, peering through the glass. "Are you staying?"

Keith patted the end of the guitar case which was leaning against the wall beside him. "I got custody of Claudia," he said. "A responsibility I'll be glad to be done with. I think I'm going to just run it past Chris's place and go on home. Unless you were really asking for help?"

Greg shook his head. "Sandy's staying, and that's all the extra hands I need. Take baby home."

Outside, a half dozen bodies were blocking the stairs as they shared a pep-pack. They made way for Keith to squeeze by, but only barely, and then went back to passing the stick and giggling. Keith headed down the street toward where his flyer waited.

Halfway down the block, his ears pricked up at the sound of quick, light footsteps behind him. Keith spun around, suddenly on alert, to find himself confronting a redheaded girl in a black leather jacket, short boots, and black jeans. In the streetlight, she was a black ghost with a sallow yellow face.

"You're not the singer," she said, her features contorting with surprise.

"No."

"Damn. Is he gone already?"

"I'm afraid so," Keith said, and started to turn away.

"Wait," she said. "You have to tell me something. He's a *Memphis* colonist, isn't he? He has to be."

"No," Keith said. "He's not." The denial was automatic and emphatic.

"But you're all from the Project, aren't you?"

That denial was automatic, too. "He's from Oregon. I'm from Illinois."

"I can read," she said, pointing toward his shirt.

Keith looked down to see his AT-Houston ID dangling from his shirt pocket. "Look—" he began, giving himself a mental mule-kick as he unpinned the badge.

"It's okay," she said quickly. "It wasn't any secret in there. And I'm a friendly."

"Look, ah—"

"Jinna."

"Jinna," he echoed. "Like I said, Chris is gone. I'm just playing porter for him. Sorry to disappoint you."

She took a step closer. "I'd really like to meet him. Couldn't you take me along where you're taking that?"

"Sorry. I can't help you."

Her voice shifted into a husky timbre. "I haven't given you a reason to yet."

"Look—"

"Yes—look," she said, opening her jacket. Underneath, she was naked—or nearly so. From her small rounded breasts to her slender waist she was heavily skin-painted, a feral jungle of flowers and vines intertwined with a sinuous green python. The snake's glowing eyes—a jeweled piercing through the left nipple, lit with its own light—argued for the painting being a permanent laser tattoo.

She let the jacket fall closed and stepped closer, within arm's reach. "Is that your flyer?" she asked "Take us up to a thousand and put it on auto. I'll give you a thank-you in advance."

Keith shook his head. "I don't think so."

She reached for his crotch, stroked the fabric over his bulge. "You ought to find out what you're turning down. Come on, step out of the light and I'll audition."

Annoyed at his own response, he pushed her hand away angrily. "What do you want from Chris? What do you think he can give you?"

"I just want to meet him. We're twins, inside. I could tell it when he sang. We want the same things. We hurt in the same places."

Keith studied her. "What was your prescreen score?" he asked, guessing.

She held her head defiantly high. "They didn't test for what I'm best at. And you're about to make the same mistake."

"We can't get you on board," Keith said bluntly. "Nobody can. No matter how hot a fuck you are."

"I hear there were sixteen stowaways on *Ur*."

"Oh? Did you look that up on DIANNA?"

"You know it wouldn't be there. They don't want anyone to know. But I have a friend who knows someone who got on. His parents get dispatch mail every month, but they're not allowed to tell anyone, or Allied will cut them off. So there has to be a way."

"If there is, I don't know it," Keith said. In fact, there had been twenty-eight stowaways, most of them Takara construction crew or orbital staff. The irrepressible rumors were right, but they had the story all wrong. "I'm sorry, Jinna. I know it hurts. I'm hoping for *Knossos*, myself."

"I just want to meet him. To tell him I understand how he feels."

"You don't know how he feels," Keith said sharply. "Songs are stories. Stories are lies."

Her face took on a desperate cast. "You don't have to take me anywhere. Just give me his address, so I can call him. So *he* can decide if he wants to meet me. I'll still do you." She pulled her jacket open again, and the eyes glowed at him.

Keith paused, considered. "No. I don't think he needs that right now," he said, backing away into the night. "Good night, Jinna." He gestured with his free hand. "But don't read me wrong, that is one *truly* special snake."

CHAPTER 20

-|UAC|-

"... chance and fate ..."

FOR MALENA GRAHAM, IT HAD BEEN AN ADVENTURE, A HAPPY floating party. Leaving the Allied Transcon compound for the first time, riding the tram toward the city of towers, exploring the unfamiliar streets between the Rice station and the club—after six weeks cooped up in the training pressure cooker, it was all delightfully, refreshingly new.

To be sure, the Noonerville nannies weren't happy about seeing pioneers going into the city, but they did not try to forbid it. Instead, they settled for pressing locator bands on Malena and the others and extracting from them a promise to steer clear of the screamer clubs and the North End neighborhoods.

Tipped that morning by a friendly fitness instructor, Malena had industriously recruited four others for the outing, two from center staff and two other colonists, including, to her surprise, Thomas Grimes. She had half expected she would have to twist Grimes's arm, and had been unsure that she had a good enough grip to succeed.

There had been no reprise of their lovemaking of a few nights before, nor even much acknowledgment in eyes or words that the encounter had even taken place. At times, the older man had seemed uncomfortable, even embarrassed, in her presence. She had meant to press the issue and find out what was in his mind, but so far he had managed to dodge an accounting.

But when she called him at midday and told him what was happening, Thomas volunteered, "If you're going, I would like to come along," even before she could ask. That was a pleasant surprise. She hoped it meant that he had worked out whatever conflict he had over what had been, for her at least, a warm and tenderly erotic time. And though the outing was not really a date, when she dressed, she chose her clothing—outer and under—with an eye to pleasing him, and a thought to how the evening might end.

Though Thomas had been quietly reserved all night, he had hovered close by her in a familiar, if very proper, way. He sat with her on the tram, paid for her wine and chocolate cheesecake, rearranged the chairs so that she was not condemned to sit in the back of the auditorium. And through it all, he paid almost no attention to Isa, the sloe-eyed medical technician who seemed to be drawing everyone else's glances.

A gentleman, she thought. *How nice to be with a gentleman.* When the lights went down and the painfully nervous young musician stumbled his way on stage, Malena had reached for Thomas's hand, and though he started at first, they had watched most of the set with fingers entwined.

But when the rousing last number was over, Thomas had excused himself and disappeared into a confusion of bodies too dense for Malena to follow him, even with her eyes. And now the intermission had come and gone, the music was starting again, and the seat next to Malena Graham was still empty.

"I've lost track of Thomas," she said, leaning toward Isa. "Can you see him anywhere?"

Isa craned her head and looked back toward the annex. "No," she said after a few moments. "Why, are you worried about him?"

"I'm just confused."

"Did he say he was coming back?"

"He said, 'Excuse me, there's something I need to do.' Or something like that."

"Maybe he got caught in his zipper. Do you want me to check the dunnaken?"

"Oh—I suppose not. It seems silly."

"Maybe not. He's old. Old people get sick. Or maybe he said the wrong thing to the wrong person," Isa said, rising. "You never know, in a strange place. I'll give a look."

"You'll miss the music—"

Isa glanced toward the stage and grimaced. "That's okay. I must not be in the mood."

• • •

The answer to the mystery was delivered by a stranger, a white-whiskered man wearing a yellow Wonders T-shirt—the uniform of the club employees. While Isa was gone, he appeared suddenly beside her and crouched down where she was sitting. "Excuse me. Are you Malena?"

She looked up, trying to see his face in the dim light. "Yes. Why?"

"I have a message for you from Thomas?" The messenger seemed unsure of himself.

"Right, Malena. What?"

"He asked me to tell you that he had to leave, that he was very sorry, and that he would see you back at the center."

She gaped. "When did you talk to him?"

"Three or four minutes ago. I was on the counter, so I couldn't get up here until now."

Isa returned at that point, creating a traffic jam in the aisle.

"Was he sick? Did he say why he had to leave?" Malena asked.

"He didn't look sick to me. He looked anxious. Or in a hurry."

"Was he alone?"

"I didn't see anyone with him."

"Sssh," someone nearby hissed.

Malena glared in the direction of the sound. "I can't believe he just left."

"I'm sorry. He just asked me to make sure you got the message." His face apologetic, the messenger backed out of the aisle and retreated, making room for Isa to move past.

"He's not there," she said.

"Sssh!"

"I know," she said, catching Isa's sleeve and pulling her into her chair. "They just told me he left."

From Ambika's wind synth came the startling sound of a hunter's horn, a ripping echo in the hard-walled room.

"Left? What a prick. What do you want to do?"

"I want to pop him and then eat something chocolate."

Isa grinned. "Can't do either of those here, unfortunately."

"Then why don't you leave?" suggested the complaining voice.

"Well—I don't think I really want to sit here for another hour listening to this."

"Sounds good to me," said Isa. "This is college city. Ladies Night Out. We'll go find some fun on our own."

"Hooray," said their annoyed neighbor.

"What about the others?"

"I'll check." Isa leaned forward and whispered in the ear of the man in front of her. After a few side whispers, she sat back. "They're going to stay."

At that point, Ambika's instrument began barking and baying like a pack of hounds. Malena rolled her eyes. "What is it they say about those things? An ill wind that nobody blows good?"

Malena's syrupy drink sparkled with glittery stars and an orbiting comet-shaped glow bright enough to cast flickering shadows on the table.

"It's not fair," she said, holding the tall glass at eye level and staring into it.

"What's not?" asked Isa, looking past her toward the couch-lounge, where some sort of holoshow was under way.

"Oh, what a tangled web we weave, when first we practice to conceive."

Isa smiled. "Oh. *That.*"

Gulping down a swallow, Malena tipped her glass and studied the changing dynamics. "It's in the glass, not the drink," she pronounced, setting it down. "Here's what's unfair. You can have any man you want, and you may not even be any good in bed. I'm terrific and I just about have to knock them down with my chair to get them to notice me."

"Forget Grimes. He's a prick."

"No, he isn't," she said, shaking her head. "If he was a prick I wouldn't care. He's sweet. He's a gentleman. And he did this to me anyway."

"Then there must be a good reason, and you'll find out what it is tomorrow."

"I know what the reason is. The reason is me," Malena said. "I don't get it. What do men want, anyway? Besides you."

"Men want sex, power, and to live forever," Isa pronounced.

"So do I. That doesn't explain it."

"Men want to plant their seed in strong healthy women who'll raise their kids without asking too much from them in return."

"Now we're getting to it," said Malena. "They look at you and they say, 'Oooh, good genes.' Not to mention, 'I'll bet I could get it up with her.' They look at me and say, 'Next, please.' '' She emptied her glass and placed it on the reorder disk.

"Just the ones who're running on autopilot. And it's no favor to me to have that kind sniffing around."

"Gives you the prick of the litter." She giggled drunkenly at her own joke.

"Not really. Because maybe the one I want is the runt with a brain, and he's liable to take one look at the mob he has to fight through to reach me and write it off. I think you're better off than I am, really."

The drink droid had trundled by, and Malena's glass was again full of glittering stars. "Do you really want the runt?" she asked, raising her eyebrow and her drink.

Isa smiled coyly. "Sometimes."

"And?"

The smile widened. "And sometimes I want the big strong no-brain who'll fuck me till I faint. So sue me."

"Ha. I thought so."

"It's not my fault."

"No," Malena said, swirling the stars in her glass. "I don't suppose it is. So men want sex, power, and to live forever. What do women want?"

"Deep down?"

"When we're in no-brain. Screaming genes."

"You don't know?"

"I thought you were an expert. I'm asking an expert."

Isa thought for a moment. "Women," she said finally, "want babies and security."

"Ugh. Can I be a man instead?"

"You said you wanted to know."

"I take it back."

"You could argue with me."

Malena sipped at her drink. "Not when you're right."

"Am I?"

"Aren't you? It's the same game now as it was a hundred years ago, a thousand years ago. Nothing changes. We want relationships. They want friction. We want commitment. They want freedom. We want to make nests. They want to carve notches."

"In words of one syllable: We want to get them, they want to have us."

"Q.E.D."

"You left out one important fact."

"What's that?"

"When it suits us, we can be just as shallow as the next man."

Malena raised her nearly empty glass. "To mindless recreational sex."

"Say that louder and you'll have plenty of men over here."

"To vibrators I have known and loved," Malena declaimed, wobbling in her chair.

Isa laughed easily. "You know, sometimes I think the natural partner for a woman is another woman."

"Sometimes I think so, too," said Malena. "Except women's energy is all wrong for me." She paused. "Do you think Bonnie and Ambika are lovers?"

"Probably."

"What do *they* want, deep down?"

Isa pursed her lips and considered, then smiled cattily. "Talent."

He came to the table while Isa was off dancing—dancing with a round-faced woman from the next table. The cues Malena had missed had been overheard and pursued by another.

"Hi."

Malena peered up at him. Tall, clean-faced, dark-eyed, a wrestler's build. "No, I will not pretend you're an old friend. When she comes back, you can introduce yourself," she said. " 'Pleased t'mount ya, miss,' oughta do. But you have to fuck her till she faints."

He slid easily into the empty seat. "Been drinking Starshines, haven't you?" he said with a gentle smile.

"I have, until the droid cut me off. So this is as silly and suggestible as I will get tonight. Enjoy it while it lasts," she slurred. "Now, about Isa. As far as I know, she is not a lesbian, just disillusioned. Like me."

"I really didn't want to meet your friend," he said. "I came over to talk to you."

She pointed to the airchair, sitting empty against the back wall, a meter away. "Before you get either of us excited, you should know that I go with that."

"I know," he said. "You were at the concert, weren't you? At Wonders."

"Until it got silly, and the dogs chased us away. Were you there?"

"I work there. In the annex, behind the counter. You came to hear Chris McCutcheon, then?"

"Proudly. One of our own." She lifted her drink. "These are fun even when the droid leaves out the kicker."

"He's a colonist, isn't he? I know you all were from the Project, but—"

"He is *not* a colonist," she pronounced firmly. "He is a shy little librarian with one good song to his name. Which, by the way, has been playing in my head all night. *Look at me, I'm flying free, swimming in the Starshine—*"

Her visitor sat back in the chair. "That's what I *told* them. Someone at the club said he was a colonist, but I was sure that they weren't allowed to leave the grounds."

"Then you were right for the wrong reason," Malena announced. "I am living proof that they do indeed let the animals out of the cage."

"Really?"

"Really. You see before you one of the Chosen. I would get up and bow but I can't—I'd fall down first, and how would that look?"

"I guess that rules out my asking you to dance," he said with a wry smile.

"Only if you want to dance standing up."

"That's the only way I know," he said apologetically.

"And you call yourself an educated man," she said. She squinted across the table at him. "I was right. You're cute. Why are you talking to me?"

"Because I like you."

"You do? The last man who said he liked me ran away the first chance he could."

"He was a fool."

"Yes, he was. Maybe you can help me. I'm taking a survey," she said, throwing her shoulders back and taking a deep breath. "Do you like my tits?"

He looked surprised, then smiled. "As far as I can tell."

"And if I were lying naked on top of you, would I have to talk you into touching me?"

"No."

She leaned forward and whispered conspiratorially. "Then why don't you take me home and fuck me till I faint?"

"Home to where? The center? Or my place?"

"Do you have an alarm?"

He smiled. "Of course."

She pressed the button of the homing pack through the fabric of her breast pocket, and the airchair came to life and edged between the tables toward her. "What's your name?"

"Evan."

"Evan. I'm Malena. Let's go make a mess of your bed."

Malena lay back in the passenger seat of the battered Ford Courier, her eyes heavy-lidded, her peasant skirt and ruffled blouse in a jumble on the floor at her feet. Only the lacy surprises she had worn for Thomas remained in place, if somewhat askew.

She had been surprised when Evan led her to the flyer, parked in an alleyway two blocks away from the speed bar. Expecting that he lived nearby, she had primed herself for quick gratification.

But she did not mind the ride, even though Evan had had little to say since they lifted off, even though it seemed to her that they had been in the air a long time and had left the city far behind. He had not made her wait, and his hands were warm and strong, his fingers knowing. Even with his attention divided between a car and a woman, he was keeping them both flying.

Presently, he began to neglect her in favor of the Courier, just as she got that falling-fast sensation in her gut, a sensation that was unpleasantly enhanced by the alcohol and polypep soup in her bloodstream. Before her distress could mount to a dangerous level, however, there was a slight bump and the hiss of a leaky landing coupler.

"Here we are," he said, and hopped out into the night. As he came around the flyer to her door, she struggled to a sitting position and peered out through the window. There were no lights, and the light of the waning moon betrayed no structures.

"Here where?" she asked as he opened the door.

"It's a surprise," he said.

"I have to get dressed," she said, reaching for her clothes. He reached faster and tossed them to the far side of the flyer. "There's no one here," he said with a grin.

"I need my chair, at least," she said, twisting sideways in her seat and smiling up at him.

His eyebrows flashed. "No, you don't," he said, suddenly

seizing her wrist and pulling her roughly from the flyer. She fell gracelessly to the ground, barking her bare legs on the door frame.

"Goddammit, what are you— Evan, stop!" she shrieked.

Ignoring her protest, he dragged her several meters across the stony hard-packed dirt, away from the flyer. He left her there for a moment, shaken and confused, while he returned to the flyer to shut the passenger door—killing the only light—and retrieve something from the trunk.

She watched, doing nothing, her mind barely grasping the danger she was in. She could not flee, she could not hide, and only if he were horribly careless could she overpower him. Her shockbox was in the pocket of her skirt, hopelessly out of reach. The only way out was through Evan—placating him, persuading him, somehow satisfying him. And she did not know what that would take.

"Evan, it can be good without being rough," she said as he approached her. Her voice was shakier than she had hoped it would be.

"Oh, I can't fuck you," he said, circling her, his tone sarcastic, his words taunting. "I'm sure I'm not good enough for one of the Chosen."

Scrabbling in the dirt, she twisted as he moved to keep facing him. It was then that she saw what he held in his right hand—a stout stick as long as his forearm and as thick as his thumb. Fear cleared the fog from her mind.

"We can do it right here, Evan," she cooed. *Come on, come on in, come close enough for me to reach you.* She tugged awkwardly at her skirts. "It's all right. Let's do it. I can make you feel wonderful."

He laughed. "You don't know yet who I am, do you? I didn't bring you out here to fuck you. I brought you out here to kill you."

The impossible words glanced off her, unprocessed and undigested. She stared at him dumbly.

"You think you get everything you want, don't you?" he went on, his voice now calm, his tone amused. "Blessed daughter of the Earth, touched by the gods. Little queen of time and space. What's so fucking special about you?"

He moved so suddenly she could barely see him, one quick step toward her, the stick raised high. She flung up an arm as the stick came down and there was a horrible sound, *crack-*

crack, like two saplings snapping, splintering, except the sound was wet and muffled and the saplings the twin bones of her forearm.

Malena cried out in shock, wondered for an instant why she felt no pain, and then screamed as the distorted arm fell limply into her lap and a hundred million nerve endings awakened from their shock. A warm wetness spread over her thigh, and she saw with horror that her skin had been laid open by the blow, as by a razor edge. Moaning, she looked up at him wonderingly.

"You don't look so special now," Evan said, hovering out of reach. "You look just as scared as any poor slob. I saw a guy hang himself by accident once. He had the same look on his face—like he was surprised to find out he could die. Funny, it was sex that got him in trouble, too."

"Please—"

"Please what? Please let you go? Please don't kill you? Are you hoping it bothers me to see you bleeding? Dream on, Malena dear. I want it to hurt. This is the end of your life, Chosen One. I want it to last forever."

With her good hand, Malena tried fruitlessly to staunch the flowing blood. "Oh, God—"

"Save it," he said coldly. "Don't even try. You can't talk me out of it. This isn't a lark. I didn't wake up this morning and say, 'Gee, what a great day to recycle some poor trot.' I've been ready for weeks. You're a gift, a pure sugar treat for a good boy."

"You're crazy!" she shrieked. "You're fucking crazy!"

"Thank you! I'd have been disappointed if you hadn't said that at least once." He leaned in closer to her. "But you're wrong. I'm not crazy. I just hate your guts."

His arm went up, the stick came down, and the razors sliced deep into her good shoulder. She did not have the breath to scream. Blood ran, spurted, streaking dusty skin. She could not lift either arm.

"No—"

"You still don't know who I am, do you?" he hissed. "I'm the leveler. I'm the collector of debts. I'm a soldier of the Earth. I'm the hands of Jeremiah, and you're the Chosen. *I* chose you. I chose you to die."

He whipped the stick in a blinding-fast sideways stroke, and she screamed as the side of her head exploded with thunder and fire. She spun away, collapsing into a quivering huddle, the web of light in her eyes fast fading.

An immeasurable moment later, the murderous dragon's tail came down once more, across the back of her neck, shattering the bones of her spine and the delicate tissues within. She jerked soundlessly. But it was only reflex, for whatever was life and consciousness, whatever was Malena Graham, was gone. All that remained was the slow death, the quiet transformation from delicate machine to dust.

CHAPTER 21

-|GAA|-

" . . . the greater good . . . "

THE MURDER OF MALENA GRAHAM WAS NEWS THAT WOULD NOT wait for morning, and so it was a short night for many in the Project family.

Hiroko Sasaki, on Takara to receive a deficiency report from the supervisory circle and tour the nearly completed *Memphis*, went directly from her suite to the transportation office to arrange a shuttle home.

Still wearing his striped pajamas, Edgar Donovan settled in his office node and began calling contacts in the media, even as he monitored the first fragmentary reports on *Newstime* and the black traffic on the private corporate net.

A shattered Thomas Tidwell, receiving special handling from Houston corpsec, shed his Thomas Grimes persona and fled to the quiet security of Halfwhistle by means of a corporate screamer.

Sleepy-eyed morale counselors and group dynamicists, huddled in a Building H conference room, debated whether to hold the pioneers over until the shock had been absorbed or to empty Noonerville early.

An unlucky senior facilitator headed for Virginia with an insurance check and the vain hope of shaping the Graham family's public posture.

And Mikhail Dryke, heart-weary and discouraged, came back to Houston from Prainha, feeling as though it were a pilgrimage of futility. Too late, again too late. In the two hours and forty minutes between the flash alert and Dryke's Celestron touching down on the complex's runway, both the primary and secondary reasons for that journey had evaporated.

The first, of locating Graham's killer, disappeared when Rangers from the Beaumont post forced down a Ford Firefly a few kilometers short of the Louisiana border, arresting one Evan Eric Silverman. The second, of determining whether Silverman had known Graham's status, vanished when he confessed—no, boasted—in his first interview that he had killed a colonist, calling Malena a "traitor" and himself a "martyr."

On hearing the latter, Dryke's fury was matched only by his feeling of impotence. It had been obvious for months that the pioneers were at risk from the more radical Homeworlders—if not, then why were their identities and movements so conscientiously concealed? Dryke had urged repeatedly that the training centers be made closed campuses. But he had been overruled by assorted management types, Sasaki included, for reasons which had nothing to do with security.

Better to make it unnecessary for them to leave than to forbid them, he was told. Better that they see the center as a refuge, not a prison—their fellows as friends, not inmates. Better that they choose to turn their back on a world that they've decided for themselves is unfriendly. Better for morale. Better for solidarity. Better for everyone.

Except Malena Graham.

By midmorning, when Dryke reached the Beaumont post, it was already clear that so far as Allied Transcon was concerned, the murder of Malena Graham was a public relations disaster.

Here was the grieving family standing in front of their home, a sobbing Mother Caroline declaring, "Our girl was stolen from us. We never wanted her to go," and Father Jack bitterly denouncing Allied Transcon for negligence—as if Graham had been some sort of teenage overnight camper.

Here were the world media, suddenly interested in the "tensions" between Allied and the Houston community, broadcasting inflammatory interviews with Diaspora opponents, complete with footage of the compound fences, patrol boats, and watch towers. And here was clean-faced clear-spoken Evan Silverman, being interviewed from his cell by a grimly earnest Julian Minor. Dryke sat in his vehicle in the post parking lot and watched on the skylink for as long as he could stand.

"What do you mean, don't cry for Malena Graham?" Minor

asked. "This is a young woman, her life in front of her, a courageous physically challenged twenty-year-old. And you dragged her off to the middle of nowhere in the middle of the night and beat her to death."

"I don't think I want you as my defense attorney, Julian," said a relaxed Silverman. "The truth is that Malena Graham was a thief and a traitor. She was a *Memphis* colonist, a partner in a quadrillion-dollar hijacking of the Earth's treasuries. She shares in the blame for every sin and excess committed by Allied Transcon over the last three decades."

"So you murdered her as a revolutionary statement."

"I executed a criminal for her crimes."

"Will that be your defense?"

"The courts are controlled by Allied's bedmates. They won't allow the truth to clutter up their rush to judgment. Which is why I'm talking to you."

"But I've talked to you before, haven't I?" asked Minor.

"What do you mean?"

"Aren't you Jeremiah?"

Dryke sat forward, riveted.

"No," said Silverman.

"You talk like the man who calls himself Jeremiah," pressed Minor.

"Jeremiah is the prophet," Silverman said, frowning slightly. "It shouldn't be a surprise if you hear the same words from his disciple."

"Is that what you call yourself? A disciple? Is this political or religious?"

"I'll let you apply the labels as you choose," Silverman said with a shrug.

"But you're trying to say that what you did is part of something bigger."

"It is."

"Were you under orders to murder Malena Graham?"

"Execute," corrected Silverman. "My hands are Jeremiah's hands. I do his work."

"Not any longer."

"There are ten thousand for Tau Ceti—ten thousand minus one. There are ten billion Homeworlders standing for the Earth. How can they think that they're safe from us? In that ten billion there are ten times ten times ten thousand who will gladly do what I've done."

"The cost—"

"We are many, and they are few. In a war of attrition, one of us for one of them is a victory. We'll cheerfully pay that price until the last of the ten thousand is gone."

Julian Minor was scoffing with his eyes. "Do you seriously think that you can announce a plan for this kind of mass murder and still expect to carry it out?"

"Jeremiah's soldiers are everywhere," said Evan Silverman with easy confidence, looking directly into the camera. "There's no place our enemies can go that we can't reach them."

Dryke had seen enough. "Log it for me. Kill the screen," he said, and the skylink went dark. But he did not move to leave the flyer.

For, listening to the interview, Dryke had finally understood the weight of discouragement that had settled on him that morning, that had taken him under as he sat on the edge of his bed, the fading images of a disturbing dream cross-channeled with the jarring sounds and images of the flash alert.

Now the dream came back. The siege had gone on forever. Each morning he walked the ramparts, reviewing the defenses and looking out at the broad grassy meadows where the enemy's campaign tents stood and campfires burned. Each morning Dryke found a post or two abandoned, a familiar face or two among the enemy, dead allies reborn as adversaries.

Then came a morning when he woke to find himself the last bowman on the ramparts. That was the morning the assault began in earnest—uncounted enemies attacking the fortress at a thousand points. And the last archer knew full well as he nocked his first arrow that neither will nor heart nor skill would count enough to carry the day.

Writ the chronicler on the day he died, Too few on the ramparts, too many outside—

Inside the post, Dryke was stopped at a security gatelock, then escorted to a Captain Norwood's office. He knocked on the door, then pushed it open.

The office was no more than half a dozen paces in any dimension. At one end, a man in a brown uniform sat behind a small boomerang desk, beneath a Scale 3 wallscreen. "Captain Norwood," Dryke said. "I'm Mikhail Dryke, Allied Transcon."

"You're late," Norwood said curtly, pushing back his posture chair and rising. He gestured past where Dryke was standing. "I understand you know Lieutenant Alvarez."

Stunned, Dryke turned to follow Norwood's gesture. A woman with a vaguely familiar face was seated there on a cushion couch.

"Mr. Dryke," said Eilise Alvarez. "I was just telling Captain Norwood about your personal contribution to the Martinez case."

A dozen replies passed in review of Dryke's wary censor before he finally spoke. "Then I'll have to make a point of telling him my side of it sometime," he said, looking back to Norwood. "I'm a bit confused. How are the Houston Transit Police involved in this?"

Norwood settled in his chair. "Lieutenant Alvarez is representing a special operations unit working on controlling civil unrest aimed at Allied Transcon and its personnel."

"We're also seeking transfer of the prisoner to our jurisdiction on commencement-of-crime."

"Which probably won't be granted," Norwood said, nodding. "Anyway, you both asked for briefings on the Graham case, so I thought I'd spare myself the repetition. I assume you don't object?"

"No," said Alvarez.

"No objection," said Dryke. He gave Alvarez a sideways glance as he took the free chair along the far wall.

"Fine." Norwood glanced down at the desktop, which had the muted gleam of a flat tank display. "Recorders on if you've got them. Victim, Malena Christine Graham of Great Bridge, Virginia, age twenty. Oh, and she was a crip, restricted to an airchair. According to witnesses, she was picked up by Evan Eric Silverman, twenty-eight, of Houston, at a bar called Magpie's on Old Spanish Trail about ten forty-five last night."

"Twenty December," Alvarez said quietly for the benefit of her recorder.

"Silverman took the girl to a field about three kilometers west of Magnolia, off State Route 1488, where he stripped her and beat her with a dragon's tail. That's a club with a pattern of razor edges embedded in the top third. Illegal as a weapon. Silverman had a license for his—apparently he's a juggler. Cause of death: You've got your pick until the coroner wraps up. Most likely the head injuries killed her before she bled to death. Time of death is twelve twenty-one A.M. That's the twenty-first," he added. "You want to see the evidence tape?"

"Yes," said Dryke.

"Is there any point?" asked Alvarez.

Norwood opened his hands in a gesture of uncertainty. "Not for me to say. I don't know what you're after."

"All right," said Alvarez. "Show it."

The assault had been savagely cruel, and the body was grossly disfigured. It was the same kind of mindless violence he had seen in the incident at the observation platform, but turned up one notch from brutality to butchery. Looking at the evidence video, Dryke could not even tell if the young victim had been attractive.

"Jesus. Did he do all that?"

"Not quite. When they found her, the fire ants were having their fill. It's a mercy she was dead." Norwood shook his head. "At least I hope she was dead."

When the recording ended, the lights came up. Alvarez was pale, but when Dryke raised an eyebrow in her direction, she shot a withering look back.

"That's about it at this point," said Norwood, who had never turned to watch the wallscreen. "Nothing I didn't have to release to the media, really. Frankly, I'm still not clear on what you're after. There's not much here to finesse."

"What about this 'Jeremiah's hands' business?" asked Dryke.

"He *has* been talking a lot, that's a fact," said Norwood. "You obviously caught his spotlight performances. I can't let any of his private showings leave the building, but I could set you up with a screen somewhere. Are you interested?"

"Yes. If you could arrange that when we're done, I'd appreciate it," Dryke said.

"What else is there to do?"

All that was left was all that there had ever really been—the quest for Jeremiah. "Silverman's home," Dryke said.

"Being searched and inventoried now."

"What about his comlogs, his library, his personals? There could be important information in them—information that could finally give us a chance to take apart the Homeworld network. I have access to technical experts who can disarm any security traps Silverman might have left."

"What are you suggesting?"

Shrugging, Dryke said, "Mutual cooperation—our expertise in exchange for access to whatever's dug out."

Norwood frowned and leaned back in his chair. "I don't see

what standing you have to ask for access to criminal evidence. And we have our own hackers and crackers.''

''If Silverman really is working with Jeremiah, I promise you, you'll need more than a password engine and a wipe mask to get into his file library,'' warned Dryke.

''We're not amateurs, Mr. Dryke. We do this all the time,'' Norwood said with evident annoyance. ''And again, I don't see how I can justify making you a partner in our investigation.''

''Can I inject something here?'' asked Alvarez.

''Go ahead,'' said Norwood.

''I'm looking at a work load of seventy-one open property crimes against Allied facilities—which may or may not involve Jeremiah or members of the Homeworld movement. Total damage and losses runs about fourteen million dollars,'' said Alvarez. ''Will that earn me a look at Silverman's personals?''

''Yah,'' said Norwood. ''We'll work with you on that.''

''Then you may as well let Mr. Dryke have it as well. We've got a co-op agreement with corporate security, and they'll see anything we see.''

Norwood cocked his head and pursed his lips. ''All right, Mr. Dryke,'' he said finally. ''Bring on your experts.''

''I'll go make the call.''

''Wait,'' said Norwood, turning to face his wallscreen. ''V-mail, forward till acknowledged: Norwood to Unit Six. We're going to get an outside assist on Silverman's personals. Let's keep our hands off all data storage media and devices until then. Catalog in place. End.''

''Sending, sir,'' said the comsole's voice.

Reaching out to his left, Norwood touched several desktop sensors, and a list of files came up on the screen. ''Unlock fourteen through twenty-two, one viewing, sequenced, then re-lock.''

''Done, sir.''

Finally, Norwood turned back toward the others and rose from his chair. ''Okay. You can call from here,'' he said, making his way toward the door. ''When you're done, ask for file fourteen.''

''We didn't mean to chase you out—'' Alvarez began.

''You didn't. I'm due in the tank to testify in another case.'' He squinted toward Dryke. ''Let me know when you can have your people here.''

''I will. Thank you, Captain.''

As the door closed, Dryke thumbed off his recorder and turned to Alvarez wearing an openly puzzled expression. "What's going on?"

"I want Silverman's personals," she said. "I don't want blank logo and a brainwashed AIP. Your texperts are insurance."

"That's not what I mean. There's no co-op agreement between us. Or am I missing something?"

"There is now," she said. "Unless you don't want it."

"I'll take it. But I still don't understand. You can't have forgotten about Brian White since you told Norwood about it half an hour ago."

"I only told him how I knew you," she said. "I didn't tell him what I thought of your ethics. And I won't, unless you try to see Silverman."

Dryke looked at her wonderingly. "Stand still. I can't track a moving target."

"This one's different than the last one," Alvarez said quietly. "White was petty stuff, a classic bad boy. We know how to handle his kind. But Silverman's a hard-wired freakoid. And he scares the pee out of me."

"He's in lockup. Norwood's not going to let him walk."

"Not that kind of scared. But how many more are out there?" she asked. "You've got fifteen hundred employees in the compound and three thousand more outside for the next Silverman to pick from. There's no way that you can lock them all up safely out of reach."

"I know," said Dryke.

She shook her head. "I don't know how to get inside Silverman's mind. I don't even know if I want to."

"You don't want to," said Dryke grimly.

"Is he crazy? Cerebral function deficiency?"

"Was Hitler crazy?" Dryke asked rhetorically. "I don't know. I'll bet he doesn't come up CFD. He's worse. A bad combination of hate and intelligence."

"And calculated viciousness."

"That's what you get when you put those two together," said Dryke. He gestured at the screen. "Are you ready?"

"I suppose."

Dryke nodded. "File fourteen, display," he said, thumbing his recorder to on.

Larger than life, Evan Eric Silverman sat calmly in the back of the Ranger cruiser, talking to the officers in the front seats.

"This is just the beginning," he was saying. "Number one. Somebody keep score. We're going to stop them. We're going to push them right to the edge—"

It was midnight in Prainha, 4 A.M. in Northumberland, and 1 P.M. the previous day on Takara and *Memphis*, orbiting high above the mid-Pacific. But technology and the wishes of Hiroko Sasaki had erased the differences that night. The four people waiting with Sasaki in her garden meeting room were all sharing the same moment with the five skylinked to the gathering, all waiting on the same report.

"We are ready, Mr. Dryke," said Sasaki, consulting the digital slate resting on her lap. "You may begin."

"Thank you, Director," said Dryke from the tank in Houston. "I won't belabor this. We got into Evan Silverman's library about seven hours ago. The only defenses in his system were commercial repellents, which were taken down without damage to the files. About four hours ago, the Texas State Police handed over image copies of all the libraries, including Silverman's contact logs. We've parsed them six ways to November, and there's no evidence he was working with anyone else or at anyone's direction."

"Let me be certain I understand," said Sasaki. "There is no evidence of Mr. Silverman having contact with any person or organization on our Homeworld watch lists."

"That's correct."

"There is no evidence of any communication or contact with Jeremiah."

"That's correct. Understand, though, that no evidence means just that. The files could have been purged before Silverman went out that night—a good wipe utility wouldn't have left us anything."

"Was there an AIP which could be questioned?" Sasaki said each letter individually, eschewing the acronym.

"No. Silverman lived alone."

"Do you have any conclusions?"

Dryke frowned. "One thing we did find in the library was a clip file on Jeremiah—all of his pirate speeches, coverage of the tank truck gag here a few months back, and the like. I'm inclined to think that anyone who would take the trouble to wipe out damning evidence would probably get rid of the merely suspicious as well. So I expect that the reason we didn't find anything was that there wasn't anything to find. We'll run the files for embedded code, of course, before we close the book."

"It is your judgment, then, that Mr. Silverman acted alone, and on his own initiative."

"Yes. Based on what I've seen today."

"There has been speculation by the media that Mr. Silverman may in fact be Jeremiah," said Sasaki. "Is there any reason to give this speculation credence?"

Dryke snorted. "Julian Minor is an idiot. No. None at all."

"One final question: Do we know for certain that Mr. Silverman knew Ms. Graham's involvement with the Project?"

"He knew," said Dryke.

"Are you basing that on his word alone?"

"No. On the fact that he was boasting about it when the Rangers picked him up. If he didn't know before he left the bar with the woman, then she either told him or gave herself away somehow."

"Thank you, Mr. Dryke, on behalf of the committee," said Sasaki. "I know that this has been a long day for you. If you will allow me, I would like to close one other matter. Has there been any change in the status of the open gateway at the Munich operation?"

"No change," said Dryke dourly. "There've been a fistful of attempted penetrations, but all amateurs. It looks like the big fish saw the hook."

"I am told by Mr Reid that it is through the exercise of discretion that they live to become 'big fish,' " said Sasaki. "Please have the gateway closed and the operation terminated. The staff will require the navigation package to be available when they begin reporting after the New Year, and any further delays in its installation will endanger that."

"Yes, Director."

"We will contact you in the morning if we have further questions—please notify me immediately if there are new developments."

"Of course."

Sasaki touched her slate, and the Houston link was broken. There was a prolonged silence, more subdued than respectful, in the garden room in Prainha.

"Mr. Tidwell," said Sasaki at last, frowning. "Are you there?"

"Yes," came the reply, ferried across the Atlantic by the sky-link. "Yes, I am."

"Do you have anything to add?"

Tidwell's eyes were dull, and the words came slowly. "I was fond of Miss Graham. I deeply—regret—her death. That said, I do not see what I can contribute to this discussion."

One of the men across from Sasaki stirred. "Can I ask what he was doing in Houston in the first place?"

"Mr. Tidwell?" asked Sasaki. "Did you hear that?"

"I had—made a judgment—that in order to truly know the colonists, I would have to share their lives—their experience." He paused. "I meant to leave in three days, when the class was released."

"Does sharing their lives include dating twenty-year-old girls?" The question came from a woman sitting to Sasaki's left.

"I am satisfied that Mr. Tidwell's involvement in these horrible events is tangential and entirely incidental. Further, that his involvement with Miss Graham was consistent with the purposes he named," said Sasaki, her tone a sharp rebuke. "I have asked for his observations because he is in a position to speak to the present atmosphere in Houston, and for no other reason."

The woman lowered her eyes and was silent.

"While in Houston, I saw a marked and growing polarization," said Tidwell, stepping into the empty space. "Lines of allegiance have hardened. You hear bitter words on both sides, little communication between them. Emotions have outdistanced reason in too many minds. I am forced to say that I am not surprised that this happened. It was an undeclared war. No longer."

"Can you plot the curve?" asked the woman.

"Pardon me?"

"How long will the Houston operation be sustainable?" she asked. "Will we be able to move three more classes through by March?"

"I see," said Tidwell. "I am not well versed in the business of prediction."

"Noted," Sasaki said. "I would appreciate your assessment, all the same."

Tidwell loosed an uncomfortable sigh. "The undeclared war was fought, I might argue, by gentleman's rules. If Evan Silverman presages a new group of players who recognize no rules, it seems to me that it will be a near thing. There are wolves at the door."

"Thank you, Thomas," said Sasaki. "You may leave us now."

"May I ask a question of my own?"

"Of course."

"Why is Malena Graham so important? I was told today that twenty-nine people attached to the Project have died in accidents and other incidents this year, including three colonists. At least six of those deaths were murders. I am not aware that the committee was convened on the occasion of each or any of those cases. I'm beginning to wonder if you're not more concerned about my involvement than you've admitted."

Sasaki briefly showed a tired smile. "You have answered your own question, Thomas. Malena Graham is so important because she demonstrates that the rules *have* changed. She is the first colonist killed simply *because* she was a colonist."

"But what does that mean to you?" Tidwell said. "I half believe that you've been watching for it to happen."

"We have been watching for certain signs," said Sasaki. "Some time ago, the sociometric unit prepared a study of the rising curve of opposition to the Diaspora. It contained a multi-stranded prediction, specifying several checkpoints and water-shed events. Malena's murder and your assessment of the situation in Houston both fit the projection."

"Why was this study kept from me?" asked Tidwell.

Sasaki showed a flash of annoyance. "As you said yourself, your province is the past, not the future. It was not kept from you. It was simply not relevant to your work."

"I would like to have made that judgment myself," said Tidwell, somewhat chastened. "In any case, I now understand your concern."

"Our concern is long-standing." She gestured with her right hand, her simple metal bracelet gleaming. "To date, all is as predicted—the changing political and social climate, the drop in options and acceptances, and now the violence."

Tidwell's expression was a troubled one. "What lies at the end of the curve? What does this mean for *Knossos*?"

Sasaki was slow to respond, and it seemed to those in the room with her at Prainha that it was less for lack of an answer than for her reluctance to voice it.

"I suppose that circumstance has now made the study relevant to your office," she said at last. "If the projection continues to hold, we will never build *Knossos*."

"What!"

"Or *Mohenjo-Daro*, or *Teotihuacán*," Sasaki continued. "The Diaspora will end with *Memphis*. *That*, Mr. Tidwell, is why Malena Graham is so important."

"Then I will hope that fortune-telling is a less exact science than history," Tidwell said. "Good night, Director."

"May I ask him one more question?" It was the woman to Sasaki's right.

Sasaki gestured her assent.

"This boy you were talking to that night—the archie you left Malena for. Did you learn anything from him?"

Eyes haunted, Tidwell slowly shook his head. "That cuts the deepest," he said. "There was nothing he could tell me, because he didn't know himself."

When Tidwell was gone, there was an uneasy silence in the garden room. Sasaki rose wordlessly and crossed the room to the dispenser for a cup of Japanese tea. One of the men stood at the window-wall at the far end of the room, looking out at the lights of the spaceport.

"That's it, then," he said finally. "We've crossed a threshold."

No one spoke.

"I'm surprised you told Dr. Tidwell as much as you did," said the woman when Sasaki rejoined them.

"It was time for him to know."

"But not the whole story."

"He is my barometer," she said. "He now knows as much as he needs."

"I don't think you should have soft-pedaled it," said the man at the window, returning to his chair. "The truth is, we'll be lucky if they don't find a way to stop *Memphis*."

"I can't accept that," said Matt Reid, skylinked from Takara. "We can't just sit still and let them come get us."

"The study makes clear that we can only hasten our decline by matching their tactics," said Sasaki. "We have seen already, in the Singapore incident, that we are judged by stricter standards."

"Maybe I'm the only one here," said the supervisor, "but I don't take the study as gospel. I'm not seeing any of this up here. And I hate like hell to hear this kind of negativism on the committee."

"Takara is a special population," said the woman. "It will reach there last."

"I don't see why we can't fight this," the supervisor persisted. "And I'd put finding some way to silence this Silverman at the top of the list. It shouldn't be too hard to find someone willing to go head-hunting."

"No," Sasaki said forcefully. "It is already too late for that. Mr. Silverman made his statement with his hands. His words are merely echoes, and you cannot silence an echo."

"So we're going to do nothing," said the supervisor, disgusted.

"We will do what we planned to do, three years ago," said Sasaki. "We prepared for a contingency no one wanted to believe in. Mr. Marshall"—she nodded toward the man by the window—"said that we would laugh at ourselves for fools the day that *Knossos* sailed. Is there anyone on the committee who truly believes we will see that day?"

She looked at each of them in turn. No one spoke.

"I accept the inevitability of the inevitable, the reality of the real," she said. "But this is no surrender. *Memphis* must sail. We cannot allow the success of the Diaspora to depend on a single ship."

"Is there any better news from *Ur*?" asked the woman.

Sasaki shook her head. "The trouble continues. There is no danger to the ship at present, and apparently little danger any more that they will turn back. But the new governor holds out little hope for a return to normalcy."

Marshall shook his head. "If he can't deliver, then we may have picked the wrong boy to overthrow Milton."

"The truth is that there is little we can do from here to influence events on *Ur*," said Sasaki. "The threat of a communications embargo is rather a feeble lever. Our focus must be on that which we can control—the future of *Memphis*."

"Are you putting Contingency Zero in effect?" asked Marshall.

"Yes. As of this meeting. Your individual responsibilities are contained in locked files which were transferred to your private libraries earlier this evening. The key is 'Lights out.' " She smiled wryly at Marshall. "That was your phrase, as I recall."

"Last one on the planet, turn out the lights," Marshall said. "Yes. That was me."

Sasaki continued, "When you review your files, keep in mind that the first priority will be to establish a firm timetable for the move—"

The slate on Sasaki's lap suddenly began to chirp insistently. At the same time, the skylink displays blanked to white, and the black-bordered box of a flash alert appeared in the center of each. In the center of the box appeared C. Gustav Feist, site director for the Munich center. His face was flushed, and his hands slashed the air as he spoke.

"Director Sasaki," he said hoarsely. "Where is Dryke? He won't answer his page. Where is he?"

"He's gone to bed, I presume. He may be off-net. What is happening, Mr. Feist?"

Feist's eyes were pleading with the committee. "The gateway was closed, just as he instructed. Closed! Not thirty minutes. The com staff swears to it. None too soon, I thought. Now this."

"What are you talking about?"

"You haven't been told?" Feist looked away from his camera as he listened to someone off-screen. "*Gott in Himmel.* It's still going on."

"*What's* going on?" Marshall demanded.

"It must be Jeremiah," Feist said agitatedly. "There's a virus in the engineering network, tearing up the development systems. We can't freeze it, we can't kill it, and it won't let us shut down. I've got to go. We're being brain-burned, Director. Brain-burned while we're talking."

CHAPTER 22

-|AAC|-

".. . visions of Gaea ..."

IN A PRIVATE ROOM IN A PRIVATE PLACE, A PRIVATE MAN PUT on his mask and went to work.

He was David Eng and Roberto Garcia, Lila Holmes and Sandra Stone. His alter egos lived in an apartment overlooking the Chicago River, and a stately house on Avenida Manquehue in Santiago—claimed offices in anonymous towers on the fringe of Phoenix and in the heart of Vancouver.

There had been other names through the years, a dozen years now, a parade of identities, some invented, some borrowed. There had been a chain of locked rooms and secret spaces, inhabited only by obedient machines put in place by trusted hands.

And behind those masks, another mask—the constant, the connection. His name, taken from a man forty years dead, was never spoken, for no one knew better than he how the nets were watched, what tricks could be played with the bit stream of the skylinks. He spoke with other voices, always changing voices, but those who heard him knew that the words were Jeremiah's.

A construct in a silicon engine, an idea in the mind of a man, a weapon in a war of deceptions—Jeremiah was all of those. In the beginning, Jeremiah had been nothing more than these. But now the mask had been in place so long that the man who wore it had nearly disappeared, and it had become more and more difficult for him to leave the shadow places where Jeremiah was real and face the light outside, the world where he himself was real.

Necessity rescued him from that struggle. So much demanded

Jeremiah's attention, so many clamored for an audience, that there was little enough chance even to escape into sleep. The world never slept.

He had allowed himself but three hours this night, the merest nap. Yet when he awoke, he found nearly one hundred new messages awaiting him, captured and forwarded by the relayers, coders, and recorders, collated and sifted by the comsole's secretary.

A third of them were reports from members of the Homeworld network. Another dozen announced new volunteers to join the order of battle. Fully half were answers to queries issued earlier. The remainder were nuggets of gold: a scattering of technical, financial, and logistical gifts offered for his consideration.

But the message list was only the beginning. Also waiting in queue were more than seventy news stories collected by the secretary's search engine, as well as a hyperlog of real-time intercepts of new and ongoing skylink conversations. Too much. Far too much. He could not review it all, not nearly so. His spies were too good, his sources too many.

Undisguised, the sheer volume of traffic would have been a threat to the operation's survival. But he had learned many tricks, invented several others. Intercepts were fragmented and dumped to null skylink addresses for his unregistered receivers to pluck out of the air and rebuild. Reports came in as innocent-looking packets quickposted as delete-on-receipt to the subscription services. Messages relayed from the four "mail drop" sites were laundered through a high-traffic business front.

But that was not the only danger.

Once, he had had it all in his hands, knew every thread in the weave. No longer. This thing he had created had its own heartbeat, and though he still guided it, he no longer controlled every movement. More and more of the correspondence was in the hands of Lila, the secretarial engine. More and more of the ancillary reports were archived unseen. The growing archive troubled him. It represented missed opportunities, needless errors, eager volunteers frustrated by his silence and driven to act on their own.

But he was only one man, one person pretending to be five, one mortal attempting to live up to a myth. He could not be everywhere, could not scatter his energies on a thousand points of light. His focus had to remain at the center: Sasaki, Dryke,

Memphis, the strategy for a killing blow against the Diaspora. The window was starting to close, and he could not bear to fail.

Mustering a decisiveness he did not feel, he began to sift through the priority items in the queue, dispatching them from the displays at a rate approaching one a minute. Even as he did, new messages and stories appeared on the list, underlining the Sisyphean futility of the task.

But making its way to him that moment was a message which would make him forget that futility for a while. Originating with Katrina Becker in Munich, it was following a tortuous path to reach him—bounced twice to a DBS, its headers stripped and replaced by a relayer, back-coded into a transparent file on DIANNA, and then unlocked with a key that had been sent weeks earlier.

When it appeared in the queue, his face brightened. And when he read it, he laughed and clapped his hands together in a moment of celebration.

For sometime while Jeremiah had been napping, the Munich virus had gone to war.

It had been months in the making, as almost all operations were. It had begun with a suggestion from without, as almost all operations did.

"Tell me your ideas, and Jeremiah will tell you when the time is right," was the message which went out to the network, to newly vetted friends. And they looked into their own lives for the special opportunities offered there, building for Jeremiah a catalog of choices.

"I can do this to hurt them," they said. "I can do this to help."

Katrina Becker had come into the fold more than a year ago. Her vetting had been unusually prolonged, for the special opportunity she represented was dangerously attractive. Becker was a systems security technician in the engineering section at AT-Munich, the primary technical center for the Diaspora. Through her, he could have access to the closed world of *Memphis*'s operational and management engines—to the delicately tuned mind of the ship itself.

From the first, he had viewed Becker with dark suspicion. Nine years into a career with Allied, she claimed a change of heart prompted by a book she had read and a man she had met. The book was Danya Odon's *Earthsong*, an obscure collection of nature-experience poems. The man was Peter Corning, an obscure rad-left Bundestag member from Schleswig-Holstein. One sensitized her to the "organic wholeness" of Gaea, the other to the "soft fascism" of Allied Transcon.

Or so she claimed.

It took three months and several significant leaks of technical material from AT-Munich before Jeremiah was satisfied that her conversation was sincere. It had taken many more months to pick apart the secrets of the engineering network and build a virus capable of surviving its defenses.

Even then, he had hesitated. To use Becker to deliver the virus would be to sacrifice her. She was willing, even eager, but he had no one similarly placed, no way to replace the intelligence she delivered. Without a guarantee of success, and with a plenitude of other options, Jeremiah held both Becker and the virus in reserve, waiting to be convinced that the time was right or her usefulness was about to end.

Then came Dryke's transparent attempt to trap him with the open gateway into the test environment. Jeremiah had at first been amused, then insulted. Did Dryke think that he could not tell the difference between real and calculated carelessness? Did Dryke think he would expect anything in the test partition except antibodies and backtracers?

Ego prodded him to answer the insult by making Dryke look foolish. But it was the fact that the delivery of the finished command package to *Memphis* would bring Becker's usefulness to an end which finally swung the decision.

The day after the gateway opened, the virus was hard-coded in a tamper-sealed chipdisk and ferried to Becker in a delivery of perfume from a Belgian company. Two days later, it was installed in the Munich network. It had been waiting in hiding there ever since, watching for its trigger key. When the gateway was finally closed, the countdown began.

The virus was meant to alter the command package in a subtle way, modifying a calculation here, a data point there, changing a pointer, closing a loop. If it had succeeded, no one would have known of its handiwork until *Memphis* herself, basking in the spotlight of what was to be her sailing day, refused to leave the Earth.

But an antibody program, monitoring cryptographic checksums and integrity keys, spotted the change and came hunting.

In response, the virus abandoned its stealthy subversion and went wild.

All solutions are contingent. Content in his lesser victory, Jeremiah traced the virus's progress by monitoring skylink traffic between Munich and Prainha, Munich and Houston.

"We tried to tag it and it stripped the tags. When we finally got system control back, we tried to freeze it and it self-destructed," the Munich systems supervisor reported to Dryke. "But there must have been a fragment hiding where we couldn't get it, because when we came up again, it went right after us again and broke our control just like that."

Jeremiah nodded to himself. In fact, there were five copies of the virus in the system, each waiting their turn to wreak havoc.

"It's running through the libraries now," he heard Feist tell Sasaki. "We're taking nodes out of the network the hard way, pulling blocks and cutting cables as fast as we can. But Mods Five and Six are completely gone."

More good news. Mod Five was the navigation archive, Mod Six ship management. The only plum left was Three, the command engine.

But the biggest self-satisfied smile came later, when a weary Dryke told Sasaki, "Jeremiah did what we expected him to do. But he didn't use the door we had open, and we didn't get him. His virus was better than our antibodies."

"We are facing a major reconstruction because of that, Mr. Dryke." Sasaki's voice was brittle. "It was your job to prevent such a disaster. It was your job to protect our Malena Grahams. And you failed at both."

"Don't you think I know that?" Dryke snapped back. "You want to give this assfuck job to someone else, go ahead and do it. He beat me. All right? Jeremiah beat me. You got someone else that wants to take a shot, bring 'em on."

It was not until the excitement in Munich began to fade that Jeremiah thought to ask who Malena Graham was.

Lila's answer was straightforward and chilling. "A *Memphis* staff counselor, killed last night near Houston. You are implicated. Stories are in the queue and marked."

There were dozens of stories, for the murder had taken place fully six hours earlier. Troubled, Jeremiah viewed the stories one after another from the top of the queue, trying to grasp what had happened. Not one of them left him untouched.

When a State Police medtech described in graphic detail the condition of the corpse, Jeremiah's mouth went dry, and his hands trembled. When Mother Alicia recalled that her daughter was "naive about people, because she wanted to love them," Jeremiah wept with her. And when Evan Silverman proclaimed proudly that he was "Jeremiah's hands," Jeremiah rose out of his chair and raged at the screen.

"Liar—liar! You're no part of me. Not one fragment. Bastard animal—" Then a horrible fear overtook him. "Lila! Search the archives. Is there anything about this man? Have we had any contact with him?"

"I'm checking," it said. "Done. There are no entries except for those connected with Malena Graham. We have had no contact with Evan Silverman."

That calmed him somewhat. "We're going to do something about this, Lila," he said. "I won't let what he said stand unchallenged. I won't let them think I wanted this."

"Yes, sir."

"I'm going to go real-time. I'll need you to map out an interrupt. Pick a local station—everyone else can get it from them. I'll need at least three minutes."

"Yes, sir. I'll let you know when it's ready."

While he waited, there were more stories. The State Police had the only crime-scene documentaries, but were refusing to release them—a station in Dallas was suing. ("That one," he told Lila. "They'll hear me out. Put it through them.") The Allied Transcon complex was locked down and in mourning, and Hiroko Sasaki was rumored to be there. (He checked other sources: She was still in Prainha.)

But the stunner was one of the late arrivals: a synth-image recreation of the girl's last hours by the current affairs show *Headliner*. Somehow they had obtained a recording of the concert which had drawn Malena out into the city, and found her in an audience shot.

With that and Silverman's interviews as templates, they were able to animate a mockumentary, showing "Malena" walking with her friends from the tram station to the club, leaving the bar with "Silverman," sitting in his flyer, and, ultimately, lying dead on the ground.

In keeping with *Headliner*'s reputation for heavy-handed journalism, the commentary was moralistic and overblown ("But Malena Graham could not resist the temptations of her youthful freedom . . ."). The ham-fisted essayism extended to using a song from the concert as ironic counterpoint to the images: "Look at me, I'm flying free—"

"Good God," said Jeremiah. "Lila—who is that?"

"The performer is Christopher McCutcheon, an archaeolibrarian with the *Memphis* hyper project in Houston."

"I want to hear the whole song."

There was a pause. "I'm sorry, it doesn't appear to be available."

"Someone has it. Call *Headliner*."

"I could contact Christopher directly."

"No," said Jeremiah. "Call *Headliner*. Buy it if you have to."

"Yes, sir," said Lila. "By the way, the interrupt you requested is ready now."

"Keep it current," said Jeremiah. "I'm not."

Jeremiah sat back in his chair, hands folded in his lap, eyes unblinking, and watched the recording through to the end. When it was over, he watched it a second time.

"Kill it, Lila," he said. "No archive."

Then he rose and left the warren and its screens and queues, left the house, his heart full of pain. His triumph had been stolen from him, trumped by the mocking images which had flickered across the displays. It did not matter if the damage in Munich would delay *Memphis* ten days or ten months. No amount of time would be enough to dissuade them. They would never turn from their course.

All the proof he needed was contained in the final four minutes of the concert. The last song Christopher sang was the embodiment of unreason, a précis of cultural insanity. Its words revealed every folly of the Diaspora, every bitter truth that poisoned the sweet romance of adventure.

There were no other Edens, no golden paths. There was no glory in a shabby death a long way from home. The final, brutal indictment was the son's tragically misguided choice—no, not a choice, a received obligation—to carry on his father's quest. *Delicta maiorum immeritus lues.*

Yet the audience applauded the waste of lives, acclaimed the embrace of pointless suffering, absolved the father through his son's blind emulation of a suicidal self-sacrifice.

And the singer accepted the accolades as though that were what he had meant all along.

The agony of Malena's parents came through to him with new force. "We tried to talk her out of it," Mother Caroline had said to the reporters. "We pleaded with her to stay. But she wouldn't listen. What can you do? What can you do when they've made up their mind?"

Her helpless feeling echoed his own. He could not touch them. He could not reach their minds or turn their hearts. You will leave me, and I will lose you. That was what Mother Caroline faced, what every family faced. That was the fear which had eaten away at the dreamy idealism of the Diaspora in the years since *Ur.*

"As far as I'm concerned, she was a runaway, as much as if she'd gone to the streets," Father Jack had said. "Someone caught her eye with a shiny trinket and a bit of candy and she was gone. She took everything that we'd given her and threw it away. I'm sorry if it sounds hard, but she was dead to me from that day on."

How many wounds had been left by eight thousand final partings, how many families shattered? How many mates and lovers and children and parents still nursed anger and hurt that they were abandoned? How many that they touched had learned to view the new ship taking shape in orbit as a threat?

"She was a terrific girl," Father Brett had said. "She brought so much brightness to my life, and now she's gone. I know we were going to have to say good-bye soon, but I feel cheated. We were expecting her home for Yule, did I say that? And I still half expect to hear her at the door. I loved her and she's gone. I really haven't been able to think about anything but that."

Malena was gone. But the rest of the ten thousand were still here, could still be saved, their families and friends and lovers still spared. Mother Caroline and Father Jack had surrendered, accepted a reality they hated, and their daughter had paid the price. If he, Jeremiah, surrendered as they had, the price paid would be far greater.

When he returned to the house after an hour's walk, he stopped to watch the hummingbirds darting through the air around the bright red feeder. There were three nesting pairs this season, the most in several years. The frantic energy in their tiny bodies was a marvel, their speed on the wing a delight.

But this morning, he could not feel delight. He descended

into the warren, still grasping for an answer. The queues had ballooned again. The new additions included the Houston site director's first statement, still under way, on the murder. As Jeremiah joined the cast, the director was condemning Silverman and "all those who share his curse of hate and arrogance of virtue."

"We know his kind," said Carlos Vincenza. "We've seen them outside our gates, waving fists and hurling rocks. We've heard their voices, bleating about Mother Gaea and the selfishness of the pioneers. But is there any act more selfish than the one Evan Silverman committed in that field? Is there any explanation besides jealousy for denying someone else a gift you could never appreciate, or stealing a reward that you could never earn?

"They call themselves Homeworlders. Better we should call them homebodies. They protest their own history. They stand against the future. Their life strategy consists of pulling back to the smallest defensible locus. They want to give up nothing, risk nothing, and preserve everything. They've made their lives petty and meaningless, and they want ours to be as empty.

"But we have goals and dreams, and we have the right to pursue them. The cost is being borne by those who choose to bear it. The sacrifices will be made by those who choose to make them. We ask only one thing from you: *Let us be.* Turn your back if you must, but let us go. It means nothing to you, but everything to us—as it did to Malena Graham."

As Jeremiah watched Vincenza, his expression turned harder and grimmer. "Lila," he said when it was over, "what has Allied said about Munich?"

"Nothing received, sir."

"What has Sasaki said about it? Or about Malena Graham?"

"Nothing received, sir."

"Is the interrupt still ready?"

"Yes, sir."

"Bring up the translator and animator and give me a countdown," he said.

"Yes, sir. Translator up, Converter up. Counting down: five— four—"

"This is Jeremiah, speaking for the Homeworld."

The anger was still bubbling within him, and he welcomed it. "My heart aches this day for those who knew and loved Malena Graham. Her death was brutal and tragic. But the greatest pain must be the knowledge that her death was unnecessary.

"Who is to blame for what befell Malena Graham? I have been accused. But my goal from the first has been to dissuade—not destroy. I love this world and all its creatures, mankind most of all.

"Who, then? Her parents, for failing to control her? Evan Silverman, for succumbing to the hate that filled him? Hiroko Sasaki, for dangling the universe before a naive girl? Or Malena herself, for the choices she freely made?

"As every parent can witness to, life is a journey from dependence to rebellion to responsibility. Every parent knows that their child will have to face temptations and make difficult choices. You want them to choose well.

"But how do they learn to choose well? They learn from the rules imposed on them from the beginning. If the rules are too strict, what they learn is to escape. And they learn from the examples that surround them. We are sometimes surprised to discover that they have learned more from our example than our words.

"Did Malena Graham choose well? She forsook her family for strangers, the richness of a vast bountiful world for the closed spaces of a tiny metal shell.

"Her father has called her a runaway. But what was she fleeing? Was she abused and belittled? No. We can see that she was loved and nurtured. Was she bitter and unhappy? We are told that she was vibrant and joyful. Why, then, would she make such choices?

"The answer is that Malena Graham was a victim not of a murderer's hand, but of a poisonous idea. An idea born in the harsh years of the great Repression, when the family of man turned cold in spirit as well as flesh. An idea as false and foolish as a ten-year-old's notion that his problems will end if he only leaves home.

"*Come with me to the stars*, whispered the demon. *Come with me to find a better place.*

"Malena Graham listened. Many good people listened. They saw so much more clearly than we, or so they believed. They saw a burning Earth, an old and weary Earth, a sickly Earth. They saw disease-riddled bodies and fear-divided communities.

"And they dreamed a child's fantasy of a magic land inhabited by the pure and the loving. A fantasy that became a crippling obsession, a roadblock on the way to responsibility.

"Who is responsible for Malena Graham's death? We are all responsible—Evan Silverman perhaps least of all. Every one of us who thought the demon harmless. Every one of us who thought the fantasy amusing. Every one of us who failed to notice our children slipping away.

"Malena Graham is dead, but her death will have meaning if only we can read the warning in it. Malena Graham is gone, but there are nine thousand nine hundred ninety-nine more tragedies that can still be averted.

"I say this to the family of Earth: When a child goes astray, a good parent will use a firm hand to bring them to heel. The greater the danger, the firmer our hand must be. We must speak the hard truths. We must set limits. Those who see must act, or those who are blind will stumble.

"I say this to the pioneers of *Memphis*: We have learned from our mistakes. The Earth is healing. The disease which divided us has been defeated. Now we will correct one last mistake, by saving you from yours. This day, I have struck at the heart of *Memphis*, in the most protected refuge of Allied Transcon. And I will strike again, and again, until the fantasy is shattered and the demon destroyed—because I love you.

"Listen to me: There are no other Edens. This Earth is all you need. You may not leave."

CHAPTER 23

-|GAC|-

"... notions of progress."

IT WAS THE EMPTIEST, LONELIEST NIGHT CHRISTOPHER MC-Cutcheon could remember.

Outside the house, a drenching winter rain was sweeping the dusty streets, the fat droplets beating against the windows when the wind gusted. Hiding out from the storm in their vehicles, two stalwart microcam crews, competing independents, waited at the mouth of the cul-de-sac, hoping Christopher would make an appearance or agree to an interview. It was a small mercy that there were only two—the morning after the concert, there had been eleven cameras waiting for him when he started for work.

The attrition was largely Allied's doing. As part of its response to Malena's murder, the company had gone to war with the media on his behalf. Management dispatched spin doctors and jackmen to divert their attention elsewhere, and loosed its attorneys to end the use of the bootleg concert recording (the source of which was still not known, though signs pointed toward Papa Wonders).

No doubt he was becoming old news, and soon even the last holdouts would lose interest. Still, he felt trapped. The house was at once the only place where he was guaranteed privacy and the last place he wanted to be.

Christopher knew, though it was no comfort, that his dilemma was largely self-created. He had squandered most of the compassion offered him in the wake of Tuesday's horrors. Brittle-tempered and bitter-tongued at best, inconsolably self-hating at his worst, he had exhausted the sympathy of his friends by the end of the first day and the patience of his supervisor by the end of the second. She banished him from the complex late Thursday with orders to take the weekend off and see a staff facilitator when he returned Monday.

" You're all turned inside out, Christopher, with the ugly parts on the outside and the good stuff tucked away," was her blunt assessment. "Get your attitude adjusted and come back in tune, because I need you on task."

The oddest part, looking back, was that he had known exactly what he was doing. As if he wanted to make them despise him as much as he despised himself. As if making them reject him would confirm his harshest judgments of himself and make him feel as miserable as he thought he ought to.

And he had succeeded. He was quite alone, and he had never felt quite so awful.

Jessie was somewhere in the city with John Fields, the fifth time in two weeks they had disappeared on a formal evening date. And Loi was in the moon room's whirlpool with a new playmate, the lion-maned son of a Dallas client. From time to time, Christopher could hear the splash of water, a titter of laughter, from behind the privacy-opaqued glass door.

It should be me in there with her, he thought wistfully, wishfully. *Could have been.*

Loi had been home Tuesday night when Tidwell delivered him to the front door. She had seen him struggling with his conscience, witnessed the body blow as he learned that his name and music were linked to a bloody murder that was top of the queue on every net. She had offered him motherly consolation and caught the full force of a broadside of bile for her trouble. He had been too busy being unapproachable, unlovable, to accept the comforts she offered.

No, he could not blame her for leaving him to his own devices—though, in truth, neither could he quite forgive her.

Or himself, he realized. *Or I wouldn't be sitting here in the pit making myself listen to them play.*

"Music," he said.

" What kind of music?" asked the house AIP.

"Loud music," he said, sinking down further in the cushions.

Better alternatives were scarce. He had already run the list of programs in storage without finding anything that could command his attention. Daniel Keith was locked in a late-night con-

ference with Karin Oker and the senior selection staff; he would
not be free until after Saturday's memorial service and Sunday's
postponed send-off ceremonies.

And Christopher's usual diversion had no appeal at all—he
had not picked up the Martin since leaving the stage at Wonders,
and it seemed unlikely he would again soon.

"This is no good," he said aloud.

The music ceased. "What would you like?"

"An answer."

"I'm sorry. I did not hear the question."

Christopher snorted. *Baiting the house AIP? A game for ten-
year-olds. Is that how low I've gone?* "Show me the mail list,"
he said.

The frozen patterns on the main display faded and the list
sprang into view.

"Kill one through five," he said, scanning. "Parasites. Kill
seven. Tell eleven to fuck off."

"That would be considered rude."

"I know. Do it, anyway." He squinted up at the wall. "I'm
gonna be brave. Show me number eight."

The list vanished, and the face of Lenore Edkins appeared.
He was in his Building H office, and frowning.

"Christopher—I had hoped to tell you myself, but apparently
you're not in the complex today," Edkins said. "Good news can
keep as well as bad, but I thought you'd want to know. Maybe
you've already guessed. 'Caravan to Antares' will be in the
Memphis hyper. Through the front door. You're relevant now."

Edkins tried a smile. "For what it's worth, I think you could
have cracked in on artistic merit—the best work I've seen from
you. Anyway, congratulations. Maybe the circumstances aren't
the best, but I know how much you wanted it."

Somewhere in the middle of the message, Christopher's mind
switched off, and something wild and ugly took hold of him.
Giving voice to a cry that began as a growl and ended as a
shriek, he seized an onyx carving off the end table. In a single
seamless motion, he came to his feet and hurled the carving
overhand with all his strength at the wallscreen.

His throw was wild high, and the carving buried itself with a
small puff of white dust in the soft plasterboard above the screen.
It was over that quickly, the impulse grounded in one explosion
of sound and movement, leaving him feeling drained and
wobbly-legged.

As he stood staring wonderingly up at the hole, Loi appeared at the door of the moon room. She was dripping wet and wearing only a troubled expression.

"Are you all right?" she asked,

"Sorry," he said, turning toward her. "I'm all right. Go back to your friend."

She looked past him briefly, her glance taking in his redecoration. "Then what was the screaming about?"

"I was celebrating," he said wryly. "Primal victory cry."

"Celebrating?"

He dropped into a chair. "I'm going to live forever. The company just told me so."

Her gaze narrowed. "Are you under?"

"No," he said, trying to manage an embarrassed smile. "Unless self-pity is a drug. Which it probably is. Please—go on back to your friend. I really didn't mean to disturb you. I'll—I can leave the house if you want."

She frowned, studying him. "Only if you need the distance. Not for me."

"I'll be okay."

She hesitated. "Mark won't be staying," she said. "We can talk later if you need to."

Looking at her glistening body, Christopher remembered something Daniel had said when struggling to explain why he wasn't comfortable around Loi. "She'd make a lousy lifeguard," he had said finally. "She'd kneel on the edge and hold out her hand, but she'd never jump in to do your swimming for you." Christopher had bristled in loyal defense, only later realizing that Daniel had been right.

But it was a trait, not a fault. Or if it was a fault, it was an innocent one—of expecting from others what she expected from herself. Loi had built her life on self-reliance. To need rescuing was a humiliation; to offer a rescue, an insult. The edge of the pool was as far as propriety would allow. It said something about how she saw him now that she was offering her hand a second time.

Shaking his head slowly, Christopher said, "Thanks, but I don't think you can help."

"Don't close me out, Chris."

Plea or caution? He couldn't quite decide. While he debated, she retreated two steps and disappeared behind the closing door. A moment later there was a splash.

Caution, he decided.

"Would you like to see any further mail?" asked the AIP.

Christopher laughed brittlely. "No."

"Would you like to select alternate music?"

"No." He was silent for a long moment, trying to read the feeling in his body without putting words to it, trying to grasp his experience of his own life. *Is this where you want to be? Is there anything right about who you are this instant?* he asked, and the answers were reflected back to him as echoes of sorrow. *No. Not the tenth part.*

Then what are you going to do about it?

Male laughter in the distance. He drew a slow deep breath, his eyes closing briefly. "Judy?"

The AIP responded to its name. "Yes, Chris?"

He sighed. "See if you can reach Eric Meyfarth."

Meyfarth did not call back, Jessie did not come back, and Mark did not leave until after midnight.

By that time, Christopher had retreated to the darkness of his bedroom, trying to pretend he was tired. When Loi slipped into his room, he tried to pretend he was asleep. She stood by the bed for a long time, watching him, saying nothing. Just when he thought that she was about to leave, she spoke.

"Would you like some company?" she asked gently.

He opened his eyes and looked up at her, his eyes suddenly damp. "Yes," he said hoarsely, pulling back the sheet.

Loi slipped into bed easily and snuggled against him in a position born of compromise and experience, lying on her side with one arm hugging his chest, one leg hooking over his. Her skin was silky and warm, and her hair smelled faintly of spa oils, but not at all of Mark.

Despite their nakedness, the embrace was chaste, the intimate space they shared the creation of two friends, not two lovers. She wrapped him in a safe, comfortable cocoon built from her love and her body and her energy, and her presence was balm for his pain. He was so grateful for the gift that he almost began to cry.

"I called Dr. Meyfarth," he whispered, the words an offering.

"Sssh," she said, turning her head to kiss his shoulder. "Sleep."

Christopher closed his eyes and listened to the echoes of his unhappy thoughts, now fading beneath the sound of their breathing, each breath deeper and more tranquil than the last. Sooner than he would have guessed possible, he was asleep.

Loi was gone when he woke in the morning—she did not like to share a bed for sleeping, so he was not surprised. But the touch of peace that she had given him remained, nestled against the resolve he had found on his own. Between the two, it was a little easier that morning to face both the day and himself.

Eric Meyfarth did not make it easy.

"I got your message," he said when he called back. "What's up, Chris?" His tone, like his expression, was pointedly neutral.

"Can I see you?"

"That depends," said Meyfarth. "Why?"

Asking had been hard enough. Christopher had not expected to have to explain himself. "Because if I saw someone else, I'd have to waste all that time getting to where we left off."

"I appreciate the compliment," Meyfarth said dryly.

"I didn't mean—"

"But I'm not quite persuaded," he went on. "The last time I saw you, you were a bit skeptical about my usefulness."

Christopher looked away. "I wasn't ready to be helped."

"True enough. What's changed?"

"Nothing. Except for the worse. And that's what has to change. I don't want to feel like this."

"You said much the same thing a few weeks ago, in my office. But you broke your contract with me and walked out when it got tough."

"I—" The quick defense died on his lips. "I guess I did. Old habits die hard."

"Sometimes they don't die at all," Meyfarth said. "What assurance do I have that you're serious this time?"

Knitting his brow and frowning, Christopher considered. "I don't know. None. I have to hope you'll trust me. Which comes harder the second time around, I suppose."

Nodding, Meyfarth said, "You know that I'm going to go right back to the sore spots, right back to your father and your family."

"I know. I just don't know how much I'll be able to help you."

"Why is that, Chris?"

"Because I don't know how much I know."

"Ah," said Meyfarth. "I'm confident that, at some level, you remember everything that's important to remember."

"How can you say that? You can't know."

"No, I can't—not with complete certainty," said Meyfarth. "But it's something I've come to believe about people. Inside every one of us is the frightened four-year-old, the nine-year-old explorer, the restless adolescent, and the twenty-year-old dreamer we once were. Remembering is easy. It's the forgetting that we have to practice."

"It comes naturally enough to me."

Meyfarth shook his head. "You're self-taught, I assure you. The heart of your problem is the pretense that all you are is what you are now. You've been living unconnected to your past."

"I just don't archive things like other people do," Christopher said defensively. "Look, I have trouble remembering what happened two years ago, let alone twenty. I wish I had more stories about my childhood. I wish I had more stories about my father. But I don't. I'm lost when the conversation turns to people telling funny anecdotes on themselves. I just don't remember that sort of thing. I don't know what I was like when I was ten. And I don't have anyone to help me remember."

"You don't need anyone," Meyfarth said simply.

"I need *some*thing. You, anyway."

Meyfarth shook his head. "*You* know where the gold is buried. I can only guess. If you need a map, you have to look in your own life. Have you ever kept a diary? Letter archives? Any family video albums lying around?"

"No and no. Not many pictures." He paused. "And when I look at them, I can only see this little boy that I can't really remember being."

"Because you won't let yourself. If you were connected to your past, those pictures would make you *feel*, not remember," said Meyfarth. "You're a curious one, Chris. You don't even get emotional about your emotions."

"That's not true—"

"It is. Which is why they all come out as anger."

Christopher looked away.

"You need to be reconnected, Chris."

"How do we do that?"

"*We* don't. You do." Meyfarth pursed his lips. "I was hoping to get what I needed talking to you. But the trust is coming a little hard, Chris. I think you're going to have to show me something before we can pick up our sessions."

"What?"

"How long has it been since you talked to your father?"

"Uh—a few weeks."

"Your sister?"

Wincing, Christopher admitted, "A couple of years."

"Okay," Meyfarth said, nodding. "Here's my offer. I can slot you at two, Monday—if sometime between now and then, you give your sister a call and ask her what kind of kid you were. Or something equally risky. What do you say?"

Christopher's wince deepened into a grimace. "We're not close."

"I didn't expect that you were, considering."

"This one's not my doing. My sister isn't exactly my biggest fan. I never have quite figured out why."

"That doesn't matter," Meyfarth said. "Your sister holds a piece of you. Reach out and claim it back."

Christopher met the arty's gaze with a wondering look. "I never looked at it that way."

"Probably she hasn't, either."

It was hard to believe that any piece of him which Lynn-Anne Aldritch might hold could be of much value. Because of their history, she was more like a cousin—a cousin who had seemed like a friend in their uncritical youth, but who had drifted away on the judgments of maturity. And all the growing up that seemed to matter had taken place in her absence.

Lynn-Anne was fifteen when Christopher was born, a dark-eyed, thin-bodied girl who rarely smiled, at least for a camera. The four of them—his father, Lynn-Anne, Deryn, and himself—were not together long, and Christopher remembered little of the time they were. Lynn-Anne left the B Street house when he was five, first taking an apartment in Portland, and then late admission to Bennington College, a continent away. And she never really came back into his life.

After Bennington, it was New York Metro for a year, Toronto for two, and then back to New England, settling at last in Bangor. Somewhere along the way, she replaced their father's surname with their mother's, bringing her in line with custom. She had never married, in fact had always lived alone, except for her first few months in Toronto, when she joined a household of women on exclusive Center Island.

Christopher remembered the trip to visit Lynn-Anne there, a memory highlighted by the quaint hubris of the CN Tower and the vertiginous delight of its upper lookout. There was a less vivid remembrance of an earlier trip to a weary, noisy New York.

She always sent something at Yule, never on his birthday. He went her one better and remembered both occasions, but his gift-giving was duty-driven and the gifts chosen almost at random—he knew so little of her life that he had no idea what would truly please her, and Deryn could offer little help.

Once every few months there would be an unexpected call or, if Lynn-Anne was in the middle of one of her depressions, a morose letter. He would answer with earnest but stilted missives which—at Deryn's prodding—invariably contained an invitation to come home for a visit.

But the invitations went ignored and unanswered. As far as Christopher knew, only once in twenty-two years had Lynn-Anne returned to the West Coast—a decade ago, for the funeral of Grandmom Anne, Sharron Aldritch's mother, in Seattle. But after coming five thousand klicks across the country, Lynn-Anne chose not to come the one small step farther to Oregon; she was back in Maine before either Christopher, then in school in San Francisco, or their father, at home in the ridge house, even knew of the death.

That was the break point. Perhaps understandably, the Aldritch-Martins had never taken Christopher into their hearts as a grandchild—the circumstances were unhappy, the link tenuous. Grandmom Anne was a name to him, little more, and he was not greatly surprised to learn he had been excluded.

But he would not have expected his father to be kept in the dark, or Lynn-Anne to join the conspiracy of silence. That was the first time Christopher realized how hard the lines were dividing what was left of the family, and the first time he realized that he and Lynn-Anne stood on opposite sides of one of those lines.

He missed one birthday, she the next Yule. With no protest or apology from either side, the remaining threads tying them together broke one by one. Without those threads, the semblance of kinship and friendship between them simply slipped away.

There was never any formal declaration, no doors slammed. But silence was its own message.

That was the gap he had to bridge. And all he had to throw across it were words. Two words.

"Hello, Annie."

It was a jolt to see how she had aged. The picture he carried frozen in his mind was of her at the rail of the Toronto harbor ferry, pointing out the sights, or standing on the balcony of her 94th Street high rise, watching the two-mile-long shadow of Columbus Tower sweep across the city—a brave-eyed wry-mouthed woman in her twenties, living what seemed then like an adventure.

But fifteen years had taken the courage from her eyes and twisted her mouth into a cynical pout. She looked at him wonderingly for a long moment before she spoke.

"Christopher," she said. "God, but you're looking worn."

That was the second jolt. The picture he carried of himself was also frozen, locked in the first time he looked in the mirror and no longer saw a boy, with no allowance made for further aging.

"It's been that kind of year," he said ruefully.

Lynn-Anne passed on the opportunity to invite him to explain. "So, you've joined the real world at last," she said. "Life is the great leveler. You don't know how much comfort I take in that."

"I wanted to wish you happy holidays," he said. "Are you going to do anything special?"

"I don't celebrate a winter holiday anymore, Christopher," she said with a politely tolerant smile. "I didn't believe in most of it, and the rest has been a disappointment. It's rained for Solstice Moon three years running, Santa Claus is just a nice old man with whiskers, and I'm still waiting for Jesus to decide he wants me. Hardly any point, wouldn't you say?"

"I had my doubts about Santa Claus early on," Christopher said with a gentle smile. "But it's still a good excuse for catching up with people you've been neglecting."

Though she was only forty-two, Lynn-Anne had mastered the dowager's raised-eyebrow look of skeptical disdain. "This may come as a surprise, but I don't feel neglected," she said. "It isn't an accident that I moved here, you know. And I do know where you are and how to use the link. Besides, I hardly think that's why you called.''

He frowned. ''Why do you think I called, then?''

Leaning forward, Lynn-Anne collected the cup on the table before her. ''Based on past experience, you either want something from me or you're going to apologize for something you've already done to me,'' she said, and raised the cup to her lips.

It was an attack, and yet said so quietly, so gently, that he hardly knew how to respond. ''I need your help,'' he said. ''I need your help understanding what happened to our family.''

Her laugh was unpleasant. ''We don't have a family, Christopher. We only have relatives.''

He stared at her for a long moment. ''Maybe that's right,'' he said. ''But if it is, I don't know why.''

''Why does it matter?''

''Because I'm trying to build a new family,'' he said. ''And I seem to keep tripping over pieces of the old one.''

''Give it up for a loss,'' she said shortly. ''McCutcheons don't know how to love. It's a birth defect. Their hearts are too small.''

''I don't want to believe that.''

''Of course not,'' said his sister. ''You think you can have what you want, just because you're you and you want it. You always have.''

''Why are you angry at me?'' he asked beseechingly. ''I don't understand what I did to you.''

Frowning, she shook her head. ''Be careful what you wish for. I might tell you.'' She set the cup down before her. ''Thank you for the holiday wishes, Christopher. And the same to you, just as sincerely meant. Good night.''

And the screen brightened to white.

''Damn you!'' Christopher exclaimed, bouncing up from the couch, jangling with frustration. Satisfying Meyfarth's conditions was no longer uppermost in his mind. Lynn-Anne had seen to that, with her genteel sniping and infuriating dismissal.

He waited five minutes, composing himself, composing his words, and then called back. As he half expected, this time her AIP answered over the simple blue and black identifier screen.

''I'd like to leave a message,'' he said resignedly.

''Ready.''

''Surprise, surprise,'' Christopher said. ''It looks like you're just as good at avoiding the past as I am, Annie. I thought you stayed out there because you didn't like us. I never thought it was because you were afraid of us.

"We were a family once, on B Street. You were part of it. I was part of it. Maybe it didn't last very long, but it was important. You're a witness to my life. I need your memories to help me sort it out and put it in order. And if there's some grudge you're holding because of something I don't even remember, I need to know that, too.

"You used to tell me stories about our mother, and that was important to me. You knew her. I never had that chance. Buck and Annie didn't even consider me a relative. But I needed to know what part of her is in me. I needed her to be real—"

Unexpectedly, the display brightened, and Lynn-Anne's face appeared. "You don't have any right to call Sharron 'Mother,' " she said, her eyes flashing angrily.

"You thought I did then."

"I've learned things since then," she said. "Hard things."

"I know that in most ways Deryn was to me what Sharron was to you. But Sharron gave me life. She made half of me. I've always felt that I had a father and two mothers."

"Wrong," Lynn-Anne said curtly. "You had a father and a keeper. That's all."

"Look—"

"You really *don't* know your own history very well, do you, brother dear? I ran away the day you were born. I spent five weeks on the coast, Cannon Beach, Nehalem, Tillamook, before they found me."

"Why?" Christopher asked, brow wrinkled in puzzlement.

"Hurt feelings. While Deryn was pregnant with you, it seemed like I didn't exist. William fussed and fretted and hovered and dictated every detail of what she did, so you'd be healthy. You were such a big production it was pretty obvious that he wanted you because I wasn't good enough, that he wanted you a lot more than he wanted me. So guess what—I was rooting for you to die. Then Deryn would go away and everything would be the way it was."

Christopher blinked. "I never heard anything about that."

"Who would tell you?" she asked. "But you went and survived, even came two weeks early. As far as I could see, it was only going to get worse once you were actually born, so I left. I was just two months short of majority when they dragged me back."

"But then you stayed for five *years*."

"Yes," she said, and glanced down at her folded hands. "And you even lived through them." She looked up. "Does that shock you? That I thought about killing you?"

He swallowed. "Yes."

"Just remember, this was your idea," she said, and settled back in her chair. "I had never been around a baby. I didn't expect you to be cute. Deryn let me hold you, and I felt—protective. You were so tiny, so helpless. And then Deryn told me that I was the closest connection you had to your mother—to Sharron—and that you needed me. That Sharron—that my mother would have expected me to help." Lynn-Anne fought off a tear with an angry shake of the head. "Stupid me, I believed her."

"She wasn't wrong," said Christopher. "I looked up to you. I loved you."

She was silent for a moment. "Past tense," she said finally. "Or didn't you notice?"

"I *do* love you—"

"Don't rush to judgment on that," she said. "Deryn *was* wrong. She was told a lie and passed it right along. All part of the plan." She shook her head. "He started working on you as soon as you could talk. I finally left because I couldn't stop it and I couldn't stand to stay around and watch it anymore."

"Working on me?"

"Pushing, pulling, twisting, programming. The sculptor at work, creating a self-portrait." She studied him with a critical gaze. "For a piece of statuary, you actually do a fair imitation of a person."

So sharp the scalpel, so deep the wound. She was an artist. He gaped, amazed. "Why do you want to hurt me?"

"Why do you care what I think?" She pulled a yellow-wrapped cigarette from a sleeve pocket and lit it. "I was eight when Mom died. You notice things at eight that you wouldn't notice at five, even if you don't understand them." A deep, breathy drag. "They had a fight, the night before, and then she came and held me."

"I remember you telling me."

"She knew I didn't like it when he yelled at her. Usually, I was the one crying. This time she was. She said, 'I'm sorry, sweetheart. So sorry. I won't make the same mistake again.' It was the last time I saw her."

"It happened in the lab the next day," he supplied.

She smiled faintly. "Yes. The toxicity lab. A lovely irony. Grandmom Anne came and got me from the city school, took me to the hospital. I remember how pale she was, how frightened. By the time we got there, my mother was dead. William was arguing with the doctors and barely noticed us. So Anne took me in to say good-bye."

Lynn-Anne's eyes were unfocused and bright with tears. "I touched her hand, and it felt so wrong that I ran out of the room crying that it wasn't her. I didn't know until later that it was the hand where she'd injected herself." She looked hard at him. "You know she did it on purpose, don't you? You don't still believe it was an accident."

"I don't know," he said. "I still wonder why she would do it. A moment of weakness, because they had a fight? That doesn't explain it. There were better choices. If she was unhappy, she could have left, moved out, even divorced him."

Lynn-Anne was shaking her head in dissent. "You don't leave William McCutcheon until he's ready to let you go. Sharron Aldritch was a very bright woman, but not a very strong one," she said. "She killed herself in a moment of clarity and strength, because she knew that it was the only way that she could escape him—the only way she could deny him. I'm as sure of it as I am of anything in this world. And I hate him for it."

Tight-lipped, Christopher nodded. "I guess if I believed that, I would have to hate him, too. But I don't see him that way."

"You can't," she said with a sad smile. "Please don't pretend on my account."

"I'm serious. Sharron gave me something precious—a piece of herself. I love her for that, even though I never knew her."

"She gave you nothing," his sister said harshly.

"I am what I am partly because of her—"

"What makes you think she wanted you born?"

He stared. "They harvested her eggs when they knew she was dying—she wanted—"

"No," Lynn-Anne said sharply. "I saw them take her to surgery. I remember, because I thought it meant she might be okay. They harvested the eggs after she was dead."

A deep frown creased Christopher's face. "So I was confused," he said. "It doesn't matter whether it was before or after. The point is the same. She gave us a gift—"

"What makes you think that she knew?"

"Deryn told me—" He stopped short. "Was *that* the lie? Is that what you meant?"

Lynn-Anne showed a smugly satisfied smile. "The light dawns. Yes, that was the lie. The fight was about you, Christopher."

Though he heard the words, the meaning eluded him. "What are you saying?"

She laughed at his puzzlement. "Think about it. You'll figure it out eventually. You see, you're just like your father, Christopher. You're just not as good at it."

The screen went white.

And though he tried for more than an hour, she accepted no more calls from him that night.

CHAPTER
24

-|UGG|-

"All sins are justified . . ."

THE MEMORIAL CONVOCATION FOR MALENA GRAHAM WAS nearly over when Mikhail Dryke returned to the auditorium. Sasaki was at the podium, a slender but powerful figure in her wide-sashed black and red kimono. Rather than create a distraction by returning to his seat in the front row, Dryke found a spot along the back wall and stood there.

Dryke had resisted Sasaki's plans to address the convocation in person, just as he had resisted the decision to hold the Block 1 pioneers over for two days at all three centers. Both actions seemed foolishly defiant, a challenge and invitation to any fanatics who might have been inspired by Evan Silverman's example. Neither Sasaki's movements nor the Project's internal schedules were made public, but Dryke was under no illusions that he could ensure either remained a secret.

The gathering made a lovely target, and Sasaki's presence vastly sweetened the prize. When com services could easily place her "in" the auditorium with an Oration hololink, it seemed to Dryke a foolish risk for her to leave the controlled environment of Prainha for the urban front lines of Houston. When Sasaki dismissed his objection without discussion, Dryke could not help but read it as confirmation that she had lost confidence in him.

But he had been wrong—wrong about the decision, and perhaps wrong about the meaning. Because of his everyday access to her, Dryke realized, he had lost sight of the power of Sasaki's mystique, the calming influence of her quiet leadership. Since the word began to spread that she was coming to Houston, and especially since her arrival three hours ago, Sasaki had worked a transformation on the mood of the center more profound than that managed in three days by the center's army of counselors.

And now, with the closing words of her panegyric, she was sealing the change.

"There have been many rumors—many more, no doubt, than have reached my ears," Sasaki was saying. "I have heard that Malena Graham's place on the ship's roster will be filled by her sister. That her body will be carried on *Memphis* for burial in space. That she anticipated her death and recorded in her diary a hope that she would be interred on a world of Tau Ceti.

"I must tell you, perhaps to your disappointment, that these rumors are false.

"Malena Graham's diary was filled with anticipation of her life on *Memphis*, with reflections of the dream and the goal that we all share, with the private thoughts of the heart and the spirit. She had no inkling of what was to come.

"Malena Graham's family has requested that her body be returned to them for burial near Franklin, in Virginia. The coroner's office of the Texas State Police has already complied with their request. Her body was never in our custody. Nor would the police have recognized any claim to it we might have made.

"And I have decided that Malena Graham's place on *Memphis* will be filled by a random draw from the qualified alternates— which is the usual process by which vacancies are filled."

Despite the inhibiting solemnity of the event, a scattering of voices was raised in unhappy protest. Dryke was shocked, but Sasaki remained unperturbed, holding up her hand to ask for silence.

"I know that Dr. Oker's office has received several hundred messages urging that Malena's place be left vacant, as a memorial," she said. "I sympathize with the sentiment. But I cannot believe that Malena would want us to deny to another, in the name of honoring her, the gift that she had been so grateful to receive herself."

The audience marked its agreement with applause—well short of universal, but louder and more emphatic than the protests which had preceded it.

"Over this last year, our family has lost a dozen members to accident and incident," Sasaki went on. "We mourn them and remember them, but we carry on.

"If we leave Malena's place vacant, we are as much as saying that we could have done without her, that her contribution to the community—and therefore her death—were trivial and meaningless. And that is not so.

"If we make an exception for Malena because of the way she died, we are raising a memorial not to her, but to her murderer, for making her unique. And that I will not do."

This time, the applause was spontaneous, spirited, and strong. She had won them back.

Sasaki continued, "A meaningful memorial to Malena Graham would respect her commitment to the Project and preserve her contribution to our community. It would leave her joined to the *Memphis* family as more than a memory. It should be a *living* memorial.

"I can tell you now that we have an opportunity to create just such a memorial."

Dryke, knowing what was coming, marveled at Sasaki's flawless control. The auditorium was absolutely still, spellbound, all attention focused on the woman on the stage.

"All of you who have endured it know how thorough Selection's biomedical testing is," Sasaki said. "Many of you also know that Malena Graham was a childhood victim of poliomyelitis. She did not think that remarkable, and it was clearly no obstacle to her selection.

"But it did make her different, and that difference is now a blessing. Because of her polio, when Malena Graham came here, she was among the several dozen new arrivals subjected to an additional battery of tests to evaluate their reproductive health," said Sasaki. "She was given a hormonal accelerator, and a few days later, eight ova were collected. Two of those eggs were consumed in the testing. But the remaining six were not needed and were placed in cryostorage for future tests, if necessary."

As those listening began to realize where Sasaki's words were leading, Dryke began to see heads bob and joy-tearful smiles appear on the faces of those standing near him. The funeral spell was shattered, the blanket of gloom dispelled. The applause grew from scattered knots to spreading waves as the audience came joyfully to its feet.

"That future use will come, time willing, on the first colony world you found," said Sasaki over the rising tumult. "For I direct that Malena Graham's eggs be added to the gamete bank aboard *Memphis*, and ask you to take her essence with you to Tau Ceti—not as a memorial, but as a legacy. And when the first child is born of her line, then you may give her an epitaph worthy of the dream she dreamed, and a fate better than that which befell her here:

"*Non omnis moriar.*

" 'I shall not altogether die.' "

It was a challenge to reach Sasaki in the friendly crush that followed, and a greater challenge to separate her from it. Finally, Dryke resorted to deception and professional prerogative, catching her arm to tell her that there was a security alert in the complex, and then hustling her away to a private room on an upper floor.

"I'm sorry, Director. There is no threat," he said when they were alone. "I have to leave the center shortly, and I needed to talk to you before I did."

"Does this have to do with your disappearance from the convocation?"

"Hugh sent up a package from the data analysis lab at Prainha, eyes-only. I went out to collect it from the courier and to find a tank."

"And?"

"And I have some news that I hope will do for you what your eulogy did for those people downstairs. We've located Jeremiah." He said it pridefully, looking at her expectantly.

But Sasaki's reaction was disappointing. Her eyes widened briefly—surprise?—and then narrowed into a questioning, almost disbelieving gaze. "Located or caught?"

"Located. That's why I have to leave. I'm taking four locals from security and the two top systems texperts with me."

"Where is he? *Is* it a he?"

"The Pacific Northwest. Oregon. I'm not sure on the other."

She frowned. "Then this is hardly an authoritative identification, is it?"

"No. Not yet. We have two addresses, one a business. We'll sort it out when we get there."

"He tracks you," Sasaki said, fretting. "He will be gone before you arrive."

"He tracks my screamer," said Dryke. "Which is leaving any minute for Chile, with appropriate disinformation on the bounce. I'm going off the net until I have him. There'll be nothing out there to point to where I am, and I'm telling no one but you."

"He may already be gone."

"The line's been active within the half hour."

She nodded, accepting the point. "What was the break? Was it Katrina Becker?"

"No. Becker has been immovable." Dryke smiled coldly. "No, it was the bragging that got him. We backtraced his rant over the Munich hit past the Albuquerque node which had stopped us the last time. This time we had more ears to the ground and matched to a dedicated line."

"How easily?"

"What?"

"I remind you of your discourse on the art of fishing, and the lesson of the great fish."

Dryke stared, the self-congratulation leaving his face. "I have a good feeling about this, Hiroko."

"You are too valuable to lose to a feeling," she said. "If an Evan Silverman was willing to kill a Malena Graham for such little gain, would a Jeremiah hesitate to kill you?"

"I won't give him that chance."

Frowning, she wrapped her arms around herself. "Mikhail, I am most serious about insisting that you examine your judgment. You received the failure of the Munich operation and the death of Malena as personal defeats. You may have perceived them as blows to your prestige. Am I unreasonable to think that Mikhail Dryke might be so eager to restore himself in my eyes that he would alter the equation of risk?"

He looked away, up toward one corner of the ceiling, and sighed. "No," he said finally. "You're *not* unreasonable."

"Thank you."

"But you're wrong," Dryke added. "This is Jeremiah, and I can get to him."

Her hands slid down the sleeves of her kimono until her arms were crossed over her chest in a more forceful pose. "Despite the week's events, I do not require vindication of your competence, Mikhail. And I do not welcome assurances spoken by the voice of personal pride."

Dryke felt himself bristling. "We've been closing in on him all year. Every time he spoke, every stunt he pulled. There were already signs pointing in this direction. This is consistent with all of them."

"And it is exactly when all is as expected that the wary may become inattentive, and a trick most effectively employed. I ask only that you exercise prudent caution."

To be reminded by Sasaki of such an elementary principle stung Dryke's pride. "If you really believed in me, you wouldn't need to ask that."

"Have I lost the right to question you, Mikhail?" she asked, eyebrow arching. "What message should I read in your defensiveness—insecurity, or impatience? Either would be reason to send someone else in your place."

Drawing a quick breath, he squeezed his eyes shut for a moment, then looked at her and nodded. "You're right. My apology."

"Not necessary," she said, relaxing. "But accepted."

"It *is* personal. I don't deny it," said Dryke. "I want him. But that won't make me reckless. Just the opposite—I'll be that much more careful. I've been chasing Jeremiah long enough. I want it to be over."

"As do I," Sasaki said. "As do I. May your journey be fruitful. Report to me at first opportunity."

"I will. But there's something else we need to settle. Do I still have authority? Will you support me?"

She studied him for a long time, her eyes deep crystal black and unblinking. "Yes."

"Thank you."

"But be sure. Be very sure."

"I will." He glanced at his watch. "The others should be ready. I have to go," he said, and started for the door. Then he paused and added, "I nearly forgot—"

"Yes?"

"Word came in while you were in the convo. The command and navigation package is safely aboard the ship."

That earned a smile. "I am glad to hear it."

"Feist says that the virus turned up with every archive copy of the package on site in Munich. All five of them. Every time they tried a restore, the virus would come up, look for its parent on the main net, and go crazy when it came up missing."

"Then consider yourself vindicated," said Sasaki. "Can you tell me now where the operational copy was stored?"

Dryke grinned. "In a bulk cargo cask in the holding yard at Palima Point, waiting for a cheap ride to orbit."

"Tagged as what?" Sasaki's eyebrows were frowning.

"As the personal freight of a new Takara immigrant, one Atsuji Matsushita."

"Did he know?"

"The only person who knew was Matt Reid, who had to make the intercept."

"And the awkward questions from Mr. Matsushita, wondering what's become of his socks?"

"For the price of his immigration fee, Mr. Matsushita was prevailed upon to help smuggle some contraband up to the colony," said Dryke. "Believe me, he'll be too scared to ask any questions about its disappearance."

An hour later, Dryke's team boarded the tube at the DFW transplex. Already dispersed through the waiting line, the five men and two women ended up scattered between six different compartments on the two-car train.

Dryke, with an end seat in number 9 of the second car, was able to watch through the window as the containerized cargo and luggage slid on board below his feet. He wondered if the team's kits had passed railway scrutiny; the bags did not carry the Federal Weapons License scanner tags to which he and the corpsecs were entitled. Although that limited their options, it also avoided a verification call-out, which could alert Jeremiah of their approach.

At the Phoenix interline station, the team separated into two groups. The texperts drew the longer route, the Midlands tube back to Chicago, then west again to Seattle, where they would wait for Dryke's call. Dryke and the four corpsecs stayed on board for the coast run to Portland.

The elderly woman at his left was garrulously inquisitive, but Dryke was not interested in conversation. Before long, he detached the eyecup display and carpieces from his slate and donned the slender headset which held them, pointedly withdrawing to the artificial reality they created.

But it was hard to make the time pass quickly, impossible to calm his inner restlessness. The correlation files and quicksearch reports stored in his slate were dry as a brittle leaf. And the DBS link of the expensive Korean-made slate was useless a hundred meters underground. The train was isolated from the direct broadcast skylinks, except for what the National Railway chose to relay from surface antennas—and to sell by the minute to its captive audience. But Drake could not afford to have his account show any activity, especially not aboard a tube.

He realized suddenly that he was tired. The adrenaline that had sustained him through the preparations was gone, leaving him weary-limbed and energyless. His kit contained antifatigue tablets, but it was just as well that they were out of reach—Watchman worked as advertised, but exacted a horrible price when it finally wore off.

He realized, too, that he had missed two meals that day and had nothing with him to fill the void. The thought was enough to awaken an empty-bellied hunger which had lain dormant to that point.

Extracting the stylus from his holder, Dryke began to doodle idly on the slate—filling the frame with patterns of nested diamonds, blanking it to fill it with concentric circles, then with the squares of a chessboard grid. It did not amuse him, but it occupied him, and that was almost enough.

He thought ahead to Jeremiah, ahead to the mission. There was little doubt in his mind that the team would succeed. The end of the chase was in sight, if not yet in hand.

But, oddly, there was little pleasure in the anticipation. After all the travel, all the trauma, he would have thought he'd be happier. Even his curiosity had been dulled. He no longer cared to know what moved his adversary, what tricks and tactics had prolonged the siege. The weariness ran deeper than blood and muscle. It had infected his spirit as well.

It's time to move on.

The thought surprised him. Move on to what? *To serving Mikhail Dryke. To carrying on a normal life.* But he wondered if he knew how to do either. *To keeping all those promises consigned to the future—Castillo de San Marcos, Loches, Peveril Castle. To walk the ruins of the Great Wall from Shanhaiguan to Jiayuguan and the edge of the desert—*

"Are you a historian?" asked the woman beside him.

"Eh?" He turned toward her. "Excuse me?"

She pointed toward his slate. "I was wondering if you were a historian?"

Dryke looked down at his lap and laughed despite himself. The last sketch that had come from his deft fingers and idle mind was a half-completed plan for an assault on a mountain redoubt he had labeled Fort Jesus.

"No, ma'am," he said, his voice soft and weary. "Not a historian. Just a boy playing soldier."

She left him alone after that, even though he might have ultimately welcomed the distraction. The thoughts that possessed him were black and joyless. *Victory is a more difficult art than war.* Which American President had said that? Wilson? Roosevelt? Gingrich? Dryke could not remember. Others had learned the same lesson. The Duke of Wellington explaining to Lady Shelley: *I always say that, next to a battle lost, the greatest misery is a battle gained.* An old secret, indeed, now being revealed to Dryke.

It was a decision he did not want to make, wrapped in questions he did not want to answer. If there was a Katrina Becker in Munich, an Evan Silverman in Houston, a Javier Sala in Madrid, who might there be in Prainha, or Kasigau, or Takara? How long would it take an organization which had intercepted company mail and jammed *Newstime* to find where their Prophet was hidden?

Would the people who had knocked down a T-ship and spilled poisons on the ground be any less bold in trying to reclaim their leader? Could he rest easy knowing that his enemies played breathless electronic tag on the nets unimpeded, and found the Project's defenses as intimidating as the Maginot Line?

There were a hundred questions, and yet they were all the same question: How long would it go on if he let it go on? He hoped that circumstance would save him from having to find an answer, save him from touching that place inside where white fire lived and no act was forbidden.

All of the decisions were coming hard.

They had two targets, each difficult in its own way: the Peterson Road house, a hundred klicks outside the city, and Pacific Land Management, ten stories up in the heart of Portland's financial district. Dryke had too few troops to cover both at once— the small size of the team was part of the price for moving quickly and quietly. Nor could they touch local law enforcement for help. There was no way to control what went out into the net. There was no way to know who was Jeremiah's friend.

One or the other. It had to be one or the other. But if they chose wrong, Jeremiah would have a chance to run. And a man like Jeremiah with a network like Homeworld could run for a long time.

But which one was Fort J?

It came down to probabilities. Pacific Land Management had nineteen registered partners, twenty-eight comlines (counting eight on the building's SkyLAN), and its fingers in half a billion dollars' worth of land and real estate in four countries—a splendid foundation for the infrastructure of a revolution. By contrast, the Peterson Road house had a modest four comlines, an overdue property tax bill, and a reclusive owner with legitimate connections to most of the state's business and political leadership.

Dryke chose the Peterson Road house.

He hedged his bets by calling the texperts down from Seattle and leaving one, the brooding man named Ramond, to play stakeout at Pacific Land Management. But the rest went with him to Hoffman Hill, a six-hundred-meter summit just six klicks from Peterson Ridge and belonging to the same whorl of valleys and steep-sloped tree-covered fold mountains. Hoffman Hill was a nearly ideal staging area—just a one-minute dash from the target for the armed and armored Beech Pursuit that Ramond and Dru had leased for them in Seattle.

By that time, all of them were well into their second dose cycle of Watchman. While Dru set up sky monitors and spotting snoops on the ridge line, Dryke huddled with the others in the predawn chill to lay out the logistics. They made a skeptical audience.

"We come in from the top, he's got a lot of room to hide. We come up the road and hit his gate, and he'll sky," said Loren, the most senior of Dryke's recruits.

"I know," said Dryke. "That's why we're going in both ways."

"I'd sure rather be doing this with fifty bodies than five." Loren's frown was dyspeptic. "What do you know about the defenses?"

"Boundary fenced and a hailer. That's all that's on the books. I'm sure that's not all there is."

"Anti-air?"

"Maybe."

"How many people up there?"

Dryke reached down to the open kit by his feet and tossed the corpsec a clear-skinned frag helmet. "Can't tell you. So flash goggles, bug-heads, and torso armor for everyone. And keep your fagging heads down."

"Are you sure you don't want to just pump a rocket or two

into the house from here?'' asked Liviya with a grin. She was
cradling her frag helmet under her arm like a basketball while
she checked her pistol.

"I'm sure," Dryke said. "Dru will do battle management
from here if it comes to that. But I really don't want this drawn
out. If it's not over in five minutes, we're going to be in more
trouble than I want to think about." He looked up through the
trees at the brightening sky. "Any questions?"

"I want another look at this guy's picture," Loren said.

Dryke keyed the frame and wordlessly handed Loren the slate.

"With five minutes warning, they'll be able to dump all their
files and break both ends of every link," Dru called to them
without looking up from her work. "Five seconds would be
enough if it's all volatile storage."

"We're not going in for files. We're going in for Jeremiah—
or whoever speaks with his voice."

"If we have to shoot to stop someone—" Liviya began.

"Then shoot straight," Dryke said. "Any more questions?"

In the silence, Loren handed back the slate.

"Dru, anything?" Dryke called to the texpert.

She shook her head. "Outside lights went off a minute ago.
Two comlines active, looks like background traffic. Might be
there. Might not. Nothing conclusive."

"Do you have the tracer ready?"

"Yes."

"Send it."

"Will do."

With the skylink's cellular narrowcasting and active message
routing, every personal receiver sent regular updates to Central
Addressing, so that the net would know where to "forward" the
owner's messages. Trace queries—ordinarily not processed without a court's "order to locate"—retrieved the current address in
the system.

"For whatever it's worth, the tracer's still pointing here," Dru
announced a few seconds later.

Dryke nodded grimly. "Let's go find out if it's worth anything."

Like chrome hummingbirds waking to the dawn, the team's
three cars rose from the muddy track of Lawrence Road and
fanned out over the forested slopes.

Loren and Liviya's skimmers stayed at treetop level, swinging north and west in snaking arcs that kept them below Fort Jesus' horizon. Dryke took the Pursuit straight up along the slope of Hoffman Hill and exploded skyward, clawing for the altitude he would need in a look-down shoot-down scenario, showing Fort J only the armored underbelly of the flyer.

But there was no response from Peterson Ridge—not when the skimmers flashed over the boundary fences, not even when the Pursuit's climb flattened out and turned over into a heart-stopping dive.

"No delta," said Dru, watching the comline traffic. A burst coder carried her words to all three vehicles. "Repeat, no delta, nothing to squash."

As the double dome of the house grew larger before him, Dryke saw the two skimmers slow and drop down into invisible gaps in the trees and disappear.

"Unit Four on station, all clear," said Loren. A breath later, Liviya logged in a near-echo.

Still there was no response.

The purr of the Pursuit's engines climbed to an annoyed whine as it braked for touchdown. With a last-second sideslip, Dryke dropped it on the concrete scorch pad in front of the garage, blocking the middle half of the double-wide door.

"System lock," he said. "Code Eben-Emael."

"Locked," said the autopilot AIP.

Dryke flipped down his own bug-head and climbed out on the left side of the flyer, keeping its bulk between him and the house. He looked to see if Loren had come up the road into position and was answered with a wave.

"Liviya?"

"Ready."

"Going in."

Crossing the yard to the front door under the gaze of the house's many windows was an act best done without thinking. Once on the porch, Dryke waved Loren forward and waited until the black man was alongside the Pursuit.

"Dru?" asked Dryke.

"No change."

"What?"

"No change?"

"Ramond?"

"Nothing is happening here, Mr. Dryke."

"This is bad. This is very bad," warned Loren. "Maybe we ought to wait until we know it's clean."

"Goddamm it, he's gone," Dryke fumed, reaching for the door. "We're too late."

"Oh, man."

Dryke touched the controls and received a shock—the door was unlocked.

"Son of a bitch," he said, staring. "Dru?"

"No change."

"Not even a fagging burglar alarm?"

"Nothing."

Dryke puffed out a breath. "No one else comes in," he said, and stepped through the doorway.

Inside the Fuller were the ordinary private places of a man of some means, but few affectations. A gentleman's kitchen, tidy and highly automated. A morning-facing breakfast nook, with a hummingbird feeder hanging outside the windows. A working study dotted with motion toys and engineering models. A dark bedroom with an empty, neatly made bed.

Stinger in hand, Dryke moved warily from room to room, wrestling with a mixture of heart-thumping fear and squeamish embarrassment, waiting for a nasty surprise and fearing he had already received it. The house felt empty, like a set piece, a fabrication.

"Nothing yet," he said. "Loren—check the garage."

In a moment he had his answer. "Got one Avanti Eagle and one Honda SD-50, as registered."

Dryke swore. "Then where is he? Does anyone have anything?"

"Could have been picked up by someone," Loren said. "You want some company in there?"

Frowning, Dryke tipped the shield of his helmet halfway up. "I suppose. Liviya, baby-sit the Pursuit, will you?"

While he waited, Dryke drifted back to the study, the most interesting room. When Loren joined him he was sitting in the chair at the console, playing with a model of a self-lifting crane.

"Bastard got away from me again," he said, his voice almost emotionless.

"I did a space inventory on the way through—not a very good house for playing hide-and-seek."

"No. And I'm tired of that game." Frowning, Dryke discarded the model on the desk. "I guess we can have Dru take a look at this, anyway."

"Somebody's going to have to come pick me up," Dru reminded.

Under the weight of Dryke's disappointment, it seemed like a major decision. "Liviya—no, better keep the flyer here. Ah, who's in Unit Four?"

"Zabricki."

"Just a moment." Loren leaned closer and peered at the console. "Dru? You still showing traffic on the lines into here?"

"Sure," she answered. "The same background stuff—ad frames, financials, junk fax. Intermittent but steady."

Puzzled, Loren swung his head toward Dryke. "Where's it going to? This system's not logging anything."

"What? There must be an AIP trashing it."

"Even that would show as activity."

Loren and Dryke stared at each other for a long moment. Then Dryke stood and flipped his shield back down into place.

"Zabricki, Dru, stay put," Dryke said. He raised a questioning eyebrow at Loren. "Where?"

"Down," said Loren. "Has to be down."

"Let's find it."

"Look for natural seams, inside corners. I don't think there's any wall volume unaccounted for. Probably in the floor."

"Kitchen," said Dryke, his eyes lighting up. "Parquet floor. Come on."

The seams were almost perfect, the door almost invisible. It filled the rectangular space between the pedestal counter and the sink cabinets along one wall. Dryke stood looking down at it with hands on hips, chewing on his lower lip.

"How much do you want to bet there's another way in?" Loren asked. "Tunnel to the woods? To the garage?"

Dryke shook his head. "Doesn't matter. He's not here." He sighed. "What do you think, voice command? Through the house AIP?"

"Probably."

"And what else?" Dryke scanned the kitchen. "A lot of control contacts here. Some unlikely combination—"

"I can't imagine them taking the chance of someone trying to make some toast and raising the door instead."

"And I can't imagine him not building in a safety net. AIPs can be corrupted."

"We can force this," Loren said. "There's a power chisel in my skimmer."

"No," Dryke said, walking to the sink at the middle of the rectangle. "If we force it, the files are sure to be dumped." He turned on the cold water and splashed a double handful on his face. "It wouldn't be anything you could do by accident."

"It wouldn't be anything that would open it while you're standing on it," Loren said with a grin.

The water still running, his face still wet, Dryke stared sideways at the other man. "No, it wouldn't," he said slowly. He touched the sweep contact on the wall behind the sink and watched as the faucet head swiveled in a circle to sweep away particles loosened by the ultrasonics. "But all you'd need is a little interlock, a pressure sensor—"

As the sweep cycle ended, Dryke stepped back from the sink, retreating past the edge of the door. From there, stretching out across the countertop, he could barely reach the contact behind the sink. But he could reach it.

With a faint whir, the floor began to rise, the first few centimeters straight up, then canting toward Loren. Dryke jumped back and stared.

"He must have longer arms than I do."

Loren was marveling. "Son of a bitch. How did you know where the switch was?"

"Because I know him better than I want to."

The panel stopped rising when it made a sixty-degree angle with the rest of the floor. Beneath it was a lighted passage, a carpeted stairway.

"Stay here," Dryke said to Loren, and started down.

He descended the stairs cautiously, the edge suddenly back in the game. Halfway down, he crouched for a peek into the room below.

Where the walls should have been, he glimpsed a golden-red desertscape, a flash of light on water, the brilliant greens of a fern-filled rain forest. The whole chamber was a tank, ten meters across, with earthscape murals playing on the shell. At the center was a large-scale table display, an interface controller with its multicolored screens, a curved desk.

And, in the high-backed chair beside the desk, a man. He was facing the stairway and looking directly at Dryke.

"Lila, begin," said the man in the chair.

His breath still caught tight in the binding of his surprise, Dryke descended the last few steps as an automaton. The man in the chair had but a passing resemblance to Jeremiah—his face beardless and too lean, the hair thinner and darker. But there was something in the eyes that was the same.

"I expected you, Mr. Dryke, but not this soon. Take off your hat and stay awhile—"

There was something oddly theatrical about the man's demeanor, something scripted about his words and tone. But where was the audience?

"Did you get that?" Loren was calling from the kitchen. "Mr. Dryke, did you get that?"

Dryke heard him through the helmet, not the coder. "Get what?" he called back.

But Loren was already descending the stairway with quick steps. "Dru says all the lines from here are lit up. Land and sky—Dru? Dru? Damn, I'm losing her. This place must be shielded." He stopped short of the landing and blinked. "Jesus Christ. There's somebody here."

"Ready," said a woman's voice from nowhere.

"Thank you, Lila," the man said calmly. "This is William McCutcheon, speaking for Jeremiah and the Homeworld—"

The whole chamber is a tank. Dryke spun around and looked at the ceiling behind him. A three-eyed camera limpet hung from the ceiling above the stairway.

"As you can see, I have visitors this morning. As you might guess from the weapons they carry, I did not invite them. Mikhail Dryke, chief of the security forces for Allied Transcon, has invaded my home to arrest me. My crime—"

"No!" shouted Dryke, whirling. "No more fucking speeches!"

Behind him, Loren wordlessly retreated halfway up the stairs. "Dru?" Dryke heard him saying. "Dru?"

"Do you really think that you can stop us?" asked McCutcheon. "That your efforts have made any difference at all? Do you think I count so much, that you have only one enemy? I'm just one link in the chain, one cell in something larger. When I'm gone, someone else will step in to take my place."

"And someone else will step in to take mine," said Dryke. Something had snapped inside him, like a switch being thrown.

He no longer cared if his words were being broadcast to the world, no longer could bear to be taunted and lectured.

"You don't understand what you're fighting." McCutcheon's tone was dismissive.

In that moment, Dryke realized that he had made the decision on the train. He realized, too, that if he let McCutcheon go on talking, the moment would slip away. Later, he would want to tell himself that he had been driven past the edge by rage and fear, necessity and fatigue. But the truth was that it was a willful act. He touched the white fire and let it fill him. Only afterward did it burn.

"Wrong, Jeremiah. I do." He raised his gun and pointed it at the middle of McCutcheon's chest. "This is for Malena Graham."

He fired four times, four neatly spaced and carefully aimed shots, then lowered his arm slowly to his side. He stood, swaying on his feet, and watched the shattered shell of William McCutcheon die, and felt cheated because triumph tasted as bitter as defeat.

Ripping his helmet off, Dryke threw it aside, turned his back, and started up the stairs. Loren was staring at him. "Dru?" Dryke said as he reached the kitchen. "How much got out?"

"Just the first ten or twelve seconds," she said. "I jammed the skylinks and Ramond got the lines through Pacific. What happened?"

"Can you put a message up for me to the Director?"

"I can do better than that. I can get her direct."

Dryke shook his head, aware of Loren's watching eyes, though he would not meet them. "I don't want to talk to her," he said. "Just tell her for me that Jeremiah is dead."

CHAPTER 25

-|CUC|-

"... the footprints of lost souls."

DR. MEYFARTH'S COUNSELING ROOM HAD BEEN A COMFORTABLE space, an almost cluttered space. But since Christopher's last visit, the clutter had vanished, and everything that remained was now pure eggshell white—the cradle couch, the low table with the recorder ball, Meyfarth's molded chair, the padded corner pit, the carpet, the ceiling, the walls.

It was now a confrontational environment, offering no distractions and allowing only one focus—the interaction between technologist and client. Christopher wondered briefly if Meyfarth had made the change with him in mind. But this time, he needed no encouragement to talk.

"She wants me to believe that my father bullied my mother to the point that she killed herself, and then went ahead and did what he had to, to get what he wanted. I've been thinking about this since Saturday night, and I just can't accept that picture."

"Then don't," Meyfarth said. "The facts aren't clear, and you're not obliged to share her beliefs."

"I think the facts *are* clear. My father loved Sharron—my mother." The amendment was a conscious jab at his sister, whose cutting words were still playing in his thoughts. "I know he did, no matter what Annie says."

"The point is, that's your sister's particular family grief. Accurate or not, it doesn't have much to do with you."

"Lynn-Anne thinks it does."

"None of us is responsible for the circumstances of our birth. That doesn't heal your relationship with Annie, I know," said

Meyfarth. "But you don't have to make peace with her to come out ahead."

"How's that?"

"You can take away from this the understanding that she's bracketed you and your father together and that the hostility she shows you is only partly your fault. In fact, it's safer for her to vent that hostility on you than on him, so you can probably expect more of the same if you try to press contact."

Christopher nodded slowly. "If she could learn to separate the two of us, then maybe we could work out whatever real grievances she has with me."

"It would be a good starting point, at least."

"And I'm sure there *are* some," Christopher added.

"There almost always are, between siblings," said Meyfarth. "In any case, I think we can let this go for now—unless you'd rather not."

Christopher crossed an ankle over his knee as he answered. "No. This doesn't feel like it touches my problems with Jessie and Loi."

"On the whole, I agree," said Meyfarth. "What *is* the climate in the house now? When we talked Saturday, you led me to think that it wasn't very pleasant for you."

A wry smile formed on Christopher's lips. "Not very pleasant for any of us, I guess. Loi surprised me this weekend—kind of took pity on me. But Jessie—I can't get near her. I can't even get her attention. Almost as though she has her back to me, if that makes any sense." He gazed intently at the carpet beyond his feet. "And it hurts," he added quietly.

"Is she still seeing John?"

Christopher's head bobbed slowly in affirmation. "I expect her to tell us any day now that she's moving out," he said. "I'm not quite sure why I didn't see it before, but she's never been as serious about the trine as Loi and I were."

"Are you sure you're being fair? She wanted to have a baby with you."

"But only as long as it looked like it'd be easy," Christopher said, raising his head and looking plaintively at Meyfarth. "She wants a lot, you know? But what is she giving back?"

"What *does* she want? 'Listen to me. Tell me your feelings. Be affectionate.' That's too much?"

"This was the first bump we ran into, and she's already given up on me."

Meyfarth cocked his head and said nothing, inviting Christopher to follow the thought.

"It's almost like we were a comfortable place to light, and she was paying her keep by running the house and being cuddly. But it's not comfortable anymore, so she's ready to move on. A butterfly. Pretty, but—"

"No commitment?"

"No commitment."

A skeptical smile flickered across Meyfarth's face. "You opted out of your marriage at the three-year option. So what do you know about eternal love?"

The dig was neither unexpected nor unfair. "I've been thinking about my marriage, too," said Christopher. "Trying to learn from experience, you know? Maybe there's no mystery here. Maybe it's just like the first time—right idea, wrong people."

"I think that lets you off the hook too easily, Chris."

"No," he said, shaking his head and smiling dolefully. "I was counting myself as the chief wrong person."

"Are you ready to give up?" asked Meyfarth. "Is that what we're talking about?"

"I don't know," Christopher said tiredly. "Why don't you ask me a different question?"

"All right," Meyfarth said, settling back in his chair. "There *is* something you said earlier that I'd like to go back to. You said your father loved Sharron. How *do* you know? You weren't a witness to it. And Lynn-Anne was."

The question stopped Christopher for a moment. "I didn't mean a hard question," he said, and sighed.

"Did he tell you he did?" the arty suggested.

"No. I don't think so. He wasn't comfortable talking about her. This is strange, because I'm sure I'm right, I'm just not sure why. I think that part of it—a big part—is that he never married again. As though it wouldn't have been right to replace her. Never even came close, as far as I'm aware."

"He had a child—you—with another woman, and lived with her for fifteen years. That isn't close?"

"I don't think they were even lovers," said Christopher. "They never acted like they were." A pause. "Did I tell you Deryn wouldn't let me call her 'Mother'? She always kept the lines drawn. 'I'm not your mother, I'm your incubator,' she'd say. And laugh. But somehow it never felt like a rejection." He smiled bitterly. "At least, not until she left."

"Did your father love *her*?"

"What? Deryn? No." Christopher frowned. "Yes. But not the same way."

"What way?"

"He—" Christopher stopped and studied his hands. "I don't suppose I really know how it was different. It just seems like it would have to be."

"That he would have been closer to Sharron? More affectionate? Happier?"

"Yes." An afterthought. "It's hard to tell when my father is happy."

"Funny," said Meyfarth. "Loi once said that about you."

Christopher looked up sharply. "Are you going to start that, too?"

"What?"

"Telling me I'm like my father. I'm not. I've told you that— we can hardly survive a weekend together."

Meyfarth nodded in a way that somehow was an acknowledgment rather than agreement, pursed his lips, and considered. "Christopher, I see something here, but I'm not sure you do. Maybe it comes from sitting on this side of the room for so long—the patterns come to be familiar."

"Patterns?"

Meyfarth nodded. "Families have a way of reinventing the same mistakes."

"Spell it out, will you?"

"Lynn-Anne lost her mother, early. You lost your mother—"

"No. I told you, she—"

"You lost your mother early," Meyfarth repeated. "I don't care what semantic games you played in the family." He paused. "Lynn-Anne blames your father for her mother going away. Do you blame him because yours did?"

"No." The answer came quickly, emphatically. "*She* left *us*."

"Broke her contract. Flew to Sanctuary and never came back."

"Yes."

"Do you hate her?"

Christopher shook his head slowly. "No."

"Why not?"

Shakily, he drew a deep breath. "Her job was done, really. It was like saying good-bye to a good teacher. You don't want to, but when it's time—"

"A good teacher?"

"A very good one."

"Did you love her?"

His eyes moistened. "Yes."

Meyfarth waited, but Christopher did not fill the silence.

"This isn't a good sign," Meyfarth said finally, offering a compassionate smile. "We're down to monosyllables."

"Then ask better questions."

There was a crackle in Christopher's voice, something potent, something uncontained. Meyfarth studied him levelly. "You said your father didn't like to talk about Sharron. Does he talk about Deryn?"

"No."

"What's the last thing he said about her?"

A shake of the head. "I don't remember."

"The last thing you *can* remember, then."

Christopher was squirming as though pinned to a dissection table. "He just doesn't talk about her."

"Anything."

"He won't talk about her when I do." The words came out in a rush, a little ampoule of poison bursting.

"When did he talk about her?"

"I don't know."

"When she left? What did your father say when Deryn left?"

He shook his head again, frowning. "I don't remember."

"You don't *want* to remember." The words were a needle.

"I don't want you to try to make me hate him."

"You touched it a moment ago, didn't you? When you said you loved your mother. Tell me what he said."

Pleading. "I can't remember."

"Ask your fifteen-year-old self. He remembers."

Suddenly, he was up out of his seat and shouting. "I don't *want* to remember!"

"Then you don't want to be well," Meyfarth said calmly. "What did you say to him? When you knew she was going."

Christopher's eyes were seeing somewhere else. "I asked him to make her stay," he whispered. "He said—"

"Yes?"

"Oh, God—"

Meyfarth's voice turned hard. "You have to speak the truth about your own life, Christopher. If you don't, the lies are going to own you forever."

A shivery breath escaped Christopher's lips. His face was knotted with pain.

"He said—" He swallowed and started again. "He said we were better off without her. She wants too much," Christopher said, his voice rising. "He said, why should I try to stop her? I'll be glad to say good-bye."

He blinked hard, squeezing out the tears that were welling in his eyes. "God damn him."

Fists clenched, shivering, Christopher stood in the middle of the room, staring at the blank white wall on which he seemed to see his life. But it was not until Meyfarth rose from his chair and wrapped him in a quieting hug that Christopher began to cry in earnest, and let himself feel at last the pain of a crippling cut which had never healed.

Christopher drove back to the center dazed and benumbed, the flyer's radio merely noise in his ears.

"Top news of the hour: from Diaspora Project headquarters in Prainha, Brazil, word that the certification flight of the starship *Memphis* will be delayed at least a month. The shakedown mission, a round-trip sprint to the orbit of Pluto, had been scheduled to begin February 5. Although Project officials would not comment, simple math indicates that the ship's announced sailing date of April 1 is also in peril.

"The announcement came from Takara construction crew chief Benjamin Burns, who had this to say: 'You have to remember that *Memphis* is a different ship than *Ur* was—a third bigger, more complex, with hundreds of modifications to every major ship system. So even the old hands up here are really doing this for the first time. And it has to be *right* the first time, so we're not going to let ourselves be rushed by an artificial schedule.'

"Burns announced no firm date for the test flight and refused to give specific details about the reason for the delay. But Anne-Lee Adams, a space system analyst with Grodin Associates, pointed to claims made last week by Homeworld spokesperson Jeremiah·

" 'In my view, this confirms the rumors and reports of a major sabotage incident at Allied Transcon's Munich center. For them to acknowledge it at all means that the damage must have been quite serious. I expect we'll see this one-month postponement turn into a much longer delay before the story has run its course.' "

The news barely penetrated Christopher's consciousness and distracted him not at all from his thoughts. Though Meyfarth had mercifully found an extra forty minutes to spend with him, that time had bought him only a measure of composure, carried him only a tiny step toward peace. The walls of denial were still toppling, and his eyes hurt from the light that was shining in.

He could see all the way back, all the way in. He could no more close his eyes to it than he could stop breathing, though both had their temptations. There was nothing soft beneath him to catch him when he fell. There was nothing firm enough to carry the weight of his life.

Tear apart the memories and assemble them anew, all the sharp edges restored, the polish removed. Too many pieces to hold at once. Too many connections to make between them.

I thought I was a happy kid. I thought I'd come through pretty clean—

Truth was a solvent for illusion, but there was nothing tidy about the process, nothing cheap about the price. He had bought a dose of truth that morning and paid for it with the rawness of his throat and the battered ache in his body.

And the hardest truth was that it was not over.

It was not just the work ahead—sorting untouched feelings, touching disowned thoughts, assembling all the pieces into the picture he had so long rejected. It was the knowledge that all of that work would only solve half of the equation. For the other half, he would have to look to William McCutcheon.

"It's a hard choice, confronting a parent," Meyfarth had told him. "You have to risk losing the relationship that you have in order to get a better one. And that's difficult for some people to do. Unsatisfactory as that relationship might be, your definitions of love and self and family are all tied up with it. You're going to need some support from outside and some strength from inside. Don't force a showdown now. Give yourself time."

Time to heal. *But how much healing can I do when the blood is still running? How long can I live with this much pain?*

Waiting in his skimmer in the security check line at the south entrance to the compound, Christopher wondered if it wasn't time to go back to riding the tram.

Ever since the Homeworld assault on the NASA Boulevard checkpoint, it had been more trouble than it was worth to try to bring a private vehicle through the relocated gate. Sentinel now took control of approaching vehicles the moment they crossed the security threshold, and the open-gate on-the-fly check had been replaced with a stop-and-go double-gate inspection. It was like putting a navigation lock on a busy river, with the predictable result traffic was always backed up, no matter what the time of day.

But after last week's concert, he had turned to the skimmer as a way of hiding from the media who followed him onto the tram. The nosy suspicion of the sentries was less of a nuisance than the nosy intrusion of the reporters. But the cul-de-sac had been empty that morning, miracle of miracles. If the miracle repeated itself tomorrow, he would leave the skimmer in the carport.

Presently, he was first in line, the outer gate opening for him. Sentinel eased the skimmer forward, then closed the outer gate behind it. At that point, Christopher was sealed in a square cell formed by the double gates and the flanking gatehouses.

Ordinarily, it took only a few seconds for the red-eyed laser to strobe the code plate on the skimmer, the bomb sniffers and telltales to pronounce it clean, the telescopic camera in the left-side gatehouse to scan Christopher's face and check it against the hyper.

But this time, the kill-Q alarm came on, a sirenlike sound that startled Christopher. The skimmer settled to the ground, its lifters shut down. While he gaped in surprise, doors on both gatehouses yawned, and brown-uniformed guards hurried out through the openings. In seconds, Christopher found himself looking out at four hard expressions, four unslung assault rifles.

"Christopher McCutcheon"—he heard the words over the skimmer radio—"this is Captain Jackson of base security." In truth, it was Sentinel; "Captain Jackson" was merely a stern-voiced AIP.

"Yes."

"Please get out of your vehicle."

Numbly, his face proclaiming his bewilderment, Christopher obeyed. As he did, a blue-striped Security flyer coasted to a stop beyond the inner gate, and one of the corpsecs stepped forward.

"Would you come with me to Building 100, sir?"

The inner gate opened a walk-through to the flyer, but stubbornness rooted Christopher's feet. "What's going on?"

"If you please, sir," the corpsec said, nodding toward the flyer.

Reluctantly, and still without any conception of why he had failed the check, Christopher allowed himself to be bundled into the flyer and whisked off to Building 100—the security office. He only braved the obvious question once, not knowing if they could hear him, not knowing how to penetrate their professional distance. "What did I do?"

No one answered.

At Building 100, they left him waiting in the flyer, watched by more of the hard-eyed Corporate Security officers. Presently, a broad-shouldered man wearing a steel-gray jumpsuit emerged from the building and joined him in the flyer.

"Christopher McCutcheon?" the man said as the flyer lurched forward.

"Yes?"

"I'm Donald Lange, site security," the man said. "You're wanted at another location. I'm going to escort you."

"Wanted where? For what?"

"I'll tell you once we're in the air."

"In the *air*?" Christopher tried to shake his fog. "I don't have any clothes."

"That won't be a problem," said Lange.

They took him to a six-seat screamer already warming up on a taxiway. Christopher, Lange, and two corpsecs boarded. In less than five minutes, Houston was falling away behind them.

"Now can I know where we're going?" asked Christopher, turning away from the small window.

In lieu of an answer, Lange turned his seat and locked it so that it faced Christopher. From the small case beside him, he retrieved a flip-flop slate and plugged it into the SkyLAN port on the right armrest. Finally, he placed a black-banded eyecup headset on his head, tugging the display down into place.

"Recorder on. Analyzer on. This is a contract compliance interview, clauses 29 and 33. Donald Lange, examiner. Christopher Alan McCutcheon, subject."

Christopher's mouth suddenly went dry, for he understood the references, if not the reason. Clause 29 was the Non-Disclosure section of his employment contract—a comprehensive collection of thou-shalt-nots Keith called the Twenty-nine Commandments. Clause 33 was the Corporate Property and Enterprise section—or, more simply, the theft and sabotage clause.

"This is about Malena Graham, isn't it? It wasn't my fault, I thought you knew that. I thought the company was on my side."

"The purpose of this interview is to help determine whether grounds exist for termination, civil prosecution, or both," Lange went on, ignoring the question. He was looking at the slate, and his words had a scripted ring. "Lying to an examiner, or refusing to answer, is itself sufficient for termination-for-cause, with forfeiture of the full probationary bond and all pension and insurance rights. Answer the questions as completely and truthfully as you can."

"I want to know where we're going," said Christopher stubbornly.

Lange looked up. "You're in a company aircraft, on company time, involved in company business. That should be enough for now."

"To hell with your compliance interview. I resign," Christopher said. "I want out of here."

"You have a ten-day notice provision in your contract," Lange said. "Sorry."

"The hell—you *kidnapped* me, you son of a bitch."

"Was force used against you? Were you threatened?"

"No—"

"Suspend," said Lange. He flipped up the eyecup and leaned forward in his seat. "Look, if you want to cut your own throat, that's fine with me. But if we'd already decided you were dirty, we'd just toss you. Answer the questions, and if you're clean, you'll be okay. As for where we're going, Mr. Dryke, the head of security, wants to talk to you. But I can't tell you where he is, or they'll have *me* in that chair on the way back. So what's it going to be?"

Christopher didn't know how much of what Lange was saying he believed. Not many people came back from compliance interviews—a CCI notice looked a lot like a termination notice dressed up in due process.

But it would be hard enough finding a civilized position fresh from being fired by Allied Transcon. If he blew away the bond in the process, he'd be locked out of virtually all of the front-line openings. No one with a multimillion dollar data investment to protect was going to let an unbonded librarian near a password.

And besides, he *knew* he was clean.

"I'm sorry," Christopher said, his face pickling as he said the words. "Ask your questions."

Lange nodded. "Resume."

• • •

But Lange did not want to know about Malena.

That fact wasn't immediately clear, because Lange started there. Had he ever met Malena Graham? Whom did he know in Nassau Bay? In Training? In Selection? Had he taught any tutorials to the Block 1 pioneers? How many times had he been to Wonders? What had he told Bill Wonders about his job? About Allied Transcon? About Malena Graham? What had he told Evan Silverman?

After every question, Lange would pause, as though reading the voice analyzer's judgment in the eyecup display. Try as he might, Christopher could not read Lange's face. His expression never changed, never betrayed what he was seeing.

But it was not hard to read the changing focus of the questions. What do you know about communications processing? Data storage structures? System security? Have you ever hacked a net to which you did not have legitimate access? Created a private gateway to a net on which you were working? Broken a transmission cipher? Designed a virus?

It was hard to answer some of the questions, and more than once Christopher's hesitation showed. No systems jockey with any curiosity escaped technical adolescence without taking a look under the hood now and then, and he had enjoyed a perfectly healthy curiosity.

Before settling on data structures and information archaeology as his specialty, he had tried or mastered most of the hacker's rites of passage—cracking private family files, remotely switching on a friend's or neighbor's or interesting girl's videophone, sending "ghost" messages on the net. And he had used that knowledge more than once in his professional life to make an end run on an intractable systems administrator or a witless structures engineer.

Everyone did it. Everyone. But he hesitated, because he knew how the truth would sound to ears tuned to suspicion. And then he told the truth, because he knew that a lie would sound still worse.

Whether coincidence or not, from that point onward Lange started fishing for a confession. What do you think of Jeremiah? Are you a member of Homeworld? Do you know anyone who is a member? Do you know anyone who you think might be sympathetic to their cause? What about Bill Wonders? Loi Lindholm? Deryn Falconer? Daniel Keith? William McCutcheon?

Those questions Christopher fielded more easily. His opinions of Jeremiah were less than passionate, and a series of increasingly amused repetitions of "No" did for the rest. He did not try to tell Lange he was fishing in sterile waters.

Then, just as Christopher was beginning to feel comfortable, things took a nasty and surprising turn.

"How often did you discuss your work with your father?"

"Almost never," Christopher said.

"What did your father want to know about your work?"

"As I just said—"

"You said you talked about your work sometimes. What did you talk about?"

"All he wanted to know is if I was happy with what I was doing, and if the work was going well."

"On May 7, you traveled to Oregon and stayed two days at your father's house. What was the purpose of your trip?"

Christopher allowed his incredulity to show. "A family visit."

"Why?"

"Because he invited me. Don't you ever go home?"

"What did he want to talk about that weekend?"

Christopher frowned. "The Twenty-ninth Amendment. Seral stages. The mean annual rainfall of northwest Oregon. We went hiking," he added by way of explanation.

"Did you talk about Homeworld activities?"

"No."

"In August, your housemate Loi Lindholm went to Europe for five days, visiting Brussels, Paris, and Geneva. Why did she make that trip?"

"August? Ah—she had a commission debut and went to some business-card kiss-and-snack parties," said Christopher.

"What did she take there for you and whom did she deliver it to?"

"What?" His face wrinkled in puzzlement. "Nothing. Her trip didn't have anything to do with me."

Lange rolled on, undeterred. "Five times in November, your father left messages for you on your personal account. What instructions did he give you?"

"Wait a minute," Christopher said warningly. "Wait just a minute. All that means is I didn't want to talk to him."

"But then you took a call from him at your workstation in Building 9. Was that because you needed to warn him about the Munich gateway?"

The picture suddenly snapped into focus, and Christopher

stared at it with a collision of horror and helplessness, astonishment and rage. "What are you saying? Those are all just things that happened." He clawed at the safety restraint, but it would not release him. "This is crazy! What are you saying?"

Lange sat back in his seat and watched Christopher's futile struggle, listened, but was unmoved.

"I'm not saying anything," he said lightly, pulling off the headset and closing the slate with one finger. "I'm just asking questions."

Christopher should not have been surprised when he saw where their journey had taken them, but he was, all the same. He knew with the first glimpse of the little Forest Grove hubport, knew with the first breath of air as they crossed from hotwinged screamer to waiting flyer.

But until the thin ribbon of U.S. 26 and the scattered houses of Manning flashed by below, until Tillamook State Forest spread out beneath them and a mist-wrapped Hoffman Hill loomed out the right-side windows, Christopher refused to accept the knowledge.

At that point, though, he had no choice but to embrace it. They were taking him home.

There were four vehicles already crowded into the clearings flanking the house, and easily a dozen people in sight—ferrying cases from inside to the square-backed silver van, standing talking in knots of two or three, or just watching as the flyer bearing Christopher floated in to settle on the much-trampled grass between the muddy track of the old road and the garage.

Christopher had long since given up demanding—or even pleading for—explanations. He docilely followed Lange inside, sat in the living room chair Lange pointed him to, watched mutely as white-gloved men and women meticulously erased any signs of the intrusion with vacuum and buffer and an endless supply of square yellow cloths. How long had they been there? Where was his father?

Presently, Lange returned, trailing behind a black-haired dart-eyed man with a wrestler's build and a soldier's walk. Christopher stood up to meet him.

"Are you Dryke?" he asked.

"Yes."

"What are you doing here?"

"Getting ready to leave," said Dryke. "I'll take the rest of your questions when you've answered mine. Come with me, please."

He led Christopher to the office and, asking Lange to wait outside, closed the door behind them.

"Sit at the desk."

Moving tentatively, Christopher complied.

"Ask the AIP if it knows you."

Christopher swallowed. "Hello, Lila."

"Hello, Christopher," Lila said. "I wasn't told you would be visiting. How long will you be staying?"

"I don't know," said Christopher, looking to Dryke.

"Ask for your messages."

"Lila, are there any messages for me?"

"No messages, Christopher. Should I update your address to this location?"

"No."

"Ask it to replay the last message sent to you by Jeremiah."

"I never—"

"Ask it."

He did, and the center panel of the comsole darkened into an image of William McCutcheon. "Hello, Christopher. This is your father. You're not being paid enough if you're still working at this hour—"

"Lila, you made a mistake," said Christopher. "That's my father."

The display went white. "I'm sorry, Christopher," said Lila. "Which Jeremiah did you mean?"

Suddenly fragile, Christopher looked up into Dryke's intent gaze. "It made a mistake."

"No," said Dryke.

"You think my father is Jeremiah?"

"There isn't any question about it. Do you expect me to believe you didn't know?"

"I don't believe *you*."

Dryke nodded. "Lila, show Christopher Jeremiah's last transmission."

It was his father again, sitting in a room Christopher did not know. "This is William McCutcheon, speaking for Jeremiah and the Homeworld. As you can see, I have visitors this morning. As you might guess from the weapons they carry, I did not invite them. Mikhail Dryke, chief of the security forces for Allied Transcon, has invaded my home to arrest me—"

"Lila, where is my father?" Christopher asked suddenly.

"He was shot by Mikhail Dryke on Sunday morning," Lila said. "I infer that he is dead."

With a cry of anguish, Christopher vaulted out of the chair and lunged at Dryke. The older man turned the charge aside easily, spinning away and giving Christopher a shove that carried him hard into the wall. By the time Christopher picked himself up and turned, he was facing five men and three weapons.

"Fagging bastard. Where is he? What did you do with him?"

"Buried him in the earth," said Dryke. "I would tell you where, but that could prove awkward. I'm sorry." He turned to one of the newcomers. "Tell Ramond I want the rest of the house files wormed out and this AIP reset. Now."

The man nodded and left, and Dryke turned back to Christopher. "I don't know that I believe what you told Donald. Even if I did, I don't know how much sympathy I'd have left for you. You'll understand that if you have any idea of the grief that Jeremiah caused.

"I do know I don't trust you. I can't. If it was my choice, you'd be going with us, and disappearing, at least until *Memphis* sails. But it isn't my choice this time, and my orders are to move you out and cut you loose," he said. "Lucky you."

He stepped closer. "But I'll warn you right now, don't come near Allied property, or anyone in the Project. I don't think I even want to hear that you're back in Houston. That would put thoughts in my head that you don't want me to think.

"Your resignation will be final in ten days—thank you for that, it's tidier. You'll even get one more check, I suspect. But your passes, codes, and credits are dead as of now. You can send someone to pick up your car."

They kept him waiting in the bedroom while they finished their work. When the only noises Christopher could hear were outside the house—voices, the banging of equipment being loaded, the whistle of lifters—he opened the door and found himself alone.

He walked through the silent house slowly and reached the front window in time to watch the last vehicle, the silver van, clear the scorch pad and disappear over the treetops. He stood at the window for a long time, though there was nothing more to see. His body jangled with an impotent fury. They were gone, and he could not touch them.

And his father was dead, and he did not know how to feel.

CHAPTER
26

-|AAU|-

"I must walk carefully."

CHRISTOPHER COULD NOT STAY IN THE HOUSE. IT WAS TOO UN-comfortable, too jarringly wrong, to be in his father's space and not feel his father's presence.

Even the characteristic smell of the house—part aromatic cedar from the closets, a hint of sesame oil from the kitchen, his father's soaps from the bath, the char of burnt wood from the fireplace—had been upset by the cleaning. It smelled now of alcohol and cleanser, and another faint chemical scent—the strongest in the kitchen—which he could not define.

Heedless of the temperature outside, Christopher went through the rooms opening all the movable windows and both doors, changing the blowers at the top of each dome to exhaust. Then he left the house behind and walked into the forest, his fists buried deep in the pockets of a jacket borrowed from his father's closet.

For a time, he ordered himself not to think, allowing the mountain to wrap itself around him. The air was damp and cool, the ground soggy underfoot. There was a steady patter as drops of water fell from the tree crowns high overhead to the carpet of trillium and humus. A few birds called lonely sounds from the branches far above him. Now and again, his approach flushed a nimble-quick chipmunk from a tangle of ferns and brush.

The farther he went into the forest, the more his steps slowed. His purposeful passage, tramping a line through the wildness, became a quieter communion. He threaded his way between the gray-white trunks almost as a ghost.

Where did they take you, Father?

He had no thought of searching for the grave, no hope that even a forensic expert would find it. Dryke had undoubtedly been too thorough for that. Christopher's sense of futility was such that he had not even called the police. What could they do with no body, no witness, no evidence?

Even Lila had been silenced, as Christopher had learned when he finally tore himself away from the window.

"Lila? Do you know where they put my father's body?"

"Would the speaker please identify himself?"

"This is Christopher. Christopher McCutcheon."

"Thank you, Christopher. To use verbal command mode, I will need a sample of your normal speech. Would you please talk to me about your day?"

Vainly hoping that some part of Lila's customization had been missed by Dryke's wormers, Christopher had invented for Lila a more pleasant morning than he had lived.

"Thank you. I have a sufficient sample now. Will you be the primary user of this AIP?"

"No," he said. "The primary user is my father."

"Thank you," Lila said, and then stole even that faint hope away. "What is your father's name?"

No, involving the police was pointless or worse. What did he need them to do? He already knew enough of what had happened, exactly who had done it, perhaps even a piece of why. But his testimony was valueless. He knew nothing firsthand. It was only a story.

A wild story. What would a thoughtful prosecutor make of such a tale from a distraught young man whose life had been disintegrating around him? If that prosecutor talked to Meyfarth—and, of course, he would—he might quite reasonably decide that the most likely suspect was Christopher himself.

The best he could hope for was that they would believe him enough to declare his father missing. But what was the value in that? Only his father's attorneys and accountants would care, and nothing seemed less important at the moment than matters of business and family finance.

Justice? Punishment? Revenge? Words of primal myth and melodrama, the classic passions of the wronged, and yet they, too, seemed not to matter much to Christopher. Perhaps it was too soon, the shock too fresh, the loss too new. He had not even cried.

Or perhaps the passions and tears both were knotted in the confusion of unsettled issues. He had been cheated of his own confrontation with William McCutcheon, robbed of a reckoning over the lies which lay between them. Lies which now appeared to be only the lesser part of the deception his father had worked.

A fat drop of water falling from above hit the back of Christopher's neck and made a cold trail under his collar to the vicinity of his shoulder blades. Christopher shivered, suddenly realized that he was hunchbacked against the chill, the jacket nearly soaked through. He turned back, guessing at the direction. When he crossed paths with old Johnson Road a few minutes later, he allowed it to lead him back the long, easy way.

The truth was that he did not understand well enough who his father had been—whether William McCutcheon had, in fact, been murdered, or had fallen in what amounted to a duel. Christopher did not know if it was right to love and mourn him, or to hate and curse him. He still did not know how to feel.

"Hello, Christopher," Lila said as Christopher entered.

The house was barely warmer than the woods, and Christopher hastened to close the windows. "Hello, Lila."

"I am glad to see you again, Christopher. Can you tell me if something has happened to Mr. McCutcheon?"

That froze Christopher in midstep. "Mr. McCutcheon?"

"William McCutcheon, your father. The owner of this house."

Christopher took several uncertain steps toward the office. "What's going on here, Lila? When I left, you were as dumb as a toaster."

"While you were gone, I appear to have received a message from Mr. McCutcheon," said Lila.

His breath caught. "What? Is he alive?"

"I don't know, Christopher."

"What other possibility is there?"

"The message may have been composed earlier and stored until after a trigger event or a specified time. It's even possible that I sent the message to myself."

Sliding into the chair at the comsole, Christopher said, "Let me see it."

"I'm sorry. I do not have a copy of it. I would not be able to show it to you if I did."

"Damn it, who's in charge here? Do I have primary user status or not?"

"You have visitor status, Christopher. Mr. McCutcheon is the primary user."

Which meant that the initialization Christopher had completed before leaving the house had been erased and replaced. "Then tell me what you do know. What the message was and where it came from."

"I only know that several of my directories are restored, and the time stamp on my command files is only a few minutes old. That's what I would expect to find if I had received a self-executing command file."

"Do you remember Mikhail Dryke being here?"

"No."

"Do you know who he is?"

"Yes, Christopher. If he was here, that is a reason for concern."

"What are you doing now besides talking to me?"

"My first instruction is to try to locate Mr. McCutcheon."

Christopher frowned. "What if you can't find him?"

"I have contingent instructions. Do you know where Mr. McCutcheon is?"

"My father is dead." It was easier than it should have been to say.

"His death has not been recorded, and his skylink address is still active and pointed here. How do you know that he's dead?"

"Because you told me, two hours ago. And Dryke confirmed it. What else did my father tell you to do?"

"I'm sorry, Christopher. I am not allowed to tell you."

Christopher felt a quick flash of impatience. "Look, Lila, Dryke already knows, unless the message came in by parachute—I can't imagine that they're not still monitoring this house. What good does it do for him to know and me to be in the dark? And if you're going to be carrying on with Homeworld business, I want to know."

"I'm aware of the monitoring, Christopher. I've been instructed not to place you at risk."

"Maybe I want to be put at risk," Christopher said, the thought springing new into his mind as he spoke it. "Maybe I'm going to want to draw Dryke back here. Lila, was my father Jeremiah?"

"Yes, Christopher. Your father used that name."

"Why that name?"

"I don't know the significance. But your father's grandfather was named William Jeremiah McCutcheon."

"I never knew that," Christopher said. "I never knew *him* The face and voice—that was you?"

"I coordinated the simulations."

Christopher was silent for a long moment. "What if I said I wanted to take over my father's work? All of it."

"A successor has already been selected."

The words stung, even though his offer had been more an arguing point than any serious intention. "Selected by who? You?"

"Mr. McCutcheon made the selection."

Not good enough. Still not good enough to earn his respect. Was that the real message of the secrets? He had spent his whole life trying to be the best. *I never would have guessed how little being good at what I do would matter—*

"Lila, why didn't my father tell me what he was doing?"

"I'm sorry, Christopher. I don't know."

No easy answers. He had allowed himself to hope someone from Homeworld would appear to offer kindly explanations and refuge, to acknowledge a debt and pledge a bond of kinship. But he saw now that it was not going to happen. He was not going to be embraced by his father's friends—by Jeremiah's friends. If his father had not welcomed him, had not trusted him, how could he expect that anyone else would? He would have to find answers to his other questions on his own.

"Lila, what's the status of the house library?"

"The house library is empty."

"Hidden files? Protected files?"

"I'm sorry, Christopher."

"Is there *anything* left? Anything from my father? Anything about my father? About my family?"

"Mr. McCutcheon kept personal files in off-line storage, not as part of the house library," said Lila.

Reason to hope, however feeble. "Then Dryke may have taken them. Where were they? What medium?

Books," Lila said.

Christopher did not have to be told where to look. He went directly to his father's bedroom, to the long shelf below the west-facing window and the long row of hardcover books atop it. He had noticed them during his imprisonment, even picked one up and glanced briefly through it.

He had noted them as curiosities, both because books in general were rare and because the particular form of these books was unusual. For, with one or two exceptions, the books were all Portables—traditional print volumes with their contents duplicated electronically in the binding for access by a computer. The Portables were designed to be shelved on special bookcases, "plugged in" to smart ports, although the shelf in his father's room was not one such.

It was a transitional technology, predicated on the notion that traditional readers would resist surrendering their words-in-boards for slates, but might welcome having the contents of their libraries on-line for quick reference. Never more than a modest success, the Portables had all but vanished from the marketplace before Christopher was born. They survived only as collectibles, and he had not known his father was a collector.

Scanning the titles, Christopher found historicals, art books, Locke, Eiseley, Kant, a biography of John Muir, and one fiction best-seller, Wolf's *Lord of Sipán*. And that was all. "Nothing personal here. Dryke must have taken them," Christopher said. His voice was heavy with disappointment.

"Did you find any books?"

"Yes—"

"Would you count them, please?"

Christopher's eyes skipped down the line. "Thirty-one."

"Then none are missing. They are all there."

"But I don't see any journals, any diaries, any albums—"

"There are none to find, Christopher. The bindings are standardized. The texts vary in length. So there is always unused space in a Portable's chipdisk. Each of those books contains more than its cover admits to," said Lila. "As much as several hundred kilobytes per book."

"That isn't very much."

"It is when you are only storing words, Christopher."

Shaking his head, Christopher said, "I didn't know this was possible, and cultural media are supposed to be my specialty."

"If you had known, then probably Mikhail Dryke would also have known, and the books would be gone."

Christopher's face screwed up into a mystified frown. "Lila, how did *you* know about this? It had to be in the restored files."

"Yes, Christopher."

Tentatively, he reached out and pulled Clark's *Indian Legends of the Pacific Northwest* from the ranks. "But only some of your files were restored."

"Yes, Christopher."

He looked up from the book in the direction of Lila's voice. "Then this was important. He wanted me to know they were here. He wanted me to read them."

"Yes, Christopher," said Lila. "After he was dead, and only if you asked about them."

"Who else?"

"I am not allowed to show them to anyone else."

"Not even Lynn-Anne?"

"No."

He pulled more volumes from the shelf, carefully making a stack in his arms. "I want to see them now."

"There is one condition. Mr. McCutcheon asked that you read them all, or not at all."

That brought him up short. "Why?"

"I'm sorry, Christopher. I don't know."

Though the archive had been opened to Christopher, he saw very quickly that it had not been created for him. Save for a few decades-old "letters" from a father to his new son, it was not even addressed to him.

And instead of the systematically organized, theatrically perfect deathbed soliloquy Christopher had expected, the archive was a fragmented and incomplete potpourri, a scattering of the thoughts and reflections and memories of a man of complexity. It was his attic, the bottom drawer of his rolltop desk, the notes scribbled in the margins of his days.

Together, they said, "This was my private world, which I never shared with you in life. This is who I was."

Christopher rooted himself in the seat for two hours, reading his way through the first six volumes of archiviana. Then, as dusk was settling over the ridge, he pushed back from the desk and retreated to the kitchen to fortify his body with its first food since breakfast.

He also needed the break to fortify his determination. Reading William's private archives was akin to raking a mine field in search of a lost treasure. Dangerous forces were concealed beneath the surface. Inevitably, he would stumble on them. There was no way to predict when, no way to prevent the intersection, no way to protect himself. Not if he wanted to reclaim the treasure. Not if he was to honor his father's final request.

So far, there had been more wonder than pain. He had found nothing about Sharron, nothing about Deryn. He did find a self-conscious episodic letter which began "Dear Christopher" and spanned more than four years. The contents of the letter explained little and illuminated little more. But it was fascinating all the same, for it was filled with details of a sort that he would not have thought his father would take the trouble to notice.

But he had taken the trouble, not only to notice, but to record.

The letter began two years after Christopher was born, and the tone was both self-conscious and oddly apologetic, as though his father felt he had been caught procrastinating. It was written in simple language, as though his father was speaking to the child he was, not the adult he would be.

But it offered a snapshot, all the same: a portrait of a cheerful, self-amusing two-year-old who knew the alphabet and could count to thirty, and who liked to "play a game"—saying words and seeing them appear on the screen—on the old computer in Lynn-Anne's room.

Because such things were important to his father, Christopher expected the catalog of the hundred and one landmark achievements of childhood—the ever-changing answers to a parent's "Do you know what my boy can do now?" But he was surprised to hear about the soft-stuffed gray mouse that went everywhere with him until it disappeared on a family trip to Long Beach—and about Traveler Pup, the bow-tied hound who succeeded Friend Mouse.

Friend Mouse was beyond remembering. But Christopher remembered Traveler Pup with a twinge and a tug. He could see it, worn and worried, its bow tie gone, its golden fur gone gray with handling, lying in the basket of toys in the corner of his room on B Street. But he could not remember what had become of it. Surrendered without a thought during a housecleaning, most likely, the emotion imbued in it leached away by time.

The letter's entries were spotty, tantalizing, maddening. Snapshots. An imaginary friend named Birdy, who flew away in the winter and then came back to live in a ground nest Christopher built for him beside the house. Christopher forming letters on the white brick of the backyard patio from twigs collected in the yard and broken to size. Even his own words, unremembered but resonant:

"Do you know what, Dad? It takes a long time trying to grow up. It goes age to age, and I want to skip some ages."

That was the one that drove him away to regroup, that threatened to upset his precarious balance. The dirty little secret of growing up, Moyfarth had said. And Christopher had been in such a hurry to learn it.

Presently, he returned to the comsole and read through the last of the letter. It ended without explanation or closure in the middle of Christopher's sixth year, its last anecdotes—of his trials with an older and more aggressive neighbor child—offering no clue as to why the project was abandoned. The next item Lila presented was date-stamped a full three years later.

"Wait—what's going on here?" Christopher said in surprise. "Isn't there anything between this and the last?"

"No, Christopher. I'm proceeding in strict chronological order, as Mr. McCutcheon directed."

"Show me a file directory."

"I'm sorry, Christopher. I don't have a directory available."

Lila's mechanical politeness was becoming an annoyance. "I can take these somewhere else, you know."

"Yes, Christopher. But you would not be able to read the files without my assistance."

"Then I'll take a can opener to you first and see how you do it," Christopher said irritably, coming up out of the chair and then kicking it out of his way.

He walked to the window and stood looking out through his own reflection, his hands tucked into his back pockets. House rules, he thought. Still his father's house, still his father's rules.

"All right," he said finally. "He wants you holding my hand, I guess that's the way it has to be. Tell me this. Is there more like what I was reading coming up? More addressed to me? If so, I want to skip ahead to it."

"Christopher, there are very specific restrictions on how I may access this material. I may not look ahead, skip ahead, or redisplay already viewed sections. I may not store, mail, or copy any part of it, or allow it to be filmed off the display."

He sighed and made a reluctant pilgrimage back to the chair. "Do you have any idea why there's such a gap?"

"I'm sorry, Christopher. I don't. Is it important?"

"You tell me," he said. "Continue, please."

• • •

Before long, Christopher was convinced that it was important. For, in everything that followed, he found himself discussed in the third person, rather than addressed in the first. It seemed that—for some reason—any thought of him ever seeing his father's words had vanished in the interim.

But, curiously, Christopher discovered his father spoke most clearly when he was not speaking to Christopher directly. His father's voice became a more familiar one, his language liberated from the prison of childspeak. And though there were as many gaps and mysteries as before, the thoughts he did record seemed less guarded, closer to the heart.

I can see Sharron in his eyes and hear Deryn in his words. They are both inside him, pulling at him to follow, his father had written just weeks after Deryn broke her contract and left for Sanctuary. Christopher thought he read both fury and fear in his father's words, the latter an unexpected complexity. His father afraid. It was nearly an oxymoron, as bewildering as burning water.

Infuriatingly, that brief entry was the only allusion to Deryn's departure. It was, in fact, one of the few times either woman was named, and—to that point at least—the only time they were spoken of together. For all their presence in the archives, it was almost as if Christopher's mothers had never existed.

He had waited in vain for the kind of reminiscence of Sharron that he had sought from Lynn-Anne, for the kind of reassurance that would erase his sister's bitterness—and his own ambivalence—from his mind. Through the long hours leading up to midnight, he had kept wondering when something would touch his still-untapped pain and break loose the logjam of anger and grief he could sense but not reach.

But before that happened, he was ambushed by a simple, self-knowing confession:

> *I have loved one cat, one woman, one child. They've all left my life, but they haven't left my heart. And the cats and the children and the women who hover on the edge of my world can't get in. That space is already taken.*

The cat was Dorian, the big gray who had owned the B Street house until the day he simply failed to return from a winter walk. The woman could only be Sharron, for Christopher could give damning witness to the way his father had kept Deryn at arm's length.

And though he tried desperately to find a reason to believe otherwise, Christopher knew in the first moment the words fell under his gaze that the child his father spoke of was Lynn-Anne.

In that moment, hurt and alone, he hated both his father and his sister more than he had known possible.

This time, the kitchen was not far enough away. Christopher retreated outside, to the wooden deck which squared off the curves of the twin domes at the back of the house. Overhead, thin high clouds were making a ghost of the gibbous moon.

It was not that Lynn-Anne was first in her father's heart which cut so deeply. He granted her that as right of precedence. It was the thought that she had won from their father something that Christopher never could, that she had stood in the way of his having any standing at all. It was the realization that his father had knowingly imprisoned him in a losing game.

There was no comfort in knowing that Lynn-Anne's jealousy had blinded her to her real status, costing her exactly what she blamed Christopher for stealing. There was no joy in the contemplation of how much her defection had cost William McCutcheon. That they, too, had been cheated only made the whole muddle more tragically foolish.

His father had changed after Lynn-Anne left, though at the time Christopher had not seen it. There was proof of the change even in the spotty record of his father's notebooks. It explained the end of the long letter. It explained the three-year silence, coinciding with the trips east, now seen as attempts to win his daughter back. It explained the emotional distance when the entries resumed.

The picture was clear. For his first five or six years, Christopher had been an intimate part of his father's life. But after that time, he was never more than an important part. And he had spent the succeeding years trying to earn back something he had once had, without ever grasping exactly what was missing—or why it had been taken away.

So much of Christopher's history with his father finally made sense. His own eternal sense of inadequacy. The paradox of his father's studied indifference and his obsession for control—the endless auditions for an approval he would never give. Even his father's curious relationship with Deryn, by his choice alone less than it could have been, an arrangement rather than a marriage.

Numbly, he wondered—was this the whole point of the exercise, for him to learn that his father did not love him? If so, then it was a cowardly act, and a cruel legacy. And there was no reason to mourn such a man.

The high clouds were blowing off, and scattered windows of star-dotted sky were starting to open. Christopher sat on the railing, back resting against the wall, his arms crossed tightly across his chest, looking up into the fragmented sky for pieces of a pattern he could recognize.

It struck him then that his father had left him neither a gift nor a message, but a final test. *See what you can do with these,* his father was saying. He had bequeathed Christopher the task of assembling into a picture the thoughts and moments captured in the archives, and the harder task of drawing out the meaning. What more fitting legacy could there be, considering his profession? Christopher had performed the same synthesis a hundred times on the lives of strangers.

There was something of love in the challenge, as there had always been. Never the unconditional embrace, never the final security, but always *something* of love, nonetheless. His father had tried to love him without ever making himself vulnerable. And because his father did not trust him, he had tried to control him.

Was still trying. *Read it all or not at all.* Why? Because his father had feared that Christopher would stop before seeing everything of importance, would draw the wrong conclusion or be led to too harsh a judgment. The same manipulation as always, coming from an even colder, safer distance.

The temptation to answer with rebellion was strong. But such a rebellion now would be an empty, self-defeating gesture. William McCutcheon was gone, immunized by death against Christopher's venom. And there were seventeen volumes left.

There has to be something more, he thought as he went back inside the house, something meant for him. There has to be some reason for the exercise beyond destroying the last illusions of a twenty-seven-year-old child.

These fissured cliffs, grading from brown to white to red, appear to me as a great wound carved across her face, as

*the wrinkled features of the crone. How could such feeble
rivers cut such canyons? The wind is a ghost, water a chi-
mera. The element that escapes our eyes is time—time in
such measure that only the earth herself is witness.*

*Who remembers these tablelands rising from a dying sea?
Only Gaea. Who recalls the march of life preserved in these
canyon walls? Only those to whom the gift has been passed,
whose substance preserves the fragile past in a precarious
present. We have left our mark here as surely as have wind
and water. My heart beats in rhythm with the land. I am
its eyes, shaped from the clay and touched with the spark.*

There were dozens more like it, and a yawning, eye-weary
Christopher hardly knew what to make of them. Prayerful poetic
reveries to the experience of nature seemed hardly to belong to
his picture of William McCutcheon.

Christopher knew that his father had treasured the privacy that
the forest estate assured him, that he had a speculator's eye for
land. But these essays went far beyond that. Embodied in them
was a whole world of thought into which Christopher had only
had rare glimpses. And, though it was not easy to accept, there
was as much emotion in such passages as there had been in his
father's letter. Perhaps more.

The only way he could make sense of them was to think of
them as coming from Jeremiah. But even that was an imperfect
answer, because it merely confirmed the fact without explaining
it. The man who had written, "These switchback mountain
streams tumble through crazy folded hills growing ever wider,
ever calmer, as though milked of the energy needed to sustain
the conquering fecundity of the forest," could have written any
of Jeremiah's speeches on the price of the Diaspora.

Indeed, there were any number of entries that read like
sketches for such a speech, echoing the metaphor of desiccation:

*In whose eyes is the butterfly more beautiful than the
chrysalis, a glittering jade jewel flecked with gold? The
price of the transformation is destruction, the transaction
final and absolute. The beauty that was vanishes, consumed
as the fuel for flight and freedom. In just this way, an unchecked hunger to expand will drain the life from the Earth,
sacrificing this jade and azure jewel for that poor prize.*

But was there a way to marry Dryke's Jeremiah to Christopher's father, and make the two merge into a single image?

He sat back in the chair, hands folded in his lap. "All right, Lila. I give up. What's the secret?"

"Excuse me, Christopher?"

"Five down, a nine-letter word meaning 'mercy.' I want a peek at the answers in the back of the book."

"I know no such word."

" 'It droppeth as the gentle rain from heaven upon the place beneath. 'Tis mightiest in the mightiest: it becomes the throned monarch better than his crown—' " His voice trailed away as his memory failed him. "Must be the way you were raised."

"I don't understand, Christopher."

"You're helping him tell this joke. What's the punch line?"

"I don't believe these records constitute a joke, Christopher."

"Never mind," he said with a sigh. "Keep it coming."

Fighting fatigue and frustration, Christopher stubbornly persisted in his task as the wee hours of morning slipped by. His eyes burned and blinked, his focus wandered. The words on the display blurred into an extended non sequitur.

The same world that seems crowded to some seems empty to others . . . What drives them? The ignorance of men empowered by the arrogance of gods . . . There is a bloodline of expansionism which can be traced through history, and they are its youngest, most vigorous branch . . . The return of sexual liberty will blunt the rush and restore the balance. Repression is the engine of ambition . . . Hysteresis is the enemy. We are forever responding to conditions that no longer obtain . . . If I can make fear a stronger force than the fantasy of freedom . . .

And finally he fell asleep in his father's chair in his father's office in his father's house, leaving one last essay unread on the comsole display.

They pass by the windows as ghosts in a silted fog: chinook, silver, sockeye, steelhead. Their struggle seems to defy all reason. Once a lifetime, they fight their way upstream with a single-minded fervor we would find frightening in our own kind. They suffer the most grievous injuries, but though they may weaken, they do not falter.

Torn and bleeding, they attack the obstacle again and again, until one or the other is bested. Those which survive fight on, taking no note of those which fail—there is nothing that can be done, and still something yet to do. The next obstacle is just ahead.

And when they reach the quiet pools and spawn, the fire goes out. The fight has exhausted them. The spirit has passed from them to the eggs. Once the task is accomplished, they are content to swim in aimless circles until they die. Never, ever, do they ask, must it end this way? Such a question is beyond their capacity to conceive. This dimly apprehended call rules their being.

But I ask the question, because I have no wish to join them—or to live in the world that they will leave behind.

CHAPTER 27

-|AGU|-

"... I knew no fears ..."

IN THE CREATION TIME, SAID A TALE DERYN ONCE TOLD, COY-
ote subdued the monster of the Columbia for the animal people.
The wisest and smartest of all animals let Nashlah swallow him
and then cut out the monster's heart.

"A new race of people are coming, and they will pass up and
down the river," Coyote told the monster. "You may shake their
canoes if they pass over you, but you must not kill all of them.
This is to be the law always. You are no longer powerful."

Thereafter, though the wind still blew unchecked through the
river's winding gorge, Nashlah slumbered in the deep waters.
And Eagle and Beaver and Bear and Salmon came to the river
without fear.

The world had changed, and animals no longer spoke like
men. But in fulfillment of mythic prophecy, the once-wild Big
River had been thoroughly tamed by the new race of people
which came to live along its banks. The Army Corps of Engineers had finished what Coyote had begun. The river's flagstone
rapids and net-fishing falls had vanished below the surface of
the lakes which formed behind the great dams. Its currents were
now shaped by the needs of turbines and barges, rather than by
gravity and geology.

But the salmon, Chief of the Fishes, still ran—over the concrete falls and ladders, under the barge props and jetboat hulls,
through the silted, oft-polluted water. And when Christopher
woke in the chair, stiff and twisted, his neck and back aching,

and found his father's chilling essay on the comsole display, he knew where he had to go.

His father had taken him to Bonneville Dam once before, a dozen years ago, to look down into the long generator bay in the north powerhouse, to marvel at the navigation lock slicing through the Oregon shore. They had spent less than an hour in the visitor center on Bradford Island, and a spare few minutes of that on the lowest level, where the fish ladder's underwater windows and the counting room were located.

Dimly, Christopher remembered dirty water and silver fish which all looked alike to his eyes. But it seemed his father had seen something more.

To someone traveling upstream from Portland, Bradford Island appeared as a mere sliver of land, flat and forested with red and white transmission towers. It was the sole natural barrier in the string of dams and powerhouses spanning the two-and-a-half-kilometer width of the river; the smaller Cascades Island had been created when a third channel was carved out of the Washington shore.

The Corps maintained a flight control zone over the site, so Christopher was forced to merge the Avanti into the I-84 flyway and dive down with the wheelies at the Bonneville exit. A few minutes later, he was climbing out of the car in the nearly empty parking lot outside the visitor center.

"Lila, when do they open?" he said, his DBS band relaying the query.

"In half an hour, Christopher. Winter hours are ten A.M. to five P.M."

He was not well disposed to waiting. "Damn."

Even though the building was closed, the courtyards and walkways behind it were not. The walkways paralleled the fish ladder, the surface of which appeared as a staircase of tumbling water, passing beneath a small bridge and curving out of sight. Leaning out over the railing, he tried to peer down through the turbulent water into one of the cells. It was impossible to see anything but swirling silt and a chaos of bubbles.

His arms crossed and ungloved hands tucked in his armpits for warmth, Christopher settled on a concrete bench and waited for the silver flash, the white-foam splash of a sockeye or coho breaking water for an upstream leap. But in half an hour of watching the ladder, not once was he rewarded with that sight.

If there was life in the churning cells of the ladder, it was hidden below.

Finally, a stoop-shouldered brown-clad ranger appeared to unlock the lower-level doors behind where Christopher was seated. The ranger seemed surprised to find him waiting there.

"Morning," he said, holding the door open as Christopher approached. "I don't usually have company this early, 'specially not between Winterfest and the New Year. Welcome to Bradford Island—"

Christopher brushed wordlessly past him.

The lower level was much as Christopher remembered. The center of the room was filled with museum-style exhibits on the life cycle of genus *Oncorhynchus*. On the wall by the fish counting room, digital displays cataloged the traffic by species—day, month-to-date, and year-to-date.

But the focus of the room was the Living Theater—a row of large viewing windows which looked out into the ladder itself. Spaced across the longest wall, each window marked a bend in the ladder's serpentine underwater path. An electronic map of the maze appeared above, its color-coded tracking lights marking the progress of several shad, three steelhead trout, and one solitary chinook salmon.

Christopher came to the railing at the window the chinook was approaching. The water rushing by beyond the glass was a soupy yellow-green, as though it were some bilious particulate stew. A small American shad, a wriggling silver submarine, fought its way around the turn and vanished into the liquid fog. Another, darker fish squirted by, tail fins beating furiously.

But the solitary chinook in the ladder seemed stuck midway down the last leg of its maze, its bright white marker edging forward and then easing back.

"Come on, come on," Christopher said aloud.

"This is the slow season," a voice said behind him.

It was the ranger, come to check on his curious visitor. Christopher turned at the rail to see him standing beside the exhibits in the middle of the room. "What?"

"Chinook and steelhead pretty much quit running by the end of November, and the king won't start up again till March, at least. That's worth seeing. Still fill up the windows at the peak of the run, day and night, like the river's half quicksilver. Those-uns are stragglers—not likely to get where they're going, or to make anything of it if they do."

Christopher settled his buttocks against the railing, hands grasping the wood to either side. "Sounds like I'd be better off talking to you instead of waiting for the show to begin," he said. "How long have you worked here?"

"Twenty-two years next May."

"That long? Then you were probably here the last time I was," Christopher said. "In '81."

Nodding, the ranger said, "Probably was. Hope you picked a better day back then."

"I was with my father," Christopher said. "He just died a few days ago." He could not understand why he blurted that out to this stranger. But when it was said, there was a sudden tightness in his throat that made it hard to swallow.

Sage and sympathetic eyes answered him. "That's hard. I guess you'd like me to leave you be."

"No," Christopher said quickly, suddenly afraid to be alone. "You must know a lot about salmon, working here that long."

"I know my piece. Used to work the counting room over there, before they brought in the AIP. Fifty minutes on, ten minutes off, eight hours a day with an eye on the window and a hand on the tally bar. I can tell one fish from the next, I guess."

"That sounds incredibly dull."

The ranger stepped forward, tucking his hands in his back pockets. "People thought so, but it never seemed so to me. I put in six years as a counter. It was kind of like being plugged into the river, to the whole cycle of things. No two days alike."

An impolitic chuckle escaped Christopher. "Really?"

"Laugh, but it's true. And when I was done, I was done. Never took my work home to my lady," he said with a self-amused smile. "Never any complaints about the guys at the office." The ranger looked past Christopher and nodded toward the window. "There. Looks like she might make it this time."

Christopher turned back just as the thick-bodied shape of a chinook salmon, tail fins thrashing the water, hove into view at the right edge of the window. The upper third of the body was freckled with black spots. Below them, behind the pectoral fin, a triangular tear the size of Christopher's palm flapped in the current, baring red flesh beneath.

There were rips and notches in the tail fins and first dorsal as well, and the silver skin seemed pale and flaccid. The chinook hovered for a few seconds before the window, then was swept backward into the maze. The tracking lights marked its retreat, and in less than a minute it flashed past the next downstream window, its body at an odd angle, making only the most feeble effort against the current.

"Not much longer for that one," the ranger said, clucking. "Probably failed at The Dalles, upstream, and been kicking around Bonneville Lake with the spring running down. They won't feed in fresh water, you know, no matter how weak they get. Odd thing is they'll take a fisherman's fly, even though they're fasting, but that's as far as it goes—say, are you all right?"

Christopher barely heard the question and could say nothing in answer. While the ranger rattled on and the salmon tumbled past, the tightness in Christopher's throat had returned, quickly growing into a strangling ache beneath his ribs. His throat was raw, and each breath hurt more than the last. He took his air in little gasps that were chopped off with sounds like sobs.

Clutching the railing and struggling for air, Christopher blinked away tears in a feeble effort to staunch them, until his cheeks were shining wet and the anguished sobs unmistakable. He sleeved the moisture away, infuriated that he did not know what had triggered his crying, and even more that he could not stop it.

But fury, like embarrassment, was a feeble weapon against the flood of pain, and his defenses crumbled. Racking, body-wrenching sobs seized him, and aching primal sounds tore free from prisons deep inside him. He slipped down to a seat on the stepped floor, clinging to the railing like an anchor with one arm, tear-blurred eyes hooded behind the wall of his hand—one final, feeble grasp for dignity in the midst of the kind of naked moment that shatters dignity and pretense and self-deception.

And when Christopher sensed the ranger beside him, felt the uncertain touch on his shoulder, and heard the kind-voiced question "You want to tell me about it?" all he could think to say was *I hurt*, and that seemed too mean and petty a thing to share.

It was hard to escape the ranger's unwelcome solicitude, and harder still to persuade him that he did not want to be left alone. The arrival of other visitors, a family with two children in tow and an infant in arms, was the first wedge, destroying the illusion of privacy and reminding the ranger of his other duties.

"Look, you want to come upstairs, I can let you sit in the

staff workroom awhile," said the ranger. "Seems like you need to take a little time to pull together."

"I'm okay," Christopher lied, his voice unpersuasively hoarse and thready. "I just got clobbered by an old memory, that's all. My father used to take me fishing up by The Dalles."

The ranger frowned, teetering between resistance and acceptance. "We've got a counselor over at the administration center," he said. "Maybe I should give him a call."

"No," Christopher said, pulling himself to his feet. "I'm all right. Just go back to the desk and be your smiling self." He turned and looked up, feigning interest in the fish tracker.

Rudeness did what diplomacy could not. The ranger hesitated, then finally walked off. When he disappeared into the elevator, Christopher hurried to the stairs.

From the plazalike observation deck atop the center, Christopher could look down four stories into the fish ladder, as well as downstream toward the Beacon Rock monolith and across the island to the dry, quiet spillways of the dam. By the time he had made a slow walking circuit of the deck, he also had a clearer view of what had spilled from him downstairs.

His father's death had been remote and somehow sanitary, easily denied, curiously unaffecting. Moreover, there had been no one but Lila to talk to, no one to help him catalyze his emotions. Consequently, he had managed to pretend that he was whole, ignoring the growing sac of emotional pus. The sight of the blooded, failing chinook had slashed it open, the two-edged blade of futility and finality doing the damage.

But other questions, more important questions, remained unanswered. His father's ruminations on the blind, all-sacrificing drive of the pioneers were unsettling. It was clear to Christopher that his father had meant it as more than metaphor—Jeremiah's actions were proof of that. He had seen something out there to fight against, something tangible and threatening.

Which made no sense to Christopher. There were some poetic parallels, to be sure, but there were also fatal—even foolish—incongruities. There were no dissenting chinooks barricading the mouth of Columbia, no coho plotting to destroy the fish ladders. The salmon's migration was an expression of their being, an uncontested conation pointed toward survival, the sole moral barometer of evolution.

The human Diaspora, by contrast, was the rough-and-tumble marriage of romance and hubris, blessed by the twin gods of technology and opportunity. Choice was the key variable—a minority's choice, it was beginning to appear, but choice all the same. In evolutionary terms, *Memphis* was merely a whim, no more essential a part of the human pattern than the colonization of the Americas by the Asiatics or the subsequent invasion by the Europeans. Economics and natural resources, national and international politics, greed, glory quests, idealistic visions—surely they were enough to explain humanity's mythical "frontier spirit."

Conation on the one hand. Choice on the other. It was ludicrous to think that they could be part of the same thing. And yet his father had believed it, and his father was not a fool. His father had believed it, and that belief had killed him.

Christopher's questions pointed back toward the Project, and he could only think of one person there who might be both able and willing to answer them.

As soon as he cleared the Bonneville flight control zone, Christopher gunned the Avanti and pointed it skyward.

"Lila?"

"Yes, Christopher?"

"Would you see if you can get through to Daniel Keith at AT-Houston?"

"Secure or direct?"

Christopher considered. "You still know some of your routing tricks?"

"Yes, Christopher."

"Secure."

"Calls into Allied Transcon should be assumed to be monitored. A voice-only connection should be untraceable for three minutes."

"Do your best. Put it through."

It took but a second for the green bar on the dash to glow. "Keith," said a voice.

"Daniel, this is Chris."

An ominously long silence followed. "I don't think I can talk to you, Chris."

"I'll call you later, then. At home."

"No."

"Why not?"

"I think you know."

Christopher had been half prepared for this. "Daniel, you have to know that whatever they're saying about me is a lie."

"Then why did you resign?"

"Who says I did?"

"Chris, Loi called me last night, worried about you. She asked me if I knew where you were."

"Why didn't she call *me*?"

"She did. You're off-net. The call just came back to the house," Keith said.

Christopher looked at his bare wrist dumbly. "I lost my band." Lange or the sentries must have taken it from him, but he had no memory of that.

"Doesn't matter. The point is, I asked a few people a few questions, as a favor. My curiosity wasn't exactly rewarded."

"Damn it, Daniel, corpsec murdered my father."

Another long silence. "I can't discuss that," Keith said finally.

It was such a surprising answer that Christopher's mental wheels stalled as he tried to embrace it. "I need to see you."

"I'm sorry," Keith said curtly. "I can't help. Call Loi, will you? She deserves better."

Calling Loi was a duty which had tugged at him more than once since Dryke and his people had left the ridge. Something had always intervened—most often the sobering finality of being severed from his life in Houston, paired with the stark futility of trying to reclaim any part of it. Thinking about Kenning House only evoked feelings of helplessness and rootlessness. He wanted to go home too much to be able to admit to Loi—even to himself—that he could not.

Instead, he called Skylink Customer Service and changed his residence pointer to the Avanti, which had a comsole almost as powerful as the one in Houston. The next distraction was replacing his personal phone—now that he had noted its absence, he felt naked without it.

Lila steered him to an executive supplies retailer in one of Portland's older mall-malls, who offered him a Brazilian-made four-channel wrist phone at Pacific Land Management's customary generous discount. Outside in the car, he completed the process, initializing the phone with his account number and checking that his directory was intact. When the confirming message came back on the bounce, his last excuse was gone.

294 *Michael P. Kube-McDowell*

"Lila—Skylink is owned by Tetsu Communications?"

"That's correct."

"Which is a corporate sibling to Takara Construction, Allied's primary contractor for *Memphis*."

"Yes. Both are subsidiaries of Kiku Heavy Industries, Ltd., a Tokyo-based private stock corporation."

"How hard is it for Skylink to listen in on the traffic that they're carrying?"

"It is quite easy, Christopher. Mr. McCutcheon used it only as a last resort, and always with encryption," Lila said. "If you need to send a message, I can handle it more safely."

"That's all right," Christopher said. "I just wondered." He touched his phone, and the command bar glowed. "Message to Loi Lindholm. Hold to end, then send," he said, then paused. "Begin."

"Hello, Loi. This is Chris." His heart was racing, even though he did not have to fear her response. "Daniel said that you were worried," he said, speaking slowly. "I'm sorry. I—these last few days have been the hardest days of my life. Allied's thrown me out. They think I'm a security risk. And my father—" The tightness threatened to return, and Christopher found other, safer words. "I'm staying at my father's for a while. I need to figure out what to do.

"I miss you. I wish to God I could come home." He swallowed hard. "End of message."

The delivery acknowledgment came back on the bounce.

"Well, Lila—do you know anywhere I can buy a life transplant, cheap?"

"I'm sorry, Christopher. I do not."

He sighed and squeezed the throttle. The Avanti edged forward. "Then I guess I'll just come on back to the house."

For no good reason he could divine, only twice during the drive did he think about crashing the car at full throttle into an approaching ridge.

Curled up on the couch in front of the high-D TV, propped up by pillows and a flask of Puerto Rican rum, Christopher let the sounds and images wash over him.

The TV came up with a pop station out of Los Angeles preselected. But he made no effort to search through the channels, for he was no more interested in one offering than another. He was escaping, and he knew it—and it hardly mattered where he escaped to, so long as he got away.

So a chat show on lesbian incest, with a bioethicist, a Catholic Reform priest, and the national director of Family Love dueling at close quarters, was as good a diversion—no better, no worse—as the seven thousandth rerun of a medical comedy. He remained a passive observer of both, asking no questions and voicing no opinions during the former, declining his part as a heavily bandaged patient in the latter.

He was feeling a bit more participatory during a half-hour pitch for the Because You're a Woman diet, drawing gargoyle faces on the men and undrawing the clothing of the women. Even the insanity of Denali Devil's Downhill amused him, at least until a grinning Irish skier missed a gate at the seventeen-thousand-foot level and fell off the mountain at what the announcer straight-facedly called a "high terminal velocity."

Emboldened by liquor and pity, Christopher risked a glimpse at Current Events, morbidly curious about what they were saying now about him, about Malena Graham, about Jeremiah. He was almost disappointed to find that Current Events wasn't saying anything at all—not so many as five of the nine hundred stories in the Current Events stack had anything to do with the Diaspora.

Displacing them was a juicy drama—the collapse, just after midnight, of a centuries-old room and pillar salt mine a thousand feet under the trendy Melvindale section of Detroit. Sixteen square blocks had subsided ten meters in a jolt, dropping short-stack condos into their own basements and folding a crowded spin club flat.

One hundred sixty-three were known dead, and at least six hundred were missing, including the Detroit city manager, a noted poet, and three members of the Detroit Pistons basketball team. What's more, officials feared that the collapse had burst thousands of containers of colloidized hazardous waste stored in the mine in the 1990s. The Archbishop of Detroit, with wages-of-sin solemnity, called it God's warning to Sodom.

Death in the night, earthquakelike devastation, holiday-season tragedy, toxic poisons, missing celebrities, government neglect, holy vengeance—it was a news executive's wet dream. Christopher watched the coverage with a rum-flavored bemusement, finding black humor in the absurdities of the event, the stupidities of the reporters.

Christopher's mood had turned increasingly savage, cynical. It was already unpleasant sharing his mind with such thoughts, and promised to grow uglier still. He needed an escape from his escape. When it finally came, it was from a most unexpected source.

"Christopher, are you awake?" Lila asked. On the TV, dancers writhed to a backbeat.

"Sorry to say."

"Daniel Keith is calling."

He looked dumbly at his band. "My phone didn't ring."

"It's a station call to the house, Christopher. Shall I put it up for you?"

Christopher uncrossed his legs and pulled himself closer to vertical. "Sure."

Keith's face came up in a box on the TV. "Hello, Chris."

"Hello yourself." He shook his head, mostly to clear it. "Surprise, surprise. After this morning—"

"Yeah. I didn't want to be that short. But I couldn't talk. I couldn't even tell you that I couldn't. Not till I could get out of the complex."

"You home now?"

"No. Look, Chris, the hair on my neck is standing up just being on the line with you. There's been a lot of talk around here the last day or two, very strange stuff, none of it official. I didn't know how much of it to believe. I guess you told me. Your father was Jeremiah?"

"So I'm supposed to believe. I swear I didn't know."

Keith nodded. "I might be the only one in the center who'd believe that," he said slowly.

"I need some answers, Daniel."

"You want some wisdom? Don't ask the questions."

"My father left notes that have me confused. I have to know if what he believed was true."

"Why?" It was a cautionary, challenging question. *Why do you have to know? Are you sure you want to know?*

"So I can let go of it. So it'll let go of me. Will you meet me somewhere?"

Keith frowned and looked away momentarily. "Are you coming back to Houston?"

"I can't," Christopher said. "Meet me in Portland. No, better, San Francisco."

"I've got no reason to come west. And I need a reason. A

good reason. There's a limit to how much of a friend I can be to you now. I'm sorry. That's just the fact."

"I know. Where, then?"

Keith was silent for a time. "I think I'm going to go up to Chicago and visit my parents when we finally get cleared to leave. Nobody around here's gotten their winter holiday yet."

"When?"

"Not tomorrow. Probably not till Friday."

"I'll be there Friday. Call me."

"I don't know," Keith said, shaking his head.

"Please, Daniel. An hour. Half an hour."

"Why do you think I can help?" He almost sounded angry.

"I went out to watch the salmon at Bonneville Dam this morning."

"Oh? Were they helping each other?"

"I need to know why it's happening. I need to know why we're doing what we're doing."

Keith looked cross, distracted.

"Will you talk to me?"

"I don't know," Keith said. His tone hardened the words to a *no*.

Christopher chose to ignore the subtext. "Friday in Chicago. I'll call you."

"No," said Keith, shaking his head. "Don't. Maybe I'll call you. I have to think about it. Let's leave it at that."

There was nothing to be gained by pushing him. "All right. We'll leave it at that."

"Thank you." Eyes lowered, Keith looked as though he were unhappy with himself. "I don't know why I called you this time."

"I'm glad you did."

"Sure. Chris—"

"Still here."

Keith did not look up. "If you've got nothing better to do, you might ask DIANNA about von Neumann machines."

He signed off before Christopher could reply.

CHAPTER
28

-|GCC|-

"Sweet promises were made."

AFTER MONTHS OF WORKING ON AND WITH THE *MEMPHIS* hyper, it was hard to go back to DIANNA. The sluggish query engine, the restricted cross-citations, the lack of original source texts were all painfully obvious to Christopher. But he was reluctant to use his father's specialty accounts, and besides, Keith had pointed him specifically in that direction.

The name of Johann von Neumann was one with which Christopher had at least a passing acquaintance. In fact, it was hard to pass through any sort of technical education and not brush up against the Hungarian savant at one or more points.

In quantum theory, there was Neumann algebra with its critical analytical tools—rings of operators and continuous geometry. In economics, political science, and military strategy, von Neumann's game theory and minimax theorem still held center stage. In theoretical mathematics, there was the von Neumann who solved Hilbert's fifth problem and offered a persuasive proof of the ergodic hypothesis.

In computer science, von Neumann was there at the stone knives and bearskins beginning, introducing stored programs and advancing logical design in the ENIAC era. In meteorology, he anticipated the greenhouse effect in his studies of planetary heat balance. And in the history of technology, there was "Johnny" of the Manhattan Project, designing implosion lenses and solving hydrodynamic problems for Fat Man, the first plutonium bomb.

But the lead which Keith had given Christopher pointed in a different direction, to a comparatively unheralded collection of

298

papers published a decade after von Neumann's death. *Theory of Self-reproducing Automata* was a speculation on a daunting engineering challenge—the design and construction of a "universal constructor."

Von Neumann envisioned the universal constructor as an advanced cybernetic device capable of making any sort of artifact, including a copy of itself, from the specifications programmed within it and the raw materials found without. The pattern of cross-citations showed his influence on his contemporaries.

But the citations which interested Christopher were not from von Neumann's century, but from Christopher's own. Fifty years ago, as the elements which would lead to the construction of *Tigris* were starting to reach critical mass, a weak countermovement arose.

The amorphous opposition had no coordinating focus, no political center, no activist arm. All it had was a unifying argument—presented philosophically by some advocates, pragmatically by others. The first starships should be von Neumann machines, they argued. A crewed starship was too expensive, too complex, too premature, too risky. Send machines first— ship-sized robot probes which would pave the way for starships to follow, or even take their place entirely.

Some called for a few complex "prospector" probes, which could collect and relay information which could shape later decisions. Others wanted many expendable "pathfinder" probes, which could gauge the dangers of such a journey. The most ambitious proposed "caretaker" probes, which could oversee the terraforming of one planet while dispatching their clones to do the same for other worlds.

The proposals varied, but the message was the same: Let machines be our eyes, our hands. Let them go in our stead.

Christopher saw that there had never been any real chance that the machines-first movement would carry the day. Human ambitions must be satisfied in human time frames, and none of those on the point were willing to step aside in favor of a machine or an heir. But, just as clearly, contained within this largely forgotten debate was the intellectual genesis of the Homeworld movement. It was their *Federalist*, their *Das Kapital*. The seeds of revolution.

There was a time Christopher would have welcomed the discovery. But now it was the answer to the wrong question. *I need to know why we're doing what we're doing.* Daniel must have misunderstood or been deliberately obtuse. It was not the answer he needed. In fact, it didn't seem to be about the same thing at all.

At dusk Friday, they met on the Burnham Park levee, near the children's playground at Thirty-third Street. Between the restless waves of Lake Michigan, the howling Chicago wind, and the screamers climbing out of Meigs Island just to the north, they had all the privacy they could ask for.

"Are you here to talk me out of something, or are you ready to help me?" Christopher asked as they started off at a slow walk along the top of the concrete barrier, known locally as the Great Wall. With global warming, Lake Michigan had risen almost a meter in the last century, swallowing the city's beaches and forcing construction of dikes all along the waterfront.

"Did you take my suggestion?"

"It wasn't enough."

Keith sighed, pushing his hands deeper into his coat pockets. "What do you want to know?"

"What are you really selecting for?" It came out in a half-shout as a commuter screamer passed overhead with a roar.

Shaking his head, Keith said, "We're not doing the selecting. Not really."

"Who is?"

They covered another thirty meters before Keith spoke. "There are a hundred thousand genes in a mammalian cell," he said. "A hundred thousand genes, and enough unexpressed DNA between them for a hundred thousand more. Full of fragments, copies, oncogenes, nonsense sequences that code for no known proteins, programs for traits which haven't been needed in ten million years. It's where tails on babies and hind legs on whales come from. A chemical library that rivals the hyper. Not a bad analogy. The hyper is everything we know. The DNA is everything we are."

"Not everything."

"Everything. Why is one man addicted to alcohol and another never tempted by it? Look in his cells. It's all there. All our weaknesses. All our predispositions. Biology *is* destiny, Christopher. Clinical depression? Homosexuality? Look in the cells. Genius? Madness? They're there, too. An athlete's muscles, a musician's ears, the poet's heart—just different little bits of clockwork chemistry. Love? A neurochemical cycle—runs about six and a half years. Ever hear of the seven-year itch?"

"I can't argue physiology with you," Christopher said. "But we're learning from the first day we're alive. That's part of what we are, too."

"Sure. But mostly we're learning how to get what we want. You asked why we do what we do. I would have thought that was obvious. The meaning of life is to make new life. Nothing more. We just never understood the scale on which the drama was being played."

"What do you mean?" Christopher asked, grabbing at Keith's elbow.

Keith stopped and turned to face him. "You look at recent history and ask how we could do so many things that are anti-survival. Ocean pollution. Resource depletion. Ozone destruction. It isn't just that we didn't know. We kept right on after we did know. Because none of that matters. None of it. In the last hundred meters you give it everything. Because in this race, if you hold back, you die."

"Are you answering the question I asked?"

"You still don't see it?"

"No."

Keith turned away and resumed walking, and Christopher hurried to keep up with him. "The Creator has a master plan, Christopher. And we've been following it for four billion years. It carried *Eusthenopteron* onto the land and *Deinonychus* into the air. It's why whales beach themselves and cats climb trees. Do you want to know who God is, Christopher? God is two hundred and seventy-one codons on the twenty-first chromosome of the Chosen."

"In the Church of Sociobiology, maybe. I'm not a believer."

Nodding, Keith said, "That's fine. But it's a funny thing about Nature. She doesn't give a high hoot what we believe. Everything goes on just the same."

"Biology is destiny."

"And purpose."

"What happened to free will? What about our choice? Doesn't it count? Doesn't it exist?"

Keith stopped and gazed at Christopher, his head cocked at an angle. "Choice is noise on a picture with this scale," he said. "I'll gladly trade choice for destiny and purpose. Don't you understand, Christopher? *We* are the von Neumann machines."

• • •

Later, as they shared a bench and a bottle of Canadian wine outside the shuttered Field Museum of Natural History—the irony of that was not lost on Christopher—Keith explained himself in less metaphysical terms.

"Whatever it was in the beginning, we're now talking about a three-gene complex. Pieces or variants of it have been found in thirty-one species, all but three of them chordates. There's every reason to think that it's found its highest, purest expression in us. I think of *H. sap.* as the trustee of the Chi Sequence.

"The name doesn't mean anything, really. That's what it was called when it was a very minor mystery in comparative biochemistry. But you won't find anything about it in *Medbase* or the *NIH Index*. They've been sanitized—papers withdrawn, copyrights and biopatents bought.

"Three genes, A-B-C. Three messages. Direction—the where. Motivation—the why. And the activator, the little thirty-three codon sequence that says, 'Go-go-go.' "

His initial objections having been beaten down into silence, if not surrender, Christopher had listened with the kind of stunned amazement seen on the faces of young children after their first magic show. It was not his credulity which was being tested, but the agility of his mind. He was being shown marvels, and they had power and poetry even if he did not believe they were real.

"It's funny what happens when you only get one Chi gene expressed," Keith was saying. "All the people through history who felt the call of the night sky. All the fanciful invention of heavens and wheels within wheels. They were pointed in the right direction, but never understood why.

"And the way life here has spread into every possible nook and crevice, obeying the second part of the code. B for babies. B for be fecund. Go forth and multiply. Fill the world with your progeny.

"And the activator, the trickiest of all, the one that flips the ambition switch to high. A-positives have to find their own directions, their own reasons. But the restlessness that sends them looking comes from inside. Hillary had it. Thor Heyerdahl. Earhart. You don't need a microscope to make a list. But if we had a sample of their DNA, we'd find it, right there on the twenty-first chromosome. I don't doubt it for a minute."

"So the Chosen really do exist," Christopher said.

"Not the way you mean it. Three genes gives eight permutations, not even considering mutations and unexpressed recessives. Nothing is ever as simple as a geneticist says it is," Keith said, showing a smile. "But the triple actives—the pure Chipositives—they're the core of the Diaspora."

"And the Chi-negatives? Are they the core of Homeworld?"

"Who knows?" Keith said, interrupting his answer for a swig from the bottle. "Homeworlders don't tend to present themselves at the lab for testing. But if I were going to guess, I'd say that they're mostly B-positives—they're the most hidebound, the most sessile."

"That makes it sound like the different combinations have recognizable personalities."

"Not officially," Keith said. "But of course they do. A gene that's not expressed in structure or behavior wouldn't be important. I've processed more than two thousand applicants. I can call them eight times out of ten. These aren't just genotypes. They're human archetypes. It's affected how I deal with people, actually. When I meet someone for the first time, all I see is their Chi attribute."

"What is it you see?"

"I told you part of it already," Keith said. "Think of the A gene as ambition, the B as the breeding instinct, and C as the Call, and you can just about figure them out yourself."

"A-positives are adventurers," Christopher said slowly. "B-positives are nestmakers. C-positives—what, hear voices?"

"More or less. I call them the dreamers. Pure faith, pure reason, pure art. Priests, physicists, and philosophers."

"Do the traits combine?"

"Of course. And there's more variation in the combinations. BCs are the good citizens—workers and soldiers. The Call expresses itself as duty, allegiance. But put ambition and the Call together and you get a Creator—an artist or an inventor."

"Loi. She'd be an AC-positive, then?"

"Probably."

"And Jessie a nestmaker. What else is there?"

"Everyone's favorite—the AB-positives. Ambition and nest making builds kings and tycoons."

"And the pure Chi-positives?"

Another swallow. "Statesmen, saints, and avatars. And there are precious few of them."

Christopher counted. "Seven. One more. You didn't answer before. Who *are* the Chi-negatives?"

"Can't you figure it out?" Keith asked, coughing. "Why do you think there are so many meaningless lives? They're the people whose bodies give them no direction, no purpose. They don't burn. They don't want. They just are—instant to instant, day to day, like some cruel joke of nature. The hollow-chested Tin Men. The empty people. The damned."

The bottle was empty, and the sky overhead winter-black. They walked back in silence toward where the Avanti was parked, Christopher withdrawn, trying to absorb—or was it resist?—what he had heard. Keith's steps and spirit seemed lighter, the difficult obligation discharged without disaster.

"I don't know what to think," Christopher said when they finally reached the car.

"Believe what you want," Keith said. "It doesn't matter."

"Doesn't it? How many Chi-positives are going on *Memphis*?"

"I have no idea."

"Ten thousand?"

"Oh, no," Keith said, shaking his head vigorously. "Even if we could find that many. Chi-positives are difficult. It's just the way they are. They're the glue—but did you ever try building something from glue alone? *Memphis* has no use for kings and adventurers. *Ur* is in trouble because we sent her off with too many kings aboard—we didn't understand yet what the rules were. And the nestmakers and dreamers have no use for us."

"So who *are* you taking?"

Keith settled back against the fender. "*Memphis* needs a core of stable, loyal, dedicated people who know their place in the plan. It needs a leavening of creative types to keep the vision alive and deal with the unexpected. And it needs wise, unselfish leadership."

"BCs, ACs, and Chi-positives."

"I told you you'd catch on."

"But when *Memphis* gets where it's going, then you'll need the others—the kings and adventurers and the rest—to build nests and empires on the new world."

"Right. So they're making the trip in steerage, where they won't be any trouble."

It took Christopher a moment to understand his meaning. "The gamete banks—that's what the gamete banks are for."

Keith made an imaginary mark in the air with his finger. "One point for the contestant from Oregon."

"So how many Chi-positives? Five thousand? Five hundred? Fifty? How rare are they?"

"I told you, I don't know," Keith said. "They're about four percent of the applicant pool. But that's a self-selected sample. Why does it matter?"

"Because of what Jeremiah said. What happens when they're gone, Daniel? Are you stealing the spark?"

A surprised laugh was Keith's first response. "And John Galt said that he would stop the motor of the world," he said. "Our poor little ten thousand, Christopher? We won't even notice they're gone."

"You just finished telling me how special they are. The pinnacle of evolution."

Impatience flashed across Keith's face. "How about a little perspective? There've been at least fifty natural disasters and a hundred wars in the Christian era alone that killed a hundred thousand or more. There was a flood in China in 1931 that wiped out almost four *million*. The Second World War killed *forty* million."

"But who were they, Daniel?" he demanded, stepping closer. "Drones and breeders? The faithful and patriotic? How many of them had a chance to shape the world? How many of them even had a chance to shape their own lives? And even so, do you really think it doesn't cost us anything when a whole race, a whole generation, is exterminated?"

Keith held his hands palm-out in supplication. "It's only ten thousand. Not a race. Not a generation. Do you know how long it takes the world population to replace ten thousand people? An hour. Forty-nine minutes, if you want to split hairs."

"You said it yourself. They're self-selected. The manifest for *Memphis* is made up of ten thousand of the best educated, most talented, most highly motivated people we've produced. If this is where it's all been pointing, how can it *not* make a difference? You can't have it both ways. The birds are still here, but the rest of the dinosaurs are gone. Sometimes the torch passes."

"That's fear-talk," Keith said, straightening from his casual pose. "I expected better from you."

"Really? Is that why you brought the gun?" Christopher's hand closed around the neck of the bottle in a fighting grip. "And please, don't insult my intelligence. I saw it when you paid for the wine. How close did I come to being dumped into the lake?''

With a slow, deliberate motion, Keith reached into an inner pocket and retrieved the contoured shape of a shockbox, which he laid on the roof of the car. "I wouldn't come down here at night without something. It had nothing to do with you.''

"I'd like to believe that, Daniel, except I don't know what you're up to. I can't figure out why you told me what you did tonight.''

"I told you the truth. Everything you asked.''

"I know. You told me things I'd have been months finding out.''

Keith shook his head. "You'd never have found them. There isn't even anything in the hyper.''

"You're not helping your case. Nobody tells this kind of secret as a favor. We've been friends, but not *that* good of friends. What do you gain? Or are you supposed to kill me now?''

"No.'' Keith took a sideways step away from the car and the gun.

"Then tell me what's going on, goddammit,'' Christopher said, looking around nervously. "I'm getting very jumpy out here. Why did you tell me?''

"Because you're Jeremiah's son. But you're also Chris. I took a chance because I thought you would listen.''

"What?''

"I wanted you to know you don't have to be afraid of us. I want you to let us be. Don't try to stop *Memphis*, Chris. Please.''

Christopher stared. "Son of a bitch,'' he said under his breath. "Son of a bitch. My father was afraid I wasn't enough like him. And now you're afraid I'm too much like him.''

"I don't know what to think, Chris. I really don't.''

Shaking his head, Christopher dropped the bottle where he stood and made for the door of the Avanti. "I'm leaving,'' he muttered. When he reached the car, he knocked the gun to the ground with a careless, angry swipe of his hand, then pulled the door upward.

"Chris—''

He settled in the seat before looking back. "What?''

"I can't be sorry about Jeremiah. But I'm sorry about your father.''

Christopher looked at Keith with blazing eyes. "My father was a king.'' He said it pridefully, with a hint of a challenge.

"Yes. I think he was."

Nodding as though satisfied with the concession, Christopher brought the car to life, the door still open. Then he seemed to take a deep breath, taking the control wheel in both hands as though he needed it for support. He looked over his shoulder out at Keith. "What am I, Daniel?"

Keith came a step closer. "I was expecting you to ask that a long time ago—and you're not going to like my answer. The truth is I know you too well to see you that simply. I can see all eight attributes in you—including Chi-negative."

"Then how do I find out?"

"You can't," he said, shaking his head.

"Doesn't the company know?"

"No," Keith said. "That's one of the questions that got me in trouble. You were an employee. You were never sampled. And there isn't a lab anywhere outside Allied that knows what to look for."

"You knew I'd have to know."

"I was hoping you wouldn't need to be told."

"Why?"

"Can't you feel it? Didn't you say, 'Yeah, that's me,' at some point in the list?"

"Sure. Three times."

Keith frowned. "Then the key is your mother. Maybe you can figure it out from there."

"Maybe," Christopher said, little hope in his voice or his eyes. He sighed and jerked his head toward the empty seat beside him. "Can I drop you somewhere?"

The invitation was an apology and a peace offering, and Keith's acceptance the signing of a truce. But they had little more to say to each other. From the time they lifted off to the time Keith climbed out in the driveway of his parents' Stone Park home, only once was the silence broken.

"One more question?" Christopher asked as they bore across the Loop.

Looking out the side glass at the Daley Tower, Keith gave a slight nod.

"Were you ever sampled?"

"BC-positive," Keith said. "Hardworking and loyal to a fault." He turned back and showed a wan smile. "Most of the time, anyway."

"But they didn't take you."

"My choice."

"What's that mean?"

"I'm putting in my turn at the wheel," Keith said. "There are a lot of us doing it. I've been promised a place on *Knossos*."

It was midmorning when Christopher reached the house on the ridge. After stowing the Avanti in the garage, he stopped in the bathroom to splash his face and in the kitchen to start coffee. While the coffee was brewing, he collected the Portables from his father's bedroom and carried them into the den. He stacked them in three columns on the end of the comsole before settling, cup in hand, in the chair.

"You there, Lila?"

"Ready, Christopher."

"Any mail? Any messages?"

"No. There are no new messages."

"What about for my father?"

"I am handling Mr. McCutcheon's correspondence."

"Still pretending he's not dead?"

"I am doing what he asked me to."

"I don't suppose you'd care to let me see what it is."

"I'm sorry, Christopher. I can't do that."

"Have you heard from my father?"

"No. Your father is dead."

"Does anyone besides us know that?"

"No."

"You haven't told anyone while playing secretary for him?"

"I am conducting your father's business according to his instructions."

"Doesn't matter. I'll bet the only people you told knew him as Jeremiah. And Jeremiah's not allowed to die, is he? Who's the new Jeremiah, Lila?"

"I can't answer that, Christopher."

"Right." He sipped at his caramel-colored coffee, still steaming. "Do you know anything about a will?"

"A will is registered with the Oregon State Probate Court. Since no death certificate has been filed, the will has not been presented."

"Who's the executor?"

"You are, Christopher."

It was only technically a surprise. "I guess I know better than to think he'd ask me. Was he planning to ever tell me?"

"It's not required by Oregon law, since an executor may refuse the appointment."

"Know anything about what the will says?"

"No. The only knowledge I have of it comes from checking the court registry."

"It doesn't matter," said Christopher. "That's how he was going to get me back here, wasn't it? That's why he left the archives."

"They were for you to read after his death."

"So you said. Well"—he patted the top of the nearest stack—"I'm ready to see the rest of them."

"I'm sorry, Christopher. I don't understand."

"I want you to show me anything and everything about my mother that you have in your files or can find anywhere, including these archives."

"Checking. Your mother is Deryn Glenys Falconer?"

"Sharron," he said impatiently. "I'm talking about Sharron. My father's wife."

"Checking. Full name is Sharron Ria McCutcheon, née Aldritch?"

He stared at the display in surprise. "You had to check that? He didn't think it was important enough to restore?"

"I do not know what information was not restored, Christopher, nor why it was not included."

"Are you saying you don't have *anything* about Sharron?"

"I'm compiling biographical information from several sources. I'll have a report for you in the next thirty seconds."

"I don't want anything from outside. I want to know how *he* saw her. I want to see her myself. Where are the family albums? Didn't he keep anything of hers?"

"Not in my records, Christopher."

Seizing the nearest Portable, Christopher pulled open the drawer and pushed the book into the empty data port. "What about there?"

"This volume is *Wild Animals of North America*, published by the National Geographic Society. It contains no archives."

"What?" Quickly, Christopher swapped another book into its place. "What about that one?"

"This volume is *Ptolemy's Daughter: The Art of Sabra Adams*, by—"

"I can read the goddamned titles."

"It contains no archives."

"What's going on here, Lila? These are the same books I read from on Tuesday, aren't they?"

"Yes, Christopher. Those files were erased as you read them, on Mr. McCutcheon's instructions. I find no other files."

"Son of a bitch," he breathed. "Why didn't you tell me? If I'd known I was only going to have one chance to read them—" He stopped, seeing the answer to his own question.

—I'd have photographed the screen, or transcribed the entries, or read them into a recorder. And then I could have shared them with anyone. For your eyes only. This tape will self-destruct in ten seconds.

"You did tell me."

"Yes, Christopher."

"No other files marked for access by me, or no files at all?"

"I find no files at all."

I can see Sharron in his eyes and hear Deryn in his words. They are both inside him, pulling at him to follow. Follow where? They had both found a way to leave him, but by very different ways to very different destinations.

They are both inside him—

You never wanted me to know who I am. You closed all doors but one, barred all paths but the one that would lead me back here. You tried to draw my eyes from her by shining more brightly. What is it you didn't want me to see? You knew, you bastard, you knew all the time. Did you want me to like you, or just to be like you?

"What's the magic word?" he asked suddenly.

"Excuse me?"

"What is it I have to say to earn the prize? He wanted me to take his place. The will gives me the castle. I know it does. You have to give me the crown. I'm the one he picked, right? He'd rather have given it to me than anyone, if only I could pass the test."

"I can't answer that, Christopher."

"But you know, don't you? You know."

"I can't answer that, Christopher."

"You wouldn't lie to me, would you? Silly question," Christopher said. "Of course you would, if he told you to. I should take you down and clean you out so you're working for me. Except someday a call'd come in and we'd be right back where we are now. Son of a bitch."

"Mr. McCutcheon is the primary user."

"Mr. McCutcheon is dead, you crystal moron."

"I know that, Christopher."

"Miracle! She knows something. How about something useful? Tell me about the Chi Sequence."

"Checking. No information."

"Did my father love me?"

"No information."

"Where's my father's body?"

"No information."

"Who is Jeremiah?"

"I can't answer that, Christopher."

"How did my mother die?"

"No information."

With a wild swipe of his arm, Christopher sent the neatly stacked books cascading onto the carpeted floor. "Then you're not much goddamn use to me, are you, Lila?" he said, coming to his feet. "Between what you can't tell me and what you won't tell me, not much goddamned use at all."

The decision was made in that moment, but the arrangements took more than a week to complete, with another week's waiting tacked on after that. The delay gave Christopher a chance to measure his motives and consider his choice. No better options presented themselves, even if some doubts did.

He used the time well. Not knowing when he might be back, he revisited his favorite spots in the Northwest—postcard-beautiful Boiler Bay, where basalt cliffs and chaotic Pacific waves created a dramatic tapestry; Bridal Veil Falls, one of the hidden treasures of the Gorge, which he had discovered in the company of an adolescent love; the winding climb up to the high lodge on fog-wrapped, snow-cloaked Mount Rainier.

While he was in the house, there were issues to research, logistical and technical problems to resolve, and still a few doors to knock on. He allowed Lila to present what she could gather about Sharron from public sources; he called his mother's brother and father and tried to break through the wall of resentment; he took several of the Portables to a hack shop in Seattle to be cracked and copied.

None of his efforts yielded more than a few drams of insight, but, oddly, every failure only made what he was about to do seem more right and reasonable.

There were also financial matters to settle. A final Allied pay-check appeared in his account, as Dryke had said it would. Christopher transferred the full amount to the Kenning House account, as much an attempt to preserve his place there as a reaction against the source of the funds. And paying for his ticket and poundage on the Horizon shuttle from Los Angeles proved a challenge. His credit lines had shrunk when his resignation was posted, forcing him to juggle advances and accounts to cover the fare.

Paying for his seat was only slightly harder than booking it; the shuttles were inexplicably full in what should have been the post-holiday lull. The alternate route, through Technica, was no better. He even checked flights from Hawaii and Florida. Except for premium fares, which Christopher could not afford, every North American commercial shuttle was sold out through the end of January. He ended up booking for February 6, almost a month away, though he also bought a place on the six-hour standby list.

The extra expense proved worthwhile. In midmonth, just as the waiting was starting to wear on him, the notification call came through. There had been a cancellation for the 10 P.M. flight to Horizon—could he be there?

"I'll be there."

He had rehearsed the ritual often enough in his head that he was able to move quickly. In but a few minutes, his bag was packed with his clothes and the very few objects he wanted from the house. He loaded the bag in the Avanti, which he then moved safely away from the house. Disabling the alarms and extinguishers took a little longer, but he had already scouted the systems and acquired the necessary tools.

By that time, Lila's curiosity had been aroused. But the next step was to shut off all power to the house, which squelched her questions. Only then did he bring out the two ten-liter tins of accelerant. Changing into some of his father's clothes, he splashed every room, with special attention to the spaces he had occupied. He wanted it to burn hot and fast, leaving only ashes and enough mystery to prompt an investigation.

There were risks, but the only risk-free course was surrender. If his father's body wasn't found, if the investigation focused on arson rather than William McCutcheon's disappearance, if Allied and Mikhail Dryke chose to silence Christopher rather than intervene—if, if, if. There were a hundred things that could go wrong. But he could not leave his life or his father's death in limbo. There was something he had to prove—to the homunculus of William McCutcheon that lived inside his head, to Mikhail Dryke, and to himself.

Only when it was time to strike the spark did he hesitate. Standing on the front step before the open door, back in his own clothes and holding the lighter and the bundle of chemical-spattered clothing in his hands, he found his heart racing, his lungs aching as though he had just run up the ridge road from the gate. *Do I have the right to do this?* jostled with *Can I see this through?* for first place in his insecurities.

The revelation of two weeks ago was slipping away. He had to make himself say it out loud to break the paralysis that had seized him.

"I don't ever want to come back here."

Flame touched cloth, which flared happily into life. Christopher quickly tossed the bundle through the doorway, turning his back and retreating across the lawn. As he climbed into the Avanti, he stole a peek back, and was rewarded by a flickering orange glow playing behind the first-story windows of the far dome.

Christopher circled the house at treetop level until the second-story windows exploded outward in billows of gray smoke and gouts of yellow-red fire. Then he turned away, banking toward Portland, refusing to look back. He kept the Avanti on the deck to keep its movements off the air traffic monitors, settling into the I-26 surface traffic as he approached Banks. It was hard to hold his speed down when what he wanted to do was run.

The last detail was the Avanti, which he knew he could not keep. He left it at the curb on Killingsworth Street, four klicks from the city's transplex, with the passenger door unlocked and the travel log's memory wiped. The flyer was baggage at this point, and he did not care if it was stolen, stripped or impounded.

Keeping his pace brisk and his thoughts disciplined, Christopher hiked to the transplex and the tube station. He was invigorated by the freedom that came with action, by the peace that came with purpose. The police might soon be searching for him, Dryke could soon be hunting him, but he did not care. In a few short hours he would be beyond their reach, for Horizon was not his final destination. This journey would not end until he reached Deryn's arms and Sanctuary.

CHAPTER
29

"These ships are frail"

PRAINHA HAD BECOME A PRISON FOR MIKHAIL DRYKE.

In the moment he fired the first bullet into Jeremiah's body, he had understood that Sasaki would not approve. He had recognized that, by passing on the opportunity to simply collect Jeremiah, he was crossing a significant line. He had known that the decision would look different in Prainha than it had in the underground room.

And though Sasaki had said not one word in reproach, her actions argued loudly enough that Dryke had been right. It began with Sasaki's explicit order that Christopher McCutcheon be left free and alive. She had never interfered with Dryke in that way before, and he read the message clearly: *I can't undo what you've done, but I will not permit you to repeat the mistake.*

"We can't kill all our enemies, Mikhail. I do not consider the son a risk," she had said. "Separate him from us and leave him there." She neither invited nor accepted Dryke's counsel on the decision.

Another clue: In the two weeks since the event, no official announcement of Jeremiah's death had been made, even within the Project. The committee and senior security staff knew, and the Houston center was rife with apparently unsquelchable rumors. Marshall had offered token congratulations; Matt Reid had gratefully welcomed the news. But that was the extent of it.

Even more telling, it seemed as though he was being insulated from the real work of his own department. Part of it was his own doing—there was no place for him in the everyday opera-

314

tion of Corporate Security unless he shouldered aside one of his own handpicked lieutenants.

But Sasaki seemed determined to keep him from his accustomed role as fire fighter, as well. She had placed the entire First Directorate under travel restrictions, meaning that he needed her explicit permission to leave Prainha. And there was always some new reason why he couldn't leave. He spent his days chasing down problems which were beneath him and sitting through meetings to which he had nothing to contribute. He understood that, too. She wanted him in sight at all times, on his invisible leash.

The maddening part was that there were problems that cried out for his attention.

Item: In the street outside the twenty-six-story building housing the Tokyo training and processing center, the carnival of militant demonstrations continued its daily run. The strategy of the mostly youthful protesters consisted of blocking the street and baiting Tokyo police, Corporate Security, and—in absentia, since they had largely ceded the battlefield—the starheads. The police and security had shown restraint, even in the face of taunts punctuated by hurled bags of excrement.

The starheads, however, had not. There had been flyby shootings, gas grenades lobbed from blocks away, kamikaze drivers. Just three days ago, a small group of starheads had slipped into the fifteen-story tower facing the Allied building, taken over the roof, and rained thousands of marble-sized steel bearings down on the throng. In a particularly vicious twist, the starheads had begun shouting amplified insults down into the walled canyon just before the hail reached the ground.

Five demonstrators were killed and more than a hundred injured by the hail, some horribly so, with cheeks torn open, eyes splattered like eggs, facial bones shattered, skulls fractured as they turned their faces up to look for the enemy. In the riot that followed, the Allied building was breached and a fire set in the main atrium, and seven more died, including one policewoman and three starheads found dead by their own hand on the rooftop.

Item: In Cologne, Greens and Homeworlders together were trying to shut down an Allied-owned specialty metals plant by lying down in front of the haulers trying to leave the plant, which was producing both molded and machined parts for *Memphis*. More than three hundred had been dragged away from in front of the wheels and arrested, but there seemed to be no shortage of volunteers to replace them, even after a woman and a teenaged boy were crushed when one omni driver lost patience with the game.

Item: Yvonne Havens, director of operations at Kasigau Launch Center, had abruptly and unexpectedly resigned within the week. After the fact, she informed Sasaki that she had done so to "ransom" her mother, who had been kidnapped from her apartment in Cairo by a group calling itself Jeremiah's Hands. Emboldened by their success, the terrorists had just taken the husband of a HELcrew launch chief and the daughter of the supervisor of Vehicle Manufacturing, making the same demands.

There were mitigating factors in all three situations. The Tokyo center was effectively mothballed, anyway, under Contingency Zero, but it was important to keep up appearances. The metals plant had completed more than ninety-five percent of its Diaspora contract, including all of the critical high-stress system fittings. And Kasigau's efficiency had never been what it should have been under Havens.

Still, it was not in Dryke's nature to discount such threats or to entrust others with the responsibility of responding to them. But he was faced with doing both, because Sasaki "needed" him in Prainha.

He would have been more upset, except for the odd conviction persisting that, with Jeremiah dead, it should be over. He did not have the old fight in him; he was merely annoyed, not aroused, by the news coming in. Even so, he would have talked to Sasaki about it, but she had disappeared beyond barriers of bureaucracy. His former access had dried up; he did not see her and could not get to her.

Overlooked and underworked, Dryke was left with time to wonder, more time than he cared for. Had he any taste for alcohol or other drugs, he probably would have used them to shorten the day. But his fetish for control in his life was too strong to permit him that escape. Were he less duty-driven, he might have declared his war over and gone home. But he could not abdicate, even though it was harder each day to see any reason for his being there.

He no longer knew what Hiroko wanted from him or what she wanted him for. At times, he wondered if she was merely keeping him on hand to throw to the wolves when the snarling and howling grew too loud. Dryke had neither expected nor wanted to be greeted as a conquering hero—he felt too much ambivalence himself for that. But neither had he dreamed he would find himself recalled in disgrace, spinning out his days as the pariah of Prainha.

At midmonth, Dryke was granted a brief, tantalizing glimpse into what was happening in the inner circle. It came in the form of a visit from Roger Marshall, one of two outsiders on Sasaki's seven-member advisory committee.

Though Marshall came and went from Prainha at will, Dryke had had only glancing contact with the billionaire California real estate developer. He knew him only as a well-dressed, well-mannered, well-spoken man. A reasonable man, as Dryke defined the term. Someone who listened before he questioned and thought before he answered.

Dryke knew a little more about Marshall's company, Cornerstone Management. The problems of building a residential superscraper overlapped a great deal with the problems of building a starship, and Cornerstone had shown itself the reigning master of the former art, with Marshall the financial wizard who made the deals go. Marshall and Co. had put up Daley Tower in Chicago, the Gold Coast complex north of Sydney, and several other headline projects. Of the dozen or so architectural monuments around the globe which rivaled *Memphis* for cost and complexity, Roger Marshall had had a hand in five.

His expertise was unquestioned, but Dryke had always wondered at his interest. The committee was unpaid and unsung, second only to Sasaki in influence but invisible behind her. It seemed an odd place to find a Roger Marshall, unless he simply considered the Project as an interesting hobby, interesting enough that he was content with a secondary role. Dryke had no idea what a man who commanded wealth on Marshall's scale did for self-indulgence.

That day, Marshall appeared at Dryke's office without warning. "Good afternoon, Mr. Dryke," he said, showing a friendly but measured smile. "Is there any chance I might steal you away from here for a while?"

It was like asking Sisyphus if he had any interest in a five-minute break. "A pretty good chance, I'd say. What's the problem, Mr. Marshall?"

"Roger, please. I understand we're processing a lot of the

pioneers through Prainha,'' Marshall said, folding his arms over his chest. "I'd like to talk to some of them. I want to get a handle on how they're coping with all the disruption from C-Zero."

The first part was both true and common knowledge. Twenty-seat T-2s packed with colonists were flying out of the castle a dozen times a day, day after day. But for the twin bottlenecks of security screening and ferrying them from the low-orbit stations to Takara, the pace would be even brisker.

The second part was both insulting and puzzling. *Have I been demoted to tour guide now?* Marshall did not need Dryke's permission to visit Building 5, where the arriving pioneers were being assembled into groups, taken through a T-2 mock-up and orientation, and given a place to wait comfortably until their flight was called. And Training Section could provide far more knowledgeable escorts than he.

But Dryke acceded to Marshall's request, all the same. They took a wirecar over to Building 5, where Dryke ran interference with the harried Move managers. Then he stood in the background while Marshall talked with a group of Block 2 pioneers waiting for their midafternoon launch. One confessed to annoyance, one to apprehension. But the rest were almost defiantly eager—for them, the adventure had already begun.

"We're not going to let them stop us," one woman told Marshall. "This is something that belongs to us, and nobody has the right to take it away."

Marshall did not seem to have to hear much to satisfy him. After fifteen minutes, he shook hands, wished luck, and took his leave.

"Walk with me, will you, Mikhail?" he said to Dryke when they were outside.

Mystified, Dryke sent the wirecar back and fell in beside Marshall. The unscreened sun was fierce. After a few dozen steps, Dryke was perspiring.

"It's going surprisingly well," Marshall said. "Surprising to me, in any case. Nine thousand colonists, a thousand or so from Training—that's a lot of bodies to move in less than a month. A lot of coordination. And so far, none of our watchdogs have barked. That's a credit to you."

"It's all being handled by staff," Dryke said, already starting to feel the midday heat. "I haven't had anything to do with it."

"Take the compliment and forget the blushing. You'd be

blamed if they screwed up," said Marshall. "Besides, I haven't gotten to the tough parts. Tell me about the centers. What's happening in Tokyo?"

"Tokyo is closed down, for all practical purposes," Dryke said. "The work that could still be done there under siege conditions isn't worth the risk to our people. We have a hundred or so security officers and a couple of dozen operations techs inside, which is about the limit we can support from the air, with the roof pad."

"It's important to protect the building," said Marshall. "We do want to go back there—or at least be able to sell the building—when *Memphis* is gone and things have quieted down. What about the other sites?"

"Still more or less normal, except for the absence of the pioneers. Munich can thank the German government. Houston has its own airfield and its own housing, of course—they can probably ride out most anything so long as the fences hold."

Marshall nodded. "It's good to know that we're still ready to fight on some fronts. This new strategy—I guess I'm a bit more of a scrapper than Hiroko. I hate to see us cede anything. Did you sign off on Contingency Zero?"

"It wasn't my call."

"And if it had been?"

Dryke was wary. "If it had been my call, I wouldn't have put the training centers in urban sites in the first place. We're a lot more secure here than they are in Houston."

Nodding thoughtfully, Marshall said, "Maybe we should be keeping those people we just talked to here, then. Maybe shipping everyone up to Takara and *Memphis* is an overreaction."

"That's where they're going eventually," Dryke said, wiping the sweat from his forehead with his sleeve. "And as you said, that part is going smoothly, at least. No harm, no foul."

The scream of a T-ship passing overhead distracted them briefly.

"Some of us have noticed that you've been taking a back seat since you reeled in Jeremiah for us," Marshall said.

"Resting on my laurels," Dryke said. A touch of the bitterness slipped out with the words.

Marshall smiled. "I knew Bill McCutcheon. Were you aware of that?"

Eyes widening, Dryke admitted, "No."

"Well, you would be soon, I imagine. I assume that you're

building a matrix of his contacts, looking for the rest of the
Homeworld leadership.''

"Yes.'' The truth was that he had not been able to work up
any sense of urgency about what was certain to be a massive
undertaking, and so had not even begun.

"He beat me to a parcel of land in Mexico a few years back,''
Marshall said. "I offered him more than it was worth, too, but
he wouldn't sell it to me. He never did anything with it, either.
A lot of his holdings were undeveloped, as a matter of fact.''

"Oh?''

"If ten percent of what he owned produced income, I'd be
surprised. He was land-rich and cash-poor. Not your traditional
land speculator, though. More a land investor. Up until the last
few months, he bought more than he sold—which is the hard
way, since you don't realize any gains until you sell.''

"What was that about the last few months?''

"Bill moved ten or twelve parcels since August. Knowing
what we know now, I suppose he needed operating funds—but
I'm not telling you anything you didn't know. I imagine you're
following the money, too.''

Dryke squinted sideways at his companion. "Why did you
want to see me, Mr. Marshall?''

"I always valued your perspective, Mikhail,'' Marshall said.
"Just because the Director is looking past you at the moment,
I didn't see any reason I couldn't avail myself of it on my own.''

Dryke could find no argument with that. "What do you want
my perspective on?''

"Has Homeworld been eliminated as a threat?''

"I wouldn't assume so.''

"Nor would I. How would you characterize our strategy at
this point?''

Lips pursed, Dryke considered. "A controlled retreat under
cover of darkness. Abandoning a vulnerable position for a more
secure one.'' It was clear now that their conversation was a
footnote to an argument that had taken place behind closed
doors.

"But we're most vulnerable now—halfway between.''

"Yes.''

"If they find out what's happening before we're finished, it'll
be like showing a gimpy leg to a wolf pack.'' There was no
need to define *they*—it embraced Homeworld, the media, and
any other opponent or obstacle.

"It wouldn't look good, no."

"And it could happen."

"Disinformation campaigns are always vulnerable to the truth."

"Yes," said Marshall. "Do you know why I wanted to talk to the pioneers?"

"I assumed it was for the reason you told me."

"I spoke with Karin Oker this morning, and she told me something that raised the hair on the back of my neck. According to her, when the early call to report went out for the Block 2 and Block 3 pioneers, more than seven hundred—almost twelve percent—opted out. Quit on us."

It was a stunning, disturbing figure. In past calls, including those for *Ur*, no more than two percent had failed to report. "I hadn't heard that."

"That's seven hundred leaks waiting to happen. I know the calls didn't contain any damning information, but the circumstances are damning enough. Someone's going to talk, and someone else is going to figure out what we're up to," Marshall said. "I'm wondering if perhaps we ought to announce it ourselves before that happens."

"What does that gain us?"

"I know, it sounds like shooting yourself in the foot," said Marshall, flashing a crooked, humorless smile. "Here's my thinking. In his last address, Jeremiah hammered at the importance of keeping the colonists here. But once we've whisked them all away off-planet, there's only one way to do that, and that's to disable or destroy the ship. We've done our enemies a favor, really. Instead of a hundred strategies and a dozen attack points, they can concentrate on one goal and one big, fat, inviting target. Do you agree?"

"Yes."

Marshall stopped and faced Dryke. "Then it seems to me that we can best protect the ship by making sure anyone and everyone knows that there are already three thousand people aboard, with more arriving every day. Considering how the Homeworlders feel about losing them, the pioneers are as good as hostages. They won't dare a major assault."

"It doesn't add up that way to me," Dryke said with a shake of his head. "If they stop *Memphis*, they stop *Knossos* and *Mohenjo-Daro* and *Teotihuacán* as well. The numbers don't look that bad—sacrifice a few thousand to slam the door on tens of thousands. If they were really sure of themselves, they might warn us in advance, tell us to evacuate the ship. But I don't think that'll happen. I don't think they're going to be as worried about who's aboard as we'd wish they would be.''

"Then why haven't they done it yet? What's holding them back?''

"I think that Jeremiah held them back," Dryke said slowly. "I think he believed that he had the compelling case—that the ethical and logical correctness of his position guaranteed eventual victory. He wasn't dueling with us. He was debating with us.''

"Evan Silverman wasn't debating. Those people in Tokyo aren't debating.''

"No. Jeremiah saw the writing on the wall. He knew he was running out of time. The game's being played by different rules now.'' *Rules that Silverman introduced, and I ratified.* "Matt Reid brings up this every time we talk. He agrees—the question isn't if, it's when and how. It's entirely a question of logistics now. As soon as they figure out a way to take a shot at *Memphis*, they will.''

Marshall's cheek twitched, and his gaze narrowed. "Is the ship safe?''

Dryke placed his hands on his hips and cocked his head before he answered. "I could run out a long list of precautions that we've taken and send you away happy and reassured. But it's not the doors we bar that we have to worry about. It's the one we don't. It's the surprise. Is the ship safe? The truth is, I don't really know.''

Well into the second century of the Space Age, it was no secret that the best way to destroy a space habitat was to throw things at it. The things did not need to be big, complicated, or explosive, so long as they were thrown hard enough. A few kilometers per second was just fine, as everyone who remembered the inglorious end of *Freedom* knew.

Just nine years after it was completed, the American space station's main module was shattered—and three astronauts killed—by an in-falling bit of space flotsam. According to one reconstruction, a fifty-gram binding rivet lost during the construction of the first Japanese direct-broadcast platform was the probable culprit.

But it was very hard to throw things at *Memphis*—as hard as throwing a bowling ball out of the bottom of a well. Most of the major habitats, including all but two of the satlands, were part of the "Ring of Pearls," only two thousand kilometers above the Earth. *Memphis* was riding along in tandem with one of the exceptions—just ten klicks west of Takara, in Clarke orbit, thirty-six thousand kilometers above the blue Pacific and the atolls of the Gilbert Islands. Nothing orbited higher save for a geophysical survey satellite or two and traffic bound for Mars or Heinlein City.

Being at the top of the well was a considerable advantage. The fastest operational missile—the Asteroid Watch's nuclear-tipped Stonebreaker—would take nearly an hour to arrive from low orbit. The Peace Force's aging "shotgun" battle-suppression satellites could not do much better—their hypervelocity railguns would bridge the gap in twenty-six minutes at closest approach.

But orbital mechanics was not *Memphis*'s only defense. The universe threw things, too, especially at starships traveling at an appreciable fraction of the speed of light. *Memphis* had several layers of protection, including an ion deflector, the plasma bow cushion, and a particle defense system built around a pair of HEL free-electron lasers. Twenty-six minutes was more than enough time for the big gyros to turn the bell-shaped starship and bring the PDS to bear.

And against the one threat *Memphis* was not expecting to face in deep space—laser weapons—Reid had deployed around the starship several agile crane-trucks bearing huge square scatter plates in their construction grapples like shields. Dryke thought of them as the Knights Peculiar.

In that context, sabotage from within shaped up as a more likely prospect. But the memory of Javier Sola was strong, and putting a bomb aboard *Memphis* would be no mean feat.

The loyalty of the Takara workers, already securely anchored by community pride, was guaranteed by a simple expedient—the finishing crews were made up solely of those who had been selected to the mission. The small fleet of buses which ferried workers and materials across the ten-kilometer moat to the ship was owned by Transcon and operated by Diaspora pilots. And Governor Wian was allowing Matt Reid to supervise the screening procedures in the satland's euphemistically named immigration and import office, Takara Welcome.

No possibility was too wild to take seriously—not even a pocket nuke smuggled into Takara and detonated there, turning the satland into a giant fragmentation grenade. Even the one scenario which most troubled Dryke, involving the hijacking of a Takara shuttle and its use as a 120-ton battering ram, had been covered nine ways to Sunday.

Secure without, secure within. The slogan was displayed in English and kanji throughout the Project quarter on Takara and *Memphis*. Seen so often, it had become a state of mind, a statement of reality. It would be unfair to say that Reid's team was cocky, but they were confident.

Which is why the attack on *Memphis*, when it came, was every bit as much a surprise as Dryke had projected.

The black cylindrical satellite had been on station three and a half degrees east of Takara for nearly three months. It was listed in the Highstar registry as Slot 355, 177.5° East, Hughes TC-2000—a dedicated data communications satellite owned by RJR Financial Services, Wilmington, Delaware.

In adspeak, the TC-2000 was referred to as a mature technology—which in this case meant it was guaranteed to be slow, expected to be reliable, and presumed to be a bargain. In spacespeak, the TC-2000 was disparagingly referred to as a tin can. Compared to the huge Skylink 4 and Nikkei N-2 com platforms at 175° east and 5° west, the little satellite was a mouse among the lions.

But the mouse had a secret: It was not the satellite that RJR had ordered, that Hughes had built, that the United Parcel Service had accepted for delivery to a towing and retrieval company on Technica. It was, instead, a seven-year-old TC-2000 which had been originally built for the Royal Sultanate of Brunei, but was never placed in service. It had appeared on the secondary market in midsummer, offered by the People's Revolutionary Government of Brunei during a budget crisis—a bargain Jeremiah could not resist.

When Taiwanese technicians were finished modifying it, the TC-2000 featured a high-thrust ascent engine concealed behind the antenna skirt, an extra guidance package wired to the satellite's transponder 4 relay circuits, and five hundred kilos of enhanced chemical explosive. For all that, it weighed just eleven kilos more than the satellite it was to replace. The switch was made at the UPS depot outside Miami, at the price of a Corvette sport flyer for the depot chief and a joybird's enthusiastic friendship for the driver.

Three days after Dryke and Marshall's conversation, a man in a white turtleneck and brown duck pants walked into an RJR office in Hong Kong. He inquired about certain new stock offerings and applied for a modest life insurance policy. Both transactions were bounced to the home office on transponder 4 of the satellite in slot 355. A monitor program took note, a nanoswitch closed, and the mouse roared.

Trackers at Highstar saw the satellite start to move in its orbit within seconds. But *Memphis*, looking ahead in its orbit past the bulk of Takara and the clutter of Skylink 4, saw nothing, even after the Highstar alert was received.

It was well past midnight in Prainha, and Matt Reid's call roused Mikhail Dryke from a light sleep. Barefoot, hair tousled, with only a pair of half-jeans hastily added to the briefs and T-shirt he slept in, he ran down the stairs and through the halls to the orbital operations center.

By the time Dryke reached it, the center staff had a plot up on the main window, and the danger was apparent. Relative to the starship, the satellite was already moving at nearly 1,500 kph, on a looping path that would hide it behind Skylink 4 or Takara for most of its journey. The orbital mechanics were tricky, but predictable. By the time the satellite skimmed over the top of Takara, it would be just a few short seconds from its target.

"Takara's got nothing to knock it down with," Reid was saying, his face grave. "We're turning the ship now"—Dryke could hear the alarms sounding in the background—"but it looks like the only shot we'll have will light up Takara as well."

"How much can the skin take?"

"I don't know. Probably not enough to take the spill. I've got someone on the line to Governor Wian's office. Wait—I've got the PF on another channel."

Reid did not mute the link to Prainha, and Dryke listened as he talked with the Peace Force monitors on Technica.

"Yes, that's right. We've got a threat to Takara and *Memphis*. Can you help us? No, our angle is bad. A destruct on the Hughes? No, I don't think so. Beth—are you on with RJR? Ask them if they've got reentry destruct on the satellite."

"Range, five hundred ten kilometers," said an AIP voice in the background.

"They say reentry destruct failed," said a woman.

"Shit," said Reid. "Look, RJR can't control it and they can't destroy it. Can you do anything from the line?'' He was talking to the Peace Force again.

"Not enough time,'' Dryke said to himself, studying the plot of the several satellites.

"What? Was that you, Mikhail?''

"Matt, there's not enough time. We can't burn Takara—''

"Funny, that's what Wian says, except he's shouting.''

"Can't we move the ship?'' The question came from behind Reid, or from one of his open links—Dryke could not tell which.

Reid shook his head. "All we have are station-keeping thrusters. The drive is dead cold. Mikhail? What about the castle? Are we above your horizon?''

Dryke quickly got the HELcrew boss on a second window. "Just above, the long way through the atmosphere,'' he reported back. "Between the scatter and the absorption, the boss says the best we can do is a suntan.''

"Range, three hundred kilometers.''

"Anybody seen the oars for this boat?'' a gallows humorist muttered.

"You're going to have to throw something at it,'' Dryke said.

"Yeah. Any ideas what?''

"How about the Knights Peculiar?''

Reid turned away from his telecam. "Martin—plot collision intercepts for CT-5, CT-9, and CT-10. Plug in the masses—I need to know what happens to the pieces afterward. See if you can get me a deflection that'll throw both of them clear.'' He turned back to Dryke. "I knew I should have played more billiards when I had the chance.''

"Three-body no-cushion bank shot, on a warped table. Nothing to it.'' Dryke's words were clipped, his worry undercutting the joke.

"Range, one hundred ninety kilometers.''

"I can give it a pop with CT-9,'' Martin called. "The others are too far away.''

"Get it moving, then.''

"Already is. Matt, I'll do my best. But to knock it clear, I not only have to hit it, I have to hit it square center. Otherwise it'll just blow by and kick the truck into a tumble.''

"Mister, either you hit it fucking square or I'll put you outside to walk home.'' The words were said calmly. "Bobby, bring up the PDS, just in case. Track it all the way, and if Takara slips out of the hairs, do me a favor and fry the damned can.''

"Sure," the tech said with a grin. "I'll cover Martin's butt."

"You toast that Hughes and you can cover my grandmother," Reid said. "Mikhail, you still with us?"

"Yeah," said Dryke. "So glad to see you're all taking this so well."

"Range, eighty kilometers."

Reid said, "Yeah, well, there's one other thing. The section has authorized me to tell you that we all quit."

"No, you don't," Dryke said, matching Reid's deadpan. "If you're still there in two minutes, consider yourselves fired."

"Noted. All right, everyone. Let's be sharp. Marty?"

"On track."

"Bobby?"

"I'll pick it up off Takara's horizon."

"Range, twenty-five kilometers," said the AIP.

Reid nodded, looking at a display off-screen. He drew a deep breath and pursed his lips. "Funtime," he said under his breath. "Here she comes."

Six and a half kilometers from *Memphis*, CT-9 glided stalwartly toward Takara, carrying the reflector before it as though it were entering the lists for a joust.

It went into the duel with two disadvantages—size and speed. At a spidery twenty-nine tonnes, it was only two-thirds the mass of the satellite. And even after a full minute of acceleration, its propulsion systems—designed for construction, not interception—had pushed it to a paltry few tens of meters per second. Since the equations being solved and plotted on *Memphis*'s bridge depended entirely on the mass and velocity of the objects and the location of the starship, those were meaningful disadvantages.

But CT-9 also had one meaningful advantage: a guiding intelligence. The satellite's engine had finally burned out; it was coasting now, committed to its trajectory. Only the truck could counter and adjust, and so it sped in its own plodding way for the spot where the satellite would meet it.

The intercept point was just four kilometers from *Memphis*. If the two objects meeting there were perfect, incompressible spheres, the satellite would follow the track on Martin's display and miss the earthside curve of the hull by less than a hundred meters. Elementary physics of inelastic collisions.

But these were spacecraft, not billiard balls, and no computer on *Memphis* could predict the outcome.

"Range, twenty kilometers."

The chatter on the starship's bridge had ended. Dryke watched the panoramic and the tracking plot on his display wall, both relayed from *Memphis* via Highstar. They said enough.

"What—"

Something was happening to the truck. The shield had broken free from three of the grapples and was twisting to one side. A moment later, it went spinning away down toward the Pacific night like a discus. As it vanished, the Hughes appeared, a twinkling star skimming Takara's moonside pole. Dryke's breath caught.

"Range, ten kilometers."

"Eight—"

"Five—"

The satellite closed, the Hughes rose, and for an instant—but only an instant—they merged. The violence with which the truck was hurled aside, spinning crazily, underlined the missile's frightening speed. If it was deflected at all, no one watching could tell.

"Oh, shit—" said Dryke.

Suddenly, the Hughes brightened, as though it were caught in a spotlight. Dryke's mind locked, and he watched without understanding. Then the display wall strobed blinding white, like a giant photographer's flash, as the satellite exploded.

The panoramic went black, and Dryke could barely see through the afterimage that the tracking plot had splintered into dozens of diverging lines, some heading directly for *Memphis*. One second, two, three, four—whatever was going to happen should have happened.

"Matt?"

There was no answer. Then the tracking plot suddenly vanished, and Dryke realized that he was hearing shouting, cheering, the bubbling over of giddy relief. "Bridge link," he said quickly, and the scene came up in window 1. Reid was being hugged by someone. "Matt?"

Reid escaped the hug and turned toward the cam. "I guess you've still got a starship, Mike. You can fire us now."

"Firing's too good for you," Dryke said. "Besides, I wouldn't want to deny the Director the pleasure of firing us all at once. Did the ship get tagged?"

"We had a little bump, so we must have taken something. But it can't have been much, because all the important lights are

still green. The chief engineer's on his way out in a boat to take
a look.''
    "What happened there at the end?''
    Reid looked over his shoulder. "Marty?''
    The tech looked sheepish. "The reflector was blocking the
truck's rendezvous radar, and I wanted a little insurance for a
center hit. I thought it was worth a hundred kilos, so I threw
the reflector away.''
    "Highstar's gonna ticket you for that.''
    "Ticket, hell,'' said Martin. "Do you know how long it's
been since I did this to my shorts?''
    Reid laughed. "I'll buy you a new pair.''
    "I'll pay the ticket,'' Dryke said. "Get us a report on damage
ASAP, will you?''

    The postmortem was not a happy gathering. Marshall was
there, and Oker. Talbot, the construction manager, and Reid
were linked from *Memphis*. Edgar Donovan was fresh in from
Los Angeles. Dryke was nursing a cold fire and trying to hide
it; at the opposite end of the table, Sasaki was hollow-eyed and
startlingly frail.
    They heard from Reid and Talbot first. The ersatz missile had
been detonated by the PDS lasers 2.1 kilometers away from the
ship. The explosion was a mercy—it hurled the bulk of the disintegrating satellite away from, rather than toward, the target.
Fifty-eight fragments, the largest the size of a child's fist, escaped the HEL beam and tore through the fringe of the aft struc-
tural skirt. It looked worse than it was—no critical systems had
been hit, and no pressurized spaces had been breached.
    Then Sasaki ordered the links closed. "We did not deserve
the luck which befell us,'' she said to the others. "This is unrestricted war, and we were not prepared. We were not prepared, and no one stood ready to help us. Governor Wian bears
a measure of the blame—he has been unreasonably opposed to
allowing weapons or weapons platforms on Takara. I believe he
has sufficient reason now to reconsider—''
    "He'd better,'' said Marshall, the only one present who would
dare interrupt Sasaki at that moment. "Who knows if there are
any more sleepers parked up there?''
    Sasaki's gaze flickered in Marshall's direction, but she did not
otherwise acknowledge him. "Our opponents are still strong,

still determined, and growing desperate. We must take *Memphis* where they cannot reach us, at the earliest possible date."

"We've got an opportunity here," Donovan injected. "The real damage isn't serious. How serious do we want the official damage to be?"

"Will anyone who counts believe it?" Oker's expression was skeptical.

"I hear that the explosion was visible all around the Pacific rim," said Marshall.

"It's number one on the nets," said Donovan. "Even though they're starved for facts. That's the best time to feed them bull-shit—if you can get there before they start producing their own."

"This discussion does not interest me," Sasaki said. "Issue what statements you wish. Mikhail, I would like to hear from you."

Dryke looked down the table to her. "This feels like the Kasigau incident. A variation on a theme."

"The same mind?"

"No. But someone schooled under it. Someone's taken Jeremiah's place at the helm." He frowned and looked away. "Goddammit, it didn't do any good to kill him."

She nodded. "Mikhail, I am sorry. It is possible I was wrong about Christopher McCutcheon."

Shaking his head, Dryke said, "I can't gloat. It looks like I was wrong about Anna X."

"What do you mean?"

He touched his earpiece. "I heard from Horizon a few moments ago. The McCutcheon kid passed through there five days ago on his way to Sanctuary." He stood up, driving his chair away from the table. "With your leave, Director, I'm gonna go correct those mistakes."

CHAPTER
30

-|AAG|-

" . . . a sunless morn . . ."

TEN AND HALF AGAIN HAD COME TO THE SPRING GROTTO TO
hear the story, but the story could not be told with voice alone,
or heard only with the ears.

To tell it as Deryn told it required eyes, sad sparkle laughing—
hands, signing soaring—a body fluid and supple. She moved
among them as a breeze in the many-tiered chamber, hovered
as a spirit in the field of firepoint stars beyond the sky windows,
rested as a stone on the tumbledown cascade of the waterfall.
She told the story from the heart, not from memory, and invested it with her love.

" 'Will you stay with us?' asked Cho. She was first among
Asa's daughters, and the boldest. 'Stay in the golden house, and
be our guiding fire.'

"But Tetsu said gently, 'Is this as much as you've learned, to
keep me as an idol in a monument?'

"Cho was shamed, but the others begged Tetsu to stay. They
offered their houses and their worship and their love. Tetsu refused all but the last.

" 'I have been away long enough,' she told them. 'I am going
back to my home in the Earth.' "

It was then that Anna X appeared at the arched Spring Corridor entrance. She entered the grotto silently, advancing several
steps toward where the audience was seated, but stopping before
she intruded on anyone but Deryn's attention. Deryn noted her
presence and wondered, but went on without a pause or a break.

"Asa had learned the most from Tetsu, and acceptance was

331

the first of those lessons. 'How shall we remember you?' she asked.

''Tetsu smiled, and stole a tear from Cho's cheek with a touch. 'When I am in the Earth, I cannot hear your voices, for the air is too thin,' she said. 'I cannot know your thoughts, for they belong to you alone. I cannot use your gifts, for I am in all and of all, without form. Remember me with your lives.'

'' 'You will forget us,' cried Cho.

'' 'I am in you and of you as much as the river and the cliff and the forest. I will not forget you.'

'' 'Is there nothing we can give you?' cried Cho, her heart breaking.

''Tetsu took the child in a mother's embrace. 'I will feel you walking in the world above my world, and hear your footsteps like the echoes of your heartbeats,' she whispered. 'And when you gather with light hearts in the circle and dance to the celebration songs, your feet will speak to me of your joy. That will be gift enough.'

''And so we dance. *And so we dance*.'' Deryn smiled and spread her hands wide. ''Blessed be. The tale is done.''

They applauded warmly, and several—among them the two youngest children and the oldest crone—came to thank her with a hug. Anna X waited calmly until Deryn was free and then led her by the elbow toward White Corridor.

''Next time, I'll have to come in time to hear the whole story,'' said Anna X. ''You hold them in your hand, seven or seventy. It's a gift.''

''You have it wrong,'' said Deryn. ''They hold me. I'm never tired, because they send back to me as much as I give them.''

''Never tired? If you ever decide to conduct a workshop on that bit of magic, put my name down first.''

Deryn smiled. ''Did you come to listen, then?''

''I came to tell you that you have a petitioner in the Shelter.''

A look of surprise crossed Deryn's face, and her steps slowed. ''Claiming as what?''

''Claiming as your son.'' Studying Deryn's expression, Anna X added, ''You don't have to see him, of course.''

Deryn closed her eyes, the better to see a memory.

''*Have* you a son?'' Anna prompted.

''No,'' said Deryn. ''But I will see him.''

• • •

In contrast to the open-door policies on Horizon and New Star, but in keeping with its own founding purpose, Sanctuary was a virtually closed society. Long at or over its design population, Sanctuary accepted only a handful of new immigrants a year—all women. Only Hanif discriminated so openly (against non-Moslems), though Takara and the Soviet colony-sat, Lukyan, were in their individual ways nearly as effectively closed.

But the isolation of Sanctuary went even further. It and Takara were the only satlands which did not cater in some way to tourists, and Takara had Diaspora traffic to replace the lost revenue. Sanctuary restricted visitors of either sex to a portion of the inner ring of the old-fashioned wheelworld, called Entry by residents and "Mama's doorstep" by annoyed shuttle pilots.

The Shelter was part of Entry. Its forty small one-a-beds, clustered adjacent to the docking spar, were a buffer between Sanctuary and the outside world. For the wounded who needed only a place to hide and heal, the three-by-five compartments were cocoons. For the hopefuls who had reached the final stage of scrutiny by Anna X and the Council, they were way stations. And for petitioners hoping to visit women who had already crossed through Shelter, they made passably comfortable prisons.

The Shelter guide met Deryn as she entered the Sanctuary side of the warren. "Your petitioner gives his name as Christopher McCutcheon and claims you as his mother," she said. "But the indexes don't support a blood relation. Did you have an unreported male child?"

"After a fashion," said Deryn. "Where is he?"

"In 24. You can talk to him from the guide room—this way."

"Thank you," Deryn said. "I'll see him in person."

The guide flashed a grimace of distaste. "As you wish. We'll monitor."

"That's not necessary," she said, giving the woman's hand a reassuring squeeze. "He is no danger to me."

Beside the door to Shelter 24, a small screen showed Christopher sitting quietly near the far end of the compartment, keeping company with his thoughts. Deryn paused before the screen, trying to clear the image of him at fifteen from her mind and replace it with the image before her—a young man, but a man in full maturity.

The darkness cast in his features seemed now more of knowledge than of fear. The softness in his face had been chiseled down to something harder—and perhaps because of it, he was a measure more handsome in flower than she had expected. His spark of alertness was as bright as ever, even in repose. But the joyful innocence was missing, or hidden behind the mask of—what? Sadness? Behind the mask of the purpose that had brought him there.

He looked up as she entered, and his eyes seemed to brighten when he saw her. Showing an uncertain smile, he rose from the seat. He tried to say "Hello," but the word came out as a noise lost deep in his throat.

Smiling back, Deryn opened her arms, and he came to her. He was the taller by nearly ten centimeters, but he let himself be small in her embrace. There were no words, but something words could not have captured passed between them. She felt great turmoil, great pain, and great relief swirling inside him.

"You always did give the best hugs," she said, drawing back a step at last.

"I've missed you."

"My memories of you are full of love," she said. "Why did you come, Christopher?"

He seemed disconcerted by her directness. "Do you follow the news from Earth?"

"No," she said. "I find it's never about me."

"Consider yourself lucky, then," he said, but did not elaborate. "Deryn, my father's dead."

Deryn heard the news with both surprise and understanding. The surprise was the strength of the wave of regret and loss. She was caught for a moment in a time and a place she had renounced, and the breath she drew to quiet her center was quavery.

"I'm sorry," she said, squeezing the hand she had never released. "Will you tell me about it?"

"I have to," he said.

They perched on the edge of the settee-bed, and he began, marrying fact and supposition in his narrative. The story he told went further than Deryn could have guessed, and its quiet drama and horror awakened her protectiveness.

But Deryn kept that emotion contained. A father's death and a son's grief, however immediate at that moment in that room, were dwarfed by the other dimensions of the account. Deryn began to hope the Shelter guide had ignored her wishes and monitored the conversation, for there were parts of it that Anna X would need to hear.

She tried to listen as though she did not know him, to hear

him as Anna would. But Deryn could not forget whom she was listening to, and wondered at how the child she had borne—this child of such promise, now a man of such paradox—had become a witness and a victim and now a player in such a tale.

Toward the end, Christopher became careful about his words. Deryn understood that he was not yet ready to ask what he had come to ask of her, that he was not yet sure of her. But she was ready to be asked, and gently stole the torch from him when the chance came.

"You're here to do more than tell me William is dead."

He nodded. "I thought you should know. But that isn't the whole of it."

"And the rest is—"

"I came here to find out what you can tell me about Sharron." She cocked her head and studied him. "And?"

"And what your geneticists can tell me about myself. I'll pay for information, people's time, any testing—whatever."

"The first I can understand, though you may be disappointed," she said. "But why do you think that anyone here can answer questions about the Chi Sequence?"

"Because you're conceiving children here with one parent," Christopher said. "And it's a good bet that parthenogenesis requires more than a casual acquaintance with human genetics. If you want to deny it—or you're obliged to deny it—I guess I understand that. If you really don't know, I guess someone'll come bursting in here any moment to stop you from finding out. But let me tell you what *I* know, and maybe we'll see where to go from there."

"I remember the rumors and the jokes. You won't need to repeat them for my benefit."

"This is more than rumor," said Christopher. "This is a matter of record. Angela O called for parthenogenetic research in her Womyn's Manifesto long before there were any satlands. The year before this station was completed, the Sanctuary Committee—of which Angela O was a member—purchased a copy of the complete data base of the Human Genome Project.

"Four of the five geneticists given grants by the Free Womyn's Guild to work on problems in parthenogenesis stopped publishing, even privately, after Sanctuary opened. Two came up here openly, with the first wave. It's a safe bet that the other two came here as well. On top of that, you've admitted at least eighteen first-rank geneticists in the last twenty years, including one who was with the Project in Munich for a time." He shook his head. "If you don't already know about the Chi Sequence, you at least have the tools to find out."

"Why does it matter, Christopher?"

He stared at her uncomprehendingly, and she saw in that moment the part of him that had not yet grown. "I have to know who I am. I have to know what to be."

"No geneticist can tell you," she said.

"I don't think you understand how deep this runs," he said. "It's the difference between a pointless life and a life with purpose."

"Who's judging, Christopher?"

"I am."

But he was not, she knew. He was looking for a new Authority, a new compass. He did not know how bright was his own fire. He did not trust his own wisdom.

"I know how deep it runs," Deryn said. "I saw your father crush your confidence a hundred times by withholding his approval, by telling you how you could do better instead of how well you'd done. I remember when you were five and spent an entire afternoon creating what you called a movie—a poster covered with a dozen crayon drawings, complete with titles and credits. You were so proud. I hung it on the kitchen wall."

"I remember," Christopher said.

"Do you remember that when William came home, he took it down and told you to put it in your room? That he ripped off a corner in the process, and how you started to cry? That I found your 'movie' that night in a corner of your room, torn into pieces and crushed into a ball? That runs deep, too, Christopher."

His face, sulky and defensive, told her that resistance had set in. "I know about my father. I need to know about me."

She shook her head. "But you're asking the wrong question. It isn't who you are. It's who you want to be."

"That's what I'm trying to find out—who I am at the root. What my part is. What I got from Sharron."

"What will you do with that knowledge if you get it?"

"Then I'll know what it will take to make me happy." He said it with more hope than confidence.

"Will you?" There was more she wanted to say, but he had stopped listening. He so feared the responsibility of choosing for himself—so feared being wrong—he could not hear the inner voice. And that voice mattered far more than hers.

"I never told you about when I met your father," she said at last.

"Yes, you did." He looked puzzled. "How you heard about what he was doing from the doctor in Tacoma—and came up to the house to introduce yourself. The *Mary Poppins* story."

She smiled. "That was your father's version—official family history. And it was true, as far as he remembered. So I never contested it, and even repeated it a time or two. But I actually met William years before that. And not only William. Sharron, too."

He gaped in surprise, his defenses breached. "You did? When?"

"It was a party on Long Beach—there still was a Long Beach then, the big Easter storm was still a few years away. '55, I think it was. Ten years before I signed the contract to have you."

"Please tell me about it—"

"I wouldn't have brought it up if I didn't mean to," she said, and patted his hand. "There was a party with a capital *p* at Carl Walter's big old place near the north end of the peninsula. I really didn't belong—so much so that I didn't know who all those people were, though everyone was Somebody. Carl had those kinds of contacts, all through Oregon and Washington."

"How did you know him?"

"I was a friend of the family, Carl's daughter's favorite tutor, visiting for a few days on a face-to-face. I would as soon have gone up to Ledbetter Point for a few hours, but they wanted to introduce me around.

"William was there with Sharron, being William—being charming and earnest with strangers and neglecting those he could take for granted. Sharron looked as out of place as I felt, so I sat down next to her and we started talking."

"Did you have anything to talk about?"

Deryn laughed, remembering. "More than we had time to cover. We talked for almost four hours with never a lull. No one knew us, no one bothered us, and we didn't mind one bit. We understood each other. She felt like someone I already knew. Have you ever had that happen with someone? An acquaintance of mine calls them 'friendly mirrors'—you see the parts of yourself that you like in them."

Christopher was sitting forward, eager and hopeful. "Can you remember anything Sharron said?"

"Everything I remembered, I made sure I shared with you at

one time or another in the house on B Street. I just let you think it came from your father," she said. "I remember less now. Sharron told me stories about Lynn-Anne, who had just turned three. About the house they wanted to build in the woods. About the poems she was writing, and about how no one had any use for poetry unless it was set to music. She seemed very glad to have someone to talk to. I didn't know how to read that then."

"She was lonely," Christopher said slowly.

"I think so. For a certain kind of company. For a certain kind of attention."

"Did she say anything about having more children?"

"I don't remember so," Deryn said, slowly shaking her head. "Nothing either way. When William was finished holding court and came to collect her, she introduced me. By that time she felt like a friend. She was living a quiet life, but her heart and her mind were alive. I admired her. It seemed like she had more focus than I did, more purpose. I went away with a lot to think about. I was only five years younger than she, but I felt like a child by comparison."

"Then later, my father didn't remember you."

"No."

He shook his head. "That's such an amazing coincidence."

"No," she said, smiling at his innocence. "Not coincidence. It goes deeper than that. If I had never had that conversation with Sharron, I would never have become your host. I wasn't registered with an agency, you know. I had never thought of hosting. And it was only by chance that I even heard of what William was doing—about Sharron's eggs. There's the coincidence. Everything else was purely intentional."

Realization began to light Christopher's eyes. "You knew what he wanted already."

"Of course. He wanted another Sharron. And that's what I was. Or could appear to be." She took his hand and held it tightly. "You see, in my mind, I didn't agree to have William McCutcheon's baby. I agreed to have Sharron's. I did it for her, not for your father. That's why I never wanted you to call me 'Mother.' Sharron had precedence. I was only finishing what she'd begun."

He was quiet for a moment, and his face showed his struggle to grasp the meaning, the cascading implications, of what she had said. Deryn wanted to leave then and let the solvent of that revelation work at softening the bonds of his comfortably patterned thoughts. But when she stood, saying gently, "I have to leave," he clutched at her presence like a skirt.

"*Did* she begin it?" he asked. "Or was it all my father, like Lynn-Anne believes?"

"I wish I could answer that," she said, her faint smile apologetic. "But I don't know myself. Knowing him, I have to say he was probably capable of the theft. But I also believe she was capable of the gift. In the absence of proof, I chose to think the best."

"Thinking the best where my father is concerned isn't the easiest thing right now."

"I know," she said. "Christopher, I'm expected somewhere. I'll come back when I can."

"I'm sorry." He joined her standing. "Can I ask what you do here?"

"I'm a storyteller. A kind of teacher."

He smiled in a foolishly pleased way. "Do you tell them about Coyote?"

"But of course," she said, smiling back. "The young ones seem to like the animal stories best. Heaven knows what they understand from them, though."

"I wouldn't mind hearing you tell them again," he said. "Or would that only embarrass both of us?"

Touching his cheek lightly, she shook her head. "All a good story requires is a good listener. But I'm late, now. Perhaps when your petition's been heard you can join us in the grotto—"

The intrusion of reality dispelled the nostalgic haze for both of them, reminding them where they were and why, and there was an awkward distance in their good-bye. But as Deryn passed through the corridors on the way to her home, she found herself crying for William and Christopher both, and wishing she could find a way to cut the string that joined them.

Anna X heard Christopher's petition in the morning. Deryn supported it, the Shelter supervisor opposed it, and in the end the council approved it, grudgingly, and with restrictions—a fifteen-day admission, no renewals. But Deryn won the one point that mattered to her—permission for Christopher to come to her quarters on Summer Corridor.

The other issue, of turning Sanctuary's midwives to searching their records and Christopher's cells for the Chi Sequence, was resolved in private between Deryn and Anna X. Here there was no compromise—the answer was an unequivocal no.

"What tools we may have are for our purposes," Anna X said. "Your son's problem neither concerns us nor serves us."

She accepted the decision. Christopher's narrow focus on mechanistic answers and deterministic choices was, it seemed to her, a final attempt to evade taking charge of his own life. The clockwork man, his future written in beads on a genetic string. Locus of control now internal—but unconscious. *How can I be wrong if I'm only doing what I must?*

Anna X's decision might actually be a blessing. Perhaps, Deryn thought, denied the midwives' aid, he will be forced to find better tools with which to look within.

Christopher did not see it that way.

To Deryn's surprise, Anna X allowed Christopher a chance to object in person. Deryn accompanied him to the Circle Room, though she made no attempt to either coach him or forewarn him.

"Deryn presented your case to me," Anna X said, sitting back in her comfortable bowl-cushion chair. She had covered up for the occasion, her high-collared full-sleeved long robe hiding all but her face. Deryn could not remember when she had last seen her so armored with clothing. "We are not interested in whether *Memphis* leaves or stays, whom it carries away, or why they go. It is completely without relevance to us."

"That's not true," Christopher said. "The Chi Sequence is relevant to the decisions your geneticists make. You can't afford to ignore a script that powerful."

"We know more of genetic scripts than you realize," said Anna X. "Male genetic scripts rule the planet beneath us— scripts which program men for destructive competition with their kind and destructive oppression of my kind. The modern era's ethics, politics, and economics are all shaped to acquisition and domination, the ultimate goal of which is control of women's bodies. Testosterone provides more than enough explanation for *Memphis*. You are still pawing the ground and marking the trees."

They might as well have been speaking Hindi and Urdu for all that they understood each other. He knew the words, but he could not grasp her context; she heard only her translations of his arguments. Deryn saw him growing frustrated, not only with his failure to persuade her, but also with their inability even to agree on the facts. But then, he had long had an unreasonable faith in the power of reason, and too little grasp of the power of emotions.

"So what you're really saying is that you won't help me because I'm the enemy," he was saying, his tone sharp and impatient. "I've got an outie, not an innie, so anything that helps me must harm you. It must, or I wouldn't want it, is that it?"

"No. Not the enemy," Anna X said, ignoring the rest. "But your goals are not our goals, and we have the right to focus our resources on our own goals. Our midwives are busy enough with the work they have now. We accepted your presence here as a courtesy to Deryn. But this is *our* world, organized for our needs, guided by our choices. You cannot expect us to abandon that commitment to champion the cause of a visitor."

And as quickly as that, it was over.

For the rest of the day, Deryn left Christopher alone in her home. She had obligations—a class in rhythmic language at the school, a meeting of the Code circle to set sentence in a minor case, a bit of healing work to which she had promised to lend her hands and energies.

But even if she had not been obliged to leave him, Deryn would have tried to find a reason to do so. *So difficult, so difficult,* she thought. *The balance within as precarious as the balance without.* There was great danger that he would fix on her as the new object of his emotional fealty. She could not allow him to think that her life had stopped when he appeared.

He was struggling to stand, burning from within. She could not catch him if he fell, nor protect him from the flames. She could not allow herself to treat him as her child, for he was all too ready to return to that comforting security. *To love and say no is the hardest thing—*

That night, he talked about his family for the first time since he arrived. They were sitting in Deryn's teaching ring, a circle of cushions in a carpeted corner of her flex space. He had picked a spot where he could lean back against a wall; she sat cross-legged and straight-backed a third of the way around the circle. Between them was a low table bearing a woven basket of dried flowers and brown field grasses.

"This business about men and women—what Anna X said this morning," he said. "Does everyone up here believe that?"

"There's nothing that *everyone* up here believes," said Deryn with a half-smile.

"Most, then? You?"

"What we think is conditioned on what we know, and what we know best is our own experience," she said. "My experience is that men and women are different enough that I can say I prefer to be with one and prefer not to be with the other."

"What kind of difference? Or is it one of those if-you-have-to-ask-you'll-never-understand things?"

She shook her head. "It isn't sexual, which is what everyone thinks. For me, it's something about balance, or focus. Men make me jangle. They confuse me. I change around them, and I don't usually like the changes. Their presence is a demand, somehow."

Smiling, she added, "We're not angels, mind you, and Sanctuary is no utopia. But I find it a very calming place to be. In fact, that's how I think of it—a place to *be*, not a place to do. Which I suppose is part of what Anna X was saying. Do you think she's wrong?"

"I don't feel like the kind of man she's talking about," he said. "But that's nothing new. I had a friend who saw all his relationships that way. But I could never see mine that simply. They always seem so much more complicated than that, even when I think they're going to be simple."

"Did that include your trine?"

"And my marriage before that, and Vanessa before that, and Patti in Vernonia. They all started easy and ended hard."

"Your trine is still alive, isn't it?"

"Only a technicality. Only a matter of time. Jessie's locked on someone new, and Loi—I don't think I'm important enough to Loi for the amount of trouble I bring. Anytime I want, I can call and hear the death sentence. I wouldn't be surprised to hear that Fields is already living there."

"I wondered why you hadn't wanted to call out," she said. "Now I'm wondering why you're content to just let it happen. Is it over for you, as well?"

He gazed into the basket of curled leaves and crisp petals. "Jessie was so—so agreeable, so accommodating, at first. It seemed like she was happy making us happy. I guess I never thought she was going to want more. I don't even know how to win her back, because I never had to win her in the first place. Does that make sense?"

He had been spoiled by easy answers, she saw, by mind mechanics who pronounced their verdicts as quickly and shallowly as an on-air psychologist. Even if they were right answers, he lost the chance to learn from them—they meant nothing to him because they were won so easily.

"What do you miss?" she asked.

There was no hesitation. "Cuddling with her," he said. "I never knew anyone so willing to cuddle and so comfortable to do it with. Loi could never sit still that long. She'd have to talk, or plan, or get up and go do something that needed doing. Jessie has a way of melting into you. We shot a lot of evenings on the couch, just wrapped together and humming along at warm." A wan, sorry smile flickered across his lips. "She made me feel good inside. It was easy and I thought it'd always be there."

Deryn nodded understandingly. "Is she happier now?"

He nodded glumly. "It seems so."

"Then let her be."

"Why didn't she tell me what she wanted at the beginning?" he said with sudden anger. "Why did she let me think she was happy the way things were?"

Deryn made a bowl of her hands between her knees. "Years before I met your parents, I was in love with a man twelve years older than I," she said. "He was very sure of himself and very much in command of his life, both things I admired then. He was an executive with a company that took very good care of him, so he could take very good care of me. We went to Hawaii, to Rio. He surprised me with presents, never extravagant, but thoughtful, perfect.

"We'd been together six months when he asked me to go with him to a doctor in New York. He wanted me to have an operation so that I could give him more pleasure during sex. He'd had such a woman in London, in one of the Triangle clubs. I didn't even know such things were done.

"I can hardly believe it now, but I almost said yes. He was, I thought, a wonderful man. He loved me, he was giving me so much, why shouldn't I do this for him? The closest I got to the downside was thinking, 'Even if we break up, whoever comes next will appreciate it—'

"But when he left the next morning and it was just me by myself, everything changed. I had never had any surgery, never even broken a bone—no medical problems more serious than the flu. But I was going to volunteer to let someone cut and sew my body in the name of better orgasms. I was angry that he wanted me to do it. I was hurt that he wanted what a joybird had given him more than what he and I had shared—which up to that point I had thought was pretty wonderful.

"So I called him at work and told him I'd changed my mind," she said. "I never heard from my 'wonderful man' again. He moved on to someone else, a friend of a friend of a friend. A few months later, they went to New York for two weeks. When they came back, she was so happy with herself that she couldn't wait to tell everyone. I was still so miserable that I was actually jealous. And I had no idea why.

"It took me fifteen years to forgive myself for almost giving in and to understand how he managed to find someone who would. It's the dirty little secret Anna X leaves out of her speech—that female scripts are just as destructive in their way.

"We'll do anything when we think we have to have a man—trade any favor, tell any lie, take any edge. I said we weren't angels. Most women are just like most men—trying to get what we want, trying to strike a bargain. It sounds to me as though you and Jessie just couldn't agree on terms. Don't wish you could make her be different than she is. If you do love her, wish that she'll be happy."

Christopher had been silent, amazed, through Deryn's long unburdening. "I guess my heart's been too small for that."

"Hearts can grow, with proper care," said Deryn with a gentle smile.

He nodded, lips pulled tight in a frown. "It's almost time to take me back to the Shelter."

"Almost," she said, uncrossing her legs and rising gracefully to her feet. "But not quite. Come on. There's something I want to show you."

The Moon Chamber lay wheel-out below Spring Grotto, thirty meters of stairs and a double pressure hatch away from the corridors and compartments. Dimly lit and chapel-quiet, the chamber was a great open square bonded on all four sides by catwalk. The pale light seemed to rise up from the center space, like the glow from a fire pit.

Deryn led him by hand to the edge of the catwalk, and he looked down, unsuspecting. His breath caught, and he held her hand tightly as he swayed with sudden vertigo. Below their feet were the stairs, slipping past as the great wheel of Sanctuary turned. The transparent wall of plaz a few meters below their feet was invisible, except for the diffraction of dust pits and scratches.

"Isn't it wonderful?" she murmured. "There's one below every grotto—one each for Sun, Moon, Earth, and stars."

The dark limb of the Earth had appeared, dotted with spiderstrings of fuzzy light which outlined continents. It sliced across the field of stars like a shadow.

"Look," she said, "the forest fire in East Russia is still burning."

Following her lead, they stretched out prone on the carpeted catwalk, heads propped on hands and peeking over the edge, like kids looking down from an upper bunk. The Earth rode past and was replaced by more stars, their glory and plenty and variety unguessed by any earthbound viewer. Ninety seconds later, the satland's spin brought the planet into view again.

"And I didn't think I liked riding a Ferris wheel," he said with a breathless joy.

"No view like this one anywhere on Earth."

"Which way is north? I should know the constellations."

"It took me weeks to learn to spot them up here," she said. "There's thousands more stars to fill in the patterns and spaces. There—Orion, off to the right. Can you see it? That reddish star is the shoulder—"

"I see it. Oh, God, this is beautiful—"

They stayed as long as their time allowed, through half a dozen reruns of the panoramic movie, each fractionally different from the last as Sanctuary spun along in its orbit. Christopher left the Moon Chamber reluctantly, and part of him stayed behind, still caught in wonder. The proof of that was the smile that lingered on his face all the way to the door of Shelter 24.

"It gives you a different way to look at things, doesn't it?" he said when he had hugged her.

Deryn did not know just what he spoke of, so she simply agreed. But when she came to get Christopher that next morning, he seemed more at peace, and his first words were to ask how he might arrange to call home. She thought that a heartening sign, never dreaming that chaos was following close on the heels of the new calm.

CHAPTER 31

-|CCC|-

"... worlds to know ..."

CHRISTOPHER HAD COME TO SANCTUARY KNOWING THAT HE would not be allowed to stay. But almost from the moment he arrived, the thought began forming that he also did not want to stay.

The suspicion was strengthened when first Deryn, then Anna X, shrugged off the Chi Sequence as inconsequential. It crystallized into a certainty in the Moon Chamber when, watching the darkened globe and the brilliant stars roll by, he suddenly understood that Anna X was right.

Earth had seemed so far away, the bustle of its billions shrunk to a pattern of lights in the night. And the stars that *Memphis* would soon reach for were unimaginably, unbelievably more distant. In the blink of the mind's eye, scales shifted, values changed. What was Earth to Sanctuary? A foreign land in the grip of unfriendly forces. What was Sanctuary to Earth? Even less—a carnival ride in history's sideshow. What happened on Sanctuary did not matter except to those few who called it home.

I don't watch the news. It's never about me. How many more felt that way, not only around the wheel, but around the world? It was the turning away, the turning inward. Daniel Keith had described it, and Jeremiah had feared it. Sanctuary was the vindication of a prophecy, the anticipation of the human prospect. It would spin along in its orbit year after year much as it was now, growing older rather than growing, ever more fragile in structure and frail in spirit. And someday, it would fail.

It was the future of the Earth, in microcosm. He required no further proof from Daniel, Deryn, or the midwives—from Sharron's memory or his father's legacy. Synthesis was his art and his magic, and the synergy was clear. The twilight of the will was approaching.

That being so, what was the best use of a life? The curtain would not ring down for decades, perhaps centuries. In that time, billions would pass through the whole cycle of existence, and most of the passages would be made in pain. Against that background, what was the moral act? Was it enough to simply take a turn on the wheel and then step aside?

In a life of watching, Christopher had learned to measure his expectations. Wanting little placed the goal within reach. Wanting nothing too badly mitigated disappointment. The path of least resistance beckoned. If he could not be happy, he could at least hope to temper the pain.

But that, too, was a turning away, into emptiness, into numbness. There was a better choice at hand. *I'll gladly trade choice for destiny and purpose,* Daniel had said. Better still to *choose* destiny and purpose, to negate the tail-chasing pointlessness with a summary act of will. The moral act was the same in either conception of the world. A quiet life ending in a quiet death was a song sung in silence. To have meaning, it had to be heard.

In that light, the choice was easy, inevitable. Mercifully, there was still a chance to choose. He would go home and apply what tools he had to rebuild his family and rehearse his song. There was time for a child, for the treasures of his father's world. And then, Gaea willing, he would join Daniel on *Knossos* in the first breath of the new century.

The phone in Deryn's apartment was a simple videocom, barely smarter than an interactive TV, meant only for local messaging. To call out required the help of a tech in the Sanctuary communications center, which required in turn the permission of both Deryn and the station censor. And though Deryn left him alone with her blessing once the arrangements were complete, the censor remained on the line.

He had been off-net long enough that skylink greeted him with almost effusive cheeriness and a subscriber-update menu when he signed in. There were a dozen messages waiting, including blue-bar mail from Loi, Daniel, and the Vernonia District of the Oregon State Police. "Too many to wade through now," he murmured. "Give me Loi's."

It was so long since Christopher had seen her face that he almost failed to listen, savoring the sight of her.

"I got your message, Christopher. I'm sorry so much has come down on you," she said. "Take what time you need and do what you need to do. Come home when you can." There was some tenderness in her tone, if not in the words.

He smiled to himself. "Call reply," he said.

A dozen or so seconds later, Loi's face returned to the screen. She was tousled and raccoon-eyed, and a beautiful sight.

"Hello, Loi."

"Christopher?" She squinted off-screen. "Prodigal lover, it's after four in the morning."

"I'm sorry—"

"Never mind. Bad manners to do it, worse to complain. Where are you? *How* are you?"

"On Sanctuary. I didn't think about the time difference. I'm not even sure what standard we're on."

She did not seem to need any explanation about his whereabouts. "Chris, this is showing a conference call. Who else is on?"

"The station censor. Probably being looped, too—I don't know if this lag is normal."

"Special treatment?"

"Not that I know of," he said. "I've missed you, Loi."

"The house has been empty. Jessie moved out this weekend."

"She went to John's?"

Loi nodded, then rubbed an eye. "Kia was here last night, but mostly I'm alone here now. Are you coming back soon?"

"Tomorrow, I think. I haven't talked to the Entry staff about openings on the shuttle yet. And I may have to borrow a nickel or two for the fare."

"It'd be worth a nickel or two to have you back," she said. "Let me know. Chris, have you been avoiding Daniel Keith?"

"Why?"

"He came by the house tonight, late, wondering if I knew how to reach you. He said he had to reach you before seven tomorrow morning. I mean this morning. He must not think me very bright, because he said it three times."

"Everyone's off-net up here. You need special permission just to order out for nachos," Christopher said. "I'm surprised that Daniel tried to get me, though."

"You've been popular with the oddest people. The Oregon

State Police called. A lawyer in Portland. Roger Marshall even asked about you.''

"Who's Roger Marshall?''

"The L.A. developer. He called to talk over a commission for the lobby of Daley Tower. He said he was sorry to hear about your father, wondered how you were doing.''

"I'll be damned," Christopher said. "How did he hear about that? Unless they moved faster than I thought—Loi, I've got to go. I've got to find out what this means, and this phone can only do one thing at a time.''

"You're still in trouble, aren't you, Chris?''

"Some. It'll all sort out. Maybe it already has.''

She knew the optimism was misplaced. "I have a lot of friends. Come on back and let's fight it together.''

"I like that idea,'' he said. "I like it so much I had it myself a few hours ago. Look, when did this Marshall call?''

"Ah—Friday. Three days ago. Chris, I think you'd better talk to Daniel first. It's almost five o'clock. And he seemed upset. Angry might be a better word.''

"Do you know what he was upset about?''

"No. If I was going to guess, I'd say it had something to do with what happened to *Memphis*.''

A chill touch prickled the skin on the back of Christopher's neck. "What happened to *Memphis*?''

"You don't know?'' Her expression turned grave. "Homeworld hit it with some kind of missile yesterday morning. A hundred and six dead, twenty percent destroyed, two-to-three-year delay, according to some reports. Some are saying she'll never leave.''

It was there on all the services, just as Loi had described, complete with Takara-supplied pictures of twisted metal and construction plastic. The list of the dead had not been released yet, but the reports showed their bagged bodies stacking up in Takara's medical stations.

"Oh, no. No, no, no,'' he breathed to himself, angry tears welling as he watched. "Not *Memphis*. Why couldn't you have just let them go? Why couldn't you have just let her be?''

With a full day already passed since the event, the live coverage had deteriorated into talking heads debating in a vacuum. No reporters had been admitted to Takara, *Memphis* had been turned away from prying eyes, and the flow of information from

Prainha had tightened down to a trickle. That helped Christopher escape becoming a prisoner of the screen.

"Did you pick this story up for local use?" he asked the censor.

"They did two hours on it yesterday morning."

While I was still on vacation, he thought.

Time was slipping away, but he was not ready to face Keith, knowing what he must be thinking. Instead, Christopher went back to the mail stack and tried to focus on problems he could touch, and to answer a nagging question raised by his talk with Loi.

The first message from the Oregon State Police informed him that there'd been a fire on the ridge, that his father could not be located, and would he contact Detective Brooks with any information he might have? The second, the one with the receipt tag, was only a day old, and a bit more terse. An investigation into William McCutcheon's disappearance had begun, and Christopher's participation was considered crucial—would he please make himself available within the next forty-eight hours to answer questions?

But still no fugitive warrant or grand-jury subpoena, which meant no body. Which meant no way for Marshall to know that William McCutcheon was dead—except hearing it from either Allied or Homeworld.

Christopher could not tap DIANNA from orbit, and he was not welcome in Sanctuary's library, which probably didn't contain the data he needed in any case. But he sent a query through to Codex, a subscription information service, and had an answer in a few minutes: Roger Marshall was a member of the Diaspora advisory committee.

Surprised as he was by that discovery, it explained plainly enough how Marshall knew. But the rest of it made no sense. Was there some kind of message in Marshall calling Loi? An apology? A confession? Or just a bit of carelessness? Christopher could not make the picture come together.

The clock caught his eye, warning him that he was running out of time to reach Keith. Keith's message gave him a clue what to expect: It was short and foul, beginning with "You shitmouthed son of a bitch—" and going downhill from there. It was time-stamped several hours before Loi would have seen him; Keith's emotions had apparently cooled, though his judgments had likely hardened at the same time.

In the end, Christopher could not let those judgments stand
unchallenged. He was surprised to find Keith on the move, in
his flyer rather than his bed. But Keith's cold tone and hard
words were no surprise. "Fag off, I don't want to talk to you."

"Fine. Just listen. This is the truth: I only just heard about
Memphis. I didn't have anything to do with it."

"Do you think I'm that big an idiot? You don't get another
chance."

"How many ways can I say it? I feel sick about *Memphis*. I
didn't do it, I didn't know about it, and I didn't want it to happen."

"This is Dan Keith you're talking to. I know you, remember?
Sorry. Your eleventh-hour conversion fails to convince."

"Daniel, I know where the last verse of *'Caravan'* came from
now. And it wasn't a lie."

That slowed him—Keith blinked confusedly. "What do you
mean?"

"Daniel, read my lips: I didn't do it."

A blank stare turned to a hateful glare. "You did it to me."

"What are you talking about?"

"They're not taking me. They're not taking me, and it's your
goddamned fault. Because of your fucking father. Because I
thought friendship fucking counted for something. They're not
taking me, do you understand? Because of you I've got to stay
here." The flyer beeped an out-of-lane alarm at Keith, and he
slammed his palm against the dash. "Shut up!"

"What are you talking about? *Memphis* isn't going anywhere.
And you weren't going on *Memphis* in the first place."

"Fuck it," he said sullenly.

Christopher did not understand what had just happened. "I'm
coming back to Houston tomorrow. If you're in trouble because
of me, I want to help."

"You, help me?" Keith's snicker was nasty.

"I haven't done anything against the Project. Not one thing,"
Christopher said. "But they've done to me. They killed my father and stole his body. They took away my job, screwed up my
career, and helped me screw up my family—not that I needed
much help in that department. And do you know what? I still
want them to make it.

"They were wrong to be afraid of me. I was wrong to duck
my tail and run. That's over. I'm coming back, and I'm going
to stand toe-to-toe with Dryke or anyone else I have to until

reality sinks in. And if I need to scrap for you at the same time, I will.''

Keith was silent, his eyes on the road.

"What's going on, Daniel? Why are you up at this hour of the morning?''

When Keith finally spoke again, his voice was muted. ''I don't know why the hell I believe you,'' he said. ''I must be as big an idiot as they make, I guess.''

"Sorry. The line forms behind me.''

"I don't know why I'm telling you anything,'' Keith said, rubbing his cheek roughly. ''There isn't anything you can do to help me. And there won't be anyone here to talk to by the time you arrive.''

"What do you mean?''

"They're shutting down the training centers. All the small fry are being let go. They're sending half the talent to Prainha, including me. The other half—four hundred people—is going up to *Memphis*. They've been flying out all night. You can guess why we're needed in Prainha—they're shipping people upstairs, too.''

"Why?''

Keith turned his head away to the right and drew a ragged breath. ''Vincenza told the press that we're sending technicians and engineers to help with the reconstruction, management to inspect the damage. That's bullshit. I know the list. It's the fraternity. And I can't get anyone to admit it, but I know they're not coming back.''

"That's crazy. Where can they go?''

Keith's gaze was faraway and sad. ''Tau Ceti.''

Christopher gaped. ''In what?''

"You really don't know, do you?'' Keith said, turning back. ''*Memphis* isn't hurt. Not that badly. But they're not going to take any more chances. They're going to move her. Everyone knows that. The only question is how far. I think they're going to load her up and light her up the first chance they can, and not look back.'' His mouth twisted into an acerbic smile. ''That's what I'd do, if I was Sasaki. And she's at least as bright as I am.''

His own future vanishing with his friend's, Christopher found himself hollow and numb. ''Why are you going to Prainha?'' he asked finally.

"Because I'm like you. I want them to make it no matter what they do to me," he said. "I'm almost to the gate, Chris. I can't stay on."

"Wait—how's the Houston staff getting to *Memphis*?"

"Through Technica, I think. On the big bus. Jesus, Chris, you're not going to try—you don't think you'll get near them, do you?"

"Why not? How many stowaways on *Ur*?"

"Sixteen. Trust me, they all had better plans than this."

"Things are going to be crazy on Technica and *Memphis* both. It's the last days of Saigon, man. And I think I ought to be able to pass myself off as a Project archie, don't you?"

A long hesitation. "No," Keith said. "Too many people from here know about you and Jeremiah."

"Then—"

"Shut up. The Munich people are going through Horizon," Keith continued. "You'll have a better chance there, as a Houston staffer caught away from the center when the orders came through."

Christopher had run out of words. "Thanks. You didn't owe me that."

"I know," Keith said. "I said a better chance. Your chances are still piss-poor. Do me a favor, will you? Try not to let me find out if you make it. I want to be able to think it came out either way, depending on my mood."

"Sure," said Christopher, his throat hot.

"I'm up. Time to go. Have a life, huh?"

"I'll try. Better days—my friend."

"Fuck you very much."

Christopher didn't know how long he sat there, wet-eyed and stiff-backed, after the phone blanked. He had prepared himself for a marathon, but the only race open to him was a sprint. Last call, everyone in the blocks. But his feet, like his thoughts, were churning in mud.

Ready to go?

No!

Gun in the air—

Wait!

But the starter paid no heed. The race was on. He had to start moving or walk away, disappear into the tunnel.

I have to get to Horizon.

That was almost an executable thought. The missing operand

was Deryn. Without her permission or presence, he seemed to be able to do nothing on Sanctuary.

Where did Deryn say she was going?

Sanctuary's infuriating phone net had no way to call *persons*, only *places*. He called all eight schools, harangued the net operator, even went to the door and called for her down Summer Corridor. Finally, out of desperation, he called Anna X.

"McCutcheon," she said. "Your timing is very good. I was about to send someone for you."

"I have to find Deryn. Do you know where she is?"

"No. Do you remember the way to my Circle Room?"

"Where we had our meeting? Yes."

"Then come here, please. As quickly as you can."

"With no escort?"

"There is a man named Mikhail Dryke in Entry, with several armed and armored friends, suggesting that we turn you over to him. I thought you might like to be involved in the decision."

Christopher ran, ignoring the startled stares.

There were six goons in Entry and who knew how many more on the twenty-four-seat Transorbital shuttle docked to tunnel 2. As near as could be told from the monitors, they were carrying splatterguns and shockboxes, both of which could be safely used inside a pressurized space, though there'd been no shooting so far. In all probability, they also carried enough cutters and shape charges to come through the bulkheads and locked doors which presently contained them.

Shelter had been emptied and sealed without incident, but two Entry staffers were still at the main desk, keeping Dryke and his men company. They were not exactly hostages, since discussions were still technically polite, with no hard refusals or locked doors yet tested. But the women's position was tenuous and their presence was a complication.

"This is the man who killed your father?" asked Anna X.

"Yes," Christopher said, studying the monitor with hard eyes. "Are you going to give me to him?"

"Do you want me to?"

"No," Christopher said, shaking his head. "I have to get to Horizon."

She nodded thoughtfully. "I don't think he means to allow that."

"Have you admitted I'm here?"

"We are still discussing technical issues—the validity of his police powers, the status of our agreements with Brazil and Kenya, certification of his warrants—"

"He has warrants this time?"

"Conspiracy and unlawful flight. Purely ceremonial. This is not a question of law. The paperwork is to keep up appearances. The real warrants are his soldiers and the weapons they carry."

Someone had found Deryn at last, and she came into the room at that moment. "Dryke," Christopher said to her, gesturing at the screen.

Looking up at Dryke and then at Christopher, Deryn sat down beside Anna X on the open end of the bench. "Are you going to surrender Christopher?"

"I would rather not."

It was welcome news to Christopher. But there were others in the room, all of whom had dropped into sullen silence when he arrived. Now one spoke up.

"Shelter was meant for women, not for cocks," she said. "Why are we risking our home for him? It's not our fight."

The object of the objection was unmoved. "I would not like it said that either Sanctuary or Anna X can be threatened."

"Here come the certifications," called a woman across the room, looking down at a comsole.

Anna X did not stir from her seat. "We'll take some time to study them, I think."

"Is there any other way off the station?" asked Christopher.

"Yes. Two ways. They control the passenger side of the hub, but not the freight side. And there is a small slug freighter there. There are also emergency boats, of course."

"Can either reach Horizon?"

"Either can."

"Can either reach *Memphis*?"

Several eyebrows went up.

"No," Anna X said.

Christopher looked at the docking monitor. The blue and red Transorbital shuttle was clearly visible, anchored to the slender pylon which projected from Sanctuary like the axle from a bi-cycle wheel. The white docking tunnel angled up to it from the half-gee Entry ring at a forty-degree angle, like a flight of covered stairs. "Can you keep Dryke from leaving?"

She nodded slowly, acknowledgment but not encouragement. "Dryke and the men inside, yes. His shuttle, no." She smiled faintly. "Run, fight, surrender—all three are possible. As you see, none are attractive. Do you have a preference? Or a solution?"

"Anna," Deryn said sharply, looking up at the main screen. The two women were no longer behind the desk. Two of Dryke's soldiers had them in hand and were walking them briskly across the floor to the opening of tunnel 2, at the end of which lay Dryke's shuttle.

"Idiot," Anna X muttered. "Trionna—cut the shuttle loose. Seal the lock."

On the docking monitor, Christopher saw a smoke-ring puff blow outward from the oval tunnel just a half meter from where it was attached to the shuttle. *Between the inner and outer locks,* Christopher thought, remembering his own arrival. The tunnel was flexing and shaking in long, wavelike undulations from the jolt and the flying load of the four people inside it. Meanwhile, the shuttle had drifted a few meters from the pylon, trailing the stub end of the tunnel from its main port.

Long moments later, the four reappeared in Entry, the soldiers looking more shaken than the staff. An angry Dryke ordered the women to sit on the floor, their faces to a wall, and then turned toward the nearest camera.

"Anna X, I assume that you can hear me—"

Anna X signaled to a technician with her hand. "You're an impatient man, Mr. Dryke," she interrupted. "Neither quality is a virtue here."

"I want Christopher McCutcheon. It's a simple thing. You have enough documentation to satisfy any conscience you may have. Are you going to give him to me?"

"Mr. McCutcheon is not a possession to be given away. He is a person. He petitioned for Shelter, which was granted. And Sanctuary has never given up a Sheltered person on the demand of any authority."

"Then you must feel safer than you are," Dryke answered. "Don't make this a test of strength. I'm not leaving without him."

Anna X's back was up. "Do you think that Sanctuary is a huddle of helpless women? Do you think—"

"Is two enough to make a huddle? Because there are two women here with me who don't seem particularly powerful at the moment. Two citizens of Sanctuary, I suspect—not visitors.

I imagine you can play with the pressure and the lights and the heat and maybe even gas the whole section anytime you please. I just think you should know what will happen if you do. How often have you sacrificed Sanctuary citizens for a male criminal? Would you like to put that question to a plebiscite? I'll be happy to wait."

"I know how a community aspiring to your ethics would vote," Anna X said. "Christopher doesn't have to fear that from us."

But looking at the faces around him, Christopher was less certain than Anna X sounded.

"Really. There's only one reason I can think of that'd account for that—"

"Then you have a sadly stunted imagination."

"—which is that he isn't just a visitor, after all. Maybe he's a friend. Hell, let's think creatively—maybe he's not even a he. What about that, Anna? Things aren't always what they seem, are they? Should we come take a look in your records under Homeworld? Should we look in them for Jeremiah?"

"Off," said Anna X tersely. "Self-important bastard—is the freighter ready?"

"Yes—on one-minute hold."

"We'll use it as a decoy. Send it toward Hanif. Then prepare boat 5 for launch to Horizon—"

"No," Christopher said, stepping forward. "Stop."

"Isn't that what you wanted?"

"He won't send the shuttle after the freighter. He'll destroy it if he has a way. And he'll have a way. He won't have come up here without being ready to deal with me if I ran."

"I don't want to give you to him."

"He doesn't want that, either. I only just realized."

"Explain."

"I think he wants an excuse to come in here. He'd rather have a chance to 'accidentally' kill me, with pawing through your records as a bonus. That's why he's baiting you. This isn't a negotiation."

"Have you a suggestion? Or a choice?"

"We're dealing with the wrong person."

"Explain."

"It would take too long. Let me talk to Dryke. I think I can get us better terms."

She studied him skeptically, then vacated her seat for him, standing off to one side. "Are you ready?"

He nodded.

She stepped back, out of camera, and gave the signal.

Dryke had been having his own side conversation. When he looked up, a mild flicker of surprise crossed his face. "So you are here, after all," he said.

"Shut up," Christopher said. "I want to talk to the Director. Conference, three-way, full video. You, me, and her. You can arrange it, or we can put out the call on Aurora Freenet, all hundred thousand watts' worth." He saw Anna X's eyes widen. "You decide. Thirty seconds."

"No."

"Bad choice. Because if I don't talk to Sasaki, Freenet is going to start broadcasting everything we know about the Chi Sequence and *Memphis*. Which is quite a lot."

Dryke's expression did not change. "What the hell is that to me? Just come out, McCutcheon. It'll be a lot easier to clean up around here if you do."

Christopher tried to keep the surprise off his face. Dryke didn't know. *Dryke doesn't know.* For just that moment, Christopher's confidence wavered. *Mother of Gaea, if I'm wrong—*

"You'd better check with the Director and see if she cares," he said weakly.

"I'm not playing the game, McCutcheon. You've got nothing to bargain with."

"You're a chump, Dryke, d'you know that? A first-class nobrain chump. You don't know what this is all about. You don't know what you're defending. You don't even know what you're fighting."

"You're not earning any points, McCutcheon."

"You couldn't keep count if I was," Christopher said. "The hell with you. We're taking it to the air."

"We're already on the air," Anna X said.

Christopher shot her a surprised sideways glance, and then a pleased smile. "My name is Christopher McCutcheon," he said, looking straight into the camera. "My father was Jeremiah, of the Homeworld. The first reason that I'm here is to tell you that he's dead."

He swallowed, dropped his eyes for a moment, and then drew in a breath to proceed. "He's dead now, but I'm still learning from what he taught me. You have something to learn, too. That's the other reason I'm here—to tell you a story. It's a story about a great river and the animals who explored it. The river is called Time and Destiny and God. The animals have many names, including Man.

"So you're part of the story, and so am I. It's a story about where we came from and where we're going. It's all of our stories, from before the beginning of history, all wrapped in one. Because it's the story of who we are. Some of you won't like the ending—I'll warn you about that now—"

"Christopher?" interrupted one of the women. "Someone heard you. It's Hiroko Sasaki."

"Switch," he said. "Director? Can you hear me?"

"Yes, Christopher. I hope you can hear me, as well. Mikhail, are you listening?"

"Here, Director." From his expression, he was eating his face off from the inside.

"Very well. Christopher, what is it that you want?"

"I want to see you. I want the truth about the Chi Sequence and *Memphis*."

"Nothing more?"

His chest rose and fell with several breaths before he knew his answer. "There's more, but it will keep until I see you."

She nodded. "Mikhail."

"Yes, Director."

"If he ends his broadcast now, bring him to me."

All eyes in the room were on Christopher. He sought out Deryn's with his own.

"It's a good beginning," she said, answering the question in his look. "And I know how to finish it. If you can't, I'll tell the story, when the time is right."

He nodded. That was enough. "I'd like a promise of safe conduct from Mr. Dryke," he said to Sasaki.

A moment later, he had the promise. He hugged Deryn and thanked Anna X, then turned and left, his steps curiously light. Alone, he climbed up to Entry and walked out through the door of Shelter 24 with his shoulders straight and his head high. As he did, the two staff women rushed by him, escaping into the safety of Sanctuary.

"You don't have it yet," Dryke said, glaring across the room.

"Wrong," Christopher said. "I always had it. I was just the last to know."

• • •

Christopher did not try to talk to Dryke in the shuttle, not even to ask where they were headed. Instead, he thought about the questions he wanted to ask Sasaki. There were fewer than he would have expected. Confirmation, correction, validation— those he still needed. But the unknown detail was irrelevant. The synthesis embodied the detail. The general implied the specific.

The flight was long even in objective terms, long enough that it could have only one destination. Finally, they docked at a satland which, from the glimpse Christopher got through the pilot's port and the kanji signage in the transfer chute, could only be Takara.

"The Director's on *Memphis*?" Christopher asked, turning as he walked and throwing the question back over his shoulder to Dryke. Dryke's only answer was a straight-arm, flat-palm shot to the middle of Christopher's back, shoving him forward.

Dryke and two of the soldiers escorted Christopher to a med station, where he was stripped, scanned, sampled, searched inside and out, and, finally, given new clothes—a rigger's pajamalike skinsides. He endured the exercise stoically, refusing the humiliation he might have felt.

Then he was bustled aboard another spacecraft, this one cavernous and buslike, with low, extra-wide seats that were actually uncomfortable without the work suits they had apparently been designed for. Their party of four was scattered among the forty seats—Christopher and Dryke at opposite sides of a middle row, the soldiers at opposite ends of the center aisle.

As on the shuttle, Dryke never took his right hand off his shockbox or his eyes off Christopher. The level, unflinching gaze had in it something of a carrion bird's hopefulness and something of a timber wolf's watchfulness.

For the most part, Christopher ignored him. All of his surroundings were new, and he managed enough curiosity about them to divert himself by attending to the novelty. But he could not stop his mind from thinking, from trying to weave in the last few threads. And one of those threads involved the security of *Memphis*, which meant it involved Mikhail Dryke. It was hard to offer anything, even a thought, to the man who had shot down his father. But Sasaki might not be the best to face the question he wanted to ask.

"Is Roger Marshall coming up to *Memphis*, too?"

Dryke's gaze never wavered, and his expression never changed.

"He never went through Selection, you know."

Still there was no response.

"I hear that a lot of people are going to be on *Memphis* who never went through Selection or Training. If Marshall's one of them, you might want to pay attention to whether his freight gets here before him. And if it does, you might want to make sure it gets the 'A' inspection—the kind you'd give something belonging to me."

Almost five minutes passed in silence.

"Why?" Dryke said, as though a complicated equation had ground through his mind without generating a solution.

"Because I'm not the new Jeremiah—which means that someone else is."

Another long silence. Christopher understood that it was as hard for Dryke to accept anything from Christopher as it was for him to offer it.

"Why Marshall?" Dryke asked finally.

"Do you know a good reason why he would call my home and wonder to Loi how I was dealing with my father's death?"

"Do you?"

"Maybe. It was two days after I disappeared, and two days before the attack on *Memphis*. Maybe he'd lost track of me and needed to make sure I wasn't on board somehow."

"Why?"

"Because of a promise to my father."

Dryke looked away, raising a hand to scratch the bridge of his nose. "A lot of maybes."

"Then he *is* coming," Christopher said.

The gaze firmed and found Christopher again.

"Has it occurred to you that the attack on *Memphis* was a successful one, after all?" Christopher asked. "The real damage was done to security. This panic plan puts hundreds of people on the ship who would otherwise never have gotten there, apparently including Marshall. And I'm guessing it overwhelms your normal screening procedures, too. Are you streamlining things to get people processed faster? Giving anyone a pass? Top management? The committee? Roger Marshall? Don't answer, I can't do anything with the information. Just questions."

Something had awakened in Dryke's eyes. His head tipped

back slightly, and he stared at Christopher with something closer to—fear?

One last card. "Tell me—Marshall wasn't involved in drawing up this plan, was he?"

There was a suspended moment, in which Christopher could almost see the picture in his mind replicating itself in Dryke's. Then there was a bump as they docked with *Memphis*, and the all-clear tone.

This time, Dryke preceded him down the aisle. He seemed to be in a hurry.

The suite in which Sasaki received him was neither large nor grand, but it bore a stamp. A pale-tinted hanging scroll sandwiched in translute was strung between ceiling and floor as a room divider; in lighted display recesses on the wall were a bronze horse, a gleaming metal-paper origami of a dragon in flight, and a deep-rubbed mahogany Buddah, surrounded by flowers and candles, smiling within at some untold amusement.

Other recesses were empty, but there were two trunklike shipping casks stacked in a corner of the outer room. Furniture seemed sparse until Sasaki showed him a pair of facing chairs that slid out from an inner wall as though they were drawers. She settled in one and invited him to the other with an open hand. She was smaller than he had expected, and braver—they were alone, Sasaki having sent his escorts back.

"You said that you wanted the truth," she said. "Are you equal to it?"

"How do you know, before you're tested?"

She nodded. "A good answer. Ask your questions."

"Is *Memphis* ready for space?"

"It will be, very shortly."

"When are you leaving?"

"From Takara, a matter of days. For Tau Ceti, a matter of a few weeks. We will go out for our certification flight with full crew and manifest. If the systems are sound, we will not turn back at Pluto."

"Who will be governor?"

She smiled slightly. "That duty will be mine, for now."

"And what happens here? Who takes over? Or will there be anything to take over?"

"No," she said. "This is the end of the Diaspora, as we have suspected for some time it would be. After *Memphis* sails, the

Project will fall into bankruptcy. But the vultures will find very little meat on the bones. The money is all here, in *Memphis* and *Ur*. We have bought two starships for the price of five. Many promises will be broken, and many bills left unpaid. Not even Allied has ever seen an honest accounting.''

"Why that way?''

"Because it was time. Because it was the only way the flower would blossom,'' she said.

Dryke joined them then, entering the suite quietly and standing with crossed arms beside the hanging scroll. Sasaki looked up past Christopher with a questioning glance.

"Marshall missed his flight from LAX,'' Dryke said. "He apologizes and says he has to have more time to wrap up business. His personals didn't miss their flight. I had the casks pulled out of the line on Technica and checked. The one that was supposed to be art and books was two hundred and eighty kilos of underwater explosives.''

Christopher closed his eyes, the rush of relief carrying away the strength from his limbs.

"I should have wondered why a man like that wanted to go,'' Dryke said.

"Sometimes perfection is found in the result, not in the method,'' Sasaki said. "And sometimes perfection is only possible in thought.'' She looked to Christopher. "Now a question for you,'' she said. "Do you want to come on *Memphis*?''

Her words encircled his heart and tightened until he could hardly breathe. "Yes.''

"Why?''

He opened his mouth to answer, but no words came out. The reasons were all turned around inside each other, connected at odd places, sometimes not connected at all. His motives were all suspect, shallow, trivial—or else so deep and fundamental that he could not wrap sentences around them. "I don't know,'' he said at last.

To his surprise, Sasaki smiled warmly. "Then come.''

He drew a hard breath. "No,'' he said. "I can't.''

"Explain?''

"There's someone else who belongs here before I do. A friend. Daniel Keith. He works in Selection—a BC-positive. He'd be up here now if it wasn't for me.'' He was fighting with tears. "If you're going to give me a discretionary space, I—you have to let me give it to him.''

She was studying him closely. "Mikhail, do you know anything about this?"

"Keith was on the list," he said. "He was sent to Prainha because of contact with Christopher. He's under arrest there."

"He was clear except for his friendship with this man?"

"Yes."

She nodded, looking into Christopher's eyes. "You don't know how extraordinary I find it that you would give up your place to your friend."

"I made him a promise."

"Even so, that would be rare selflessness, even here." She sat forward in her chair. "I think that we can find two places as easily as one."

A shuddery sob escaped through the smile that sprang onto Christopher's face. He pressed his palms together almost as though praying, and puffed away the rush of discordant emotion in hoarse breaths.

Rising, she smiled and touched his shoulder. "I will give you some time. Then there will be much more to say."

He twisted in his chair as she started away. "You had me tested for the Chi Sequence. On Takara. Didn't you?"

"That was the question I expected first," she said. "Yes."

"What am I?"

"Young," she said. "But you will grow." Guiding Dryke ahead of her, she started again for the door.

Christopher stood and called after them. "That's not enough," he said.

She turned and looked back. "Most of those who will make this trip will know no more."

Shaking his head, he said, "I still need to know—do I belong here?"

Her gaze appraised him. "Not if you still need that question answered by me."

He considered that for a long time, then laughed a little laugh, the joke a silent secret. "No. I suppose I don't. But did any of us really have a choice? Did you?"

"No," she said. "And still, I did what I wanted."

"I don't understand."

"Do you know T. E. Lawrence?"

"A little."

"The epigraph from *Seven Pillars*." She quoted, " 'I loved

you, so I drew these tides of men into my hands and wrote my will across the sky in stars, to earn you Freedom—' "

"You," Christopher said, throat suddenly tight, thinking not of Lawrence, nor of Sasaki. "I have one more question."

She waited.

"For him," Christopher said, looking at Dryke.

Dryke met his gaze with a look absent of apology—which, for the first time, Christopher could accept. "What?"

"Where is my father?"

There was only the briefest hesitation. "Where we found him."

Eleven days later, fulfilling a promise by Sasaki, an Allied screamer took Christopher down to the ridge.

It promised to be his last hour on Earth, and he had hoped Loi could meet him there and share it. He had envisioned a tidy closure—fierce, fervent hugs, murmured *I love you*'s, blessings and forgiveness. But it was not to be. The day before, when he called her to ask, he found her half a world away in Osaka, promoting a new timesculpt, arranging for an exhibition. She could not get away.

Her regret seemed sincere, but he could not tell her that there would be no more chances. She already knew he was leaving—he had been transferring his libraries up from the housecom all week, and a Project gofer had been by to retrieve Claudia and his other possessions. He was moving on, and so was Loi, and if it was not tidy, it was still going to be all right, in time.

Just as it was somehow right that he had ended up coming to the ridge alone.

Overhead, clouds like black lace curled down to form a dome. The house was little more than ashes, and the ashes were already dotted with green fronds. Christopher moved slowly across the charred foundation, marking where each room had been, toeing the ashes here and there but finding nothing he recognized, much less anything he wanted. Hands buried in his pockets, he wandered a short way into the woods, drawing in the familiar scents, looking skyward into the crown and watching the firs dance their slow dance in the wind, listening to the delicate sound dead needles made falling to the soft carpet of the forest floor.

Then it was time to do what he had come there to do.

The grave marker had been made on Takara, formed of the

compacted lunar soil used as satland shielding, etched with energy captured from the Sun. In silence, Christopher carried the heavy tablet from the screamer and placed it in the wet ashes above his father's tomb.

JEREMIAH MCCUTCHEON, it said.

Non Omnis Moriar

"Good-bye," said Christopher. And as the rain began and his tears ran, Loi, his father and the verdant hills all released him with their blessing.

Caravan to Tau Ceti

FOR ONE DAY SHORT OF FIVE WEEKS, *MEMPHIS* NURSED ITS wounds, real and feigned, in a polar orbit high enough to shrink the blue-white globe below almost to the size of a memory.

Inside, training continued as time and space allowed, with impromptu classes held at all hours, all over the ship. With the manifest at 218 over the design maximum of 12,000, staff and citizenry both faced relentless settling-in pains, as though the ship were a shoe and a half size too small. But, in an unfolding miracle, each day *Memphis* seemed to grow larger, as its inhabitants learned where elbows rubbed and how best to use the spaces that they had.

While the techs and mechs tuned the ship's systems, the counselors tried to tune its community. Nearly two hundred Selection mistakes were quietly corrected before the sailing day arrived, each case reviewed by Sasaki before the offenders were sent down to Takara for holding. A hundred more went out on their own through the door that Sasaki held open for them to the very last.

But at last the ship was ready, and the door irrevocably closed. There was no announcement—*Memphis* was still officially disabled, departure indefinitely postponed—and yet somehow there were anticipations in the ether. On the day that *Memphis* sailed, 56,000 massed in London at a Muslim prayer rally aimed at pulling the starship back down from the sky. In the hour *Memphis* sailed, a judge in Delaware granted an injunction barring the starship from leaving and ordering Allied to show that the son of Mr. and Mrs. Bellamy of Wilmington, missing now for nearly two months, was not aboard.

But neither the power of prayer nor the power of law would be enough to stay the captain's will or still the starship's drives. And so, in the minutes before *Memphis* sailed, two friends spoke one last time across a void wider in space than in spirit.

"I've already written my essay for tomorrow's *History Today*," said Thomas Tidwell from his house in Halfwhistle. "Do you want to hear how it begins? 'The starship *Ur* left Earth in the sunlight, to children's cheers and the sound of summer bands. The starship *Memphis* stole away in the night, in the silence of a pricking conscience.' Nicely turned, don't you think?"

"Well enough—but whose conscience?" said Sasaki from her suite on *Memphis*. "Mine is clear."

"I use you only as a bullfighter uses the cape, to draw them in, unsuspecting. I go on to make many profound observations, the meaning of which will likely escape nine in ten listeners."

Sasaki smiled. "I look forward to hearing it all tomorrow, from somewhere in the neighborhood of Jupiter."

"That will be a good distance to listen from, I expect," said Tidwell. "Have you told Governor James on *Ur*?"

"I plan to put up a dispatch when we cross out of the solar system."

"Good," said Tidwell. "Perhaps then they won't feel so alone. Perhaps it will help them take some courage and pride in what they've embarked on."

"Perhaps. But I intend to concern myself only with *Memphis*," said Sasaki. "Thomas, Captain Powell is calling me to the bridge."

"Never let your people forget that they are messengers as well as travelers."

"I will try. I trust you have no regrets, Thomas."

Tidwell shook his head. "I no more regret refusing your offer and staying than you regret leaving. And I am curious to see if knowledge of the prophecy of our genes will allow us to defy them."

"I will wish you the best in that," Sasaki said. "Thank you for your service, Thomas."

"Thank me? I should rather thank you. I was privileged to stand in the shadows beside you while you drew to yourself all the forces of a moment in time," Tidwell said. "Everyone over the age of five in 2083 remembers where they were, what they were doing when *Ur* sailed. Everyone over the age of five today will remember as vividly where they were when they heard that *Memphis* had skipped away. And you, Hiroko Sasaki, will go down in history as one of the great criminals of all time."

"There you are wrong, my friend," said Sasaki with the smallest hint of a prideful smile. "Starting today, *we* write the histories."

BEGIN CHAIN: AUG - CGG - UGU - CAA - GGU - CAC - UUU - GUC - AUA -